A VIRGIN KISS

She moved closer, tilting her chin up, offering him her mouth, but a soft cry left her lips when he took it, as if he'd surprised her, somehow, but it was an instant only, and then she was opening for him, welcoming him inside with a slick stroke of her tongue.

He toyed with her lower lip, suckling and biting at it before drawing back to revel in the way it had swollen and reddened under his attentions, the way a woman's mouth should look when she'd been thoroughly kissed, tender and glistening, the sight of it hitting him hard in his lower belly, erotic as fingers wrapped around him, stroking his aching cock.

"Do you want me, Mairi?"

She gripped a handful of the loose hair resting against his neck, the insistent tug of her fingers a command, not a request. "Yes."

He tore his lips from hers to nip at her neck, and taste the secret skin under her jaw and behind her ear. "Say it."

"I want you, Daniel."

She wanted him. Somehow, this fierce, brilliant woman wanted *him*.

She dragged her tongue over his lower lip, teased it into the corner of his mouth, tickling him with the tip and stealing his breath. Her small hands landed on his chest, her fingers curling into the damp wool of his coat, as if to keep him where she needed him…

Books by Anna Bradley

LADY ELEANOR'S SEVENTH SUITOR
LADY CHARLOTTE'S FIRST LOVE
TWELFTH NIGHT WITH THE EARL
MORE OR LESS A MARCHIONESS
MORE OR LESS A COUNTESS
MORE OR LESS A TEMPTRESS
THE WAYWARD BRIDE
TO WED A WILD SCOT
FOR THE SAKE OF A SCOTTISH RAKE
THE VIRGIN WHO RUINED LORD GRAY
THE VIRGIN WHO VINDICATED LORD DARLINGTON
THE VIRGIN WHO HUMBLED LORD HASLEMERE
THE VIRGIN WHO BEWITCHED LORD LYMINGTON
THE VIRGIN WHO CAPTURED A VISCOUNT

Published by Kensington Publishing Corp.

The Virgin Who Captured a

Viscount

Anna Bradley

LYRICAL PRESS
Kensington Publishing Corp.
www.kensingtonbooks.com

LYRICAL PRESS BOOKS are published by

Kensington Publishing Corp.
119 West 40th Street
New York, NY 10018

All Kensington titles, imprints, and distributed lines are available at special quantity discounts for bulk purchases for sales promotion, premiums, fund-raising, educational, or institutional use.

Special book excerpts or customized printings can also be created to fit specific needs. For details, write or phone the office of the Kensington Sales Manager: Kensington Publishing Corp., 119 West 40th Street, New York, NY 10018. Attn. Sales Department. Phone: 1-800-221-2647.

Lyrical Press and Lyrical Press logo Reg. U.S. Pat. & TM Off.

First Electronic Edition: October 2022
ISBN: 978-1-5161-1132-9 (ebook)

First Print Edition: October 2022
ISBN: 978-1-5161-1133-6

Printed in the United States of America

Prologue

Coldstream, Scottish Borders

July 28, 1772

Ye go poaching on Lord Rutherford's land again, Daniel's father had said to him this morning, *and I'll redden your arse tonight. Ye ken, lad?* The lord's gamekeeper was already after him—ten, maybe twelve paces behind, his old man's lungs huffing and puffing like a cracked bellows. Murdoch had caught Archie Mackenzie last week and whipped him something awful, ten bloody stripes worth, but old Murdoch wouldn't catch *him*, because Daniel was quicker than lightning, the fastest runner in Coldstream. Maybe the fastest in the county, even. Faster than Archie, no matter how much Archie bawled about it.

He gulped air as he ran, wild, gasping breaths that tore his throat on the way up, the dripping bag with the three fish he'd plucked from the pond bouncing against his thigh with every stride, leaving a damp patch on his breeches, and behind him the slap of Hamish's bare feet striking the hard-packed dirt, *slap-thump, slap-thump*, his bad leg dragging behind him, but still faster than Murdoch, for all that Hamish was lame, and got tired quick.

The other boys used to tease Hamish sometimes, called him a cripple, but Daniel had put a stop to it by thrashing 'em. Tore up his hand on one of Archie's sharp teeth doing it. It bled like the devil, too, but he'd have done the same again, as many times as it took to shut Archie's big mouth, because Hamish was the best friend he'd ever had.

They were close as two brothers. They'd sworn to it, the day he turned eight. They'd spat on their palms then clasped hands, because that was the way you did it. It didn't count if you didn't spit first. Not spitting was like cheating, and everyone knew only cowards cheated.

He danced between the patches of dappled sunlight filtering through the trees above, leaping over gnarled tree roots and ducking under the thick branches. The tree line had turned from a green blur into leaves and branches before he noticed the *slap-thump* behind him had stopped.

The mud was fresher under the trees, unbaked by the sun, and his foot slipped in the slick muck. He fell to his knees, cursing at the ooze soaking into his breeches, and peered around the massive trunk, the rough bark sliding against his palms.

Hamish was still coming, but his steps had slowed, and his face was twisted with panic. If Daniel ran now, he could save his own arse from a striping, but a real man didn't leave his brother behind, even if it meant Murdoch would tear the skin from *both* their backsides, cackling with every lash of his horsewhip, his blind eye, all white, rolling around in its socket like a runaway billiard ball.

Archie had told him Murdoch could curse a boy with one blink of that eye. Daniel had called him a liar, right to his face, too, but Archie had sworn to it. He said he'd seen Murdoch curse a boy once—one twitch of his eyeball and the boy had dropped where he stood, good as dead.

Daniel clutched at the trunk of the tree, slivers of loose bark digging under his fingernails, and muttered a few words he remembered from the bedtime prayer Mrs. Cameron had taught him. He could stop a curse that way, couldn't he? Stop Murdoch's evil spells from raining down on Hamish's head.

Now I lay me down...now I lay...if I should die...

Then, when that didn't work, "Come on, Hamish. *Run.*"

But the gamekeeper was getting closer, his huge hand reaching, clawing the air just behind Hamish's neck, the slash of his mouth opening in a bloodthirsty grin as he caught Hamish by the shoulder and wrenched him off his feet with one vicious jerk. "Got ye, ye little whelp."

Hamish's shriek bounced off the trees, everywhere at once. Heat rushed into Daniel's chest, burning him, battering against his ribs, his own shriek tearing loose from his throat, echoing Hamish's cry, as if a scream could make the man stop, make him leave Hamish alone.

He dropped into a crouch, muscles tensed to burst from the trees and pummel the man into the ground, but he had Hamish by the throat, and he was shaking him, shaking him like a hound with a fox, Hamish's body dangling from the grip of that crushing fist, feet jerking, and Daniel froze, his stomach pushing into his throat, because if he moved, that man would catch *him*, and shake him just as he was shaking Hamish, and he'd go limp and still, only his feet moving, swinging back and—

"Not a word, Daniel." A hand clamped over his mouth, the rusty taste of blood hit his tongue, and a voice, low and frantic, whispered close to his ear. "Come with me, quickly."

"No! Hamish!" A real man didn't leave his brother—

"You do as you're told," she hissed, then she shook him hard enough to rattle his teeth, her fingernails sinking like hooks into his shoulders.

He gaped up at her, tears stinging his eyes. She'd never shaken him before, had never even raised her voice to him. Had his father sent her to fetch him for a whipping? It was all jumbled inside his head—the pond, the fish, his father's warning, Hamish's feet dangling—but it was wrong, wasn't it, to shake a boy for stealing a few fish—

"*Quickly*, Daniel. There's no time to waste." She seized his arm and dragged him deeper into the woods. Tree branches snagged his hair and left long, bloody scratches on his face and arms, but she urged him to go faster, faster, pulling on him until at last they broke through the forest and came out on the road on the other side.

His father was waiting for them in their wagon as they burst from the woods, with their few possessions piled haphazardly into the bed, and that was wrong, so *wrong*, that his father should be *here* instead of pounding iron at the forge, and the look on his face...

Daniel froze. His father was a big, strong man, but he'd shrunk since this morning, his shoulders pulled into his chest, like an old man's. His father had looked that way only once before, three years earlier, when he'd taken Daniel aside and told him his mother was dead.

He wanted to go back to Hamish, where the trees were rustling in the breeze, the birds were twittering, and everything made sense, but Mrs. Cameron was dragging him to the wagon, saying...*something*, but he couldn't make any sense of it.

After that, it all happened too quickly for him to wonder anything more. Mrs. Cameron snatched him close and pressed a kiss into his hair, her arms so tight around him his lungs ached. "Be a good lad, Daniel. Promise me?"

He nodded, his words all gone, his lips numb, and let her hurry him toward the wagon. His father grasped his arm and hauled him onto the seat, and an instant later they were moving, wagon wheels creaking against the rutted dirt road.

He only looked back once, but by then Mrs. Cameron was gone, the hem of her gray skirts vanishing into the trees.

* * * *

Mairi tumbled out the window and landed on her hands and knees in her grandmother's strawberry patch. She'd tried to be careful where she landed, because strawberries were her favorite, but a crushed berry had left a sticky red smear on her hand. She spat into her palm and wiped her hand on her pinafore, but now she had a red smudge there instead.

"Damn." It was a bad word, a curse, but no one was around to tell on her, because Daniel and Hamish had gone fishing without her.

They always did, and it wasn't *fair*.

She'd given them her saddest face, begged and pleaded with them to take her along, but they'd gone off this morning without her, as happy as anything. Daniel had even been whistling.

Whistling!

He was a mean, wicked boy, and Hamish...well, Hamish was sweet, better than summer strawberries, but he'd let Daniel leave her behind, all the same. He said she was too young to go to the pond, that it was dangerous, if she fell in.

She *wasn't* too young. She was turning six years old tomorrow, and anyway, she knew how to swim.

Mostly.

But she didn't need them, anyway. She'd just go to the pond on her own, and have an adventure all by herself. She'd been doing it all summer, ever since she found out that if she stood on the bed, she could reach the latch on the window beside it. It stuck halfway up, but she could wriggle through the gap, then *plop!* She dropped right into the back garden.

She picked her way through the strawberry patch, jumping from one foot to the other so as not to spoil any more of the plump berries hidden under the tiny white flowers, their dark green leaves huddled together in threes.

Her grandmother would scold something fierce if she found out Mairi had gone to Rutherford Pond. It wasn't *really* called that, but she tried to remember to call it that in her own head, because her grandmother said you had to give the lord his due, even when he hadn't done anything to deserve it.

But she hadn't *promised* she wouldn't go, so she wasn't doing anything *bad*, not really, and she wouldn't go near the water. She'd just peek through the bushes and see if she could see Hamish and Daniel.

They were always together, whispering and laughing, because they were best friends.

Her belly had twisted with something ugly when Hamish told her Daniel wanted to be his best friend, because she wanted Daniel to be *her* best friend, but she'd worked it out in her head, and maybe it was fair, because Hamish didn't have many friends, and she had dozens and dozens of them, so it was maybe all right if Hamish had Daniel.

The pond was just through the trees, but she had to go through the brambles to get to it, and they tore at her legs, leaving stinging cuts behind worse even than splinters, but she wasn't *crying*, even if her eyes did tear up just a little. She wasn't a baby who cried at every hurt, no matter what Daniel said.

She dragged her sleeve across her eyes, and pushed her way through the thicket of weeds and scraggly bushes, but when she got to the spying place, where you could see the pond through the trees, Daniel and Hamish weren't there. No one was there. It was just the bugs chasing each other around in circles over the muddy water.

Stupid, boring pond. The only thing worse would be going back to the stupid, boring, empty cottage after she'd gone to all that trouble to get out the window. Daniel would laugh at her if he found out, but it was chilly in the shade of the trees, and she was hungry, and she didn't want her grandmother to catch her near the pond.

She turned to scurry back the way she'd come, but a branch snapped, and the leaves rustled like someone was moving through the forest, so she crept along after them, winding her way through the trees.

She walked for a long time without seeing anyone, until at last she came out at the little clearing at the other end of the wood, her boots skidding over the leaves, and there they were, Daniel and her grandmother, right there in front of her, standing on the road, Daniel tucked into her grandmother's arms. Mairi couldn't see her face, because it was pressed into Daniel's dark hair, but her shoulders were shaking, like they had when Daniel's mother died.

A chill grabbed her neck, gooseflesh prickling her skin.

Daniel looked *scared.*

But Daniel was never scared, not of anything. He was the bravest of all the village boys, the bravest boy she'd ever known. A bad taste rushed into her throat, bitter like wild cherries, but just as she opened her mouth to call out to them, her grandmother released Daniel and gave him a gentle push toward his father, who was waiting on the road in his wagon.

The reins snapped, the horses' hooves kicked up little clouds of dust, and then they were gone. She didn't take her eyes from the wagon until it faded from sight, swallowed into the tunnel of trees that lined either side of the road.

By then, her grandmother was gone, vanished back into the woods without a sound.

Mairi stood staring at the place she'd been, her mouth open, but she felt scared now, so she ran home, scrambled back through the open window and closed it tight behind her, so no one would know she'd ever been gone. She flopped down in the center of the bed, pulled the quilt over her head, and closed her eyes, but she could still see Daniel's face, and her grandmother's shaking shoulders.

Her grandmother wept that night, after it got dark, her back to Mairi, her face pressed into the pillow. Hamish didn't come back that day, or the next, or the day after that.

Daniel never came back, either.

After a while, Mairi stopped asking where they were, when they were coming home. Her grandmother never spoke of them. Mairi might have believed she'd forgotten them, but every night after they'd gone, after her grandmother tucked her into their bed, she'd weep, quiet, ragged, broken sobs that dragged babyish tears from Mairi's eyes.

It wasn't right, that they'd left like that. Not right, that they'd taken her grandmother's joy with them when they did.

Stole it.

Some days, when she woke to her grandmother's red-rimmed, swollen eyes, the fist inside her chest would clench and squeeze until the knuckles bulged and the sharp fingernails clawed at her ribs, and her heart would shrivel into a dry, empty husk to make room for it.

Those days left long, jagged, bloody scars inside her. On those days, she hated Daniel and Hamish. Other days, she longed for them both with an ache nothing could sooth.

On those days, she hated them more.

Chapter One

No. 26 Maddox Street, London

Early February 1796

Daniel prowled amongst the thick shadows at the edges of Lady Clifford's drawing room, rubbing his fingers over the smooth pearl handle of the dagger he'd slipped into his coat pocket.

It was one of two, a gift from Lady Clifford. They were fine ones, perfectly balanced, the hooked blades sharper than an eagle's talon. Pretty, too. Their gleaming edges caught the light, so whoever was on the slicing end could see them coming.

He'd tucked the other one into his boot just before he'd been called into dinner.

Ten courses tonight. Nine too many, and two hours too long. He'd eaten little, said even less, instead keeping his attention on the window on one side of the room, the sky darkening behind the thick panes of glass.

It was dark, but not yet dark enough. Not for what he had planned.

Lady Clifford and the girls—nay, not *girls*, they were *ladies* now—were dressed in blue tonight. A man might think there were only a few different shades of blue, but he'd be wrong.

Then there was Lord Haslemere, trussed up like a peacock in a waistcoat such a bright blue it singed Daniel's eyeballs. No blending into the shadows in *that* waistcoat.

Daniel was in black, as always, a dark, solitary island surrounded by an ocean of blue silk, rippling and eddying in the firelight.

"For God's sake, Brixton, I've hardly had a glimpse of your face this entire evening." Lord Lymington waved him toward the fire, a goblet of port balanced between his elegant fingers.

Daniel had refused the glass offered to him. His own fingers were rough, scarred things, too thick to be elegant. No goblet was going to change that, no matter if it did have gold filigree...angels? No, cherubs, of all bloody stupid things, etched around the rim.

"You don't intend to skulk about in the shadows all night, I hope. You're the sort a man likes to keep his eye on, Brixton." Haslemere swirled the port in his goblet, the blood-red wine dripping down the sides of the crystal bowl. "I despise it when you skulk."

Daniel slitted his eyes against the offensive glow of lamplight spilling into the drawing room, and retreated deeper into the gloom. He'd done a bloody poor job of skulking, if a dull-wit like Haslemere could still see him.

"Come, Brixton. It's baby Amanda's birthday. She's three months old today, and you haven't held her once since she was born."

Lord Gray, this time. An earl, and irritating enough with that smirk, but not as irritating as Haslemere. No one was as irritating as Haslemere.

As if he'd heard Daniel's thoughts, Haslemere gave him a provoking grin. "Don't tell us you're afraid to hold her, Brixton."

Afraid? He wasn't afraid of anything. Not villains lurking in dark alleys, not knives, swords, rapiers, or any other sharp, pointed objects. Not pistols, fists, brawls, or bullwhips. There was a reason the sight of him was enough to send London's black-hearted villains fleeing into the night. "Nay."

"Hush, Lord Haslemere. Of course, he isn't afraid." Sophia, now the Countess of Gray, approached his corner, carrying a squirming, mewling creature wrapped in a white blanket, the downy head tucked in the crook of her elbow. "Here she is. Hold out your arms."

Daniel kept his arms at his sides. If he didn't raise them, no one could put anything into them.

"Please, Daniel?" Sophia turned wide, pleading green eyes on him.

Christ. Not the pleading eyes. Anything but that.

He'd taken a pistol ball to his cheek once. It had only grazed him, but it had scorched like fire, bled like the devil, and left a nasty scar, too. He hadn't even flinched, but one glance from the eyes felled him every time, worse than a blade plunged into the center of his chest.

They knew it, too. Shameless chits.

What the devil was wrong with Gray? Why wasn't he putting a stop to this? Any man worth a damn would refuse to turn his precious infant daughter over to a conscienceless blackguard like Daniel, but Gray didn't say a bloody word, just stood there nodding.

He swallowed back another refusal and trudged toward his doom, gaze averted from the wrinkled, pink creature in Sophia's arms, the tiny, spindly fingers gripping the edge of the blanket.

Sophia gave him her most winning smile. "Hold out your arms."

No sense in fighting it. He stuck his arms out in front of him, and waited for it to be over.

"You needn't look so grim. She's a baby, not a poisonous snake."

A baby. A soft, defenseless little thing with a head no bigger than his palm. He'd prefer a poisonous snake, as no one was likely to mind if he dropped it, or squeezed it too hard. His huge hands had no business touching such a delicate, innocent creature.

The girls—that is, the *ladies*—all crowded closer as Sophia placed the squirming bundle in his arms. "There. That's not so terrible, is it?"

"Oh, look!" Cecilia beamed at him, one of her hands moving to cradle her own swollen belly. "She's smiling at you, Daniel. I'm certain she recognizes you."

"That's a yawn, lass, not a smile." Or worse, a yawn one breath away from becoming a wail. He stared down at the baby, gut rolling with every twitch of that soft, open pink mouth. He could already hear the ear-blistering shriek ringing in his head.

Sophia leaned closer to get a better look at her daughter's expression. "Nonsense. Of course, it's a smile. She loves you already."

"She does," Georgiana echoed stoutly. "Why shouldn't she?"

Dozens of reasons. Nay, hundreds. Too many to list, so he settled for a grunt.

"Doting uncle, indeed." Lady Clifford stood a little aside from the rest of the group, watching him, no part of the scene unfolding before her escaping her notice. "The first of many nieces and nephews."

She said no more, but he wasn't fooled. They'd known each other too long for that.

She didn't say, *everything's changing.* She didn't tell him he'd have to bend and twist and squeeze until he'd made a place for himself here, but the warning was there, hiding between the words she spoke aloud.

He'd long since learned to listen for what she didn't say.

He was handy with blades, pistols, and his fists, but he'd never been good for much else, especially anything tender, breakable, like the feeble little bundle he held in his arms, with her soft skull and thin, fragile bones.

"Here, ye take the wee lass now." He held the baby out to her mother before he dropped her and she shattered, his throat clenching with an unfamiliar rush of panic, and pretended not to see the disappointment in Sophia's eyes, so it couldn't reach the few remaining tender strips of flesh around his hard heart. "I'm going out."

He strode from the room as soon as Sophia took the baby out of his arms, but Lady Clifford's determined footsteps followed him down the hallway, and her soft voice stopped him before he could flee through the front door.

"Where will you go tonight?"

"Guess I'll know when I get there."

"Is there anyone in particular you're chasing? Someone I should know about?"

"Nay, but it's a dark night. Plenty of criminals on the streets, I reckon." It was true enough—criminals were a plague on London, much like rats—but it wasn't what she'd asked, and sure enough, her brows lowered and her blue eyes narrowed, just as they always did when she was annoyed.

"I would think we had enough trouble without you going in search of it. You must do as you will, I suppose, but keep in mind, Daniel, that chasing shadows won't solve your difficulties. They'll be waiting for you when you return."

"No reason to bother with them now then, is there?"

He owed her better than that, but the thick darkness was waiting for him just on the other side of the circle of light that spilled from the hallway, tempting him. He sucked in a deep breath of frosty air as the night settled over him like a familiar hand against his neck, warm and reassuring, right up until it turned into a fist, tightening and squeezing...

That was when he liked it best. Odd, how a man could become accustomed to ugliness and violence, comfortable in it, in a way he never could be in a drawing room. The night surrounding him, the damp cobbles under his feet, the wind sliding icy fingers under the edge of the collar of his cloak made sense, soothing his jangled nerves.

His steps took him past cramped alleyways toward the other end of the city. As he neared St. Giles, the stench of chamber pots emptied onto the already filthy streets assaulted his nose.

If a man wanted a fight, he'd find it here.

Or it would find him.

His quarry was nameless, faceless. A new enemy, not one of the usual scoundrels he'd reduced to a bloody smear on the streets so many times before. He'd told Lady Clifford the truth about that—he wasn't after one of their usual blackguards—but he hadn't told her *all* of the truth. He'd neglected to mention that for the past few days, someone had been chasing him.

Or not chasing so much as following him, watching him. Whoever they were, they'd kept their distance. They were stealthy, skilled at slipping around corners and down darkened passageways, someone who knew how to blend into the background, and hide in plain sight. Otherwise, he would have caught them days ago.

But they wouldn't stay hidden forever. They never did.

It could be anyone. He had a great many enemies in London.

He lingered at the junction of the seven streets where the sundial used to stand, just for long enough to be seen, then headed west down Little Earl Street toward Monmouth, whistling, but he was listening, waiting for any sign he was being followed. Not anything ordinary, like the sound of footsteps, or a glimpse of a figure darting just out of sight. Seven Dials was always a confusion of bodies and noise, especially on a dark night like tonight, but for something much more subtle, his senses honed by years of wandering these streets.

A telltale chill at the back of his neck, a spray of gooseflesh from a stranger's eyes crawling over him, following his every move—

There.

Just seconds ago, there'd been nothing, and then it appeared as if born from the mist itself, the hairs on the back of his neck standing straight on end. He didn't turn, nor did he slow, but he palmed the handle of the blade buried deep inside the pocket of his greatcoat.

He led his quarry past Monmouth Street—too many people about there, and too much light—and toward the narrow maze of streets overshadowed by tall, shabby buildings crowded together, leaning on each other for support.

He could hear the footsteps now, behind him, a muffled tread, lighter than he'd expected. His pursuer was small, then—much smaller than he was—but agile and quick.

Without warning, he darted to the right, blending into the thicker shadows cast by one of the buildings, and waited. The footsteps behind him ceased, and he imagined his pursuer pausing at the entrance to the courtyard, weighing his options. Only the faintest trickle of light illuminated the darkness here. There were people about, but the poor souls who inhabited the crumbling buildings were people of the night, just as he was, and long since hardened to others' distress.

They wouldn't come running, should anyone cry for help.

So, he waited, poised to spring, but his pursuer was clever enough to see it was too dangerous to follow a man his size into a dark alley, because he didn't appear, and a few moments later Daniel heard the distinct sound of retreating footsteps.

Running, this time.

He leapt out from his hiding place just in time to catch a glimpse of the hem of a dark cloak whirling out behind a fleeing figure, and he took off in pursuit, his much longer legs eating up the ground between them.

It was a mistake to run. He'd chased dozens of blackguards through these streets, and knew what lay behind every corner and down every alley, as surely as he knew the patterns of scars across his knuckles.

There would be no escaping him now. One way or another, this would end tonight.

His pursuer—now the pursued, the tables having been neatly turned—fled back the way he'd come, across Grafton Street toward Newport Market, then scurried into another dark courtyard adjacent, with Daniel right on his heels. When he reached the entrance to the courtyard he paused and peered into the gloom. He'd expected the man to pass through to Porter Street, where he had a better chance of losing Daniel in the crowd, but he hadn't.

He'd stopped in front of one the hovels, and seemed to be frantically scrambling with the door.

Surely, the man hadn't led Daniel to his *home*? He must know he wouldn't find any refuge there. Daniel could crash through the flimsy door with one well-placed kick.

His spine tingled with warning, but he was so close, nearly had the man in his grasp. It might be a trap—there could be a dozen blackguards waiting to leap upon him on the other side of that door—but they'd come after him either way, and he had yet to fall into a trap he couldn't batter his way out of.

The wood of the door splintered under his boot heel, what was left of it crashing into the wall behind it. The hem of the dark coat whirled past him, but Daniel caught a handful of wool in his fist and jerked the man backwards by the cape of his greatcoat, only...

It wasn't a greatcoat at all, but a woman's cloak, and the bunched wool in his hand wasn't a cape, but a hood, and inside the hood was a girl—woman? with wild locks of red gold hair, a pale face with dainty bow lips, and eyes so wide and blue they could sink a man, and make him grateful for the drowning.

He fell back a step, mouth dropping open. "What the dev—?"

He didn't see the dull gleam of the pistol until the instant before it crashed into his skull. He staggered backward, his arms flailing, grasping at air. He got one hand on the girl before a second blow sent him to the floor. His fingers went limp around the fold of her cloak, and he tumbled into a deep, silent darkness.

Chapter Two

He hit the floor with an almighty crash, like a tree falling—a tree that hits another, even bigger tree on its way to the ground.

Mairi flung herself down beside him and threw her arms over her head, eyes squeezed closed as the ceiling shuddered from the impact. Dust rained down from the low wooden beams above, but after another protesting groan, the building settled.

She crawled onto her knees, panting, and peered into the darkness above. No, no sign of the moon or the gloomy London sky. The roof was still there, then. Miraculously, it hadn't collapsed on top of them.

It still might, but at the moment it remained intact, which was more than could be said for the unconscious giant bleeding on the floor.

He was sprawled on his back, blood trickling from the ugly gash she'd given him—just one wound of many, by the looks of the scars on him. He looked like the sort to carry a weapon, likely a pistol.

Sure enough, a quick rifling of his pockets turned up…not a pistol, but a dagger hidden in a narrow, deep pouch sewn into a pocket of his greatcoat. A fine one, too, with a long, curved blade, and was that…? Yes, a pearl handle. He wasn't going to be pleased when he woke and found *this* was missing.

She sheathed the dagger, slipped it into her own pocket, and leaned over him to get a closer look at that gash. His eye was already swelling closed where the butt of her pistol had landed with a crack against his orbital bone that made her wince to recall it. She hadn't *meant* to hit him, but—

Well, no. That wasn't true. She *had* meant to hit him, but she hadn't *wanted* to—

No, damn it. That wasn't true either. She'd waited twenty-four years to see Daniel Adair brought to his knees. She hadn't quite managed that, but unconscious on the floor would do just as well.

Still, she hadn't wanted to kill him. She *hadn't* killed him, had she? She'd been careful to strike the brow bone, where the skull was thicker, and keep away from his temples, but it had been too dark to see properly, and she'd been a trifle...agitated.

She plucked up one of his eyelids and peeked underneath. Plenty of rolling and twitching under there, but just to be sure she pinched the tip of his thumb.

He flexed his fingers in response. Not dead, then.

Good. His death would put a damper on their reunion, and reunions were meant to be joyful occasions, weren't they?

She let out a bitter snort and clambered to her feet. It was a great pity they should meet again under such ugly circumstances, but when that massive hand had clamped down on her shoulder, and that ferocious face had been mere inches from her own, she'd reacted as anyone with any sense would do.

She'd struck him with every bit of strength in her body, then scurried out of the way so he wouldn't crush her when he collapsed.

Still, perhaps she hadn't needed to hit him *twice*. He'd be no use to her dead, after all. If he died, the only thing she cared about in the world would die right along with him.

She edged forward and nudged him with her toe, then leapt back again, just in case he woke. The last thing she wanted was that enormous paw grabbing her ankle.

He didn't stir, but a low moan left his lips.

Alive, and likely enough to stay that way. It would take more than a few blows to fell a man that size, for all that the blood was flowing freely from his wound now, staining the collar of his shirt with dark, rusty smears.

Still, better a blow to the head than a blade to the heart. She hadn't been the only one following him tonight, and the gentleman on his tail hadn't looked like the forgiving sort. By that she meant he had a dagger of his own hidden in his coat, and it was longer than her forearm.

Daniel Adair—or, no, it was *Brixton* now—had more than one enemy, it seemed.

If she hadn't lured the blackguard toward a dead end, Daniel might even now be pinned to the cobbles with a dagger buried in his throat. She might even have saved his life.

Ironic, really, but she hadn't done it for *him*. She'd done it for her grandmother.

Daniel wasn't of any use at all to Lillias Cameron if he were dead.

Mairi needed him breathing, so it might be just as well to bind his head wound. But what if he woke up while she was tending him, and attacked her? He'd end her in an instant if he wrapped those massive hands around her neck.

No, it was too risky. She hadn't gotten this far just to make a fatal error now.

His splayed body took up all the floor space in the tiny room, so she dropped down onto the bed in the corner and pulled her knees up under her chin.

Now what? She couldn't simply sit here while he lay there bleeding all over himself. They'd been friends once, after all.

Friends. No one needed a friend like him.

She wrapped her arms around her knees and let her forehead rest against them. For the entire journey from Coldstream to London, she'd never once let herself admit how remote her chances were of finding Daniel, but now she was here, with him laid out at her feet, the fear she'd spent the past seven days ignoring was right there, waiting for her to acknowledge it.

Odds had been against her making it this far, and this was only the first step. Odds of her making it to the second, third, fourth, or fiftieth step were even grimmer still.

He hadn't known her. There hadn't been even a flicker of recognition in his eyes when he'd seen her face. To be fair, he'd only had a split second before she struck him, and it had been years—no, a lifetime—since she'd last seen him.

She lifted her head and picked out the rough lines of his severe face from the surrounding gloom. If she hadn't known without a doubt the man bleeding on the floor was Daniel Adair, she never would have recognized him, either.

How in the world had an ordinary boy become such a monster of a man? Every inch of him was hard, tight, and...well, there was only one word for it. *Bulging.*

There wasn't a single soft surface anywhere to be seen on the man, only taut, bronze skin pulled tight over straining muscles. His legs were as thick as the wooden beams holding up the ceiling, but sturdier. If there'd been any give at all in the buckskin stretched across his thighs, she would have sworn he padded his breeches.

She'd hoped for more than cold, slitted eyes, pinched lips, and clenched fists, but there was nothing of the sweet boy in the hard man she saw before her. The playful dark eyes had turned hard and wary, the gentle hands brutal, and the dimples she'd recalled with such affection were hidden by the dark, rough scruff that covered his cheeks and chin. Or perhaps they'd vanished entirely, lost forever among the nicks and scars that spoke of a brutal past.

This was what had become of the boy her grandmother had sacrificed everything to save?

What happened to you, Daniel?

That unyielding mouth looked as if it hadn't smiled in decades.

Pity, but then one reaped as they sowed, didn't they? At least, so her grandmother had always told her. From the looks of him, Daniel Adair had reaped the consequences of his actions to an extent that should have satisfied even her vengeful spirit.

Yet she was far from satisfied, nor would she be until she and Daniel were on the Great North Road on their way back to Scotland, where her grandmother waited, silent in the face of the accusation against her, withering away in a dingy cell in the Coldstream Toll Booth.

Their friendship with Daniel Adair hadn't done either Mairi or her grandmother any good, but the past didn't matter anymore. The boy Daniel had been, and the man he was now—none of it mattered. All she cared about was her grandmother, and the blood debt this dark, violent stranger owed them.

She'd come all this way to see that debt was paid.

The frame squeaked in protest as she swung her legs over the edge of the bed and scrambled to her feet, her gaze pinned on her captive as she snatched up the pillow and fingered the thin, dingy fabric of the pillowcase.

It wasn't as durable as she would have liked, but it would do well enough.

As for the rest of the bindings...

As thin and meager as the blanket was, it was too thick. That left only the rough cotton sheet, which she ripped off the bed with one quick jerk.

It was made with the cheapest cotton, and tore easily into strips.

It was impossible to tell if Daniel was deeply unconscious, or on the verge of stirring, and she didn't want to jolt him awake until she'd secured him, so she crept across the floor on her tiptoes, breath held.

Thank goodness he'd fallen on his side when she struck him, with his legs splayed out before him and his arms flung over his head. If she'd had to drag him anywhere, this plan would have been over before it began.

As it was, she made quick work of tying his legs together at the ankles, and then, upon consideration, tying them at the knees as well. She was obliged to shift his arms slightly, but managed to drag them down onto his chest, then tie them at the wrists and elbows without waking him.

Once he was trussed up like an enormous side of mutton on a spit, she sat back on her heels to catch her breath. Yes, that would do quite nicely. It wouldn't hold him forever, of course—he didn't look like the sort of man who was easily contained—but with any luck he'd remain bound long enough for her to explain who she was, and what she wanted from him.

Long enough to remind him of his unpaid debt to her grandmother, one that had remained so for decades. It was well past time for him to make things right.

Until then, there was nothing to do but wait.

On the *bed*, as far away from him as she could get. The last thing she wanted was to find herself at his mercy again. She clambered to her knees, but as she was drawing away, she allowed herself one last look at him before he woke, and the silence erupted into chaos.

Without the snarl on his face and curses streaming from his lips, he looked different. Or, no, that wasn't it, exactly. It was more that he looked…
The same.

The way she remembered him looking, twenty-four years ago. To six-year-old Mairi Cameron, he'd been the boy who'd hung the moon and stars. Oh, he'd been a dreadful tease, of course, and she'd been furious with him often enough, but in her eyes he'd still been perfect. She'd adored him with every part of herself, in the way perhaps only a child was capable of adoring someone.

That dark hair, nearly black, with that one wavy lock that always refused to behave, and insisted on falling over his forehead, and his mouth…the playful grin was gone, yes, but she could almost imagine it now, curling the dark red lips she remembered, with the same full lower lip that always made him look as if he were sulking.

And those thick eyelashes resting against his cheeks. She'd always envied his eyelashes, far too pretty to be wasted on a boy, framing a pair of eyes darker than a midnight sky, eyes she'd seen in her dreams nearly every night since he disappeared.

Could it be that this pitiless man still had those same deep, liquid dark eyes?

If he did, she might be able to believe the boy she remembered was still there, lost somewhere inside this hard, brutal man. She rested a hand on his face, hovering over him, hope fluttering in her breast. No man with eyes as warm as those she remembered could be as heartless, as lost to all tender feeling as he appeared to be.

"Daniel?"

Don't touch him.

"Quiet," she muttered, ignoring the niggling voice inside her. It was too late, in any case—her fingertips were already on his cheek. His face was warm and prickly, the rasp of it against her fingertips coaxing a shiver out of her.

The hope was surging inside her now, beating against her ribs. "Daniel, are you—"

His eyes snapped open without a hint of warning, not even as much as a telltale twitch of his eyelid. "Oh!"

She scrambled backward, away from him, heels scrabbling at the floor, but she got a glimpse of his face, for one frozen instant.

That was enough.

His eyes were dark, as dark as a starless midnight sky.

Dark, cold, and empty.

Chapter Three

Daniel crawled back to consciousness one searing breath at a time, like a drowning man fighting to the surface of a pool of oily water. He was limp, heavy, his tongue slick and rusty. He slid it around inside his mouth, expecting to find shredded flesh where his teeth had been.

No, they were still there, right where he'd left them, but that twitch of his tongue was enough to send pain shooting through his skull, and something thick and sticky was trickling from his temple and pooling at the corner of his mouth.

Blood. Not his teeth then, but his head.

He'd been awake for some time before he opened his eyes, but he lay as still as a corpse, an instinct honed over long years of battle on the streets of London. The longer this blackguard believed him to be unconscious or dead, the better it was for Daniel.

A dead man wasn't apt to sink a dagger between his ribs.

He slitted one eye open—the other was swollen closed—and squinted into the darkness. He'd been chasing someone through Seven Dials—the man who'd been following him these past few days. He'd tracked him into a dark hovel off Newport Market, and...

Slender frame, red hair, wide blue eyes.

He peeled his eyelids back, or tried to. One cooperated, but the other gave up at the midpoint and stayed there, like a window stuck in the sill, but that single eye opening was enough to send someone scrambling for safety with a shriek that sunk into his skull like a fishhook in his eyeball.

A *woman's* shriek.

The red-headed chit? *She* was the one who'd bashed his head in, and made a bloody pulp of his eye? Such a tiny, feeble lass as that could hardly swat an insect, much less bring down a man of his size.

Nay, someone else had dealt the blow, some hulk of a man, quick and vicious. As for which big, quick, vicious villain it might be, he couldn't say. There was likely a half-dozen of them hunting the streets for him right now.

Whoever it was, he wasn't in the room. If he had been, Daniel would be dead by now. That only left him and the girl, which meant he was even now squandering his best chance at gaining the upper hand.

He squinted into the darkness, but she was nowhere to be seen. Still here, though, watching him from some shadowy corner of the room, keeping her distance. It's what he would have done, in her situation. She had a pistol, yes, but he could disarm her in an instant.

As soon as he got a hand on her, it would be over.

It was almost too easy.

Then again, he was the one bound on the floor with blood leaking from his head, wasn't he? His brain was still bouncing off the inside of his skull, his cheek was smashed against a cold, grimy floor, and he couldn't see worth a damn. His hands were bound with—he wriggled his fingers and turned his wrists—torn strips of cotton at both his wrists and elbows, tight enough that his fingers had gone numb. An experimental kick revealed his legs had also been bound, at the ankles and knees.

If she'd been the one to tie him, she'd done a proper job of it.

He didn't care for being struck on the head or trussed up like a pig, but he couldn't help a grunt of approval. No sense bothering to bind a man if you weren't going to do it right.

If he'd been anyone else, the bindings might even have held. On him, they were nothing more than an inconvenience, a delay in the inevitable. All told, the bindings worked against her, as delays irritated him, and he'd been told he was unpleasant when he was irritated.

He wedged his thumb into the knot at his wrists, and before long he'd worked it loose enough so one quick twist would free his hands from the makeshift bindings. If his only goal had been to escape, he could have gone then, but his wily, red-haired attacker and her accomplice had been tracking him for the past few days, and now they'd done their best to leave his brains scattered over the cobbles.

He wanted to know *why.* "I know you're there, lass. My head is pounding, and there's blood in my eyes. A bit of water, if you would, and mayhap a cloth?"

No response. Not even an indrawn breath, the heartless chit.

"My eye is bad. I could lose it if it isn't tended to."

There was another long pause, but his face must have been good and bloody, because he heard a rustle of skirts, then a trickle of water. He held his breath, waiting, then let it out in a slow exhale when two small feet in a pair of torn, filthy shoes appeared in his line of sight.

But she stopped a few steps away from him, just out of his reach.

"It's all right, lass." He kept his voice soft, and made a show of wriggling his arms, as if they were still securely tied. "I'm no threat to you, trussed up like a Christmas goose as I am."

"More like a Christmas side of beef."

A surprised chuckle split his cracked lips. The girl was daft, trifling with him, but she put him in mind of Sophia or one of his other girls with that lash of a tongue. "You've no more to fear from me than you would your Christmas dinner."

The lie flowed easily from his lips, as smooth as cream, just like the hundreds he'd told before, and anyway, it wasn't as if he was going to hurt her.

At least, not any more than he had to.

She crept closer, taking care to keep the hem of her skirts clear of his reach. "Keep still, and remember, if you please, that my foot is mere inches from your forehead."

Vicious. He liked that in a lass. Stronger than she looked, too—much stronger than a lady with such tiny feet had a right to be, her grip on his shoulders steady as she rolled him flat onto his back with one mighty heave, then scurried out of his reach.

He squinted up at her, eyes stinging.

Her face was a pale oval in the dim room, blurry from the blood in his eyes, but he could make out the bridge of her nose, the sweep of her chin, the high arch of a cheekbone, and the bow of a tempting upper lip, too dainty for the generous curve of the lower.

Had he seen her before? No, he'd remember those blue eyes, but there was something familiar about her.

A prickle of unease tingled at the back of his neck. The unusual color of her hair, the blue eyes, the stubborn chin teased at the edges of his memory, like the fleeting impression of a dream just as it dissipates into wakefulness.

But a great many criminals in London looked familiar to him. Maybe he'd chased her before. She might look as innocent as a wee spring lamb, but innocent ladies didn't prance around the rookeries with pistols in their reticules, nor did they know how to bind a man's wrists so tight it cut off the flow of blood to his hands.

Someone had taught the girl to tie a proper knot.

"Is that for my eye?" He blinked, letting his lashes flutter as if he were close to losing consciousness again.

She peered down at him, a damp cloth in her hand and her teeth sunk into her lower lip as if she'd only now realized how close she'd have to get to him in order to cleanse the blood from his head. "If you remain still, then yes. Otherwise, you'll find it shoved halfway down your throat. Which is it going to be?"

"My eye, please, miss." He *could* be charming, but only when his life depended on it.

Her pretty lips pinched together, gaze raking his battered face. He smothered his grunt of satisfaction as she eased closer, white fingers curling around the cloth as if it were a weapon.

That's it, wee thing. Come on...

"Don't move," she warned again, keeping a wide slice of empty space between them. She had good instincts on her, but that wouldn't matter, in the end. All he needed was to get one hand on some part of her, just one hand...

His muscles twitched as she crept closer, then close enough that she was within grabbing distance, but his eye was throbbing angrily, as if it were one instant away from abandoning his skull altogether, and he'd learned long ago not to strike unless he could be sure he'd hit his target. "Wouldn't, even if I could."

Just a little closer...

At the last minute her eyes locked on his, and whatever shadows she saw lurking under his false smile made her breath catch on a soft cry. She whirled away from him, but by then, it was too late.

He snatched up a fold of her cloak, used it to struggle to a sitting position, and fell against the wall at his back with her hem still clutched in his fist. He didn't want to hurt her, but it was either gain control or lose it, and he didn't lose.

Ever.

He tugged her closer with a quick flick of his wrist. "Come here, lass."

She stumbled, a startled gasp on her lips, but regained her balance quickly. "Let go."

"Nay." He curled his fingers in the cloth, twisting it tight. "A word of advice, lass. Never trust a man who claims you have nothing to fear from him."

"Never underestimate a lady who just knocked your brains out your ear and laid you out like a turtle flipped on its back. I would have preferred you on your knees, but a lady takes what she can get, doesn't she?"

"*You* knocked me flat?" Laughter wheezed from between his bloodstained lips. "I don't think so, lass."

She arched an eyebrow. "Do you see anyone else here?"

Curiously enough, he didn't. Just a bit of a girl who looked as if she'd topple under the weight of a muff pistol, and it had been no bloody muff pistol that had left the crack in his skull. "Not *now*, no."

"Well, that leaves me then, I suppose." She shrugged, but a smirk twitched at the corners of her lips. "I beg your pardon if I was too rough with you."

He snorted. A tongue like acid, this one, and that smirk of hers was even more irritating than Haslemere's. "What did ye tie me with?"

"The bedsheets, of course. What else? Now, I demand you release me this instant."

"Demand?" Oh, she was a haughty one, all right. "I might demand the same of you, lass."

"You might, yes, if you weren't bound and bleeding. As it is, you're not in a position to demand anything." She tossed her head, a gesture that might have been more impressive if she weren't squirming to get free.

"I like my position well enough." He curled his lips in the feral grin that had terrorized men far bigger and deadlier than this chit. Oh, she was a fierce thing, to be sure—the blood matting his hair was proof of that—but he could tear his bindings loose in an instant, if only she'd hold still. "I would have thought a clever lass like you would know to tie my hands behind my back."

"I *do* know, but I also knew I didn't have a prayer of rolling you flat onto your stomach with your arms behind you, any more than I would a horse. Or a carriage. A barouche, that is, or perhaps a traveling coach."

He snorted. "I'm big enough, aye. Mayhap you might convince me to release you, if you can make me believe you won't just up and run, and leave me here, bound and helpless."

Far from helpless, but she didn't know that.

"Do you suppose I went to all this trouble only to abandon you, now I have you where I want you, Daniel?"

Daniel. She knew his name.

That chased the smirk from his lips quick enough. "Do you know me, lass? Beg your pardon, but I don't recall having had the pleasure."

She gave him a thin, cold smile. "It wasn't a pleasure, but yes, this is a reunion of sorts."

Not a happy one, by the looks of things. If it had been, she wouldn't have come after him with a pistol. "Can't say I'm liking it much, so far, but I've never reunited with long-lost kin before. Do they always beat each other bloody?"

Something hard flickered in her blue eyes. "We're not kin."

Christ, he hoped she wasn't one of his former lovers, but it *would* explain the assault. More than one lady in London had reason enough to want to beat the devil out of him. This one, though…tempting mouth, and a mass of red curls that begged for a man's fingers, but she was a bit too delicate for his tastes.

He wasn't tender. He didn't fondly caress, or whisper sweetly. He didn't even kiss, if the thing could be avoided. He fucked, hard. That was all, and she looked as if she'd break apart with one good thrust.

"I didn't follow you for three days and lure you here to reminisce, Daniel. We have unfinished business between us."

Lure? His amusement drained as quickly as the blood from his head wound. This red-haired lass with an oddly familiar face had been following him around London for days to lure him back to this filthy little hovel?

This wasn't the impulse of a moment, then. If what she said was true, she'd intended for him to end up here in this room from the start. Once she caught his attention tonight, she'd fled to Howe Court, hoping he'd follow her here.

She'd planned a bloody ambush, and done a neat job of executing it, too.

"Who are you?" Without his intending it, Daniel's fingers loosened around her cloak—a damn foolish move, given her wiliness, but instead of putting some distance between them as any lass in her right mind would, she remained where she was.

"Don't you know me, Daniel? It has been many years, but I'd think you'd remember your dearest childhood friend."

"Childhood friend, eh?" What bollocks. He hadn't had any childhood friends. He'd hardly had a *childhood*. "Beg pardon, but I've never seen you before in my life. Your name, lass. What is it?"

"It's Mairi, Daniel." She was still, watching him. "Mairi Cameron."

"Mairi Cameron." No, the name meant nothing to him. "All right, then, Mairi Cameron." He drew her closer with a tug on her skirts. "Suppose you tell me why you've been chasing me down every dark street in London?"

Chapter Four

He didn't remember her. Not her face, her voice, or her name.

Twenty-four years was, admittedly, a long time, and memories could prove wearisome, particularly those that involved obligations so profound they demanded satisfaction.

Mairi might even have forgotten it all herself, if she hadn't spent the past twenty-four years snatching and clawing at every sliver of her memories of that time, scraping up every fragment, no matter how thin, and laying them carefully aside like fine linens in a cedar trunk until the time came to drag them out again.

Some ladies had trousseaus. She had revenge.

For him, though, it was far more convenient to forget, blood debts being ugly, messy, painful things. Or, failing that, to pretend to forget, should anyone from the past emerge, demanding answers.

Inconvenient, but there it was.

"Let's try again, lass. Why have you been following me, and why did you beat the wits out of me with the butt of your pistol?"

"Your wits, such as they are, would be intact if you hadn't closed in on me like a rabid animal intent on ripping my throat out. I did what I must to save my own neck."

"Your neck was safe enough with me, until you bludgeoned me."

If he thought her fool enough to believe that, his wits truly were addled. "I bludgeoned you *after* you threatened me, Daniel."

"I hit the floor before I had a chance to threaten anyone." His voice was as cold and flat as his empty dark eyes. "What have you done with the pistol?"

"It's someplace safe."

He eyed her, then glanced around the room, as if searching out potential hiding places, and assessing his chances of finding it before she could get to it.

"If I intended to shoot you, I would have done it by now. You were unconscious for five full minutes. I could have put a ball between your eyes then if I chose."

"A sweet, wee thing like you, shoot a helpless, wounded man between the eyes?" He took in her slight frame, her small hands, skepticism rising from him in palpable waves.

She recognized that look, having seen it on dozens of faces before. People tended to underestimate her, men in particular. It was the cloud of red hair that did it. They saw it, and...what? Mistook her for a kitten, or a fawn? She'd never been sure what went through their heads, only that they took one look at her, and made their assumptions.

The *wrong* assumptions, every time. "Are you aware, Daniel, that a tall, thin gentleman with a scarred face and a knife hidden in his sleeve has been following you? I assume he has unfinished business with you, as well."

He shrugged. "What if he does? He's got nothing to do with you."

Ah, that's where he was wrong. Everything that had to do with Daniel Brixton had to do with *her*. He just didn't know it yet. "He didn't, until I led him away from you, and back toward Grafton Street. You should be thanking me."

He snorted. "For what? Saving my life so you could finish me off yourself?"

"For diverting him. Better to be bludgeoned than stabbed, and I didn't finish anything." Not *yet*, but she would. "You're still here, aren't you?"

He didn't answer. A sliver of moon had emerged from the clouds, but his face was still cast in shadows, and she couldn't read his expression.

"He has a scar, you said? This blackguard who's been following me?"

"Yes. He followed you all the way to the entrance of Howe Court tonight. You seem to be acquainted with some unsavory characters."

"He could have been after anyone. How can you be sure he was after me?"

Dagger-wielding villains seemed to be of no more concern to him than the horse droppings dirtying every street in London. "Because *I* was following *him*, following you."

"Now why would you want to do a thing like that?"

"To keep him from murdering you, of course." Really, wasn't it obvious?

He chuckled, as if she were a precocious child, or an especially clever hunting dog. "Is that so, Mairi Cameron? I'm flattered."

"Don't be. I didn't do it for *your* sake."

"Whose, then? No lass in her right mind chases a man three times her size though the streets of St. Giles at night unless she has a reason. So, what's *your* reason, Mairi Cameron?"

Perhaps a lass in her right mind didn't, but she'd left her sanity somewhere on the road between Scotland and London. She'd burned through precious days traveling from Coldstream, days her grandmother didn't have.

The spring session of the Court of Assizes was in five weeks, and there was little doubt Lillias would be found guilty. If Mairi couldn't persuade Daniel to return to Scotland with her, her sweet, gentle grandmother would end her life swinging from a noose.

If there'd ever been a time to mince words, it had long since passed. "I did it for my grandmother, Lillias Cameron."

Surely, there must be some deeply buried part of him that hadn't forgotten what Lillias had done for him all those years ago? Surely, he still had a tender place inside him for the woman who'd loved him as if he'd been her own grandson, the woman who'd risked everything for him?

But there was nothing. His face remained hard and impassive at the name, without a single spark of recognition in those blank eyes. "What's your grandmother got to do with me?"

"She's been accused of a crime. Even now she's in prison, awaiting trial." It took an effort to spit those words out, but he didn't reward her with as much as a ripple in his expression. Not shock or horror, not sympathy—not even mild surprise.

"*And?*" He waved an impatient hand at her. "I still don't see why I should give a damn about any of this."

That dismissive wave of his hand, his *indifference*…bile flooded her throat, coated her tongue, so sour all the swallowing in the world wouldn't wash the bitterness from her mouth.

Had there really been a part of her that had hoped he'd prove to be the hero she'd thought him twenty-four years ago? Against all odds, against reason itself, had she truly believed a glimpse of her face, a whisper of her name, of Lillias's name, would justify her childish adoration of him? That the intervening years of rage and bitterness would fall away, scattering like leaves in an autumn wind?

The more fool she, then. Looking into his watchful dark eyes now, it seemed incredible that she ever could have imagined he'd be pleased to see her.

Nothing ever happened as one hoped it would, did it?

No matter. She'd accepted long ago the reality of being left behind by him, a boy she'd once loved who'd grown into a man who'd never looked back. Behind those frigid eyes, bulging muscles, and gruff demeanor, Daniel was a coward.

He'd always been a coward.

He'd have her believe he'd forgotten her. That he'd forgotten all of them. Lillias, Hamish, Coldstream itself.

It was fortunate, then, that she was here to remind him. "We were friends, once—dear friends, when we were children together in Scotland. It's been years since we've seen each other, but you were eight years old when you left Coldstream. How can you not remember it?"

"I can't remember a thing that never happened, can I?"

"Or remember one that *did*, apparently." She swallowed, but her mouth remained as dry as dust. "It's curious, really, that you could have forgotten it all, and so completely, but I suppose it's easier that way."

There was a pause, then his voice, cold-edged and dangerous, reached through the darkness. "What do you mean by that? Easier how?"

His grip on her skirts tightened, tugged, and she was obliged to move a step closer to him. "If you don't remember a debt, then you need never trouble yourself about repaying it. If my grandmother is in prison because of something she did *for you*, well, I suppose that's her problem, isn't it?" Her throat had gone as tight as a fist, clenching as she shoved more words off the edge of her tongue. "She's facing the gibbet."

"The *gibbet*? What crime did she commit?"

"No crime at all. She's innocent."

"She found herself on the wrong side of the law somehow. What's the charge against her?"

"Murder." Dear God, that word burned, like acid dripping from the tip of her tongue.

"Murder? Aye, that'll get you sent to the gibbet quickly enough."

She had to clench her hands into fists to keep from shaking him, bite her tongue to keep from shrieking at him. "Too quickly, in her case. She's no murderer. She'd sooner hurt herself than she would another person. She's spent her entire lifetime protecting those she loves, including you, Daniel."

Especially you. She was *still* protecting him, only now Lillias's misguided loyalty to Daniel would see her hanged.

No reaction from him, aside from a raised eyebrow.

"She's as much *your* grandmother as she is mine." She tried to lower her rising voice, to smother the thread of hysteria there, but all she could see in her mind's eye was Lillias locked in a cold, dark cell in the Coldstream Toll Booth—Lillias, so pale, silent, and still it was as if she were already a corpse, standing on a scaffold as the executioner fit a noose around her neck. "Turning your back on her now is no different than turning your back on your own family."

"Poor choice of words, lass. I don't have a fa—"

"None of this would have happened if it weren't for you!" She was losing control, a flood of accusations threatening to pour from her lips. It would only make it easier for him to walk away, but she couldn't make herself stop. "You *owe* her, Daniel! You—"

"I don't owe you or your grandmother a bloody thing, lass. She got herself tossed in a cell, then she can face whatever comes next."

"What comes next is a scaffold. It's nothing to you if an innocent lady is hanged?"

"Every criminal facing the noose at Newgate claims they're innocent."

"In my grandmother's case, there's no doubt of it."

"Why? Because she swore it to you? People swear by their lies every day."

"No." Inside her head she was screaming, raging at him, but her voice when she spoke was a whisper. "Because she's been accused of murdering *you.*"

Silence, so sudden and deep each of her breaths seemed deafening.

"One problem with that, lass," he murmured, his disembodied voice floating from the darkness. "I'm not *dead.*"

"As far as the Coldstream justice of the peace is concerned, you *are* dead. You died twenty-four years ago—"

There was a quick, hard jerk on her cloak, and then she was falling, her words lost in a choked gasp as the heel of her boot caught on her hem. She threw her arms out to brace herself and squeezed her eyes closed, but she never hit the floor.

She hit the wall, instead, only this wall was of muscle and bone, warm and alive, moving underneath her. Oh, *no.* She was in Daniel's *lap.* A cry rose to her lips, but before she could give it voice, a huge hand came down over her mouth. "No shrieking. I've got a wee bit of a headache."

He released her mouth, but his massive arm locked around her neck, a half dozen strips of torn cloth dangling from his fingers—his bindings, knots neatly untied. Dear God, what a *fool* she was. He'd likely freed himself ages ago, and she hadn't even noticed it.

But it wasn't the bits of cloth in his hand that made her breath seize.

It was the dagger.

Pearl-handled, the wicked hooked blade polished to a high shine, identical to the one she'd taken from his coat, because of course, *of course* he had two daggers, the second one likely hidden in his boot. Oh, *why* hadn't she thought to check his boot?

"Nice and easy, now, lass. I'm not going to hurt you."

"No?" She winced at the humiliating breathlessness, the *fear* in her voice. "Then you've no need for the dagger, do you?"

His chuckle tickled the fine, loose hair near her ear. "I don't need the dagger to hurt you, lass."

She'd never forgive herself for the whimper that escaped her then, but the forearm pressed against her neck was the size and weight of a horse's hindquarters, and her chin was the only thing that stood between it and her throat.

"You have the wrong man, Mairi Cameron. You've mistaken me for someone else."

The wisest course of action here was to *agree* with the man holding a dagger an inch away from her throat, but her tongue refused to cooperate. "No. We lived next door to each other in Coldstream, Scotland, until you were eight years old. How do you suppose I know who you are? We were best friends."

"I don't have friends, half of London knows who I am, and I've never set foot any further north than Derbyshire."

He had an answer for everything, it seemed. "You've called me 'lass' half a dozen times since you regained consciousness. Did you pick that up in Derbyshire?"

"Nay, from my father. He was from Dunkeld, near Tayside."

"You acknowledge your father was Scottish, then. That's something, isn't it?" Her heart leapt, but then crashed down again at his next words.

"Dunkeld, lass, not Coldstream, and he left Scotland years before I was born. Now, you listen to me carefully, Mairi Cameron. If you tell me the truth, mayhap I can help you, but if you keep up with your wild stories, I'll go through that door, and you may believe me when I say you'll never lay eyes on me again."

He was as good as gone, then. He hadn't believed a word she'd said so far, and there was no reason to suppose that was going to change. At this point, he'd think every word out of her mouth was a lie—

But it isn't.

Every word she'd said to him was the truth. It was all she had, and the only thing she could do was to keep telling it. "Your name is Daniel Brixton, and you're thirty-two years old." Her voice was shaking, and she drew in a long breath to steady it. "You're the only child of Ian and Aileen Adair. Your mother died of a consumptive fever when you were five years old, and you don't remember her."

He stiffened for an instant, but then his shoulders shifted against her back in a shrug. "My life has never been a secret. Anyone in London could tell you the same thing."

She bit her lip, hesitating. Bits and pieces of Daniel's life rose to the surface of her mind, details only an intimate acquaintance would know, but there were a few inconvenient holes here and there, things she wasn't certain of. If she revealed them now, and it turned out she was wrong—

"If that's all, lass, then I'll be on my way—"

"Your mother's maiden name was Thompson."

He said nothing, and she squeezed her eyes closed, praying she'd remembered right.

"Your father was a blacksmith, and you spent most of the years after you left Coldstream traveling from one village to another in England." This was supposition only, no more than a guess, really, based on the letters Ian Adair had sent Lillias. "You stopped when your father found work, then moved on again when it ended."

"I told you before, lass. Every blackguard in London could tell you the same."

He *did* seem to have more than a passing acquaintance with London's blackguards. "Your father died four years ago." Again, she couldn't be sure of this, but as the blank letters that had arrived for Lillias every year since Daniel and his father left Coldstream had abruptly stopped four years earlier, it was a good guess.

He neither confirmed nor denied this.

"Your father was living in Rotherhithe when he died. His former neighbor, a voluble lady by the name of Mrs. Burton, remembers him well. She remembered you, too, and was happy to tell me where to find you. Before Rotherhithe, it was Solihull, outside Birmingham. Before that it was Beccles, Eversham, Great Malvern, Letchworth, Kempston, St. Margaret's—"

"That's enough. Very well then, explain to me how you know every place I've lived in the past twenty-three years."

"I can do better than explain it. Release me, and I'll show you."

"All right, Mairi Cameron." The arm around her neck went slack. "Show me."

Her knees were still shaking as she stumbled to her feet, crossed the room to the bed, lifted up a corner of the tattered mattress, and slid her hand underneath it.

"Slowly now, lass. I don't like surprises, and you never did tell me where you hid that pistol."

"I *did* tell you. It's somewhere safe." Her fingers brushed against the packet of letters, tied in a bundle with a bit of string. Nineteen of them. The first had arrived the year after Daniel Adair had gone missing, and the last four years ago.

But it hadn't only been Daniel who'd disappeared. Hamish had, as well. One day they'd been there, and then, in the blink of an eye, they'd both vanished. The letters were the only fragile, tenuous link to a tragedy that didn't make any sense, each one of them a window into the past, a feeble ray of light illuminating an incident shrouded in mystery.

The letters were all blank—just folded pieces of paper, without anything written inside. All of them, that is, but the first, sent twenty-three years ago this year, and that one bore one word only.

Brixton.

All of the letters were addressed to Mairi's grandmother, Lillias Cameron, with the address written in a barely legible hand, as if the sender were unaccustomed to using a pen. Her grandmother had saved them all, tucked into the bottom of a dusty wooden box hidden under a loose floorboard beneath the bed. Mairi had asked her about the letters, over and over again, but her grandmother would only shake her head in reply.

Eventually, Mairi had stopped asking. Lillias intended to take her secrets to the grave, even if her silence meant she'd find that grave much sooner than either of them had ever suspected.

Sooner, and under the most brutal of circumstances—

"Get on with it, lass. I haven't got all night."

She pulled out the packet of letters, turned to face him again, and nodded at the only chair in the room, a spindly one he'd promptly reduce to a bit of kindling. "Perhaps you'd better sit on the bed. I'll take the chair."

He did as she asked, the bed squeaking in protest at his weight.

She perched on the edge of the chair with the packet of letters held protectively against her chest. "This is the first of them." She untied the string and carefully took up the letter on the top, the one with the postmark from St. Margaret's, a tiny village in Herefordshire, southwest of Hereford. "Open it."

He took the letter and slowly unfolded it while she held her breath. The inside of the letter was blank, but for that one word.

Brixton.

Daniel stared down at the paper for a long time. "Where did you get this?"

"The packet was hidden among my grandmother's things. She received a letter much like this one every year after you and your father left Coldstream, the address written in the same hand each time. This one—the first one—is the only one with anything written on the page."

His fingers twitched, leaving a faint wrinkle in the paper. "Doesn't make sense."

It made perfect sense to her. "There's only one way to interpret it. Your father adopted a new surname after he took you away from Scotland. This first letter provides that name. The rest seem to be sent for the purpose of informing my grandmother where you were."

"That makes even less sense. Why should your grandmother need to know where we were?"

"I assume so she could find you again, should the need arise."

And now it had arisen, in spectacularly desperate fashion.

She handed over the rest of the packet, watching as Daniel shuffled through them one by one, paying particular attention to the address and the postmarks. "That is your father's handwriting, isn't it?"

He tossed the final letter aside. "I don't remember."

It was a lie. She knew it as soon as the words left his mouth. It was curious that she could still recognize the signs of deception on his face, despite the intervening decades. But it was still an answer, nonetheless. If it wasn't his father's hand, he would have said so at once, as there was no reason to lie about it. "I don't believe you."

"I don't give a damn what you believe."

"If I'm lying, then how do you explain those letters? Why should your father write to a lady he's never met before?"

"I didn't say they'd never met, only that I'd never been to Scotland. For all I know he knew her in Solihull, or St. Margaret's, and wrote those letters to her after she moved to Scotland. Another thing, lass. If they were such good friends, why are all the letters blank?"

"I didn't say they were good friends, or friends at all. The purpose of the correspondence wasn't to nurture a friendship. It was to communicate information."

She waited, heart pounding for the boy she'd once loved, a boy who'd grown into a man she didn't know and didn't trust, to pronounce her fate. How had it come to such a sad pass as this?

Perhaps it had been a hopeless quest from the start, a fool's errand, nearly certain to fail, but Daniel was the only hope she had left. Since she'd arrived in London the day before yesterday, she'd been consumed with the search for him. Now by some miracle, here she was, so close she could reach out her hand to touch him.

The hard part—finding him—was over.

She only had to convince him to return to Scotland with her. "If you don't help me, my grandmother is going to hang. The only way to prove her innocence is for you to return to Coldstream with me, and—"

"Return to Coldstream with you? Is that why you've been following me? To fetch me to Scotland? Beg pardon, lass, but I don't fancy a trip up north to the Scottish Borders."

He shot to his feet so suddenly she jerked back, and would have toppled over, chair and all, if he hadn't seized her wrist. He didn't hurt her— surprisingly enough, given the size of his hands, the muscles of his arms straining against his coat sleeves, but the look in his eyes, the grim set of his mouth, sent her heart plummeting into her stomach with a resounding thud.

To look at him now, she couldn't believe he'd ever been that playful, dark-eyed boy with the infectious grin, but she forced her chin up, and looked him in the eyes. "Listen to me, Daniel—"

"Nay, I've heard enough. Go home to Scotland, Mairi Cameron. You're wasting your time with me."

Chapter Five

The bones of her wrist were so thin and breakable, Daniel felt as if he'd caught a bird between his fingertips.

She was a dainty one, with that pale skin and those big, blue eyes, but the girl's mind was like a gamekeeper's steel trap, and his leg had been caught in it since he'd followed her into Howe Court. The wound on his head was throbbing, the blood trickling from his forehead was stinging his eyes, and he had a splinter in his left arse cheek from where he'd crashed into the rough wooden floorboards.

He'd been hit before, beaten to unconsciousness only to wake to boot heels kicking in his ribs, but he'd never before awoken to a world that no longer made sense. This time he'd left his wits scattered on the street outside, and Mairi Cameron—a name he'd never heard before, and didn't want to hear again after tonight—was grinding them into the cobbles with her boot heel.

It was time she was made to understand she'd chosen the wrong man to play with. "Last chance, lass, and I'll have the truth this time. What's your name, and why have you been following me? What do you want from me?"

"For pity's sake, how many times must I repeat myself? I told you, I'm Mairi Cameron, granddaughter to Lillias Cameron—"

Before she could say another word, he clamped his arm around her waist, holding her as easily as he would a ragdoll, and dumped her on the thin, grubby mattress pushed against the wall in one corner of the room.

"What are you—?"

"Quiet." He scooped up the torn pieces of bedsheet, tied her wrists, and secured the other end to one of the iron posts at the head of the bed. Then he snatched up the letters scattered over the coverlet and across the floor, and took up the first letter to read it again.

He held it in front of him for some time before he realized his hand was shaking. He wanted to blame the blow to the head for his unsteadiness, but it was the familiar scrawl that had his heart thrashing against his ribs.

Brixton.

Written in his father's hand.

He stared down at the word until it began to blur on the page, then raised his eyes to the girl he'd bound to the bed. She'd struggled upright, and though the room was too dark for him to make out much beyond the outline of her face, he could see her eyes in his mind as clearly as if he were gazing into them.

Bluebells.

As familiar to him, somehow, as the hesitant scratches on the paper clutched in his hand.

He looked away, ignoring the unanswered questions piling atop each other in his head. There would be a time when they'd demand to be answered, but he'd wait until he had his wits about him, after his head had ceased its relentless throbbing and blood was no longer gushing from the gash she'd torn into his skull with that wicked blow from her pistol.

He'd do well to remember *she'd* been the one who'd dealt that blow, especially now, when she appeared so small and defenseless, as if those pale hands of hers were much too weak to hold even a bunch of wildflowers, much less a heavy pistol.

"If you've finished manhandling me, I can explain the—"

Daniel held up a hand to silence her.

Still shaking, damn it.

He moved toward the window where the faint glow of moonlight managed to peek through the filthy panes, slid to the floor, resting his back against the wall, and began once again to sift through the packet of letters.

One by one he examined them, the blood cooling on his neck and in his veins as the same address in Coldstream, Scotland, appeared again and again, written on the face of each one in his father's unsteady scribble. Ian Adair had been good with his hands, but he was a blacksmith, not a scholar. He hadn't had much occasion to write, as the shaky curves and jagged angles of each letter showed.

There was no mistaking it. As infrequently as he'd seen it, Daniel would have recognized his father's handwriting anywhere. He sifted through the thick pile, holding each letter up to the window to catch the faint glow of moonlight. Aside from the first one, each of the letters was blank, just as she'd said they were.

He set them aside, one by one, then sat still for a long time, thinking, but there was no making sense of it. He squinted into the darkness, picking out the small figure huddled in the middle of the bed from the surrounding gloom. He could wring another explanation from her—there was no shortage of words on *those* lips—but he wasn't certain he wanted to hear what she had to say.

Not yet.

He scooped the letters up into a haphazard pile in his hand, but just as he rose to stuff them back under the mattress where he'd found them, he paused, his stomach churning as he gazed down at the postmark on the one at the top of the pile.

Solihull. He hardly remembered the small village outside Birmingham, he'd been so young when he'd lived there briefly with his father.

He took up the next letter, then the next, and the next.

St. Margaret's, in Herefordshire, Beccles, Eversham, Great Malvern, Letchworth, Kempston, George Lane, in East London—

It didn't make any damned sense a girl he'd never laid eyes on before could have come out of nowhere with a handful of letters postmarked from each town Daniel and his father had lived, yet the proof of it was right there in his hand, in his own father's handwriting, a timeline of the past two decades of his life, as if his father was sending him a message from the grave.

The last letter was dated the year before his father died, and postmarked from Rotherhithe, where he'd lived the last few years of his life. Christ, those shabby rooms. He'd tried to get his father to come with him when he'd gone to Maddox Street, but Ian Adair had said Mayfair wasn't for the likes of him.

He snatched up the packet of letters and approached the bed. She didn't flinch away from him as he closed in on her—the lass was brave, he'd give her that—but she stiffened when he paused, towering over her before he took her shoulders in his hands, and lowered his face until it was mere inches from her own.

"Suppose you tell me how you happen to have these letters."

She eyed him, calculating. "Untie me first."

"Nay, I don't think so. I don't fancy another blow to the head."

"Do you suppose I'd hit you with my fist?" She held up her empty hands. "My pistol is under the washbasin."

"*That's* somewhere safe?" He strode over to the wobbly table in the corner of the room, where a cracked basin had been overturned, and beneath it, he found her pistol. "I never should have turned my back on you, lass. I won't make that mistake again."

"You never turned your back on me. I was standing in front of you when I struck you. Don't you remember?"

He grunted. "I can hardly forget with my brains still leaking out of my ears."

"Better that than your blood leaking out of your chest, or...well, perhaps not *much* better, really."

"Aye, that's right. You risked your life to save me. Or so you'd have me believe."

That stubborn chin jutted out. "Believe what you like, but it's the truth."

"Aye, lass, so you say, but I don't recall seeing either the man or the blade, so for all I know, both are a figment of your imagination. I do remember seeing *your* face, though, right before everything went dark, and this is *your* pistol in my hand too, eh?"

"As I said, untie me, and I'll tell you everything."

"You'll tell me anyway."

More than one man had begged and pleaded for mercy when facing off with him—violent, brutal men, thieves and murderers, and all of them bigger than this tiny slip of a girl with her pretty bow lips, which had, astonishingly, curled into a smirk.

It *did* make sense some scoundrel or other had been on his heels, lurking in the shadows, waiting for a chance to strike. More than one of London's blackguards would like to see him maimed or dead, and that was to say nothing of the aristocrats, but whether she was telling the truth or spewing lies made little difference to him.

He didn't trust Mairi Cameron any more than he did any other villain in London.

Or villainess.

"I'm telling you—"

"You're not telling me a bloody thing that's of any use to me, girl, and until you do—"

"*Girl?* I'm nearly the same age as you, you condescending—"

"Until you do," He repeated, his voice drowning hers. "You'll stay right where you are, tied to that bed. Now, let's try this again. Where did you get these letters?"

The pretty lips pulled down in a scowl. "I told you. My grandmother saved them in a trunk under her bed. When she was taken up for murder, I took them before the magistrate could find them."

She'd stolen her grandmother's letters out from under the magistrate's nose? In the past two weeks she'd committed an assault *and* a theft?

Christ, the chit was a bloody criminal. "Why would my father write to your grandmother?"

"I already explained that, too. We lived in the same neighborhood in Coldstream—you with your father, and me with my grandmother, up until the day you and your father vanished, without even a goodbye. None of us knew you were leaving, or where you went. One day, you were just...gone."

He dropped into the chair beside the bed, exhaustion sapping what little strength he had left. She was still speaking, saying something about having come to London specifically to find him, but he hardly heard her over the roaring in his ears.

I can't do this.

Not right now, when his wound was throbbing as if his skull were splitting into pieces. He couldn't reason his way through this thing while his jaw was clenched with pain and the dingy little room was spinning around him.

He must have looked as wild as he felt, because when he stumbled to his feet and bore down on her, grasping her shoulders, she let out a soft gasp and shrank away from him. He ignored her flinch and tightened his grip, preparing for a storm of kicking and squirming, and then, when that didn't work, extravagant weeping.

But none of those things happened. She should have been wailing and struggling in a desperate attempt to escape him, but Mairi Cameron's blue eyes were calm—much too calm for a tiny lady at the mercy of a brutal giant like himself.

Of the two of them, *he* was the one panting, his lungs squeezing in time with the rise and fall of her rib cage as he fought to catch his breath, struggling with her bindings, unknotting them with clumsy hands.

She rubbed her wrists once he'd freed her, but remained quiet as he untied the other end, her blue eyes moving over his face as if he were the ghost of someone she'd once recognized, but no longer did. "May I have my pistol back?"

He should take it with him to keep her from bludgeoning anyone else, but he couldn't leave her alone in St. Giles without any way to protect herself. He slid the chair across the room near the window, and pointed to it. "Sit."

She gave him a wary look, but did as he bid her while he strode back over to the bed and stuffed the pistol underneath the mattress. If she really wanted to shoot him it wouldn't take her long to snatch it up again, but he'd be gone before she even made it halfway across the room. "Don't even think about moving from that chair until this door closes behind me."

She nodded, but she was staring at the pocket of his coat, where he'd shoved the packet of letters. When she raised her gaze to his, she looked more panicked than she had at any other time during this strange ordeal. "You're taking my grandmother's letters?"

"Aye."

"No! I...please don't."

Her throat caught on the words, and for the first time since he'd regained consciousness, she didn't meet his eyes, but kept her gaze fixed steadily over his shoulder.

She hadn't laid a fire or lit a lamp, and the gloom had now reached each of the four corners of the freezing hovel. It was too dim for him to see her expression, but he didn't have to see her to feel her panic.

This was as close as Mairi Cameron ever came to pleading.

He shouldn't know this about some chit he'd never seen before, but he knew it, in the same way he knew the particular shade of her red gold hair, the distinct dark blue of her eyes, like Scottish bluebells, and that voice, soft and melodic, the sweet lilt of it like treacle dripping from the end of a silver spoon. That voice had a strange pull on him, as if he'd heard it somewhere before.

The hairs on the back of his neck rose, and he turned around and strode toward the door before she could tug him deeper under her spell. "I'll bring them back to you."

He'd have to tell Lady Clifford about this whole bloody mess, but given the muddled state of his mind, he didn't trust himself to explain it coherently. The letters would help.

She shot to her feet. "When?"

"Sit down, lass." He waited until she obeyed his command, then said, "Tomorrow. Wait here for me to come."

She slumped in the chair, looking so forlorn he wondered if he should just take her with him to Maddox Street, but a stroll through St. Giles at night with a bashed skull would be challenging enough without dragging along someone he didn't trust.

And he didn't trust Mairi Cameron.

"Tomorrow," he repeated, but as he closed the door behind him and ducked into the shadowy corners of Howe's Court, he hoped that by then she'd be gone.

Chapter Six

Well, that hadn't gone as smoothly as she'd hoped it would, had it?

And there was the panic again, sneaking up on her as it did with every setback, every disappointment, its fetid breath hot on her neck. It was growing more restless, weary of waiting for the moment it could sink its wicked claws into her chest, and finish her off for good.

Daniel hadn't been at all pleased to see her. No, he was far too busy pursuing a perfectly lovely criminal existence in London to bother himself over Lillias Cameron's troubles.

That he claimed not to remember either Mairi or her grandmother was a surprise, much in the same way a tumble down the stairs or a fist to the jaw was a surprise. Maybe he did remember, or maybe he didn't—or maybe he'd become so instinctively deceitful he no longer knew the difference between a lie and the truth. Maybe he woke up every morning, drank a cup of tea, put on his boots, told a thousand lies as he went about his day, then fell asleep every night with a clear conscience.

So, twenty-four years had turned sweet Daniel Adair into lying Daniel Brixton. What of it? He might lie his way through the next twenty-four years, with her blessing. She cared only for the past twenty-four years, and the next five weeks. That their joyous reunion had begun with her bound to a bed with a bloody, infuriated giant looming over her was…not quite the outcome she'd hoped for.

Her neck ached from keeping her head high, and her shoulders burned from the effort it took to hold them back, to keep them straight. Twenty-four years was a long time to bear the weight of the past, and her knees were collapsing under the burden.

Twenty-nine years old, and she was weary down to the very marrow of her bones.

And now, he'd taken her letters. Perhaps he did intend to bring them back to her tomorrow as he'd said, or perhaps he intended to drop them on the first fire he came across, and grin madly as he watched them disintegrate into cinders.

She *needed* those letters—her grandmother needed them, but unless she fancied another jaunt through the dark, seamy streets of St. Giles on a fruitless search for him, she'd have to sit about and wait while he decided whether or not he'd keep his word. The only question now was how far down into the abyss of despair she'd plummet before the sun rose tomorrow morning.

Too far—farther than she ever had before. Far enough she might never claw her way back out again. The flimsy walls of the hovel were already pressing closer, the darkness becoming thicker, the neckline of her cloak too tight, choking her. She tore at it with her fingers and sucked in one shaking breath and then another, until her heart slowed, and the beads of sweat on her neck dried.

There. Another fainting fit averted, and her without her crystal bottle of smelling salts, too.

She wheezed out a laugh as she dragged herself to her feet. Yes, that was better. Mockery was good—it made her feel more like herself. A bit of bad temper wouldn't go amiss either, so she gave the leg of the chair a shove for good measure, then strode across the room.

The bits of the torn sheet hanging limply from the iron bed frame were plenty dingy, thankfully. My, she'd come to a sad pass, indeed, being grateful for grubby bedding, but one made the most of small victories, and bright white wouldn't do.

Not for what she had in mind.

Daniel was one problem, but she had another matter to deal with, namely the scarred gentleman with the vicious blade who'd been chasing Daniel earlier this evening. If he chose to come looking, he might find his way back here, and he could batter his way through the door of this pathetic little room with one well-aimed kick. She didn't choose to share her hovel with a dagger-wielding villain, so she'd better be ready for him.

The bedframe, or the chair? A trap set just a bit farther than the sweep of the door when it swung open would be best. That way it would spring as soon as he strode over the threshold.

Right there. The bedframe, then. Yes, that would do.

Now, where to tie the other end? It would have to be the bed on one side, and the leg of the chair on the other. Neither was as heavy as she would have liked—once the door swung open, they'd both fly across the floor—but they were the only two pieces of furniture in the room.

She worked quickly, taking care to tie the strips of bedding as tight as she could, then she sat back on her heels, head cocked. It was a poor enough job as far as traps went, but she did know how to tie a proper knot.

Very pretty, indeed, and it wasn't as if the man was likely to pause to inspect the threshold. Once he'd battered down the door, he'd be much too busy attacking her to think about what was happening at his feet.

Now, for a weapon. Not the washbasin—it was too flimsy. The chamber pot, though…she snatched it up from the shelf under the table and weighed it in her hand.

Pewter. Yes, that would do.

She pocketed her pistol, though it would be best if she didn't have to use it, as he could take it from her as easily as blinking an eye. The chamber pot, though—he wouldn't be expecting *that*.

The shadows were deepest near the window, so she tucked herself into a corner there, the chamber pot clutched in her hands, the pistol banging against her thigh, every one of her senses straining, and waited.

She waited, and waited, then waited some more, the shadows lengthening, her legs aching from standing so long in one position, and her arms shaking from the weight of the chamber pot. "Damn the man, where is he?" She shifted from one foot to the other, whispering curses that would have scandalized her grandmother—

Hot shame crept over her neck into her face, scalding her cheeks. However bad things might be for her at the moment, they were far worse for her grandmother. Yes, a blackguard was likely stealing through the streets of London at this very moment, salivating at the thought of spilling her blood, but it could be worse.

She could be facing the noose for a crime she hadn't committed.

How could anyone look into Lillias Cameron's guileless blue eyes and believe her guilty of murder? Mairi had inherited the blue eyes, but they lacked her grandmother's sweetness. Oh, perhaps she'd had it once, but for as long as she could remember a pair of guarded blue eyes met her gaze when she looked into the glass. Perhaps someone might be forgiven for suspecting *her* of murder, but not Lillias.

Never Lillias.

She forgot the ache in her legs then, the awkward weight of the chamber pot in her hands, and let her mind wander back to her childhood, before

Daniel and Hamish had disappeared—to a time when her world still made sense, when her grandmother took her by the hand and led her into the fields behind the cottage to pick wildflowers. They'd fill the pretty blue and white pitcher that held pride of place in the middle of their scrubbed wooden table.

Lillias was fond of pretty things, but to Mairi it had never been the wildflowers or the pitcher that mattered. It was the quiet joy Lillias took in everything, the way she enveloped everyone around her in that same joy and comfort.

So many of those early memories of her grandmother included Daniel.

How many skinned knees and bloody noses had Lillias tended at that kitchen table? How many childish tears had she dried? When Daniel's mother had died suddenly from a consumptive fever, whose arms had wrapped around him, whose shoulder had he poured his grief into?

Lillias had been as much Daniel's and Hamish's grandmother as she'd been Mairi's.

The pitiful hovel around her and the ugliness of tonight receded further away as one memory chased another—time she'd spent with Daniel and Hamish, hazy now, yes, the memories blurred at the edges, but still there, even as young as she'd been then, hovering in her consciousness, waiting to be called forth by a stray word, a look, or a scent.

They flooded in now, crowding her head, so many at once she'd nearly lost herself in them when the door squeaked open slowly, inch by agonizing inch, and for one confused instant she had an absurd hope that somehow it would be Daniel, returned to tell her he *did* remember, that he remembered it all, Mairi and Lillias and Hamish, and the mysterious reason Lillias had made Ian Adair take Daniel away from Coldstream without delay, to leave that very day—

But it wasn't Daniel.

The flimsy door slammed open with a crash of splintering wood and hit the wall behind it with an echoing crack. The building shuddered around her, as if trying to make up its mind whether it was worth remaining upright after this second assault tonight, but this time she paid no attention to the plaster that drifted down from the cracked ceiling.

If the roof *did* decide to collapse, now wouldn't be the worst time.

The villain looming in the open doorway was bigger than she remembered, and angrier, too, snarling and spitting like a rabid dog. "Ye can tell me where 'e is, or I can beat it out of ye. Yer choice."

She clawed at the edge of the chamber pot, slippery now with the sweat from her hands. "Or I can leave you unconscious in a bloody heap on the floor. I doubt it would take much of a blow to scatter *your* brains."

It took a moment for the insult to penetrate the man's thick head, but once it did, he let out a roar of laughter, and his big, filthy hands clenched into fists.

That's right, come after me.

One step forward, that was all she needed. A single step, the more forceful the better.

Just one step...

In the next instant, it happened, and dear God, it was a thing of beauty, the way it played out so perfectly. This night had been one disaster piled on top of another, but *this*, well...she couldn't prevent the bloodthirsty grin that rose to her lips.

His shin hit the strips of torn bed sheet with his first step into the room and he pitched forward, a curse on his lips. The stumble was minor, not enough to send him sprawling, but as she'd also predicted, the chair and bed weren't heavy enough to hold his weight, and they flew across the floor, directly into his pathway.

He did fall then, and with a whimper so embarrassingly cowardly she would have laughed had she not already darted across the room, raised the chamber pot over her head, and brought it down onto his skull in a blow that left her arms shaking.

It landed on the crown of his head with enough force that it actually cracked in her hands. Shards of pewter pierced her skin, but she hardly noticed the sting.

"That did for you, didn't it? I warned you I'd scatter your brains!" She tossed what was left of the chamber pot aside and leaned down to get a good look at her victim. "Oh, that's going to leave a nasty scar, isn't it? Pity, but you aren't that pretty anyway."

But there was no time to stand about and gloat. The door was now a splintered mass of shredded wood, leaving her at the mercy of any blackguard who happened to stroll into Howe Court. She hadn't any idea where she was going to go—she'd rather worn out her welcome in London, and on her first night, too—but she couldn't stay *here*.

She snatched up the few bits of clothing she had, stuffed them into the hood of her cloak, slung the cloak over her arm, then slid her other hand into her pocket, checking for her pistol.

It was there, still loaded.

She headed for the door, snatching up one of the bigger bits of the broken chamber pot on her way, just in case he was stirring. She paused to nudge her victim with her toe, but he was just as she'd left him, only now there was a slimy puddle of blood and drool on the floor beneath his open mouth.

Two men, felled in one night, with nary a shot fired.

A tidy bit of work, there. Her only regret was that Daniel hadn't been here to see it. Underestimate *her*, would he? At his peril, the condescending arse.

And if a third London blackguard needed to be taught a lesson by a small Scottish lass tonight, well...the handle of her pistol was smooth against her fingers, the solid, reassuring bulk of it straining the worn seams of her cloak pocket.

She was more than happy to oblige them.

Chapter Seven

The blood spurting from his temple had slowed to a lazy trickle by the time Daniel reached the junction at the center of St. Giles.

If he'd been in another part of London—Piccadilly, say, or the Strand, or even Covent Garden—his swollen eye and gore-soaked hair might have attracted a glance or two, but a bleeding man staggering down Queen Street was as common a sight as an overflowing slop bucket. He could fall to his knees right now, his heart on its last wheezing beat, and no one would blink.

There were no good Samaritans here.

No one poking into his business, or standing between him and Maddox Street. Queen Street, Little Earl Street, Monmouth Street…he'd trudged this same route dozens of times, once with a pistol ball buried in his shoulder. There'd been blood spurting everywhere that time too, but it hadn't slowed him down any.

The blood wasn't the trouble this time, either. It was his blasted feet. They kept trying to turn him back in the direction of Howe Court.

It *wasn't* his conscience pricking at him. Aye, it was rattling around loose, just like everything else inside his battered head, but he didn't bother with its murmurs and scolds. Guilt was a wasted emotion, and in his business, a waste of time.

He didn't owe Mairi Cameron a damned thing. The chit had nearly decapitated him. Half the blood that used to flow through his veins now decorated his shirt in streaks of dark red, and anyway, he wasn't in the business of rescuing dainty females, especially red-haired spitfires who bludgeoned a man without giving him a chance to explain himself. She could reap what she'd sown, just like every other criminal who haunted St. Giles.

He wasn't going back, no matter if she was a wee bit of a thing, alone and unprotected, prey to every scoundrel who roamed the rookeries at night. She'd got herself there, and she could find her way out. It was no concern of his.

Now, if some blackguard left any of *his* girls at the mercy of every villain in London, he'd see to it they paid for their callousness with their blood.

But Mairi Cameron wasn't one of his girls. She was nothing to him, and her troubles were just that—*hers*.

He had his own skin to worry about.

Still, for all that she was a shameless liar, she *might* have been telling the truth about the scarred man who'd been following him. It wouldn't be the first time a bloke with a dagger chased after him, and he was in no state to defend himself tonight, with one eye rolling around loose in his skull.

He thrust his clenched fists deep into his pockets, searching for the cold pearl handle of his blade, but instead his fingers brushed the packet of letters he'd taken from her.

She hadn't liked it, him taking them. It was the only time tonight she'd begged him for anything. Not a single word when he'd grabbed her, snarled at her, growled at her. The daft chit hadn't even had the sense to plead for her life when he'd bound her hands to the bed, but if she'd had her pistol handy when he'd laid a finger on those letters, he didn't doubt she would have made mincemeat of the other side of his head without a second's hesitation.

Whatever the truth was, Mairi Cameron believed every word she'd said. Didn't matter, though, because he *wasn't* going back tonight. Tomorrow would be soon enough.

Too soon, in fact, only...

The description she'd given of the man who'd been following him had sounded a lot like Angel Nash. That bastard had been chasing him for weeks now over a little difference of opinion between them involving Angel and an associate of Lady Clifford's.

Since then, Angel had been threatening to carve out a slice of his throat if he ever caught up to him. Handy with a knife, was Angel. Vicious, too.

Still not going back to fetch her, damn it.

Except if Angel *had* seen him go into Howe Court, and had reason to think he was still there, he'd find his way back, blade at the ready, and was unlikely to trouble himself much over who met the pointy end of it.

Not bloody going—

But Angel wouldn't find *him*. He'd find Mairi Cameron, with her bright red hair and a pretty face even a man intent on carnage might take a liking to—

He spat out a curse though bloodstained teeth, his boots slamming against the dusty streets with each reluctant step. Little Earl Street to Monmouth, then on to Grafton, St. Giles rushing by him in reverse, shadowy alleys, shrill voices, the maze of streets twisting crazily around soot-blackened buildings, the thud of his footfalls coming faster and faster until at last he reached Newport Market, and slipped down the alleyway that led to Howe Court.

Someone was there already, lurking in the shadows, the outline of his shape darker than the surrounding gloom. Daniel squinted, his one good eye narrowing, the other twitching helplessly under his eyelid, but whoever it was, he kept himself well hidden.

He crept forward, his back flat against the side of the building, and waited, each breath he drew unnaturally loud in the silence, until a strange, scuffing sound met his ears, heavy footsteps followed by the drag of a boot heel over the cobbled street, a big man with a limp.

Slap thump, Slap thump...

Angel, then. No question. Angel had found himself on the wrong end of a cutlass last year, and had come out of it less a toe or two. There was no mistaking the drag of that useless foot over the cobbles.

The lass had been telling the truth. A miracle, that, but she talked enough that a truth was bound to slip out now and again.

He peered around the edge of the building, but the instant he moved all went silent again, without even a flicker of movement, except—

There. A dark shape slithered from the shadows, stealthy as a serpent but for the quiet scuff and drag of Angel's steps echoing inside the tight row of buildings looming over the alleyway.

Angel paused, ear to the door. Now was Daniel's best chance, while Angel was distracted, but he held back an instant to see how Angel was going to play this.

It was an instant too long.

In the time it took for him to draw a breath, Angel burst into a sudden explosion of action. One vicious kick, and the door flew open with a deafening crack, crashing to the floor as Angel tore it off its rusted hinges and tossed it aside like it was nothing more than a bit of kindling. The wood splintered with the blow, Angel shoving the fragments out of his way with the toe of his boot and striding forward, shouting Daniel's name and a list of all the ways he would make him suffer—slit his throat, then gut him like a pig and feast on his entrails—the usual sort of thing.

Daniel lunged for the door, dreading a shriek of terror or pain from Mairi at every moment, but she never made a sound—not then, and not throughout the skirmish that followed.

Angel, however, was making enough noise to wake all of London. There was another crash, as if someone had tossed a chair across the room, then a thud, and a resounding crack—her pistol, or the handle of his dagger?

Something hard, smashing into bone. A fist, or a boot heel?

A pitiful whimper made the hair on Daniel's neck bristle before a deafening ring, like a club striking metal, ricocheted against the surrounding brick, and then...

Nothing.

Christ, he didn't like the sound of that nothing.

He rushed for the door, boots slipping on the cobbles, stumbling over ragged chunks of wood, but skidded to a stop a few steps away from the threshold, his mouth dropping open.

Mairi Cameron was standing in the middle of the room, a cracked chamber pot in her hands, the floor around her a jumble of overturned furniture and bits of broken wood. And there, on the floor at her feet, blood pouring from a gaping hole in his ugly head, lay Angel Nash. "Oh, lass. What have you done this time?"

The chamber pot in her hand hit the floor with a hollow clang. "Nothing he didn't deserve."

"Another bludgeoning?" Daniel strode across the room, wedged his boot under Angel's shoulder and with one kick, flipped him roughly onto his back. "You've been busy tonight."

"Is he dead?" she asked, peeking over his shoulder.

He crouched down and pressed his fingers to Angel's neck, where a weak but steady pulse fluttered. "Nay. Pity." He snatched up Angel's dagger and rose to his feet.

"You're stealing his knife?"

He thumbed the blade, then tested the point with the tip of his finger. "I've always fancied it. Call it the spoils of battle, if that suits your conscience better."

"If it's the spoils of battle, then I believe it belongs to *me*." She held out her hand.

"You think I'd trust you with a blade, after what you did with that chamber pot?" He slid the knife into his coat pocket. "I won't say I'm not impressed, lass. He's a big one."

"Size is no match for creativity, Mr. Brixton." She glanced at him, taking in his height, the breadth of his shoulders. "But perhaps that's not a lesson *you've* ever had to learn."

He let out a derisive snort. Whatever lessons the streets had to teach, he'd learned them long ago. "I'm both, so I never needed to. How did you manage it this time?"

"I had a feeling he'd come back. He saw you dart down the alley, and he didn't seem the sort of man who'd give up easily. No doubt he saw me, and thought I'd be easy prey. They always do." She peered down at the bleeding heap on the floor, and shook her head. "Some men never learn."

He couldn't argue with that. He'd seen more than one fool brought low because they made the mistake of underestimating one of his girls at the Clifford School. Hadn't taught him much though, had it? He'd underestimated Mairi Cameron just as Angel had. He'd taken one look at that slender body and sweet face, and dismissed her as unthreatening.

But Mairi Cameron had proved she wasn't the sort of lass a man wanted to turn his back on. The chit was wily, clever. It didn't look like Angel even got anywhere near her. There wasn't a scratch on her, her clothing wasn't mussed, and not a single strand of her hair was out of place.

Angel, though…

He was lying in an unconscious sprawl on the floor, his legs tangled in strips of white sheet, a chair on top of him and what was left of the chamber pot lying in pieces around him. The bed that had been up against the wall now sat in the middle of the room, with the other end of the bedding still tied to its leg. "Set a trap for him, did you?"

"Yes, and not even a particularly sophisticated one."

"Lucky he never got a hand on you. He's deadly with a blade."

"Yes, I heard him shouting something about slitting and gutting and entrails. What sort of criminal announces himself before he kicks the door in?"

"He's not one of your cleverer blackguards, is Angel."

"Ah, so you do know him, then?"

"Aye. This gent right here is Angel Nash. He's as mean as he is ugly, and as dim-witted as a burnt wick." If Angel had a lick of sense, he'd have known better than to trifle with Daniel in the first place. "I'll have the pistol you're hiding in your pocket now, lass." He held out his hand. "Give it here."

She crossed her arms over her chest. "You mean to say you intend to leave me here *again*, this time without my pistol to protect me from London's wicked criminals? That's not very gentlemanly of you."

"I'm not a gentleman, but I'm not leaving you here. You're coming with me." He'd rather let her fade into the darkness and never think about her again, but there were too many coincidences about this thing, too many unanswered questions.

He was in this now, and the only way out was through it.

"You can't stay here." He nodded at the smashed door behind her.

"I can't imagine I'm any safer alone with *you*. Perhaps I'd be better off on the streets. You did tie me to a bed, if you recall."

"I recall it, aye. I also recall you tied me first. Now, the pistol, if you please, lass. We're wasting time." When she didn't make a move to hand it over, he added. "Either you can hand it over, or I can take it off you."

"You're welcome to try, if you want to risk getting shot."

"You're not going to shoot the only person who can prove your grandmother isn't guilty of murder, lass. Unless that tale you told me earlier was all a lie?" He'd have wagered his last coin on it being just that.

She paled at that reminder, and his conscience, which had suddenly sprung to life after having had the good sense to leave him alone these past ten years and more, pricked at him again. *Hard*, too, the bloody thing. "Come on then, lass. I'm not going to hurt you."

Her chin jerked up, but she'd come with him, if only because she didn't have a choice. "Very well, then, but I'm not following *you*. I'm following my grandmother's letters."

He shrugged. "Whatever prevents me from having to toss you over my shoulder and carry you all the way to Maddox Street."

She snorted at that, but she did as he bid her, flouncing down the alleyway like the Queen of Scots herself in the direction of Monmouth Street. "What's at Maddox Street?"

"My employer." It was more complicated than that, but he wasn't going to try to explain Lady Clifford to the girl. She'd find out for herself soon enough.

They didn't speak as they made their way through the rookeries toward the West End of London. The sky was still dark when they reached Maddox Street, but the moon was peeking out from behind the clouds, casting a glow over the smart white brick of the Clifford School.

"Your, ah…your employer lives *here*?" Mairi had come to halt on the sidewalk, and was gaping up at the building, her lip caught between her teeth.

"Aye," Daniel grunted as he went up the steps to the front door.

Mairi didn't follow. "What does he do? What's his business?"

He turned around. The chit had felled two men tonight without suffering a single scratch, and *now* she was nervous? "*She*. Lady Clifford, proprietress of the Clifford School. Are you coming or not?"

"This is a *school*?"

"It's a...that is, it's not..." Christ, how to explain it? "Aye, in a manner of speaking."

She didn't move, but continued to gaze up at the building, brows drawn. "It doesn't look like any school I've ever—"

The door opened then, and Lady Clifford herself stepped out. "Here you are at last, Daniel. I was beginning to worry you wouldn't make it back to us in one...oh, dear." She frowned at his swollen eye and the oozing wound on his head. "You're not *quite* in one piece, are you?"

"I'm well enough." He wasn't, but a public street in Mayfair wasn't the place to talk about daggers, pistols, and bloody head wounds.

Lady Clifford's gaze wandered to Mairi. "It's a bit early for calling hours."

"She's not a visitor." He glanced at Mairi, who was gaping up at Lady Clifford as if she were an apparition.

"No?" Lady Clifford's eyebrow arched upwards another notch. "Who is she, then?"

Daniel trudged back down the steps and grabbed Mairi's arm. "She's the lass who tried to kill me tonight."

Chapter Eight

"*Kill* you?" The fair-haired lady—for she *was* a lady, at least a viscountess, judging by her air and her elegant silk gown—swept a speculative gaze over Mairi, her blue eyes cool. "She doesn't look much like a murderer."

Daniel snorted. "The dangerous ones never do."

Mairi waited for the lady to scoff at the idea that such a wee, sweet lass like her could be dangerous, but instead a spark of interest lit Lady Clifford's eyes. "She's responsible for your head wound, then?"

"Aye. She's wily as a nest of snakes, this one."

Snakes? Well, *this* introduction certainly left a lot to be desired.

"Why, how remarkable," the lady murmured, still staring at Mairi. "It's not often *you're* caught by surprise."

"Knocked me cold with the butt of her pistol. I woke to find myself tied hand and foot, leaking blood, and with one eye swollen shut."

"*Tied?*" The lady's eyes widened. "My goodness. Not your best night, was it? Who is this young lady, Daniel?"

"This here is Mairi Cameron, or so she claims. The lass is a liar as well as a murderer."

Oh, for pity's sake, this was absurd. "I've told you half a dozen times, Daniel. If I wanted you dead, I would have shot you already!"

Daniel ignored her outburst. "This lady, lass, is the Countess of Clifford."

Mairi opened her mouth to say...well, she hadn't any idea, really. A polite "good evening" was ludicrous under the circumstances, and she couldn't force "It's a pleasure to meet you," from her lips, because it *wasn't* a pleasure. This business was difficult enough without a countess sniffing about and making an even bigger mess of things.

"I—" she began, stupidly enough, but she was saved from having to think of anything else to say by soft footfalls coming down the hallway.

"Is that you, Daniel?" A young, dark-haired lady popped her head over Lady Clifford's shoulder. "Where did you...oh." A pair of the prettiest green eyes Mairi had ever seen opened wide as the lady caught sight of her. "Hello."

"Sophia, my dear." Lady Clifford took the young lady's hand. "This young lady is Mairi Cameron."

"Or so she claims," Daniel growled again, before Mairi had a chance to say a word.

"She's, er...Daniel's guest," Lady Clifford went on.

"Nay. She's not my guest. She's the chit who tried to kill me."

"*Kill* you?" The green-eyed lady gaped at Mairi. "What, this tiny little thing?"

Daniel shot Mairi a sullen look. "She's stronger than you'd think."

The lady seemed to notice then that Daniel was covered in blood. "You don't mean to say *she* did that to you? But...how did she manage it? You tower over her!"

Daniel pointed an accusing finger at Mairi. "Sneakiness, that's how. She may be wee, but she's a crafty one, wilier than a snake."

"A *nest* of snakes, even." Lady Clifford shot an amused look at Daniel.

"It was no more than he deserved!" Mairi pointed her own accusing finger right back at Daniel. "This blackguard of yours tied me to a bed!"

"Did he, indeed?" The lady's dark head swung from Daniel back to Mairi, her mouth open. "My goodness. It's all rather exciting, really. But how did you manage such an impressive blow, Miss Cameron?"

"Ambush, that's how. The chit's been following me for days. She lured me down to Howe Court tonight, and bashed my head in with the butt of her pistol." Daniel waved a hand at his abused eye. "Knocked me unconscious, and nearly blinded me."

"Perhaps we'd better take this inside," Lady Clifford murmured. "I'd rather our neighbors be left ignorant of this particular murder attempt. They still haven't gotten over the last one."

The last one? Dear God, what sort of a place had Daniel brought her to?

Lady Clifford waved Daniel and the green-eyed lady back inside, then took Mairi's arm in a surprisingly strong grip, tugged her inside, and closed the door behind them. "Now, perhaps we should—"

She was interrupted by a flurry of footsteps, and a moment later three more ladies scurried down the hallway, the hems of their sumptuous blue silk skirts swirling around their ankles. "Has Daniel returned at last? Good lord, it's been an age! What kept you so—"

The lady at the head of the pack—a petite, dark-haired beauty with a face as sweet as an angel's—came to such an abrupt halt when she spotted Mairi that the two ladies behind her nearly ran her over.

"Cecilia, for pity's sake!" A blonde with luminous blue eyes and a stunning face grasped the first lady by the shoulders, steadying her. "I don't fancy explaining to Lord Darlington that I knocked you down, in your delicate condition!"

"Emma is right, Cecilia. You really must be more careful, dearest." The third lady in the trio was tall, with auburn hair and lovely hazel eyes. "Your balance is dreadful."

"I'd be in a better state than Daniel, even if you had knocked me down." The first lady—*Cecilia*—was staring at Daniel with a stricken expression. "I hope that's someone else's blood."

"Someone *else's* blood! Does Mr. Brixton make a habit of returning home covered in his victims' blood?"

It seemed a fair question, but Mairi regretted asking it when all six heads jerked to face her, and a moment of stunned silence fell over the group.

"Who is this?" The blonde lady cocked her head, studying Mairi's face. "I don't believe I've ever seen her before. Is she a new student, my lady?"

Student? Mairi's mouth dropped open. This place really *was* a school, then?

"No, no. That's Mairi Cameron, the young lady who tried to kill Daniel tonight." The green-eyed lady nodded at Daniel. "Almost succeeded too, by the look of him."

It was the kind of statement that should have led to horrified gasps, but the group of ladies surrounding Mairi hardly blinked. "But she's so small," the angel-faced lady said at last. "How could she kill a man Daniel's size?"

"Bashed my head in with the butt of her pistol, that's how." Daniel loomed over the lot of them, legs spread wide, his arms crossed over his chest.

"Well, to be fair, Daniel *did* tie her to a bed." The first lady—Sophia— slapped a hand over her mouth. "Oh, dear. I beg your pardon, Daniel. It just slipped out."

Now, that *did* elicit a gasp from the other three ladies, but a gasp of delight rather than horror or shock.

Daniel scowled. "Aye, I tied her to a bed, because it was the only way to be sure she wouldn't crack open the other side of my skull. I told you, she may look innocent as a lamb, but this lass is as wily as every other criminal crawling about St. Giles."

Mairi clenched her hands into fists, fury blazing through her at the unfairness of his words. "But for *me*, your servant here would be lying in an alleyway in St. Giles with a dagger buried in his chest!"

"Mr. Brixton isn't my servant, Miss Cameron. He's my partner, and if he did indeed tie you to a bed, I can only suppose he had a good reason to do so." Lady Clifford turned to Daniel. "You *did* have a good reason to do so, didn't you?"

"Aye. She tied me there first."

Lady Clifford pinched the bridge of her nose, as if holding off a headache. "I feel as if I'm missing a part of this story."

"Most of it, aye. It's a messy one."

Lady Clifford sighed. "They always are, and having so many of us here is only adding to the confusion. Girls, I don't like to be inhospitable, but I think it's time you fetched their lordships from the drawing room, and took them home."

What, there were noblemen hidden away in the drawing room? As if this passel of silk-draped ladies weren't bad enough, now they were going to toss a lord or two into it as well?

For a school, Lady Clifford's establishment appeared unconcerned with pursuing scholarship. But perhaps it wasn't a school at all, but a broth—

"Daniel, show Miss Cameron to my private parlor while I bid everyone good night, won't you? I'll be along in a moment."

"Aye." Daniel marched up to Mairi and took her arm in a firm grip. "Come on then, lass."

Mairi glanced at the front door as they passed, and a longing to flee, to leave this all behind and never look back, hit her with such force she nearly staggered with it.

But there was nowhere for her to go. She'd had only one reason to come all the way to London, and he had his fingers wrapped around her arm right now.

Like it or not, her grandmother's fate lay in Daniel Brixton's hands.

He led her down a hallway and into a small parlor or office of some sort. There was a desk in one corner, where a quill lay on top of some scattered papers, and several settees arranged around a crackling fire. It was a cozy room—much more so than she would have guessed, given how grand Lady Clifford was.

Daniel manhandled her onto the settee closest to the fire. "Sit here."

The man certainly liked to issue commands, didn't he? He couldn't seem to say a single word that wasn't an order. Still, she did as she was told, and was instantly glad she had when the soft, plump cushions opened their arms to her, cradling her exhausted limbs.

She *might* have let out a moan of pleasure then. Just a little, quiet one—

"You're a bit pale for my liking, Miss Cameron," Lady Clifford observed, striding into the room. "You look as if you could use some refreshment."

She didn't wait for a reply, but rang the bell, and when the servant appeared she ordered a tray of refreshments brought in. A strange, tense silence fell over the three of them after the servant left, and lasted until he returned with a large silver tray balanced on his hand.

"Thank you, Mason. You may go." Lady Clifford served herself and Mairi steaming cups of chocolate, then filled a tumbler from what looked like a bottle of whisky and passed it to Daniel.

"Ah, that's better. Now, then, shall we begin?" Lady Clifford brought her cup of chocolate to her lips, took a dainty sip, then set the drink aside. "From the start of the story this time, if you please, Miss Cameron."

She fixed her sharp blue gaze on Mairi, and all at once the loving embrace of the settee started to feel more like a stranglehold. "It's....er, a bit complicated."

"Yes, I gathered that. Let me see if I understand it thus far. You, Miss Cameron, have been following Mr. Brixton for several days. You tracked him through St. Giles tonight, lured him into your lodgings in Howe Court, then attacked him, dragged him into your rooms, and tied him up. Is that correct?"

Mairi blinked. "Well, yes, except the dragging part. I'd sooner be able to drag a draft horse than Mr. Brixton. He was helpful enough to fall into my room, so all I had to do was close the door behind him. Well, that and tie his arms and legs."

"I see. Why should you go to the trouble of saving his life, only to tie him up?"

"I wasn't sure how he'd react when I told him I...it seemed wiser to tie him up, just in case, but I never wanted him *dead*. I came here from the Scottish Borders all the way to London to find him. I...need him."

"You need him," Lady Clifford repeated softly, with a questioning glance at Daniel. "At last, we're getting somewhere. Are you acquainted with Mr. Brixton, then, Miss Cameron?"

"Yes," Mairi said, at the same time Daniel said, "Nay."

A charged silence fell. Lady Clifford let it stretch, until at last Mairi broke it. "I know him well. We were neighbors and...and friends until he left Scotland when he was eight years old, but he claims he doesn't remember me."

"I *don't* remember you. I don't have any bloody idea who you are, or what you're on about."

"Forgive me, Miss Cameron, but are you quite certain you have the right man? Mr. Brixton and I have been partners for years, and he's never once mentioned to me that he ever lived in Scotland."

"Because I never did. The lass is mistaken, or else she's a liar."

A murderer, a snake, and now a liar? That was beyond *enough*. "You're so certain I'm lying, Daniel? Very well, then. Answer me this. What reason do I have to lie? What could I possibly have to gain by pretending to be your childhood friend?"

"I couldn't say, lass, but I know this. There are as many different lies as there are people to tell them, and some don't need a reason at all."

"I see. So, your theory is that I've come all the way from Scotland to London in search of you for no reason whatsoever, beyond the enjoyment of your company? As charming as you are, it isn't likely, is it?"

"Nay, you're too clever for that. I'd wager you've got your reasons, but they aren't what you claim they are. If I'd been raised in Scotland, I think I'd remember it."

"Yes, I'd think so, too. It's rather a mystery to me that you don't!"

Lady Clifford had been listening to this exchange without speaking, but now she cleared her throat. "What part of Scotland do you come from, Miss Cameron?"

"Coldstream. It's in the Scottish borders, not far from Gretna Green."

"Yes, I know of it, but I can't say I've ever heard Daniel mention it. It seems as though he would have, if he'd been born there." Lady Clifford toyed with the end of the quill, her sharp gaze on Mairi's face. "Do you have any proof of your past association with Daniel, Miss Cameron, or are we meant to take your word for it?"

"Not at all, my lady. All the proof you need is in Mr. Brixton's greatcoat pocket."

Lady Clifford turned to him with a raised brow. "Daniel?"

He reached into his pocket and tossed his pearl-handled knife on the desk, along with her pistol.

Lady Clifford nodded at the pistol. "Yours, I take it?" she asked Mairi. Mairi raised her chin. "It is, yes."

"Aye, it's hers. Still has a smear of my blood on it, too."

"Is it ready to fire?" Lady Clifford asked.

"Aye, it's loaded. It's a wonder she didn't shoot herself when she struck me with it."

"I know how to handle a weapon, Mr. Brixton. Now, where are my letters?"

He reached back into his pocket, pulled out the letters, and dropped them on the desk in front of Lady Clifford. "I wasn't going to steal them, lass."

"No, just snatch them away from me, after you'd tied me to the bed. I can't imagine why I suspected your motives."

Lady Clifford held the first letter close to the light, frowning. "Who is Lillias Cameron?"

"My grandmother. The letters belong to her."

"Your grandmother." Lady Clifford shuffled through the letters, reading the name written on the front of each one, then she set them aside in a neat pile. "Forgive me, Miss Cameron, but I don't see what this has to do with Mr. Brixton."

"His father sent them to my grandmother after he and Daniel vanished from Coldstream." Mairi shuffled through the letters, plucked up the one from St. Margaret's, and handed it to Lady Clifford. "This was the first of them. Read it, my lady."

"St. Margaret's, Herefordshire. Brixton." Lady Clifford read the four words aloud, then looked up at Daniel. "Curious."

"The other letters are postmarked from towns and villages where Daniel and his father lived at one point. Ian Ad—that is, Ian Brixton sent one to my grandmother every time they moved up until last year, when he died." Mairi leaned forward, resting her arms on Lady Clifford's desk. "Even more curious, wouldn't you say, my lady?"

But Lady Clifford wasn't one to tip her hand so soon. "I grant you it's… interesting, but it doesn't prove anything beyond the fact that they knew each other."

"My grandmother has never been to England, Lady Clifford. She's never been further south than Kelso. If she knew Ian Brixton—and those letters prove she *did*—then she knew him from Coldstream."

"We only have your word that's so. No, I'm afraid I have to agree with Daniel, Miss Cameron, particularly given that all the letters are blank." Lady Clifford stacked the letters into a neat pile and pushed them across the desk toward Mairi. "If they were friends, why would Mr. Brixton send your grandmother blank letters?"

"Why would he send her any letters at all if they weren't?" Mairi's chin hitched up, but when she snatched up the letters, her hands were shaking. "The letters serve only one purpose—to inform my grandmother of their whereabouts—but it seems I'm only wasting my breath, attempting to convince you. Perhaps I made a mistake, coming to London."

Lady Clifford studied her for a moment. "The letter from St. Margaret's was the first one your grandmother received. Is that correct?"

"Yes."

"That letter was posted nearly twenty-three years ago, Miss Cameron, and the last of them more than a year ago. Why have you only come to London in search of Daniel *now*?"

She'd known this question would come, and had been dreading it. "Six weeks ago, the skeletal remains of a child floated to the surface of a fishing pond on Viscount Rutherford's land in Coldstream." She stared at the small stack of letters she'd placed in her lap, and willed herself not to cry. "We used to play there when we were children, though it was forbidden."

"A *child*," Lady Clifford repeated quietly.

"Yes. A boy, the coroner said, no more than seven or eight years old, judging by the length and thickness of the bones. Of course, the flesh had long since melted away."

Lady Clifford had gone still, listening. "Had the child drowned?"

"He had, yes. It happens more often than it should, in villages where children are permitted to run wild, but this boy…well, there was more to it, in his case. He did drown, but it was no accident. He, ah…his neck had been snapped."

"Dear God." Lady Clifford sucked in a quick breath. "He was murdered."

Mairi swallowed, nodded. "Yes. My grandmother, Lillias Cameron, has been arrested for the crime. The Court of Assizes will try her in a few weeks, and there's little doubt she'll be found guilty."

"Guilty of a murder committed twenty-four years ago? Forgive me, Miss Cameron, but that doesn't make the least bit of sense." Lady Clifford was shaking her head. "What reason does the magistrate have for thinking your grandmother murdered an eight-year-old boy?"

"Not just any eight-year-old boy, my lady. The magistrate has identified the remains as belonging to Daniel Adair."

"I don't understand, Miss Cameron. If the child's remains are unidentifiable, how can they be certain who he is, or what he has to do with your grandmother?"

Mairi scraped up a forlorn laugh from the bottom of her throat. "The magistrate hasn't troubled himself much with anything aside from finding someone to hang for the crime. My grandmother is even now locked up in the Coldstream Toll Booth."

Locked up, and *silent*.

There could be only one reason Lillias refused to offer up a word in her own defense. She was protecting someone. Who else could it be but

Daniel? Daniel, who'd disavowed her over and over again tonight—who'd pretended not to even recognize her name.

She turned to him, the injustice of it crashing down on her again, until she was shaking with fury. "My grandmother is weeks away from swinging from a gibbet for murdering *you.*"

"Well, Miss Cameron, I begin to understand why you've come all this way to find Daniel. This is all more complicated than I realized."

"Yes, and it's more complicated still. I came to London in search of Daniel to persuade him to return to Scotland with me, so we can clear my grandmother's name, and save her life."

"It's a strange story." Lady Clifford studied her from the other side of her desk. "Either you're a liar, or else you have a vivid imagination, Miss Cameron."

"Or else the lass is mad. Mayhap all three."

Mad. After twenty-four years, that was all he had to say?

She couldn't stand to hear another word—couldn't *bear* it. She jerked to her feet, legs stiff and aching, and snatched up her letters, clutching them in her hand. "I made a mistake, coming here."

She turned to the door, but Lady Clifford rose and laid a hand on her arm. "Wait, Miss Cameron. I won't have you wandering the streets of London in the dark, where any villain could get his hands on you. You'll stay here tonight. We'll discuss this again tomorrow, once we've all had a good rest."

Mairi didn't argue—she wasn't in any position to turn down a bed—but she tugged her arm free of Lady Clifford's grasp, then stood silently by the door, her back to Daniel, and stayed there until a servant came to fetch her.

Chapter Nine

"Now then, Daniel." Lady Clifford settled in the chair behind her desk and poured herself another cup of chocolate. "Do you have any open wounds, broken bones, or other injuries that need immediate attention?" He raised a hand to his head, wincing. Mairi Cameron might as well have just pried his eyeball loose from his skull with those dainty fingers of hers. It would have hurt less. "Aye, but it can wait."

"Somehow, I knew you'd say that." Lady Clifford sighed, but said nothing more—just sat with her hands folded on the desk in front of her, staring at him, and waiting.

Christ, he hated it when she did this. These endless silences were one of her best tactics. He liked quiet women—there was nothing worse than a woman who was always buzzing in his ear—but Lady Clifford's silences were like other women's endless chatter.

This one heaved and stretched until it swelled into every corner of her private parlor. She could keep it up for a good long while, too. They'd both still be sitting here at sunset, if that's what it took to loosen his tongue.

When he couldn't stand it any longer, he plucked Angel Nash's dagger out of his pocket and tossed it on the desk in front of her. It was as good a place to start as any.

Lady Clifford raised an eyebrow. "Don't tell me Miss Cameron was also carrying a dagger."

"No. That belongs to the other villain who was following me tonight."

"My, you have had an adventurous evening. One of the usuals?"

"Aye. It was Angel Nash."

"Angel Nash!" Lady Clifford placed her cup carefully in the saucer and set it aside. "Is he still after you? Rather an unpleasant sort of fellow, if I remember correctly."

"Unpleasant enough, aye. Nash might well have slit my throat tonight if it hadn't been for the lass." Mairi Cameron was a sharp-tongued, troublesome little liar, but he couldn't deny she'd proved useful.

Cursed chit. Next thing, she'd be telling him he owed *her* a debt.

He didn't want to owe anyone a damned thing. Plenty of people in London owed *him*, and that was just fine, but a debt meant another person had power over him, and he didn't give his power away to anyone.

Lady Clifford, who'd taken up the dagger to inspect the hilt, now dropped it back onto her desk with a heavy thud. "I can't imagine how she managed Angel, given she's no bigger than a hummingbird."

"Laid a trap for him. Tripped him with a bedsheet strung across the threshold. When he fell, she smashed a chamber pot over his head."

He didn't like or trust Mairi Cameron, but that had been a nice bit of work, and he approved of any scheme that ended with Angel Nash unconscious and bleeding.

"Clever girl," Lady Clifford murmured, glancing at the door through which Mairi had gone. "She would make a wonderful addition to the Clifford School."

"We've got enough troublesome chits on our hands without adding *her* into it." He didn't even want her here now—not *now*, and not tomorrow— but even he wasn't heartless enough to toss the girl out onto the streets. "The lass warned me he was after me. I didn't believe her at first, but she was telling the truth."

About this, anyway. That didn't mean every other word out of her mouth hadn't been a lie.

"What do you make of the story she told us? Do you believe she's telling the truth?"

"Nay. I don't take the word of anyone I don't trust, and I don't trust *her.*"

"Well, her story is certainly fantastical, I'll give you that. A sweet, harmless grandmother turned murderer, and taken up for a crime that occurred twenty-four years ago? It sounds like something out of one of those gothic horror novels the girls are so fond of, doesn't it?"

"Aye, just like it." He didn't like to think of anyone's grandmother swinging from a noose, especially a wee Scottish grandmother, but believing Mairi's tale meant believing that his father, the only person who'd ever cared a damn for him before he came to the Clifford School, had lied to him for years about who he was, and where he came from.

He'd been a rough man, Ian Brixton, and not the sort who'd lavished tender affection on his son, but he hadn't been a liar. It would take more than Mairi Cameron's word to convince Daniel his father had kept the first eight years of his life a dark secret.

Ian had never said a single word about Coldstream, Scotland, but...
it was odd, wasn't it, that Daniel didn't have any memories from before
the age of eight? Everything before their time in Herefordshire was hazy,
fragments of half-remembered faces.

"Well, I suspect you're right, Daniel, and it's all nonsense, just as you
said. Still, I can't see why she'd pretend to be your childhood friend." Lady
Clifford pinned him with the steady gaze that never failed to make him
squirm. "It would make sense if she'd asked for money, but what does she
have to gain from bringing you back to Scotland with her?"

He didn't have an answer for that, at least not one that made sense.

It was more than a week's journey from the Borders to London. That
was a long way to go for a bit of nonsense, and then the girl had taken
a great risk, following him as she had, and taking lodgings alone in St.
Giles, of all unholy places.

A reckless, wrong-headed, foolish risk, the kind of risk that got your
throat slit. The sort of risk only a desperate person would take—

"There's also the question of those letters."

Those bloody letters. He didn't want to think about what they might mean.

Lady Clifford poured a second measure of whisky into his tumbler and
pushed it across her desk toward him. "You did recognize the handwriting
on the letters as your father's, I think?"

"Aye, it's his." And it wasn't as if his father had ever been much of a
letter writer. Odd, that he would have written to Lillias Cameron like that.

Except he hadn't really written, had he? The letters were all blank.

"Still, anyone could have gotten their hands on those letters. Every
word she uttered tonight could be a lie just as easily as it could be the
truth. Likely the former."

"Aye. I expect so." Except she hadn't lied about Angel, had she?

There was something about the lass's face, too, some expression in her
eyes when she looked at him. She didn't flinch, or avoid his gaze the way
every liar he'd ever known did, so either she was the best liar he'd ever
come across, or maybe—

"Do you have any recollection of her face at all? Her hair? It's a rather
distinctive shade, isn't it? I think you'd remember it if you'd seen it before."

He frowned down at his glass.

Had he seen her before?

The trouble was, her face did look familiar in a way he couldn't make
sense of. He tried to think back, despite the worsening ache in his eye.
He would have sworn he'd never seen her before, but something about
her mouth, the shape of her smile, and her eyes, that particular shade of
cornflower blue, and the reddish gold of her hair...

"I think I've...dreamed of her." Christ, he sounded like a bloody fool.

"Well." Lady Clifford was quiet for a moment, watching him, then she murmured. "That *is* interesting."

"Not *her*, exactly, but..." Damn it. He couldn't explain it.

"I think this bears looking into a bit further." Lady Clifford took up her discarded quill, and fetched some paper from the drawer of her desk. "I'll send a note round to the girls, asking them to find out everything they can about Mairi and Lillias Cameron, and Daniel Adair's murder."

There was no reply he could make to that, so he said nothing.

"Winnie is in the kitchens still, readying for breakfast tomorrow. Have her look at your injuries, then go off to your bed, Daniel." Lady Clifford didn't look up from the note she was writing. "There's nothing more to be done tonight, but I think I'll pay Kit Benjamin a visit tomorrow morning."

"Aye, that makes sense." Benjamin was the chief magistrate of London. If there was anything worth knowing about Mairi or Lillias Cameron, he'd know it.

"Perhaps you and Lord Gray could track down one or two of his former Bow Street Runner acquaintances tomorrow, as well." She was still writing, her eyes on the paper in front of her. "They might have heard something about Lillias Cameron."

"About a trial way up in the Scottish Borders? Not likely."

"If the story was any less spectacular, I might agree with you." Lady Clifford looked up from her writing. "But even jaded Londoners might appreciate a story about a murderous grandmother."

He gripped the arms of his chair, a drop of liquid—sweat or blood—trickling down the back of his neck. This thing kept getting deeper, like a tide pulling him under, water flooding his nose and mouth, his chest.

Anger, frustration, fear—yes, *fear*—the man who feared nothing was afraid of a tiny, red-headed lass—simmered just under the surface, but he was too exhausted to give voice to it, too exhausted to do anything but stagger to his feet.

"Daniel?"

He paused at the door, his back to her. "Aye?"

"We'll find out the truth. I promise it."

They would—they always did—but this time the promise felt less like reassurance, and more like a threat.

For the first time ever, he wasn't sure he wanted to know the truth.

Chapter Ten

Mairi stretched out her legs and hooked her pink, shriveled toes over the opposite edge of the copper bathtub, the silky water caressing her skin.

She should get out soon—her feet already looked like two wrinkled prunes—but every time the water cooled enough for her to consider it, Jenny, one of Lady Clifford's housemaids, would appear and pour in another steaming bucket.

The only thing better than a hot, roomy bath was a warm, soft bed covered with downy pillows and protected from the cold air by heavy silk draperies. Last night had felt like drifting to sleep on a cloud. She could have easily lain there all day, wrapped up like a caterpillar nestled snugly in its cocoon.

Luxury made one stupid that way. Unless she were on her guard against the extravagant bed, the hot, scented bath, the blazing fire in the hearth, and Jenny, who appeared to be for her exclusive use only, she might be tempted to linger in London, lulled into dull, sluggish complacency.

That wouldn't do, especially when the cost of all these delights came directly out of Lady Clifford's pocket. She didn't trust Lady Clifford. Well, she didn't trust any aristocratic lady, really, but Lady Clifford in particular seemed the sort of woman who was hiding a great many secrets.

Mairi hadn't known precisely what to expect when Daniel brought her here last night. He claimed it was a school, and it looked respectable enough from the outside, but inside it had all the trappings of an exclusive London brothel.

She had yet to lay eyes on a single schoolgirl, but there were a number of beautiful ladies flitting about in silks and jewels, like flamboyant blue silk butterflies. Perhaps they weren't *quite* as ladylike as they appeared, and their four tall, handsome gentlemen companions quite as...gentlemanly.

But it was no business of hers if Lady Clifford was an infamous bawd with a household full of pretty fallen angels. She hadn't come to London to poke about in other people's secrets. She had enough of her own problems without borrowing any from Lady Clifford.

One enormous, dark-haired, surly problem in particular.

She slid further down in the tub, until the hot water tickled the bottom of her chin.

What cursed luck that her first meeting with Daniel in twenty-four years had begun with a bludgeoning! No doubt she'd put an end to any inclination he might have had to help her when she buried the butt of her pistol in his eye socket.

The trouble was, she couldn't hang about in London forever, hoping he'd change his mind. That would take time, time Lillias didn't have—

Slam!

"Jenny?" Mairi bolted upright, sending water sloshing over the edge of the tub. Dear God, it sounded like someone was trying to break the door down. "Jenny, is that you?"

No answer, but a moment later the door flew open, followed by the heavy thud of footsteps crossing the floor. Jenny had placed a lovely carved wooden screen around the tub to protect her from drafts, so Mairi couldn't see who'd entered, but it didn't *sound* like Jenny.

No, it sounded like—

"Let's go, lass. Lady Clifford is waiting for you."

Her first impulse was to cross her arms over her bare breasts, but she kept them where they were. Daniel couldn't see her, but she wouldn't give him the satisfaction of a sudden splash. "*Now?* I'm having a bath."

A snort came from the other side of the screen. "You've been having a bath for the better part of an hour. Whatever isn't clean by now will have to stay dirty. Here." He flung what appeared to be a day dress over the edge of the screen. "Put this on, and be quick about it."

"That's not mine." It was a chemise gown of very sheer, fine cream-colored muslin with intricate black embroidery along the hem and sleeves, far grander than anything she'd ever owned.

Another snort, this one accompanied by an eye roll—yes, definitely an eye roll. She might not be able to see it, but she could *feel* it. "Nay, it's Lady Gray's. She sent it over for you this morning."

Lady Gray? Who was Lady Gray? And did he truly expect her to wear a lady's dress? The lace edging on the neckline alone was worth more than she could earn in a year. What if she tore it? "No, thank you. I prefer to wear my own clothing."

The snort turned into an irritable growl. "Your clothing needed washing. Put on the dress, unless you want to come downstairs wrapped in a length of toweling."

Oh, how she'd dearly love to do just that, if only to nettle him, but she couldn't quite bring herself to appear before a countess clad only in a length of damp toweling, so she heaved herself out of the tub and reached for one of the thick drying cloths Jenny had left warming on a rack by the fire. "Yes, all right. I'm coming."

He didn't bother to answer her, but she'd hardly had a chance to run a cloth over her damp hair before she heard the distinctive sound of a booted toe rapping impatiently against the wooden floor on the other side of the screen. "What are you doing in there, lass? Building an ark?"

For pity's sake, had there ever been a more disagreeable man? "Go down without me, if you're in such a hurry. I'll be along when I'm ready."

His only reply was a grunt, but the absence of footsteps meant he'd remained right where he was, mere steps away, and quite tall enough to peer over the top edge of the privacy screen. A shiver slid down her spine, leaving a spray of goosebumps in its wake, which was perfectly ridiculous, as she didn't have the *least* reason to shiver.

She snatched up the dress and hurried into it, trying not to notice how pretty it was, how fine the embroidery, and how soft the muslin that slid between her fingers as she tugged the skirt over her hips and straightened the shoulders.

It was just the tiniest bit too long, but otherwise it fit her as if it had been made for her. There was a looking glass in the bedchamber. She could take a quick peek, just to see…

No. It wasn't *her* gown, and she wasn't likely to ever own one so fine as this one, so what did it matter how she looked in it? No doubt she looked ridiculous in any case, with her bare, shriveled toes and her wet hair hanging in a tangled mess down her back.

She gave it a hopeless swipe with another one of the towels, but unless she wanted to ask Daniel to play lady's maid and brush it out for her, there wasn't much more she could do to tame the unruly waves, so she gave up and stepped out from behind the screen.

He was waiting on the other side clutching a pair of dainty black slippers, with a black ribbon caught in his huge fist, and looking none too pleased about any of it.

She stared at the accessories, surprised. Lady Gray had thought of everything. "Are those for me?" She nodded at the ribbon and slippers.

Daniel didn't appear to hear her, nor did he make any move to hand them to her, but stood there, a dazed look on his face as he took her in from the top of her head to the tips of her bare toes peeking out from under the hem of the dress.

She gave the skirt a nervous twitch. "May I have those shoes, Daniel, or do you intend to wear them yourself?"

He blinked, then looked down at his hands. "Here." He thrust them toward her, then marched over to the door to wait, his back to her.

She stuffed her feet into the slippers—again, just a trifle too big—did her best to tie her hair neatly away from her face with the ribbon, then threw her shoulders back, her spine pulling straight. "There. I'm ready."

Daniel cast her a sour look over his shoulder, and jerked the door open. "Took your time about it. They've been waiting on you for half an hour now."

"They? What do you mean, *they*? You said Lady Clifford was waiting for me. Who else is down there?"

"The girls…er, their ladyships."

He didn't seem to think his answer needed elaboration, but Mairi stopped halfway to the door. "What *ladyships*? You mean that crowd in blue silk who swarmed us in the entryway last night? The courtesans?"

"What are you on about *now*? What bloody court—" He broke off with a rumble of laughter. "You daft lass! Those ladies are noblewomen, not courtesans."

Oh, yes, it was all very funny, wasn't it? She glared at him, hands on her hips. "Just how many ladyships are waiting for me downstairs?"

"Five. Same as last night."

"Five! You mean to say I'm meant to account for myself to *five* countesses?" Why, she'd have preferred five rabid dogs to five meddling ladyships.

"Nay. Three countesses. Lady Clifford, Lady Gray, and Lady Haslemere. Lady Darlington and Lady Lymington are marchionesses."

Marchionesses! What, were there no duchesses to be had? A duchess was all that was missing to complete the nightmare.

Daniel was still chuckling to himself when they reached the same small parlor they'd been in last night. He rapped on the door, there was a lull in the chatter of female voices on the other side, and then Lady Clifford appeared. "Ah, here you are. Come in, Miss Cameron. You too, Daniel."

Daniel stalked past her without a glance, retreated to the corner of the room furthest from the fire, and crossed his arms over his chest.

Mairi paused in the open doorway. There were only five ladies, just as Daniel had said there'd be, but all of a sudden five seemed to be a great many ladies, indeed. There were ladies lounging on every settee, ladies crowded onto every chair—far more ladies than she'd ever wished to see gathered together in one room.

"Please sit down, Miss Cameron." Lady Clifford waved her to a vacant space on the settee. "You remember Lady Gray from last night, I think? This is Lady Darlington, and on the other settee are Lady Haslemere and Lady Lymington."

Mairi did as she was told—she suspected people generally *did* do as Lady Clifford told them to—but she remained carefully perched on the edge of the settee, one wrong question away from soaring into flight.

"I've asked these ladies to do a bit of, ah…investigating into your story, Miss Cameron, to see if we might uncover anything useful."

Uncover any lies, she meant. Lady Clifford might dance about it all she liked, but she didn't trust Mairi any more than Daniel did.

"I paid a call on the Countess of Palmer this morning. Lady Palmer was a distant cousin to Lady Honora Gordon, who was the previous Lady Rutherford." Lady Darlington, who was seated beside her on the settee paused when Mairi didn't speak. "You *do* recognize the name?"

"Of course. Everyone in Coldstream knows the name Rutherford. I never saw the previous lady, as she died several years before I was born, but my grandmother knew her. She was the wife of Malcolm Gordon, the former Viscount Rutherford."

"Yes, the Third Viscount Rutherford's lady. He's dead now as well, of course, and his younger brother, Callum Rutherford, is the current viscount."

Mairi nodded. "Just so, yes."

"Do you know anything at all about the current Lord Rutherford, Miss Cameron?" Lady Clifford asked.

"No, other than that he's a neglectful landlord. He's rarely in Coldstream, preferring instead to spend his time at his London townhouse, which I believe is very grand." Mairi shrugged, but just the thought of Lord Rutherford left a bitter taste on her tongue. "I haven't seen him in the village more than a half-dozen times. His tenants aren't fond of him."

Lady Clifford glanced over her head at Daniel, and cold dread rose in Mairi's chest. She'd just said something wrong—she could see it in their expressions—but what had she said? Every word out of her mouth was nothing but the truth.

Just tell the truth. All she had to do was tell the—

"I see. And are you and your grandmother among his tenants?"

"No. My grandmother has her own small cottage in the town. She's served as midwife in Coldstream and the surrounding counties for years."

"Ah. There's no acrimony between your family and the viscount, then?"

"*No.*" Mairi clenched her hands in her lap. Lady Clifford was getting at something, but aside from living in Coldstream where the viscount's primary country estate resided, neither she nor her grandmother had any connection to Lord Rutherford or his family. "Forgive me, Lady Clifford, but I don't see what any of this has to do with my grandmother's predicament."

"You didn't tell us the truth last night, Miss Cameron." Lady Clifford's cool blue gaze seemed to penetrate right into Mairi's soul. "You left several things out of your story. Rather important things."

"No, I…" Had she left something out by accident? She'd told them about the charge against Lillias, the child's remains found in the lake—

But she hadn't told them she knew whose remains they were.

She hadn't told them about Hamish.

But how could they have found out about him from *here*, hundreds of miles from Coldstream, when even the villagers who'd lived all their lives there didn't remember him? No, it was impossible. The only other person aside from Lillias who could remember Hamish was…

Daniel. Had he remembered his childhood in Coldstream, then? Had his memory miraculously recovered, or had he remembered all along that he'd left Hamish all alone in the icy, murky depths of that pond without so much as a backward glance?

Furious, desperate tears sprang to her eyes even as her hands curled into fists. He was a liar—

"You're a liar, lass." Daniel's deep voice cut through the silence, the heavy thud of his footsteps across the room like portents of doom echoing in her head as he drew closer, until he was standing over her, looming like the monster he was. "You're a liar, and like all liars, you've been found out."

Chapter Eleven

A liar's face changed after they were caught. Daniel had seen it enough times he knew to watch for it now, that instant when they knew they'd been found out as the liar they were, and their false face melted away, like peeling a layer of skin from the bone.

He'd been looking forward to watching Mairi Cameron's pretty mask fall away since he and Lord Gray had returned from Bow Street this morning. After all the lies she'd told, there'd be nothing but ugliness underneath.

He wanted to see it up close, so when they sent her back off to wherever she'd come from, it would be right there in his head, and his bloody conscience could sink down into the depths where it had been hiding all these years, and leave him in peace.

But it was a mistake, because there was nothing ugly about Mairi Cameron, not even with those blotches of fury staining her cheeks, the bitter tears she was trying to hide turning her nose red, and now his conscience was snarling and clawing at him like a wild thing.

So, she was a pretty liar. It didn't change a damn—

"You made her *cry*, Daniel." Cecilia turned reproachful dark eyes on him, and reached out to take Mairi's hand. "Now, Miss Cameron, no one's accusing you of any—"

"The devil we're not." Christ, the girl's big blue eyes were a weapon as sure as her pistol was, only more dangerous. Another blink of those long lashes, a few more tears and she'd have them all convinced she was as pure as a newborn babe. "We're accusing her of being a *liar*, because that's what she is."

Mairi leapt to her feet so suddenly, he actually took a step backwards, but not far enough to avoid inhaling the light and woody scent of her skin. Not her natural scent, but some oil or other the maid had put into her bathwater, because he'd never met a lass yet who smelled like Scottish heather.

He didn't like Scottish heather or scrawny, ginger-headed lasses, nor did he care for a lass who knocked holes into his skull, and looked as if she'd do it again right now, if she had her pistol to hand. He didn't care for liars, and most especially, he didn't care for Mairi Cameron.

But he was a man, and thus a bloody fool, because none of that stopped him from recalling the way she'd looked when she emerged from behind that screen, all flushed and damp and frowning like some bad-tempered water goddess.

For all that she was a wee thing, with a slender waist and dainty wrists and ankles, she had a woman's curves. He hadn't prepared himself for that—hadn't known he *needed* to, until it was too late, and now every time he looked at her, he was going to smell Scottish heather and see that dewy skin and the curling tendrils of damp, dark red hair clinging to her neck.

"What did I lie about, Daniel?" Her hands were clenched at her sides, her lower lip trembling. "You might have the decency to tell me, instead of hurling accusations at me."

That he could be that weak, even knowing what she was, hardened his voice to a harsh growl. "You lied about your grandmother. She's not innocent, any more than you are."

The mask should have dropped away then, so all of them could see the darkness underneath, but that wasn't what happened. Instead, she stared at him, her throat working uselessly before she spat out, "You mean to say, Daniel, that my grandmother is guilty of murdering *you*?"

"Nay, not me, some other poor soul." Another child—God only knew who.

"You're *wrong*. I told you, my grandmother is no murder—"

"There's a witness. Someone saw her drag a screaming boy from the pond into the woods that day. Sounds suspicious, doesn't it, lass? That must be why you forgot to mention it."

That should have been his moment of triumph—his and his father's, Ian Brixton having not been proved a liar, after all—but Mairi dropped down onto the settee, all the color leaching from her face, and instead of victory some foul ooze pooled in his belly, and his conscience went at him again, sinking its talons into his already throbbing head.

"For pity's sake, Daniel." Cecilia glared at him, and, yes, Sophia, Georgiana, and Emma were just as offended. The only one who was unaffected was Lady Clifford, who gave him a curious look but didn't comment, only walked calmly to a tray one of the servants had left on a sideboard, and poured a small measure of port into a glass.

"Here, Miss Cameron. Drink this."

Mairi's hand shook as she reached for the glass, and her shoulders slumped. All the fight drained out of her, which should have pleased Daniel, but it didn't somehow.

Lady Clifford waited until she'd taken a drink before saying, "I think we've perhaps gotten a trifle ahead of ourselves. Lady Darlington is quite right, Miss Cameron, in saying we're not accusing you of anything. *Yet*," she added, with a quelling glance at Daniel. "But your story is a strange one, and demands clarification."

"This witness." Mairi's fingers were white around the glass. "What... who..."

"A lady by the name of Elsbeth Fraser. I'm afraid my, ah...associate didn't know much more aside from what Daniel just told you. Mrs. Fraser claims to have seen Lillias Cameron assaulting young Daniel Adair. She did not, however, come forward at the time of the crime, only now, twenty-four years later, which I find curious."

"It wasn't an *assault*, no matter what Mrs. Fraser claims she saw. My grandmother always kept an eye out for the boys in the village. If she saw Daniel poaching on the viscount's land, something he did *often*"—Mairi shot him an accusing glance—"she would have put a stop to it."

"Perhaps that's so, but there's something else, Miss Cameron. You mentioned Viscount Rutherford lives primarily at his London townhouse?"

Mairi blinked. "Yes."

"Would it surprise you to know he isn't in London, but at his manor house in Edinburgh at this very moment, waiting for the Court of Assizes to try Lillias Cameron for the murder of Daniel Adair?"

That announcement stole the last tinge of color from Mairi's cheeks, until she was so white Cecilia made a little sound of distress. "Oh, dear. Do finish your port, Miss Cameron. It will restore you somewhat."

Mairi did as she was told, draining the glass, but she lay her hand over her stomach once it was gone, as if she was warning it to stay put. "But... why should he be interested in what fate befalls my grandmother? He's never taken the least interest in any of the citizens of Coldstream."

"Lord Rutherford has accused your grandmother of theft, Miss Cameron. He's gone to Scotland to see to it she's held accountable."

"*Theft!*" Mairi's fingers went slack, and the empty glass tumbled to the carpet. "But...I don't understand. What is she meant to have stolen?"

"Again, my associate wasn't certain—this is all word of mouth, you understand, and Coldstream is a good distance from London—but he believes it was a piece of jewelry. Small, but theft is theft, I'm afraid. At least, that's how the law looks at it."

"First a murder, now a theft, and accused by a viscount." Mairi let out a little laugh, but it was a strange, broken sound, more like a sob. "She's certain to hang."

Lady Clifford met Daniel's eyes over Mairi's head, and he could see she was thinking the same thing he was. The girl hadn't lied to them. Anyone could see she hadn't known about the witness or the theft charge before they'd told her. Likely both had come about after she'd left Coldstream for London.

Not a liar, then. It would have been better if she had been, easier for all of them that way, but even he couldn't make himself believe she'd known. For all the wild stories she'd told since he found her in Howe Court last night, he'd yet to catch her in a lie.

"You don't look well, Miss Cameron. I think it would be best if you returned to your bedchamber to rest. Daniel, will you take Miss Cameron back upstairs, please?"

"Not *Daniel*. I'll take her." Cecilia, who evidently hadn't forgiven Daniel for his harshness, and just as evidently had decided she would champion Mairi Cameron, took her gently by her elbow and helped her to rise from the settee. "Come with me, Miss—"

"No, Cecilia dear, I think it had better be Daniel. Miss Cameron doesn't look at all steady on her feet." Lady Clifford gave Daniel a pointed look. "It would be too bad, indeed, if she were to swoon and take a fall, wouldn't it, Daniel?"

Ah. This was to be his penance, then, playing nursemaid to Mairi Cameron. "Aye. Come on, lass."

"I won't...I never swoon." But Mairi's protests were half-hearted, and she couldn't manage more than a tepid glare for him as he took her arm.

Both of them remained silent as he led her up the stairs and down the corridor to her bedchamber, but a half-dozen awkward, half-formed apologies were floating around inside his head, for all the bloody good an apology would do either of them.

He *never* begged anyone's pardon, because he was never sorry, and he wasn't sorry now. Anyone who'd heard Lord Gray's Bow Street Runner friends this morning would have thought the girl was a bald-faced liar. If he did beg her pardon, it would only be because she still looked so pale, and her fingers were still trembling, and…damn it, no one wanted to make a wee blue-eyed lass cry.

When they reached her bedchamber door, he managed a gruff, "Get some sleep, lass," and then he was gone, to the end of the corridor, down the stairs, and through the front door, without a word to Lady Clifford or the girls, and *not* because he was ashamed of himself.

He just didn't have anything to say.

Chapter Twelve

It was twenty-seven steps from the writing desk tucked into one corner of the bedchamber to the grand marble fireplace against the opposite wall.

Twenty-seven.

It was a good room for pacing. The thick oak floorboards beneath Mairi's shoes made a pleasing noise that bounced off the cavernous ceiling, then found her ears again in a faint but satisfying click.

She paused in front of the looking glass. She looked a fright, with a pallor in her cheeks, a deep, anxious crease in her brow, and teeth marks where she'd bitten into her lower lip.

But it wasn't her own face that made her flinch. It was Daniel Brixton's.

In her mind's eye she saw him as he'd looked this afternoon, the cynical twist of his lips when he'd said she was a liar, and had been caught out just like liars always were.

It had now been ten days since she'd left Coldstream—ten days her grandmother could ill afford. By the looks of things, they were ten days utterly wasted, and that wasn't even taking into account the week it would take her to get back home.

Somehow, in that time a witness and a theft charge had mysteriously appeared. There was no telling how many more fictitious crimes her grandmother would be accused of by the time she made it home, and even once she'd arrived, what was there for her to do?

Short of breaking her grandmother out of her cell and stealing away with her, she was out of ideas. All along she'd been telling herself Daniel would do what was right, that he wouldn't turn her away once he understood the fate that awaited Lillias.

Look where that had gotten her.

What could have happened to change him so completely from the boy who'd taken her by the hand to the meadow behind her grandmother's cottage to plant wildflowers, to the brutal man he'd become? When had he turned so cold, so suspicious?

Her sigh fogged the smooth surface of the glass in front of her. The when, why, and how of Daniel's life weren't her concern any longer, if they ever had been. All that mattered now was that he was a stranger to her, and he, well…either he truly didn't remember her, or he didn't want to.

It didn't really matter which. He wasn't going to help her either way. She was a liar after all, wasn't she? No one wanted to help a liar. The only way he'd come to Scotland with her now was after another blow to the head—

Thump.

The dull thud of the wooden door in the entryway slamming closed echoed throughout the house, followed by the clomp of heavy boots trudging down the hallway.

Daniel had marched grimly from the house after that strange encounter with Lady Clifford and her passel of countesses and marchionesses in the parlor this afternoon. Unless she'd mistaken that deafening tread for the footsteps of another giant, he'd now returned to Maddox Street.

The sound of voices drifted up to her, one female, faintly amused— Lady Clifford, no doubt—and another, deep and gruff, more a growl than a voice, and unmistakable.

She turned away from the looking glass and tiptoed across the bedchamber, her tread silent against the thick carpet, then eased the door open and pressed her ear to the crack. It didn't matter a whit to her what Daniel Brixton had to say, of course, but if anything had changed in the past day, she'd rather know it sooner than later, and it was only wise to keep an eye on one's nemesis—

"…consider what I asked you earlier?"

Yes, that was Lady Clifford, her voice even, without inflection, as if she were dealing with a rabid animal and the wrong tone would set it snarling and snapping at her.

"Aye."

What had Lady Clifford asked him earlier? Mairi crowded closer to the door, but Daniel, who'd had more to say this morning than she'd ever wanted to hear, had suddenly gone mute. Dear God, what a maddening creature he was. She'd end up tearing her hair from her head if she had to manage his moods every day.

But Lady Clifford didn't sound in the least perturbed by him. "Very well, then, but one thing we'll need to be certain about is…"

Is...*what*? Nothing but indistinct mumbling, as far as Mairi could hear. She pushed the door open wider and stuck her head out into the hallway, but she only caught Daniel's reply—one word, *aye*—which was about as illuminating as most of his replies.

There was more mumbling, then "...whole thing is inconvenient, but there it is."

Inconvenient. Yes, it was a very great shame poor Daniel should be inconvenienced by her grandmother's impending execution, wasn't it?

"...afraid you'll have to rely on your instincts." Lady Clifford's voice again.

Then Daniel's reply, as clear as a bell. "My instincts say the girl's a liar."

Liar. There was that word again. Did it not occur to either of them that she had nothing at all to gain from lying?

"...discuss it. I've had a servant leave a tray with a bottle of port and glasses in my parlor."

"Aye."

She waited for the soft thud of the entryway door closing, then another shuffle of footsteps before she slipped out into the hallway. She paused on the landing, listening, but the house was quiet, so she stole downstairs, darted around the corner, and crept down the corridor toward Lady Clifford's parlor.

She'd expected to hear the chink of a bottle against the edge of a wine glass, the low murmur of conversation, a half-dozen more of Daniel's mumbled *ayes* and *nays*—it would have made sense if she'd heard any or all of these things—but what she heard instead made her pause, one hand braced on the door frame.

Was that...a baby crying? No, surely not, except...

Only a baby made that distinctive thin, high-pitched squeal. She'd heard infant indignation too many times before not to know it for what it was. This wasn't a newborn child, nor was it a cry for hunger—if it had been, she would have gone in at once—but more a fretful cry, as if the poor, wee thing wanted to sleep, but couldn't work out how to drift off.

She stepped closer—the door had been left slightly open, which was as good as an invitation, really—and pressed her eye to the narrow gap. There was no sign of Lady Clifford, but Daniel was there, hovering over something near the fireplace that looked very much like a cradle, inside of which was a figure swaddled in a thick, white blanket that looked very much like...

A baby.

Why would Lady Clifford have an infant in her private parlor? Whose child was—

Good Lord. She slapped her hands over her ears as an infuriated shriek rent the air, followed by a low, gravelly pleading. "Nay, lass. Don't *cry.*" She lowered her hands and peeked through the gap again. Daniel was peering into the cradle, big hands aloft, waving helplessly, and this time she had to slap her hand over her mouth to smother a laugh.

Neither daggers nor pistols or the dark London streets could overset the great Daniel Brixton, but one squall from a tiny child was enough to send him into a panic—

"Baloo bailli, Baloo bailli,

"Ging awa peerie faires, fae my peerie bairn…"

She froze, the familiar notes of the refrain playing inside her head.

She'd heard the song hundreds of times before, just like every other child in Scotland. It was "Baloo Baleerie," an old Scottish lullaby her grandmother used to sing to her at bedtime.

"Baloo bailli, Baloo bailli

Dey'll sheen ower da cradle, O wir bairn noo…"

Daniel was singing to the child in a low, rough, yet surprisingly fine voice, the Gaelic slipping easily from his tongue and brushing over Mairi's nerve endings like the stroke of a callused fingertip.

This man, who hadn't had a single kind word to spare for *her*, who'd scowled and argued and mocked her, had called her a liar, a snake, and a murderer, was *singing* sweet lullabies to a weeping child.

With every one of his cold glares and growls, with every insult he'd thrown at her, she'd told herself there was nothing left of the loveable boy he'd once been in the cold, menacing man he'd become. It was easier to imagine the past twenty-four years had wrought an irrevocable change in him than to believe the boy she'd once loved would turn his back on her.

But there he was, right there in Lady Clifford's parlor, that same boy with the tender heart, singing with gruff affection to a wee babe, his big, scarred hands on the edge of the cradle, rocking her.

Daniel Adair *was* still there, buried somewhere inside that brutish body. Just not for *her*, and not for her grandmother.

Hot, furious tears stung her eyes. Ten days, wasted. Ten days that might well be the difference between Lillias's life and her death, squandered. She'd accomplished precisely nothing by coming here, unless one considered an evening of pacing in London's largest bedchamber an accomplishment.

Dear *God*, what a fool she was.

She turned and retraced her steps from the corridor to the bottom of the stairwell as quietly as she could, but by the time she neared the second-floor landing she was running, uncaring if anyone heard her.

She'd wasted enough time. There was only one place to go from here. *Home*. She had seven long, exhausting days of travel from London to the Borders to come up with some other way to help her grandmother.

Her feet caught in her skirt at the top of the landing, sending her to her hands and knees, but she scrambled up again, hurried down the hallway, and threw open the door to her borrowed bedchamber.

Cloak, pistol, her grandmother's letters…yes, right where she'd left them.

On her way out the door she spared one last, longing look at the bed, the cozy nest of soft bedding, but one night of dreamless slumber would have to do.

Now she'd made up her mind, she couldn't get away fast enough.

* * * *

"Why, Daniel. I didn't realize you could sing! Such a lovely bass voice you have, too."

"I wasn't *singing*. Just warning the wee lass to be quiet, that's all."

He gave Lady Clifford the fiercest scowl he could muster, but she returned a mischievous grin. "Oh? How strange. I would have sworn I heard singing. Well, whatever you did, it seemed to have worked." Lady Clifford nodded at the cradle where baby Amanda lay fast asleep, one chubby hand stuffed inside her mouth. "Now then, did you discover anything to the purpose this evening?"

"Nothing that proves the girl isn't a liar." Nothing to prove she was one, either, but no man in his right mind would credit the wild tale Mairi Cameron had told them.

Lady Clifford said nothing, just regarded him for a long moment with sharp blue eyes before saying with a shrug, "I'm certain you're right, and she's been lying to us all along. I don't suppose there's much more to say, then, is there?"

"Nay."

"I can't say I'm surprised. There's something about that girl's face I don't quite like, some shiftiness in her expression, though she did look shocked this afternoon when we told her about the witness. Ah, well, I daresay she's an accomplished actress, like most liars."

"Aye."

"Not that what I hear of Lord Rutherford is any better, either of the current viscount, or his elder brother before him. Devious, the entire lot of them. Merciless, too." Lady Clifford reached out a hand to rock baby Amanda's cradle. "I wouldn't like to find myself on the wrong side of them, would you?"

"Nay."

"Then there's the case against Lillias Cameron moving so quickly. Strange, isn't it? On such scant evidence as one witness and an unidentified body, too. But I daresay Mairi Cameron is a liar, just as you suspect, Daniel."

He grunted.

"There's some sort of trick in it, that's certain." Lady Clifford smiled down at the baby, and reached into the cradle to stroke her tiny hand. "But at the moment the only thing that makes the least bit of sense is that the girl is exactly who she claims to be. Of course, we don't know the whole story, but there is one way to find it out for certain."

"I know what you're doing. Don't think I don't." Nothing but wily women, everywhere he turned, God help him.

"Well, I should hope so." Lady Clifford's lips twitched. "I'm not attempting to be subtle, and you've watched me do it often enough to the girls. We're in agreement, then?"

"Looks like it, aye." He didn't fancy seven days trapped in a carriage with Mairi Cameron, but at least this way he could be sure he was rid of the chit.

"Ah, good. There's only one bit of business left to attend to." Lady Clifford gave him a cheerful smile. "What time will you and Miss Cameron be leaving for Scotland in the morning?"

He snorted, not bothering to hide his smirk this time. "Early. I still say the lass is lying through her pretty teeth, but no sense in wasting time."

Because if she *was* telling the truth, they'd already wasted too much of it.

"Very well." Lady Clifford tugged on the bell, then sat back in her chair. "Why don't you go upstairs and let Miss Cameron know that despite all your growling and accusations, you've decided to accompany her to Scotland, after all."

"Nay." The last thing the lass would want is to find *him* on the other side of her bedchamber door in the middle of night. "Better send Winnie, or one of the housemaids."

Lady Clifford considered it, then shook her head. "No, not this time, Daniel. I think Miss Cameron would rather hear it from *you*."

Chapter Thirteen

Mairi earned more than one curious glance when she entered the Angel Inn in Islington.

A busy coaching inn wasn't the best place for a lady who was unaccompanied by an escort or even a servant, but the mail coach was the quickest way back to Scotland, so here she was, and she might just as well get used to the gawking now, because it was a long way from London to Edinburgh, and she'd be making the journey alone.

She seemed to be always alone these days.

It was just coming on four in the morning, but there wasn't any peace to be found at the Angel even at this ungodly hour, so she retreated to a bench in the corner of the room, as far distant from the thick of the crowd as she could get and sat down, ignoring the stares aimed in her direction.

Well, then, she'd just keep her own eyes fixed firmly on her hands folded on top of her valise, and take comfort in the weight of her pistol in her pocket. There, that was better. Yes, it was perfectly *fine*, aside from the tickle at the back of her neck from the curious gazes of her fellow travelers, running over her like little spider's legs against her skin. That is, some of the gazes were merely curious. Others were calculating, assessing, perhaps, the value of her cloak, or speculating on what the small valise she carried might contain.

She kept her head down, poking the tip of her tongue into the sore spot where she'd bitten her lip bloody, and cursing her own stupidity. What had she been thinking, embarking on a wild trip to London? It had been a lifetime since she'd seen Daniel Adair.

She should have known he'd never agree to help her.

He wasn't even Daniel Adair anymore. He was Daniel *Brixton* now.

But he *had* been Daniel Adair once, and that Daniel had been her friend. He and Hamish, one the most mischievous and the other the sweetest boy in the village. There hadn't been many girls her age in Coldstream during her youngest years, and the few there were, were more interested in girlish pursuits. The boys were much more fun, even though most of them scoffed at her efforts to keep up with them.

But not Daniel, and not Hamish. At least, not all the time. Oh, Daniel had been a dreadful tease, but when he drove her to angry tears with his antics, he was always anxious to make amends. One spring, he'd given her handfuls of wildflower seeds he'd gathered at the end of the previous summer, then he'd taken her behind her grandmother's cottage and helped her scatter them about. By midsummer, their vibrant colors spread out like a patchwork quilt under the warm rays of sunshine.

She straightened her shoulders and shook the thoughts from her head. It was one of her happiest childhood memories, but it no longer felt real to her, in the way a dream ceased to be real the moment one awoke—

"Are you here on your own, love?"

Mairi startled, her back stiffening. She looked up, prepared to deliver a sharp set-down to whomever had spoken to her, but the words died on her lips when she found a pair of kind brown eyes set into a face creased with wrinkles looking back at her.

"Ach, did I frighten ye, dear? Beg your pardon. We don't mean you any harm, lass. I just thought you might like some company, being as you're on your own."

"That's very kind of you, er..."

"Mrs. Gillies, and this here is my Angus." Mrs. Gillies nodded at the man sitting behind her, a chuckle escaping her when Mairi's eyes widened at the sight of him. "Angus is a big one, right enough, but gentle as a lamb, aren't you, dear?"

Angus didn't speak, but he winked at Mairi, his blue eyes twinkling.

"We saw you come in, and I say to Angus, we'd best go and sit beside that lass, as she's naught but a wee thing, and all alone, and people tend to give Angus here plenty of space, ye see, and so here we are."

"I...that's very kind of you," Mairi said again, strangely tongue-tied.

It had been a long time since anyone had spared a kind word for her. An unwelcome stinging sensation pressed behind her eyes, but she wasn't going to *cry*, for pity's sake. She *never* cried, or at least she hadn't since...

Since she'd arrived in London, looking for Daniel. Now she seemed to be always either weeping or on the edge of bursting into tears, and here she thought she'd cried them all when Hamish and Daniel had vanished from Coldstream.

But as it turned out, there were always more tears.

That feeling of being left behind, alone and abandoned, had never quite gone away. That was the way of childhood memories, wasn't it? The happy ones shone like the sun, but the other ones, the sad ones, were as sharp as the deadliest blade—

"Ach, well, it's nothing at all." Mrs. Gillies gave Mairi's hand a reassuring pat. "What's your name, love?"

"It's Mairi Cam…it's Mairi." Perhaps she'd just keep her surname to herself. Mrs. Gillies and her husband likely hadn't heard the name Lillias Cameron, but why court trouble? A lady could never be too careful.

"Ah, then you're bound for Scotland, eh? You see, Angus?" Mrs. Gillies nudged her husband. "I told you a lass with that red hair must be as Scottish as haggis and heather."

Angus raised one bushy eyebrow, but didn't venture a comment.

Mairi couldn't help but grin at the two of them. Angus didn't seem inclined to speak, which was just as well, as his wife talked enough for the both of them. They were a perfectly balanced pair. "I was born and raised in the Borders."

"You see there, Angus? Just as I said. We're for Edinburgh ourselves, and a lucky thing it is we're here to keep you company, as I don't like to think of a young lady like yourself going all that way alone. Angus doesn't like it, either. Do you, Angus?"

Mairi chose to interpret Angus's grunt as whole-hearted agreement.

The thought of traveling alone hadn't bothered her at first—she'd made it here in one piece, after all, and she'd make it back the same way—but that was before she'd entered the Angel and gotten a good look at her fellow travelers. Coldstream's criminal element didn't hold a candle to London's.

It would be far pleasanter to have some companions to make the journey with, especially a companion like Angus Gillies, who was intimidating enough to deter even the worst sort of scoundrel—

"What the devil are you doing here, Mairi?"

Not quite the worst, then.

Of all the places in London she might have gone, of all the means of travel she might have pursued, how had he worked out that she'd come *here*?

"Well, lass?" Daniel was staring down at her, arms crossed over his chest, bulging menacingly. "It's not safe for you to run about the London streets in the dark, you daft chit."

If he called her daft one more time, she was taking out her pistol. "I don't see what business it is of *yours* where I go."

"Enough. Come with me, lass. You can explain yourself when we're back home."

If Daniel's high-handedness had been even a touch less maddening, she *might* have noticed it when Mrs. Gillies took up a worried clucking, and she *might* have seen Angus lumber to his feet, and it *might* have prevented what happened next.

But she was preoccupied with her own outrage, and wholly focused on the big, dark, churlish source of it. "I beg your pardon, Mr. Brixton, but London's West End isn't my home. My home is in Scotland, with my grandmother. I won't be explaining a thing to you, nor will I stir a single step from here."

Daniel's expression hardened. "I wasn't *asking* you, lass. I'm *telling* you."

Mairi rose to her feet, looked Daniel right in the eyes...well, more the center of his chest, really, and braced her hands on her hips. "Oh, you're *telling* me, are you? How dare you think you have the right to tell me anything?"

"Are you finished yet, lass?" Daniel waited, peering down his nose at her. When she didn't answer, he seized her arm. "Good, because we're wasting time."

"Oh, dear. Oh, dear me," Mrs. Gillies muttered, wringing her hands. "Oh, that won't sit well with Angus, it won't."

It didn't sit well with Angus, who came forward until he stood eye to eye with Daniel. "Take yer hand off that young lady. *Now.*"

Daniel's jaw tightened. "Who are *you*?" he demanded, without releasing Mairi's arm.

"My goodness, he's as big as Angus." Mrs. Gillies clutched Mairi's hand, looking between Angus and Daniel, eyes wide. "He must be a Scot."

Angus ignored Daniel's question, stepping close, so their chests nearly touched. "A gentleman doesn't put his hands on an unwilling lady."

Daniel's lips twisted in a savage grin. "I'm not a gentleman."

"No, you're not." Mairi jerked her arm free from Daniel's grip. "We can all agree on that, at least."

Mrs. Gillies had jumped to her feet as well, as if ready to go to battle alongside Mairi if such a sacrifice were needed. "Is this man your husband, Mairi?"

"My *husband*? Good Lord, no."

"He's your, ah...your betrothed, then?"

Mairi barked out a laugh. "No, he's not that either, and a good thing, too."

Mrs. Gillies sniffed. "Awfully high-handed for a man who's neither husband nor betrothed, isn't he?"

"Rather, yes. He was a friend once, you see, Mrs. Gillies, but it's heartbreaking, isn't it, the way a friendship can fade over the years as if it never existed?"

"Aye, lass. It's a terrible thing, it is." Mrs. Gillies shot an accusing look at Daniel, as if the demise of his friendship with Mairi must be entirely his fault.

"I've never had so many friends I could afford to lose one, but that's the way of things sometimes, and Mr. Brixton here has made it clear he doesn't wish to continue our acquaintance."

"I never said that," Daniel growled, one eye on her and the other on Angus.

"Not to me, no, but you said it to Lady Clifford. You told her I was a liar, and that she shouldn't trust me." Dash it, the humiliating sting was back in her eyes, and the pressure was building with every word out of her mouth.

"Listening at the door, were you? Well, if you'd stayed put until the end instead of wandering off to Islington, you would know I came to your bedchamber tonight to tell you—"

"You know, I was just thinking about you, Daniel, right before you arrived. I was remembering the time you and Ham…you took me into the field behind my grandmother's cottage to plant wildflower seeds."

Hamish had been there, too, but she couldn't bring herself to speak of him to this man she no longer knew, who wouldn't even remember Hamish's name.

"I told you I thought the flowers were pretty, so you gathered handfuls of the seeds in the summer, and you took me the following spring to scatter them in the field. Purple thistle and heather, and Scottish bluebells, and those pretty pink flowers that look like stars. I don't remember what they're called."

"Campion," Daniel muttered.

Campion? He couldn't remember her name or her face, but he remembered they'd planted campion? "They're still there, you know. The wildflowers. All these years later, they're still there, growing in the same wild profusion they did the day we planted them. That day was…well, that was the loveliest thing anyone ever did for me."

She'd spent many lonely hours lying on her back in that field of wildflowers after Daniel and Hamish disappeared, hot tears running down her cheeks. She'd missed them so terribly, the gaping hole their absence left in her life all the more painful for not knowing what had happened to them, or where they'd gone.

But she didn't tell *him* that. She'd given him enough of herself already, only to have it thrown back in her face.

"You don't remember how close we once were, but I do." This time, she couldn't keep the tears that welled in her eyes from falling. She couldn't have said whether they were tears of anger, or frustration, or exhaustion, but everything was wretched and hopeless, and her grandmother, her dear sweet grandmother who'd never hurt a soul was going to die a horrible, shameful death.

Of all the people she could think of, all the people she'd ever known over her lifetime, Lillias Cameron was the last one in the world who deserved such a fate. "I'm not asking for anything from you anymore, Daniel. You may as well go back to Maddox Street. I'm returning to Scotland on the mail coach, and I don't ever intend to come back to London again. You'll be rid of me, just as you wished to be."

"You're not going back to Coldstream alone. That's what I came to tell you tonight—"

"I'm not alone. Mrs. and Mr. Gillies are traveling to Edinburgh on the mail coach as well, and have graciously offered to keep me company. So, you see, you have no reason to reproach yourself, unless it's for all the times you called me a snake and a liar."

Mrs. Gillies turned on Daniel with a gasp of indignation. "Shame on you!"

Before Daniel could reply, the coachman bellowed a warning for the mail coach's departure. Mairi turned away from him without another word, but she hadn't taken two steps before an arm curled around her waist. "Not so fast, lass. Now, you just stay where you are, Angus. I'm not going to hurt her, but she's coming with me, even if I have to make myself a wee bit unpleasant."

His chest was like a stone wall against her back, his massive arms like bands of iron around her, holding her still against him. If she had any sense at all, she'd be terrified, but the frantic thrashing of her pulse, the sudden surge of heat searing her nerve endings wasn't from fear, but *fury.*

Yes, that was certainly fury, and nothing more than that. "I should have let that blackguard chasing you last night sink his blade into your chest!"

She felt a rumble of amusement against her back. "Nay, you made the right choice, bashing in his skull with a chamber pot. Never seen so much blood in my life, but then the head does bleed, doesn't it, Angus?"

Mrs. Gillies was staring at them, her mouth slack. "Blood? *Chamber pot?*"

"Aye, Mrs. Gillies. This lass may have the face of an angel, but she's a dangerous one—maybe even a wee bit mad. Nasty temper, too." Daniel was backing out of the Angel as he spoke, dragging her along with him. "No telling what she'd do with that pistol she's got in her valise once you were all on the road, eh?"

"Pistol?" Mrs. Gillies was gaping at Mairi, mouth open. "My goodness!"

"Best keep back, Mrs. Gillies!" Daniel whisked Mairi through the door and onto the dark street. "I can feel one of her mad fits coming on!"

"Don't listen to him, Mrs. Gillies! He's ly—"

But it was already too late. Daniel melted quickly into the deepest shadows, leaving the Angel behind, and just like that, she was once again at the mercy of Daniel Brixton.

Chapter Fourteen

It was sixty-eight miles from London to Northampton.

Mairi shifted on the carriage bench, hiding a grimace. Lady Clifford's carriage was as fine as everything else that belonged to Lady Clifford, but the superior springs and thick cushions hadn't prevented her backside from going numb.

It was the second most uncomfortable thing about this journey so far.

As for the first…she glanced at Daniel from the corner of her eye. His mouth was set in its usual harsh lines, and even the gentle breeze ruffling his dark hair couldn't offset the severity of his jawline, the menace of that lowered brow. His wasn't a welcoming face at the best of times, but the dark purple shadows of impending twilight exaggerated the angular lines, turning his habitual scowl sinister.

They'd left London before the sun rose, and aside from a rough grunt that she supposed was meant to be a cheerful morning greeting, he hadn't spoken again.

Sixty-eight miles. Ten hours, without a single word exchanged between them.

Not that the thick, endless silence bothered *her*, of course. She'd be perfectly content if he kept his grunts and growls, his *chits* and *girls* and *lasses* to himself all the way to Coldstream, and there was, after all, little to say…

Or, no. It wasn't that. It was that there was too much to say, the secrets, rumors, riddles, and lies crowding her mouth—

Stop it.

For the last time, she hadn't *lied*. Strictly speaking, every word she'd said to him was the truth. If she hadn't said *all* the words she might have, well…that wasn't a lie so much as a strategy.

A careful omission, then. Yes, that would do well enough, for now. It was too soon to tell him everything. Northampton was too close to London for her to start spewing the inconvenient truths that had been swelling inside her mouth since they'd left Maddox Street behind them.

That she should be on the verge of spewing anything at all was infuriating enough. She'd never had any trouble holding her tongue before, and it wasn't as if she were longing for a cozy chat with Daniel Brixton. He wasn't at all the sort of man who encouraged intimate confidences. If he could maintain a grim, oppressive silence for ten hours at a stretch, then so could she.

It was another sixty-three miles from Northampton to Nottingham. From there they'd head towards Sheffield, then on to Boroughbridge, Harrowgate, Darlington…

Darlington. Yes, she'd tell him everything she knew when they reached Darlington. He'd be furious, but by then there'd be little he could do about it. They'd be so far north it wouldn't make sense to turn back.

Her conscience pricked at her, but this was always going to come down to lies—that is, careful omissions—sooner or later. She'd worked too hard to get here, risked too much to let him walk away from her now because she blurted out too many truths. No, she'd give him as little information as she could possibly get away with, feed him only the tiniest tidbits at a time, the way a nurse fed a baby from a spoon, to keep it from choking, because anything less might mean failure, and that was a luxury she couldn't afford.

Darkness was thick upon them by the time Daniel brought the carriage to a stop in front of a square, sturdy building, the brick face of it freshly whitewashed, and above the doorway a heavy, wooden sign hanging from an iron pole creaking back and forth in the wind. "The Bantam Cock," she read aloud. "Are we staying here for the night?"

Daniel tossed the reins to the boy who appeared without sparing her as much as a glance. "Wait here."

That was all. No answer to her question, just a brusque order. For pity's sake, the man had spoken two words in the past ten hours, and he'd still managed to make himself tiresome. She didn't venture a reply, which was just as well, as he hadn't paused long enough to hear one, but went marching off towards the front door without another word.

Why bother wasting her breath exchanging pleasantries with a man who sent common civility scurrying for cover with one glance from those chilly dark eyes? Besides, chatter irritated him, and it was best to keep him content, at least as far as Darlington.

Longer, if she could manage it. As content as Daniel Brixton ever was, that is.

She pulled her hood over her hair, tucked her hands into the sleeves of her cloak to chase the frost from her fingers, and settled in to wait, just as he'd bid her, because she'd gotten what she wanted, and had every reason to be accommodating.

This morning she'd been in London, worlds away from Coldstream, and now she was here, sixty-eight miles closer to her grandmother than she had been ten hours earlier. Ten hours closer to rectifying whatever dreadful miscarriage of justice had seen her grandmother dragged from her home and deposited in a damp, drafty cell—

"Are you coming down, lass, or do you mean to spend the night in the carriage?"

She jumped at the deep rasp. "Dear God, you startled the life out of me. I didn't see you come—" She squeaked in outrage as his enormous hands closed around her waist. "What do you think you're doing? I don't need your help to get—"

She was down before she could finish the sentence, whisked from her seat like a naughty cat caught atop a dining table, her feet kicking in the air before he set her upright, his warm palms lingering for an instant at the curve of her waist to steady her. "I told you I didn't need any—"

"The room's ready." Daniel released her as quickly as he'd grabbed her. "Go on inside."

"Where else would I—"

But he was halfway across the innyard already, his long-legged strides swallowing the ground at his feet, so she gave into the childish but utterly irresistible urge to stick her tongue out at that broad back.

There. She felt better already.

"Good evening, madam." A red-cheeked lady with thin wisps of brown hair straggling from a haphazard bun at the back of her neck bustled from the dining room into the entryway when Mairi came in, and offered her a distracted smile. "I'm Mrs. Peckham, proprietress of this establishment. You must be Mrs. Brixton."

Mrs. Brixton? Was that who she was now? Daniel might have warned her, but then that would have required him to speak a great many words, wouldn't it? A half-dozen, at least.

"Er...yes. That's me. Yes, indeed. I'm Mrs. Brixton."

"Your husband went out to see to it James took proper care of the horses, but he bid me show you to your room." Mrs. Peckham snatched a key off a row of hooks and waved at Mairi to follow her up a steep staircase at the back of the house, pausing when they reached a closed door at the top. "Here you are."

She stood back, and Mairi passed into the bedchamber to find a small room with scrubbed wooden floors swallowed up by a massive hearth of dark gray stone. A pair of tall windows dominated one wall, and a narrow bed with a cheerful patchwork quilt the other. A small table stood beside the bed, half a candle in a pewter holder resting atop it, the other half of it reduced to a faint but pleasant scent of melted wax.

Mrs. Peckham hurried across the room to straighten the quilt, then turned back to Mairi with a tentative smile. "I hope it suits."

It *did* suit, yes—or it would have, if she and Daniel had been lovers, or at least a great deal fonder of each other than they were. The bed wouldn't even fit Daniel on his own, much less the two of them together. Not that there was any question of *that*, but even the open space available on the floor didn't look as if it would be enough for him. He'd have to sleep standing up—

"Mrs. Brixton? Will the room do?"

"Oh, yes, indeed. Thank you, Mrs. Peckham." She could hardly object to it on the grounds that her, er...*husband* was too big to sleep on the floor, could she?

"Right, then." Mrs. Peckham paused with her hand on the door latch. "Shall I send a tray up with your dinner, or would you prefer to dine—" She trailed off, eyes widening when Daniel appeared in the open doorway. "Oh, er...Mr. Brixton."

"Mrs. Peckham." He gave her a curt nod.

"I'll just, ah..." She skirted around him, breathing an audible sigh of relief when she'd gained the safety of the hallway. "Send up a tray, shall I?"

"That will be fine. Thank you, Mrs. Peckham." Mairi closed the door, then turned to lean against it, crossing her arms over her chest, eying Daniel. "Our hostess seems to be under the impression I'm Mrs. Brixton."

"You are, for now. An unwed man and woman traveling together will set tongues wagging, and wagging tongues means attention we don't want."

"You mean to say we're to pretend to be husband and wife for the entire journey?" How had it not occurred to her such an odious deception would be necessary? She must have blocked it out.

"Aye." He shrugged, as if the sudden addition of a wife were of little concern to him.

Dear God. This was close quarters, indeed, for two people who could hardly stand the sight of each other. "You could have said we were brother and sister," she grumbled. It was petty of her, but a long, sleepless night trapped in a tiny bedchamber with a silent, sullen, pretend husband loomed ahead of her.

One corner of his mouth twitched. "Because we look so much alike?"

Did he just make a *joke*? Yes, yes, he had, and that quirk of his lip almost looked as if it had been...a smile? Surely not. No, it was far more likely it was some sort of uncontrollable spasm, like a tic or a convulsion. Still, even that infinitesimal softening of the harsh lines of his face did do rather nice things to his appearance.

His mouth, in particular. If anyone had asked her to describe his mouth prior to that twitch, she would have said it was thin, tight, and severe, but it wasn't, really. His lips were full, the lower one more so than the upper, as if he were in a perpetual pout.

Objectively speaking, Daniel was attractive. Not to *her*, of course. No, he was much too somber for her tastes, much too grim, but there was a certain type of lady who'd find that thick, wavy, coal black hair of his appealing—ladies who might want to run their fingers through it to test its softness, or touch a palm to his chest to see if it was as hard as it appeared to be—

"Why are you gaping at me like that, lass?"

She blinked, dazed for an instant before scorching heat rushed into her cheeks. "Gaping at you? Why, how ridiculous. I *never* gape, but if I was, it was only because I was...I was wondering where you intend to sleep when there's only one bed, and the space between the hearth and the bed is narrower than the width of your shoulders."

Considerably narrower. Not that she'd noticed.

"I've made do with worse."

"No doubt." *That* wasn't difficult to believe. "Well, do as you please, then, but I'm going to bed." The sooner she put this day behind her, the better.

He frowned. "You just told the landlady to bring up a dinner tray."

She hadn't, actually. The poor woman had used the tray as an excuse to scurry away the moment *he* appeared in the doorway. "Well, I've changed my mind."

Daniel looked her up and down, his brows lowered, but just when she was certain he was going to say something exceedingly tiresome, like insist she had to eat, he shrugged again, and turned toward the door.

She took a step after him. "Where are you going?"

"I *am* hungry, lass, so I'm going down to the dining room for a steak and kidney pie. The stew looked hearty enough. You're sure about that tray?"

It was one of the longest sentences she'd ever heard him utter. Apparently, he could be quite chatty when it came to food. "I'm sure. I'm much too exhausted to eat." She was, too, despite that protesting growl from her stomach.

He was halfway out the door, but he turned back, his eyes narrowed. "If you're going to go to bed, then go. No wandering about."

"Where do you imagine I'd wander to, Daniel?" This was Northampton, for pity's sake, not Vauxhall Gardens.

"No telling, lass, but see you don't."

He punctuated this command with a grunt, and then he was gone.

She plopped down on the edge of the bed, something sharp-toothed and nameless gnawing at the pit of her stomach. Or maybe that was just hunger. She should have had the blasted stew sent up, but rest would be much better for her than food, and it would be easier to fall asleep if he wasn't in the room with her, listening to her breathe.

She didn't bother with a night rail, just kicked off her shoes and crawled under the covers, her limbs so heavy with fatigue the mattress sucked her down like a stone tossed into the water, deeper, then deeper still until she imagined she'd sink all the way through, and drop onto the floor under the bed.

As it was, she spent a good long time staring up at the wooden beams above her head, eyes pinned open and stomach rumbling, the memory of eight-year-old Daniel Adair's crooked smile floating somewhere above her, half-hidden among the shadows of the sloped roof, but *real* still—so real she could see it as clearly as if it were painted on the beams above her head.

She'd forgotten that smile, had long ago consigned it to the cobwebs of her mind with all her other ghosts.

But it wasn't gone.

Just hidden behind the grimace of a man who'd forgotten it had ever been there at all.

Chapter Fifteen

A man who spends his life in darkness becomes blind in the light.

Someone had told him that once, but he couldn't remember who it'd been. Lord Gray, maybe, or Lymington. It had been some lord or other, because only a lord would say something so bloody stupid.

Daniel stumbled over the hearth, crashed into the leg of the bed, and spat a half-smothered curse from between his beer-soaked lips. No port wine or brandy, and none of that claret Darlington and Haslemere were so fond of. A stout porter did just fine for the likes of him.

When he drank at all, which wasn't often. Drink addled his wits and made him clumsy, two things a man who lived or died by his fists couldn't afford to be, but not many of his enemies would bother to follow him to the wilds of Northampton to slit his throat.

Too much trouble, that.

He'd hoped a few tankards of Mrs. Peckham's dark porter running through his veins would help him fall asleep, but by the time he'd kicked his boots off and stumbled about in search of an empty bit of floor he was wide awake, and he'd made enough noise to rouse all of Northampton's dead from their graves.

A man with feet his size couldn't creep quietly about, without or without his boots.

Mairi didn't say a word to him, but she wasn't asleep, for all that she might want to make him think she was. Not only because no one could have slept through his bumbling, but because her slight body had stiffened under the coverlet when he'd opened the bedchamber door, and now he could sense her awareness in the darkness, feel her as surely as he could a hand gripping his shoulder, or the tip of a cold blade pressed to his neck.

He tossed this way and that, rolled onto his side and then to his back again, his body aching from too many hours spent sitting in that carriage, so long he'd been afraid his hands would be forever bent as if he were holding reins between them. He'd finally given up and resigned himself to sleeping with his feet flat on the floor and knees bent when something soft landed on his face.

A blanket. A moment later a pillow flopped down next to his ear. She didn't say anything—didn't ask if he wanted them, just dropped them onto the floor.

He shoved the pillow behind his head and draped the blanket over his legs. But that was almost worse, because now he was obliged to say something to her, wasn't he?

That was the trouble with kindness. As soon as you accepted it, you owed something in return, and he didn't want to owe anyone, least of all Mairi Cameron. Owing her was what had landed him in Northampton, his arse sore from the press of the hard floorboards beneath him.

If he spoke to her, then he'd have to think about her, and if he thought about her, he'd have to look at her, and once he looked at her, he'd start seeing all those splintered images in his head again—*see* them with his eyes open, as if they were real, not *dream* them, as he'd always done before.

Nothing about the waking dreams made sense. They were just faces, the features blurry, and flashing images he couldn't place—a flicker of sunlight through a thick layer of tree branches above, shouting, the smack of bare feet against hard-packed mud, rough bark under his fingertips. They were hazy, a handful of fleeting sensations, but they coiled in his belly like a serpent and stayed there, not like fists, brawls, and blood ever had.

Once a brawl was done, it was done. A tidy start, and a tidy end, and no doubt about who'd won or lost. If you were still standing, you'd won. If you were on the ground, you'd lost. Nice and clean, the way things should be.

Mairi Cameron, with her wild tales and pretty bow lips, had thrown everything off.

But it was no use, not when the pillow under his head smelled like her, like he imagined Scotland itself must smell, of earth and woods and heather, reminding him of how she'd felt trapped against his chest that first night, both strange and familiar at once.

If he'd known it would come to this, he would have left her in Howe Court without ever laying a finger on her.

"What's Coldstream like, then?" He had to shove the words out, but the hard, tight place inside him eased once he did, a fist unclenching. A few minutes of listening to her chatter was a fair exchange for a blanket and pillow, and it was easier when he didn't have to see her face, those big blue eyes filled with shadows, like she expected something from him, and he kept failing to give it to her.

She shifted on the bed, the coverlet rustling. "Small."

He waited. There was no way this lass would stop at one word.

"It's not a bad thing, just…everyone knows everything there is to know about each other. There are no secrets in Coldstream."

Ah, Mairi Cameron had secrets, then, much like everyone else did. "You have friends there?"

"Some, yes." She let out a long, slow sigh. "And enemies."

He grunted. Everyone had those, too. "People there think your grandmother's guilty?" Some of them must, the sort who were always willing to believe the worst of everyone.

Mairi was quiet for a long time, long enough the porter had time to work its magic, and his eyelids began to droop, then she said, "She's spent her whole life taking care of them."

His eyes popped open again.

"Her mother—my great-grandmother—was the midwife to the villages in the Borders, and she used to take my grandmother with her when she went out to tend to the people. My grandmother learned at her side, then she encouraged my interest in healing. In one way or another, she's been taking care of them since she was old enough to walk."

He said nothing, but he was listening now, really listening this time. Maybe Mairi knew it, or maybe she just needed to talk, but it all came out of her then, a rush of words tangled up in anger and bitterness, fear and resentment, and love, not just for her grandmother, but for all of them, even those who'd wronged Lillias Cameron by believing the worst of her.

What must that be like, to love and hate at once? For him, it had always only been one or the other.

Mostly the other.

"Of course, it's the midwife's job to care for the people, but my grandmother didn't care for them because she was the village midwife, and it's her duty. She was the village midwife *because* she cared for them. It's who she is, who she's always been."

"You admire her."

It was a foolish way to put it, when every word out of her mouth throbbed with something much stronger than admiration, but he'd never known what to do with the softer emotions.

"You admired her too, once." She laughed, the unexpected sound bursting like a thunderclap in the hush of the bedchamber, and sending him scrabbling for his blade. "All the boys in your clan did."

He sucked in a quick breath and forced his fists back to his sides. "Clan?"

"Yes. All the boys in the village were part of the clan." She rattled off half a dozen names, none of which meant anything to him. "Sometimes it was Clan Adair, and Clan Mackenzie at others, depending on who was the leader at any given time. You fancied yourselves a fierce, brutal lot."

"Not much point in a sweet, peaceable clan, is there?" His tone was gruff, but under cover of darkness his lips were twitching. Clan Adair was a much better name than Clan bloody Mackenzie.

"You were a ragged, unruly gang of naughty boys, always getting into mischief. I so wanted to be a member of the clan, but girls were strictly forbidden, and of course I was younger than you all. The other boys had no patience for me, but you and Ham—you were kinder to me, likely for my grandmother's sake."

"None of these lads had parents?" His own mother had died by the time he turned five, or so he'd been told. His father had spoken of her to him, and Daniel had tried to remember anything he could about her—her voice, the color of her hair—but it had been like trying to grasp a handful of mist. After a while, he stopped trying.

"Archie Mackenzie had a father, but he drank, and he used to disappear for months at a time. Fergus's mother is alive and still lives in Coldstream, but she was housekeeper at the big house back then, and gone most of every day. My grandmother used to look out for you all, try to keep you from getting into too much trouble."

He grunted. "Thankless job, that."

"Sometimes, but she was fond of her boys, as she used to call you, especially you and…and one or two of the other boys. You really don't remember, Daniel?" she asked, a hint of sadness in her voice.

"Nay."

"Not even…not even *me*?"

"Nay." If he'd seen *that* face before, heard that soft, lilting voice, he'd remember it.

She let out a soft sigh, but after a brief, disappointed silence, she resumed her story. "Some of the older people complained you were a nuisance. There were those who wanted to run you out of the village, but my grandmother wouldn't allow it."

The way Mairi told it, Lillias Cameron was a saint. Since he didn't believe in saints, there had to be more to it than what she was telling him. "Why should she bother with a pack of wild ruffians?"

"Because it needed doing, and because she'd been the one to help bring you into the world, and she didn't consider her responsibilities to you to be over once you were born. Because she's a good person, with a loving heart. Is that so difficult for you to believe?"

"Aye, it is. There must have been something in it for her."

"There wasn't. She'd made a promise to your mother on the day she died that she'd see to it you were cared for, and kept safe, and so she did."

"A deathbed promise, eh? That's a good bedtime story, lass, but people don't do something for nothing."

"Yes, they do, Daniel. All the time."

"Not that I've ever seen." Though to be fair, his experience was mostly limited to blackguards and villains.

Mairi didn't reply, but a few moments later another blanket floated down from above and landed on his face, a bit of warmth and comfort in exchange for...nothing.

Something, for nothing.

Neatly done, that. Clever lass.

He rose onto his elbows and peered into the darkness. All he could make out was a small lump huddled in the center of the bed, buried under a layer of blankets, but her silence was so frigid the air in the room dropped a few degrees.

He snatched up the blanket, the thick wool scratching his palms, and pulled it tight around his neck and shoulders, shivering in the sudden chill.

The hard floor, the scratchy wool and the cold anger of the woman in the bed should have been enough to keep him awake and fearing for his mortal soul, but his eyelids grew heavy despite his wickedness, and he'd nearly dropped off to sleep when a murmur from the bed dragged him back into consciousness.

Her voice was muffled, as if she'd turned her back on him, but he heard her as clearly as if she'd whispered the words in his ear.

"Once my grandmother makes a promise, she keeps it."

Chapter Sixteen

It was easier with Daniel, after their strange conversation four nights ago in Northampton. Not comfortable—Mairi didn't think they'd *ever* be that—but not quite as awkward as they'd been that first day.

Awkward enough, though.

He still didn't look at her, a circumstance that was undoubtedly best for both of them, except that he was taking such great care *not* to look at her, she had a fit of the contraries, and started trying to *make* him do so, by any means necessary.

It was diverting enough at first—a harmless amusement to entertain her as the endless miles rolled beneath the carriage wheels—until her every stratagem ended in miserable failure.

No matter how loudly she chattered at him, sighed, or shifted from one position to another, his attention remained steadily on the road in front of them. She'd never been more thoroughly ignored in her life.

It was disconcerting, rather like being invisible.

He didn't speak to her, either, at least not during the day, when they were side by side in the carriage, the unnatural silence between them dragging on until she was ready to tear her hair from its roots. They'd come nearly sixty miles today, all the way from Darlington, and he'd spoken a grand total of two words to her in that entire time.

Wait, and then, several hours later, *Nay*.

But at night, with the darkness pressing between them, a strange ritual unfolded. She'd offer him a pillow and blanket, and in return he'd put a question to her. More often than not it was a question about her grandmother, or Coldstream, but last night he'd asked her about Callum Gordon, the current Viscount Rutherford. She hadn't had much to say. The viscount spent so little of his time in Scotland, she doubted she'd know the man if she stumbled over him.

Yet for all their cozy midnight chats, the fragile intimacy between them never lasted past the sunrise. By the time he took up the reins, he'd be as taciturn as he'd been the day before. Faced with that stony silence her mouth would go dry, her tongue thick, and the same crushing silence as the day before would fall between them.

She glanced from his face to his big hands, at the ribbons resting easy between his long, thick fingers, then looked away, biting her lip. Confessions were dreadful, worrying things at the best of times, but to have to admit her, er...careful omissions to *him* was enough to freeze the tongue of the bravest sinner.

Well, this was what came of such shameful cowardliness.

Her excuses—that she'd speak when they'd gone as far north as Darlington, that she'd wait until she wasn't so tired, or Daniel wasn't so tired, or it wasn't raining, or Daniel was in a better humor—had run out, and she'd made it much worse by withholding the truth from him for so long.

Daniel wasn't ever in a good humor, it had been raining since Northampton, and Darlington had come and gone in a fog of guilty silence. Today, they'd driven through Sunderland, then on to Newcastle, but all the prodding in the world hadn't spurred her tongue into speaking. Now only a night's stay and another sixty miles of road stood between them and Coldstream, and sixty miles now seemed a great deal shorter than it had when they'd begun this journey.

"What ails you, lass? Why are you staring at me like that?"

She might flinch all she liked, but her moment of reckoning was upon her. Secrets would out, as they said. "Have I been staring at you?"

"Aye, and looking as guilty as a villain with a bloody blade stashed in his boot heel."

An objection tried to squirm past her lips, but she likely *did* look guilty, seeing as she *was*. "That's, ah...a vivid description. It's just that, well..."

"Out with it."

She swallowed. "There's, ah...something I haven't told you."

His dark eyebrows lowered. "Best tell me now, then."

Oh, no. Those lowered brows and that hint of a scowl weren't reassuring. "It's a small thing. Hardly worth mentioning, really."

"Aye, so small you've kept quiet about it for three hundred miles."

She winced. "It may prove a bit more challenging to prove my grandmother's innocence than I gave you reason to think. You see, the witness—the one who claims to have seen my grandmother dragging you through the woods the day you vanished? She, ah…she isn't lying."

Daniel's lowered eyebrows shot up—another bad sign—but he didn't speak, the only sound the rumble of the carriage wheels over the rutted road. They'd turned a corner, and the King's Head was now in sight, the lantern lit against the encroaching gloom, but perhaps she should have waited to tell him until they'd made it as far as the innyard.

Where there were witnesses.

All too soon, Daniel turned the carriage into the cobbled yard, and turned to her. "The witness isn't lying."

"No. I never said she'd lied about what she saw." It seemed prudent to remind him of that.

"I remember it differently, lass. I recall you saying she *was* lying when Lady Clifford told you about it."

"No, I didn't." She'd been extremely careful *not* to say that. "I said she was lying about it being an *assault*. I never said she wasn't there, or didn't see what she claimed she did."

"Not much difference between the two."

He didn't *sound* enraged, but he didn't know the whole truth yet. "There's…something else."

"What? I'll have the whole of it, Mairi."

There was a bit more impatience in his voice this time, but if he was enraged, it was still simmering under the surface. "There's a second witness."

"Who would that be?"

She squeezed her eyes closed. "Me."

Another silence, this one as thick as London smog, and humming with portent. It went on and on until she couldn't take it anymore, and cautiously opened one eye. "Daniel?"

"You're a witness against your *own grandmother?*"

She'd never heard him use quite that tone before, so slow and calm, as if he were speaking to a child, or a Bedlamite. It was either a very good sign or a very bad one, but she was halfway through a thorny confession. It was too late to go back now.

"I saw my grandmother hurrying you through the woods that day, too. I didn't realize at the time what was happening. I was only six years old, and, well…she took you through the woods to the road on the other side, where your father was waiting for you. You got into the wagon and drove off. That was the last I ever saw of you, until I tracked you to London."

A beat of silence passed, then another.

"Daniel?" She opened her other eye and found they'd stopped in front of the King's Head, ghostly white in the gloom.

Daniel's expression revealed nothing, and he didn't say a word, but leapt from the box and looped the ribbons around a post to secure the horses. Only then did he hold his hand out to her, his dark eyes inscrutable. "Come down, lass."

It was absurd she should be afraid of him when she'd known him since he wore short pants, his palms and knees scraped raw, grass-stained and mud-streaked. She'd seen him in fits of laugher and with tears on his cheeks—had laughed and cried with him, even—but he'd been a boy then. Now he was a man, a hard, dangerous man she no longer knew.

"Mairi. Come down, now."

She didn't move.

His face darkened, and those stern lips parted, but before he could utter a word the front door of the inn opened, and a boy darted into the yard and tipped his hat to Daniel. "Good evening, sir."

Daniel didn't reply, nor did he spare the boy a glance. The lad strode across the yard to begin unhitching the horses from the carriage, but he stopped midstride when he caught sight of Daniel's face.

The minutes slipped by, all three of them frozen into an absurd tableau, until Daniel broke the silence with a low growl. "Get down from there now, Mairi. Don't make me tell ye again."

She shook her head. "No. I prefer to remain in the carriage."

"Ye're coming down from there, one way or another." He rounded the front of the carriage and stalked toward her, his face a thundercloud.

"Oh, that's not good, that isn't," the boy muttered, watching them with wide eyes.

Neither Mairi nor Daniel paid him any attention, but continued staring at each other, both of them tensed to spring, and just waiting for the other to make their move.

The boy backed away, muttering something about blacksmiths and anvils and Gretna Green, then turned and darted back through the door, shouting, "You best come at once, Mrs. Luddington! We've got another one!"

"Ye don't make it any easier on yourself by defying me," Daniel warned, right before he lunged for her.

His arms were impossibly long, like fencing foils laid end to end, but she managed to scoot out of his reach, scrambling across the seat to the other side of the box. "I don't make it easy on myself by submitting, either."

"Daft lass." Daniel rounded the front of the carriage and advanced on her slowly, clearly intending to snatch her out of the seat himself.

"Stay where you are!" She thrust out a hand to stop him. "I'll come down on my own, but not until you stop calling me lass."

"What the devil are you on about now?"

"You speak like an Englishman until you get angry, then you sound like Bonnie Prince Charlie himself, with your *lasses*, and your *ayes* and *nays*. I don't fancy trusting myself to the mercy of an enormous, enraged Scot!"

He stared up at her, his throat moving in a rough swallow. "Do you think I'd actually hurt you, Mairi?"

She blinked, suddenly unsure. It almost sounded as if she'd...hurt his feelings? "Well, you did kick that man in Howe Court in the head."

"Who, Angel Nash? The villain who tried to murder us both? Aye, I kicked him, just as he would have done to me if I'd been the one on the ground. Have you forgotten you smashed a chamber pot over his head?" He grinned suddenly, as if he were relishing the memory.

She had done that, hadn't she? "Well, he deserved it!"

"Aye, he did, and worse." He took another cautious step toward her, his hands out in front of him as if he were approaching a wild animal. "You should have told me everything you knew about this business with your grandmother from the start. I don't say I'm not angry you didn't, but I wouldn't hurt you, Mairi. Come on down, now."

She let out a long breath. The truth was, she didn't have much choice other than to trust him. They were in the middle of an innyard in northern England under a rapidly darkening sky, and her grandmother was in as much danger as she'd ever been.

She could either take Daniel's hand, or spend the night in the carriage.

He was the only one who could help her. She needed him, and so she slid across the seat, and took his hand.

He tugged her closer, wrapping his fingers around her waist. For an instant she was certain she'd made a mistake trusting him, but he only lifted her down from the carriage, and set her on her feet. "There, that's good, Mairi."

His voice was deep, husky, and his big, rough hands lingered on her waist, the warmth of his palms seeping through her cloak and the dress she wore underneath it.

She peeked up at him, heat blooming in her belly. His fingers tightened on her waist, but just as she was swaying toward him, a piercing shriek rent the air. "Take your hands off that girl this instant, you villain!"

A large woman wearing a white apron and cap loomed in the doorway of the inn, a fireplace poker in her hand, and a fierce frown on her lips. "I told you to get away from that girl!" She waved the poker threateningly. "You may be a big one, but your head's like to be as breakable as any other man's."

A man hovered behind her. He was much smaller than the woman, even standing on the top step, his tufts of brown hair just visible over her shoulder. He was gawking at Daniel, his eyes wide and terrified.

The woman's face softened slightly as she turned to Mairi. "You've made a mistake, girl, and like as not you know it by now. We've seen it dozens of times before, being as close to Gretna Green as we are. Haven't we, Harold?"

"Dozens of times!" The little man didn't venture out from behind his wife, but he shook his fist at Daniel. "Scoundrel! Conscienceless seducers, the lot of you!"

Just then the boy who'd greeted them earlier peeked around the woman's skirts, and all at once Mairi recalled he'd been muttering something to himself, something about blacksmiths and anvils, and Gretna—

Oh. She slapped a hand over her mouth. They thought she'd been seduced by a rake, and had run off to Gretna Green to marry him!

It wasn't funny at all, but a hysterical laugh bubbled up in her throat nonetheless.

"I'm not a seducer, you half-wit." A dark scowl twisted Daniel's face. "This lady is my *wife.*"

The innkeeper's wife scoffed. "Anyone can see she's a lady, all dainty-like as she is, and you a big, rough looking brute. Poor, deluded little fool. You must be a good deal more charming than you look. A sweet-talking, charming rogue!"

"A charming rogue!" the little man squawked like a demented parrot.

Daniel, *charming?* A sweet-talking rogue? The woman had read far too many romantic stories about seducers and runaway brides.

The hysterical laugh threatened again, but she choked it back. "My dear lady, your concern for my welfare is touching, but I assure you, you accuse this man unjustly. He is indeed my husband, just as he says, and a very kind one he is. I'm, ah…very happy with him, indeed."

To give credence to her claim, Mairi reached out and patted Daniel on the chest, then immediately wished she hadn't, because his skin was warm, and even under the intimidating layers of hard muscle she could feel the beat of his heart against her palm. She made a move to snatch her hand away, but Daniel caught it and held it against his chest.

The woman squinted at Daniel suspiciously. "He doesn't look like the kind sort."

"Perhaps he doesn't, but as I'm certain a wise woman like yourself is aware, looks are deceptive. Truly, he's the best sort of man, so strong and handsome and protective. I grant you he's a bit rough around the edges, but I'd trust my very life to him."

Had, in fact, entrusted her grandmother's life to him.

"My lad here says as he was about to drag you kicking and screaming from that carriage. Doesn't sound like a happy wife to me."

"Oh, that? A lover's quarrel only. Surely, Mrs., er…Mrs.—"

"Luddington."

"Yes, Mrs. Luddington. Surely, you can understand as a married woman yourself, how disagreements can happen, particularly when one feels so deeply, and, er…one's passions are aroused." Mairi lowered her eyes modestly.

"This is a respectable business," Mrs. Luddington insisted, though some her ire had cooled. "We don't want any trouble here."

"No trouble!" her husband echoed from his perch behind her. "Get on with you!"

"But my husband is fatigued from driving all day, and we're sure to have a carriage accident if you turn us away, and that would be dreadful, indeed, as my ill grandmother is awaiting our—"

"Last thing we need is some outraged earl or viscount or some other troublesome lord on our doorstep demanding to know why we allowed his daughter or sister or cousin and her seducer into our establishment." Mrs. Luddington shook her head. "Mayhap my husband is right, and it's best if you two get on your way."

"Oh, but it's dark now, and the road is overrun with highwaymen!" If Mrs. Luddington had read any romances about gallant highwaymen recently, they were doomed. "Highwaymen carry pistols, you know, Mrs. Luddington, and my poor husband has only a dagger—"

Daniel gave her wrist a warning squeeze. "That's enough now, lass."

"Well, two daggers. I forgot the one he has hidden in his boot—"

"*Quiet*," Daniel hissed.

"And then his fists are the size of carriage wheels, and you may believe me, Mrs. Luddington, when I say he knows how to use—"

"For God's sake, Mairi," Daniel muttered, dragging a hand down his face.

Oh, no, was that too much detail about the daggers? "I mean, I...what I mean to say, Mrs. Luddington, is that I'm quite mad about him, and, ah, fiercely in love with, er...him." She rose to her tiptoes, pressed a chaste kiss to his lips, drew back, then gave him a second, more lingering kiss, as the first was a good deal pleasanter than she'd expected.

But when she went to draw back a second time Daniel took her mouth with a growl, cutting off her anxious stream of half lies and truths. His big hands cupped her cheeks to hold her still, because how could he know the moment his lips touched hers any fleeting thought she'd had about... anything at all but his kiss vanished in a wave of desire?

How could *he* know, when she hadn't?

His warm skin was tempting, the steady thump of his heartbeat against her palm reassuring, but the sensation of his soft, full lips pressed against hers was an awakening, her nerve endings screaming to life, a delirious explosion of heat in her belly, delicious and terrifying and dizzying at once.

A kiss was one way to erase the frown from his stern lips...

It was her first kiss, done only for show, which should have rendered it pathetic instead of thrilling, but it...wasn't. His lips parted slightly, and her bottom lip tingled at the hint of damp heat inside his mouth.

It would linger in her memory, this kiss, long after it was over, just as if it had been a real first kiss.

Then, in an instant, it was over, the fevered melding of their mouths broken by Daniel, and to Mairi's everlasting shame she chased after his retreating lips with such determination he was obliged to exert another warning pressure on her waist.

She lifted her fingers to her trembling lips and brushed them over the swollen skin, tracing the lingering imprint of his mouth.

Dimly, she heard Daniel offering to pay double for a room, and Mrs. Luddington, whose scruples didn't appear to extend as far as her pocketbook, snatching the coins from his hand and shoving them down the front of her bodice.

And that was that. She was hurried up the stairs and into the best bedchamber at the King's Arms, her breath still short and her lips tingling from Daniel's kiss.

Chapter Seventeen

There was nothing about the shape of her lips that hinted a kiss like that had been hiding there. Not the pale pink of them, not the bow of the upper lip or curve of the lower that warned him her kiss would threaten to drop him to his knees.

If there had been, Daniel would have noticed it days ago. He'd spent enough time staring at her mouth. Or trying *not* to stare at it at first, then when that didn't work, casting sneaky glances only so she wouldn't notice, his belly pulling tight every time she bit that full lower lip, small white teeth worrying at it until it darkened, swelled to a pout.

Nothing that warned him her mouth would be so smooth and sweet, like fine Scotch whisky.

He shoved the door closed behind him with the heel of his boot and leaned back against it, tracking her movements—the swing of her cloak, the sharp click of her shoes against the floorboards as she hurried away from him, to the middle of the bedchamber, the far side of the bed, the window opposite the door.

"Going somewhere, lass?" He pushed off the door and went after her, the thud of his boots much louder than hers.

"I, ah...I beg your pardon. I shouldn't have..." She cast a glance over her shoulder, jerking her head toward the window. "In the innyard. I shouldn't have done that."

"Done what?" He took another step toward her, then another, watching her pulse flutter under the smooth, pale skin at the base of her throat. "Kissed me? Can't say I agree."

Her eyes, wider and bluer than any woman's eyes should be, dropped to his mouth before fierce color rushed into her cheeks, and she looked quickly away. "I thought if I...Mrs. Luddington was going to send us off, and I thought if I kissed you, she'd—"

"Believe we're husband and wife, and let us stay. It worked." He waved a hand around the bedchamber, never taking his eyes off her, and took another step closer. "You're saying you didn't *want* to kiss me, then?"

"I—I don't know." She took a step back, far enough her shoulders met the glass window behind her.

"Because that would be a shame." He was close enough now he could take her hand, or stroke her cheek. He didn't do either, but his fingers itched to touch a lock of that red hair that had been driving him mad since he'd seen it peeking from the hood of her cloak, the red-gold gleam of it visible even in the gloom of Howe Court.

She swallowed. "It would?"

"Aye. You're not going to jump, are you?" He nodded at the window behind her.

She let out a high-pitched giggle, then slapped a hand over her mouth. "I wasn't planning on it." Her voice was muffled by the press of her fingers. "Should I?"

"No. I told you I wouldn't hurt you, Mairi." He caught her slender wrist between his thumb and forefinger and urged her hand away from her mouth.

God, that mouth.

He'd kissed dozens of lips, hundreds even, but none such a pale pink as hers, like rosebuds or seashells, or...well, nothing he knew a damn thing about. He didn't spend time with pale pink ladies. He'd always favored bitter over sweet, risk over comfort, red sorts of women over pink sorts, or in his worst moment, when fucking wasn't about finding pleasure so much as it was about destroying himself, ladies who prowled the deepest shadows, where everything and everyone were different shades of dark.

He hadn't been on his guard against Mairi Cameron, any more than he had been Angel Nash that night in St. Giles. He hadn't seen her coming until his mouth was already watering for her.

How did a man even kiss such dainty lips?

A man like him *didn't*. Or he shouldn't.

If she'd been anything like she appeared to be, he wouldn't, but Mairi was more than white skin and pink lips, more than blue eyes and red hair. She was a grown woman, and *fierce*, for all that she looked like a porcelain doll. So fierce she'd made it all the way from Scotland to London in one piece, risking everything for her grandmother. So fierce she'd laid out Angel Nash, then gone on to conquer Lady Clifford, and Daniel himself.

She knew what she wanted, and her kiss in the innyard told him she wanted *him*.

He'd never been one to resist temptation, and Mairi Cameron, with her pistol and chamber pot, her blue, blue eyes and her wild red curls a rippling mass of silky waves around her flushed face, stole his breath.

He raised her hand to his lips and dropped a kiss on the translucent skin, the tip of his tongue grazing the branch of delicate blue veins, tasting the frantic beat of her pulse.

Her breath stuttered. "Daniel."

Yes. He wanted her breathless, with his name on her lips. He kissed her fingertip before taking it into his mouth, teasing the fleshy pink pad with his tongue. Was she pink everywhere?

She gasped, and he closed his eyes to savor it, stroking his thumb over the long line of her fingers from her knuckles to her fingertips, and darting his tongue into the hollow between them to wring more of those gasps from her lips.

"That feels…" She stared down at the place where his mouth touched her skin. He nudged her chin up with a fingertip so he could see her eyes, satisfaction pulsing in his belly at her parted lips and flushed cheeks.

What did she see when she searched his face? The same thing he did, when he forgot to avoid his reflection in the glass? Heavy slashes of eyebrows over hard, dark eyes, a cruel twist of a mouth. She wouldn't be the first woman to want a man like him, curious to know if he was as much a savage in bed as out of it.

"How does it feel, Mairi? Tell me."

"Like…like a candle flame licking my skin."

"Does it burn?"

"Yes." Her irises had gone dark under thick, heavy eyelashes. "In the way a man's kiss should burn. Not so hot it hurts, but hot enough to wake every inch of my skin, so it clamors for more."

She moved closer, tilting her chin up, offering him her mouth, but a soft cry left her lips when he took it, as if he'd surprised her, somehow, but it was an instant only, and then she was opening for him, welcoming him inside with a slick stroke of her tongue.

He toyed with her lower lip, suckling and biting at it before drawing back to revel in the way it had swollen and reddened under his attentions, the way a woman's mouth should look when she'd been thoroughly kissed, tender and glistening, the sight of it hitting him hard in his lower belly, erotic as fingers wrapped around him, stroking his aching cock.

"Do you want me, Mairi?"

She gripped a handful of the loose hair resting against his neck, the insistent tug of her fingers a command, not a request. "Yes."

He tore his lips from hers to nip at her neck, and taste the secret skin under her jaw and behind her ear. "Say it."

"I want you, Daniel."

She wanted him. Somehow, this fierce, brilliant woman wanted *him*.

She dragged her tongue over his lower lip, teased it into the corner of his mouth, tickling him with the tip and stealing his breath. Her small hands landed on his chest, her fingers curling into the damp wool of his coat, as if to keep him where she needed him.

"You've had a man before?" She was unmarried, yes, but not a child, and so tempting, with that cloud of red hair and those seductive lips. Men must have wanted her, pursued her.

She rested her head against his chest, a soft laugh on her lips. "You really don't remember Coldstream. If you did, you wouldn't have to ask that. It's a tiny village, Daniel."

"Is that a *no*, then, lass?" His blood cooled so quickly a chill touched his neck.

"Yes, that's a no. The right, er...opportunity never presented itself." She touched a fingertip to his chest, right between his collarbones, a faint smile rising to her lips when she noticed his rough swallow. "Until now."

He caught her hands in his and tugged them away from his chest. "You've never had a lover? Good Lord, woman. Were you going to tell me, or were you going to let me crawl between your thighs and find it out for myself after it was too late? Jesus, Mairi. You don't want me as your first lover."

Her delectable lips tightened until all the pale pink color bled from them. "I would think that would be up to *me*."

"I'm not the kind of man a lady offers her...virtue to." He wasn't a man a virgin offered *any* part of her body to. How could she look at him, and not know that?

He was good enough for a rough fuck for a woman who knew what to expect from a man like him, but not for anything more than that. Christ, this was as bad as Sophia and Gray pushing him to hold their wee daughter, except worse, because he wanted to take Mairi to bed far more than he'd wanted to coo at baby Amanda.

"I've never had any difficulty making my own choices, Daniel, and I don't suppose this is any different." The desire that had clouded her eyes had cooled, anger and hurt—yes, *hurt*, damn it—taking its place.

He raked a hand through his hair. "Your husband may not see it that way, lass."

"*What* husband? I don't have a husband, nor am I looking for one. For pity's sake, do you take me for some virginal debutante angling for a title?" She regarded him in livid silence for a moment, blue eyes blazing and two bright spots of color in her cheeks.

Damn, that had been the wrong thing to say, then. "What I mean is—"

"I know what I want, Daniel. Up until two minutes ago, I thought it was *you*."

He stared at her, unsure what to do, and the devil of it was, he wanted her more now than he had before that unholy temper of hers got its claws into her. Fury suited her, flushing her cheeks and tightening her lips until all he could think about was sliding his tongue between them and stroking until they went soft under his.

Nothing for it but to retreat, and quickly.

"I'm going to the dining room. I'll have Mrs. Luddington send a tray up for you, if you like." It was an olive branch, if a feeble one, but Mairi wasn't ready for a peace offering.

She drew herself up with all the solemnity of the righteously offended, and threw the branch right back in his face. "This may surprise you, Daniel, but if I want dinner, I'm perfectly capable of securing a tray for *myself*."

"All right, then." He backed toward the door, his cock crushing any hope he might have had of leaving with dignity by insisting on remaining as hard as stone. He was obliged to adjust himself in the hallway, and even then, it gave a hopeful surge with every brush against his breeches.

He muttered under his breath as he made his way downstairs, the filthiest, most blasphemous curses he could think of, boots pounding on the floorboards, hoping Mrs. Luddington had a good, strong porter on offer.

Otherwise, it was going to be a long night.

Chapter Eighteen

Mairi hurled a pillow at the bedchamber door as soon as it closed behind Daniel's broad back. It hit the target dead center, then dropped to the floor with a harmless plop.

Her boot would have made a more satisfying thump. She should have hurled that instead.

She dropped down on the edge of the bed. It was a wide, comfortable one, with a thick coverlet and a half-dozen plump pillows. Of all the beds they'd encountered on their journey, it was the most inviting one yet.

God in heaven, what a waste.

She kicked off her boots, crawled onto the bed, and rested her head on one of the deep pillows while the last vestiges of weak winter sunlight faded from the sky, and the window opposite the bed went dark. The minutes slipped into hours, but even hours spent staring at the ceiling couldn't make that scene with Daniel make any sense.

How had it all gone so dreadfully wrong?

Or perhaps the better question was, how had they even gotten as far as a kiss? They'd left London in a state of perfectly pleasant antipathy toward each other, and for the first day of their journey, they'd been content for nary a word to pass between them.

But then, that first night in Northampton, it had all changed.

It had been a mistake, offering him that blanket and pillow. She'd only done it to prove a point, but that one small gesture had broken the silence between them. It was all that blasted *talking* that had led to tonight's disastrous kiss. The instant he'd opened his mouth, she'd begun to see him as a person, and no good ever came of *that*, especially with a blackguard like Daniel Brixton.

Then she'd gone and made it worse by kissing him in the innyard, though to be fair, she'd also been trying to prove a point then, too…

Perhaps she should stop trying to prove so many points. Yes, that would be a good start.

As for what had happened with Daniel tonight, it was for the best that he'd put a stop to it, even if his reasons for doing so had been nothing short of infuriating. Humiliating, too. No lady wanted to be rejected, especially if it was *for her own good*, as if she were a puling infant, or too dull-witted to determine that for herself. The arrogance of the man, imagining *he* was better able to judge what was best for her than *she* was!

But it was done now, and it would stay that way. There would be no more blankets and pillows, no more cozy midnight chats, and no more kissing.

Certainly, no more kissing.

That was that, then, and it was a great relief to have it all settled. Indeed, it was *such* a profound relief she remained awake for hours longer, staring at the ceiling and savoring it, until the fire burnt itself to embers, and the bedchamber became so chilly she dove under the covers, and waited for sleep to take her.

And waited, and waited, and waited…

Dash it, she was weary to the bone, so why did her eyes refuse to close? It wasn't because she was waiting for Daniel to return to the room. The longer he stayed away, the better. He was the means by which she'd save her grandmother, nothing more.

How could she be so selfish as to forget for one instant that every moment she spent trifling with Daniel meant another step closer to the scaffold for her grandmother? Hot tears of shame sprang to her eyes, and she dragged a shaking hand over her face to wipe them away.

She owed her grandmother better than that.

It had always been Lillias, for as long as she could remember. She'd never known her father, and her mother had died soon after she was born, so her first memories were of her grandmother singing to her, and later, wiping her chin, brushing her hair, and sighing over her dirty pinafores and torn hems. Her grandmother who scolded and lectured and praised and defended her, sometimes in the same breath.

When she was eight, one of the girls at her school—Fiona something, she couldn't remember the girl's name—had turned up her perfectly adorable little nose at Mairi's red hair, calling it "frightful." She'd been teased about her hair before that—which seemed curious now, given how many redheads there were in Scotland—but it had been especially painful coming from Fiona, who had long, silky hair the color of sunshine.

Oh, how she'd wanted that shiny, fair hair for herself! How she'd cursed her own wild red curls, and wished with everything inside her she'd been crowned with rays of sunshine, that she was fair and pretty, as Fiona was.

Somehow, Lillias had found out about it, and one night, when she'd sat Mairi down in front of the fire to unpin her hair, as she did every night, she'd told her, as she pulled the brush through the tangled curls in long, soothing strokes, that no one could ever make her feel ugly without her permission.

Lillias had reminded her then that she'd inherited her red hair from her mother, Lillias's own beloved daughter, who was as lovely a lady as ever graced the village of Coldstream, admired for her kindness as well as her beauty, and that Mairi was one in a long, distinguished line of red-headed Cameron women, a lineage she should own proudly.

Never allow anyone to make you ashamed of who you are.

It had been a rare, precious moment of perfect understanding between them. Even at the tender age of eight Mairi had known it for the gift it was, and she'd never forgotten it. Everything she was, she was because of Lillias. Everything she had, Lillias had given her, and everything she knew, Lillias had taught her.

It wouldn't end with her precious grandmother's neck in a noose. She wouldn't allow it.

She was still awake, her back turned toward the door when Daniel entered the bedchamber hours later. He closed the door quietly behind him, removed his boots, and stirred the fire before stretching out his long body on the floor.

There was plenty of room to accommodate him, so he might roll about and toss his long limbs around with abandon if he chose. He was perfectly fine as he was, without a pillow or a blanket. Comfortable, even.

Why, then, was guilt creeping over her like a noxious fog, and settling in the pit of her stomach? It was absurd. It was far better this way, with each of them keeping to themselves.

She closed her eyes and focused on taking deep, slow breaths.

Ten breaths later, she was obliged to squeeze her eyes closed to keep them from popping open again. Twenty breaths, and she was gripping her pillow in tight fists. By thirty, her entire body was as rigid as a plank of wood.

The trouble was, she couldn't stop thinking about the strong, steady beat of his heart under her palm, that slight hitch in his voice when he'd said he'd never hurt her.

The way she'd believed him, at once, without question.

Daniel Brixton wasn't the brute he wanted everyone to think he was, which was a great pity, really, as this would all be much easier if he *were*.

And now he was banished to the pitiless embrace of a cold, hard floor, his bones aching with fatigue after so long at the reins, the frigid draft from the boards beneath him seeping into his flesh, his thick, scarred fingers frozen to blocks of ice—

Damn it. It was no use. She'd never be able to fall asleep if she thought he was cold.

She wrestled her arms free of the coverlet, tossed it aside with a huff, snatched up a handful of blankets and threw them over the side of the bed, then tossed a pillow on top of them.

He didn't say a word, but there was a faint rustle of cloth. She peeked over the edge of the bed and saw his head was cradled on the pillow, and he'd pulled the blankets over him. The fire cast enough light over him she could see he was looking toward her, the corners of his mouth turned down in a frown.

Because *of course*, the proper response to a friendly gesture was a frown. Thank goodness she hadn't done something truly offensive, like give him *two* pillows, or offer to sing a few verses of "Baloo Baleerie"—

"Why was your grandmother dragging me through the woods?"

She blinked up at the ceiling. "I'm not sure, but something happened that day. I don't know what, but I think my grandmother *does* know. She saw something, or heard something, and dragged you out of the woods to protect you from it. Whatever it was, it was bad enough she made you and your father leave Coldstream for good."

"Made us?" Daniel snorted. "No one ever made my father do a damn thing he didn't want to do, much less someone's wee grandmother."

"If you think that, then you really don't remember my grandmother." It seemed impossible a man could forget entire years of his life, but if he didn't *want* to remember, if he'd seen something he couldn't bear to remember—

"The boy. The boy in the pond. What is…what was his name?"

The *drowned* boy. The *murdered* boy. It wasn't Daniel Adair's small body they'd pulled from the pond, but there *had* been a murder that day.

His name was Hamish. Hamish Deacon.

"I don't know." She choked on the denial, her throat closing around the words, raw and aching. "He was…just one of the boys from the village. I don't…I didn't know many of their names."

But she *had* known his.

Hamish, their dear little friend, with his big, sweet brown eyes and headful of dark curls. Hamish, who was so often covered in bruises from the swift, heavy hand of his drunken father. Hamish, who drifted from village to village, picking up odd bits of work here and there when he could, there and then gone again, often for months at a time.

It never occurred to the fine citizens of Coldstream that the remains of the child pulled from the pond could belong to Hamish, because none of them even remembered him. He'd been a lost child long before he'd drowned in that pond.

Lillias had tried to keep him with them, safe in their little cottage, but Hamish never liked to remain in one place for long. So Lillias had done what she could for him. After he disappeared, her grandmother had told Mairi she'd found a place for him, an apprenticeship with an apothecary in Edinburgh, and that Hamish wouldn't be coming back to Coldstream.

Even at the age of six, Mairi had known it was a lie. It was the first and only lie Lillias ever told her. She'd told it for Daniel, and that night, and for years afterwards, she'd wept over it.

Daniel didn't say anything more. He fell asleep soon afterwards, but she remained awake, staring up at the ceiling once again, tears streaking her cheeks, and listened to the crackle of the fire until exhaustion took over at last, and her eyes dropped closed.

The room was still dark when she woke again, jerked out of sleep by an odd noise, a low, guttural moaning, or...no, not that, exactly, but something equally out of place, primal, animal more than human—

"...*leave his brother behind.*"

She stilled, her body turning to ice. It was Daniel, and his voice... dear God, the desperation, the fear there was soul-deep and wrenching, *unbearable*, like an animal in pain, dragging chills to the surface of her skin and tears to her eyes.

"...*a real man doesn't leave his brother...*"

In an instant she was off the bed, kneeling beside him. He was thrashing about like a wild thing, damp with sweat, those awful, shuddering moans coming from deep inside him, a place he'd never been before, somewhere dark—

"*No, don't!* Don't touch him..."

She couldn't stand to leave him there alone, couldn't bear to listen to another word. "Daniel? Daniel, wake up. You're having a bad dream." She touched his shoulder, but he continued to thrash and moan, so she shook him gently. "Daniel, *please* wake—"

Without warning, his eyes flew open, wild and dark and empty. He grabbed her wrist in a bruising grip, and her heart tumbled from her chest into her belly, dropping like a stone, because he was still lost in his nightmare, and didn't know her. "Daniel! It's me, Mairi!"

"Mairi?" He peered at her in the darkness, but at last the fingers on her wrist loosened, and he snatched his hand back. "I didn't…I never meant to hurt—"

"Shhh. I know. It's all right. Come with me."

He did as she asked, still half-asleep, perhaps, because he followed her to the bed as meekly as a child, lying back when she urged his shoulders down, and letting her draw the thick coverlet over him without a word of protest.

He was already asleep when she slipped in on the other side, his words when he'd woken from his dream echoing inside her head.

I didn't mean…I never meant to hurt…

He hadn't been saying he didn't mean to hurt *her.*

He'd been talking about someone else.

She didn't sleep again that night.

Chapter Nineteen

If Daniel could fall back to sleep, he might dream of the boy again.

It should have been easy enough, falling asleep, his body worn ragged with driving and nights of sleeping on cold, hard floors.

He was warm now though, with Mairi tucked against him, one slim hand resting lightly on his chest. He hadn't expected she'd ever touch him again after that cock-up earlier, but she'd snuggled closer to him in her sleep, instinctively seeking his heat, and her hand had somehow landed on his chest.

He liked the warm weight of it on him. It reminded him his heart was still beating.

Sleep should have sucked him down into dreams as soon as his head met the pillow, but it refused to take him. Sleep was the devil that way, and dreams were worse, creeping up on you when you didn't want them, and dancing just out of reach when you did.

Or maybe he'd kept them away so long they no longer came to him when he beckoned them. Fickle bloody things. Worse than a woman, even. But then he'd never invited his dreams to haunt him before, too afraid of what they'd reveal.

Him, afraid, after years of chasing villains through London's filthiest streets and into her deepest shadows, haunting those grim corners and alleys where the forgotten people lived, the blackguards who'd gut you just as soon as let you pass, because they had nothing left to lose.

Blades, pistols, villains lurking in the dark—he wasn't afraid of them. The pattern of scars on his body was proof enough of that. Or, as Lady Clifford would have it, proof of his lack of common sense.

He'd never been afraid of dying.

Living, though. That was something else.

But a villain hovering in the dark, waiting for him to slip up and bare his throat, or a pistol pressed to his temple, a rope wrapped around his neck—they were physical threats that came from *outside* him. He could trust his body to make quick work of them.

Threats from inside his own head—thoughts, memories, dreams—he couldn't grab those, squeeze them until their faces went purple, or plunge a knife into them and watch the satisfying spurt of blood around the blade. No, he could only grope blindly for them as they scurried around him, biting and clawing like rats.

He glanced down at the head tucked against his shoulder. The darkness hid the red of her hair, but the fire lit up the fairer threads woven throughout, gilding them to a molten gold.

Mairi must know who the boy was. The boy he'd dreamed about. She must have known him—had even loved him, maybe. She'd come to London for her grandmother, yes, but maybe she'd come for the boy, too, and the truth about what had happened to him was trapped among the tangled memories inside Daniel's head.

Burying them hadn't worked. They were rising from the dead, rising closer to the surface with every dream, every voice, every face he half-remembered. Shouting, raging, and threatening hadn't worked either—hadn't laid them to rest. Men might fear him, but memories didn't. Pretending they weren't there also hadn't done any good. A man could only pretend for so long.

Twenty-four years, apparently. After that, the dead caught up to you.

There was only one way to be rid of them.

He'd have to free them. For himself, aye, but also for her.

So, he closed his eyes, and hovered there, not asleep, but not quite awake, with Mairi's small body pressed against him, her curves somehow a perfect fit for his angles, each of her quiet, rhythmic breaths tugging him closer to sleep while his frenzied brain kept him from tumbling over the edge of it.

He didn't sleep, but exhaustion must have opened his brain a tiny crack, just enough to let a glimmer of light in, because while he hung suspended between awareness and dreams, something tickled the edge of his consciousness.

Tree branches above him, flickering sunlight, rough bark under his fingernails, a roar in his ears, a queasy wrench of his stomach, and the boy's dangling feet—

No, not that. He couldn't think about the boy's feet just yet. The branches, then, the flickering sunlight, and...damp breeches, soaked at the knees.

He was kneeling in the mud, a bag against his thigh, also wet, something squirming inside it.

Fish.

They'd gone fishing that day, he and the brown-eyed boy, but a man had seen them, a man with one normal eye and one milky white one, and they were running to…to…where? Then a boy's shriek, his neck caught in a man's fist, his body limp but his feet still swinging—

A scream burned his throat, a scream without a voice, and a hand clamped over his mouth. Bile rushed into his throat, choking him, strangling him—

"Daniel! Daniel, wake up!"

He jerked upright, gagging on his own vomit. Mairi's voice was in his ear, her hand shaking his shoulder. She was leaning over him, eyes wide and pupils so huge he could only make out a glimmer of white in the darkness.

"Was I asleep?" God, his voice was wrecked, hoarse at the center, worn thin at the edges.

"I'm not sure. Your eyes were open, and you were shouting."

He was soaked, sweat pouring down his back, his pulse thundering with such force between his eyes he would have sworn someone was driving a nail into his forehead, pinning him to the pillow. He reached up to pull the bloody thing out, but Mairi caught his hand, gripped it hard.

Christ, he was shaking, his skin hot. "The boy." It came out a croak rather than a word, his tongue clumsy, and his lips too dry to make the proper shapes.

Her hand tightened around his. "What boy?"

"With the brown eyes. We were fishing."

Deafening silence, then her voice, low and strained, as if she were both speaking and holding her breath at once. "Shhh. It's alright. You're alright. Lie back down now, and go to sleep."

Her cool fingers brushed over his forehead, and he let his eyelids drop over his burning eyes.

Chapter Twenty

Daniel's throat was as dry as dust, his tongue a desert, the roof of his mouth a barren wasteland, his lips stuck together with a thick layer of spit. Better spit than blood, and there was none of that. If there had been, he'd know it. No man who'd ever woken with a mouthful of blood could forget that taste of metal, salt, and rust.

His head wasn't right, though. There was no pain, but it felt too light, like it was floating above him, bound to his body with a string instead of attached by his neck, and his eyes felt swollen.

Mairi hadn't knocked him in the head again, had she?

He could get up and see, but he couldn't be bothered, really. He was resting on something soft, wrapped in warmth from head to toe, and blessed silence surrounded him, aside from…

A trickle of water?

He cracked one eye open to a blur of white. What the devil was…*oh*.

It was a pillow. His cheek was resting on a pillow, and a dark blue coverlet was draped over him, the edge of it clutched in his fist, which was tucked under his chin like a child.

A bed, then. Seemed as good a place as any to be of a morning, only it wasn't *his* bed, or any bed he'd ever been in before. He cracked open the other eye, caught a glimpse of a slight shadow moving about a darkened room, soft footfalls and the whoosh of water being poured from a pitcher—

"Oh, are you awake? I was going to let you sleep on for a bit this morning."

The shadow fell over the bed, and a vision appeared above him—flushed cheeks, long locks of wavy red hair tumbling about pale shoulders, sleepy blue eyes…

Good Lord, but what was she doing, getting so close to him, looking like that, while he was abed, in a private bedchamber? Didn't the girl have any sense at all? Either she didn't have any idea how tempting she was, or else she wanted him to kiss her.

He'd already made that mistake once. He'd hardly gotten a taste of her mouth before he knew she wasn't the sort of lass a man could kiss, then forget about.

He'd as soon forget Mairi Cameron as he would a dagger in his heart.

She was the sort that crawled under a man's skin and squirmed about until she'd sunk so deep, he couldn't ignore her, or remember how he felt before she'd been there.

The sort he kept far, far away from.

He hadn't realized just how bloody stupid he'd been to kiss her until *now*. With that hair, the pouting pink bow of her lips, those blue eyes and those curves, perfectly proportioned to her slender frame, she was a vision out of his most heated fantasies.

"Daniel? Are you not well?"

He let her voice wash over him, let himself gaze at her lips for a moment longer before he heaved himself onto an elbow and ran a hand through his hair. "What am I doing in the bed?"

"You don't remember?"

Remember? It had been a kiss only, hadn't it? Maybe two, or...oh, all right then, a half-dozen, but that was *all*. He was nearly certain of it, only... why was his head so fuzzy?

"You, ah...you had a bad dream last night—quite bad, I think. I brought you into the bed afterward so you might sleep soundly the rest of the night."

He was in the bed? With *her*, or... "Did you sleep on the floor, then?"

"No." She nodded at the pillow on the other side of the bed. "I slept there."

"We spent the night in the same bed?" He'd spent a night in bed with Mairi Cameron, and he'd *slept through it*?

Impossible.

"It was perfectly fine, Daniel. You kept to your side, and I kept to mine." She watched him, twisting the cloth in her hands between her fingers. "Do you remember your dream?"

"Nay, I don't think so."

But he *did* remember something, just bits and pieces in hazy, broken images, just like all the dreams he'd been having for years, only he'd had them more often lately, much more often, and the one last night...he gripped the edges of the pillow, a face taking shape in his mind. "There was a boy, with brown eyes."

Her fingers stilled on the towel. "Do you...did you recognize him?"

"Nay."

"Do you remember anything else?"

He shuddered, his stomach lurching, but he didn't tell her about the man with the white eye. Not yet. "Nay."

"These dreams, Daniel." She drew closer, close enough he noticed the violet-colored shadows under her eyes. "I don't think they're dreams at all. I think they're memories."

Denials tried to claw their way up his throat, but despite being a liar as often as it suited him, this particular lie stuck in his throat like a burr. These dreams he had...they felt too familiar, too close to him to be only dreams. They were more like a distant echo of his own voice.

But believing they were memories meant believing he'd somehow lost eight years of his life. It meant believing his father, the only one who'd given a bloody damn about him before he found Lady Clifford, had lied to him, hid his past from him.

"It's sixty-odd miles from Newcastle to Berwick, lass." He tossed the coverlet aside and rose from the bed, ignoring the lightness in his head. "The sooner we get on, the better."

Mairi opened her mouth, hesitated, then closed it again, and returned to the washbasin without a word of argument, while he did his best not to watch the damp cloth moving over that soft, white skin, or think about droplets of water trailing down her neck.

They made quick work of breakfast. When they left the King's Head, Mrs. Luddington saw them out with a gusty sigh of relief she didn't bother to hide. They made good time at first, but they were both weary, and it turned into a long, slow, exhausting day.

Cold, too, with a strong, icy wind coming at them from the north, flaying his skin, the high-pitched whine of it a relentless assault on his ears. It was nearly impossible to make himself heard over the noise, but when they stopped to change horses in Alnwick he asked the question that had been on his mind since they'd left the King's Head. "The boy from my dream, with the brown eyes. Do you know who he is?"

She went still, aside from a few shallow breaths so silent he wouldn't have noticed she'd taken them at all if it hadn't been for the rise and fall of her chest. "No."

Mairi wasn't a convincing liar. The way she avoided his gaze gave her away, every time. "You're sure, lass?"

Another breath, another jerk of her rib cage. "Yes."

She grew quiet after that, the miles between them and the King's Arms in Newcastle piling up, one atop the other until they were nearing Berwick. He was silent as well, running his thumb over the smooth strip of leather between his fingers to distract himself from Mairi so close beside him, but as fine as the leather was, it was no match for *her*.

The carriage was too small. If she yawned, stretched her legs, or turned her head, he felt an echo of it in his own body. An hour ago, she'd smoothed her hair back from her face. They'd come seven miles since then, and he was still thinking about it, no matter that she was bundled into her thick traveling cloak this morning, her hood pulled low over her face, hiding every strand of it.

The darkness came on quickly, faster than it had the night before, somehow, and it was colder this far north, so cold his breath turned to white clouds of frost the moment it left his lips, the cold stealing under his hat, the neck of his coat, biting at his skin.

She'd be cold too by now, much colder than him, tiny and slight as she was, but she didn't complain of it. For all that she had a tongue as sharp as a knife's edge when she chose to wield it, she wasn't the complaining sort.

Not the talkative sort either, not today, not until he brought the carriage to a stop in front of a squat building with a pitched roof, and a wooden plaque beside the low, beamed doorway that announced itself to be the Rose and Thistle.

Thistles. They weren't far from the border now.

She roused herself and looked about, as if she couldn't understand how she'd ended up there. "I think we should go on."

He shook his head. "No. It's too dark, and too cold. You're half frozen as it is."

"I think we should go on," she said again. She was staring straight ahead, her hood pulled low enough so only the tip of her nose was visible. "Coldstream is only another twelve miles, maybe a bit further. We'll be there before midnight."

"There could be a dozen highwaymen between here and there, lass."

"There are no highwaymen this far north. No one has anything to steal." She turned to him, lowering her hood. The moonlight fell over her face, and for the first time since they'd left Newcastle, he got a good look at her, and this time it was he who was fighting for his breath.

What had happened, between the time they'd left Newcastle and now? What battle had she been fighting, between here and there? Because he could see in her face that she'd been struggling with some demons.

The few words they'd spoken yesterday came back to him then. The witness—the drowned boy, nothing but bones left of him now.

It was all lies, death and murder for the last sixty-five miles.

It was bad enough to wear anyone down, but those things had all been true the day before, and the day before that, yet she'd never looked as she did now, with her eyes huge and dark in her white face, the pretty, pale pink lips he'd kissed with such desire the evening before bitten raw.

"Please, Daniel," she whispered. "I can't...I don't want to waste any more time. I want to go home."

After that, there was nothing more to say. If she'd asked him to take her back to London right then, he'd have done it.

He turned the horses' heads away from the inn, towards the road, and with a flick of the reins headed north, toward Coldstream.

Chapter Twenty-one

The stone floor of the cottage was smeared with boot prints. Two or three different sets, maybe more, outlined in dried mud, leading from the front door through the kitchen and into the small alcove where the bed stood.

They'd trampled everything in their path when they'd come to arrest Lillias. The braided rugs had been kicked aside, baskets emptied and their contents strewn across the floor, cupboard doors left open, the bits and pieces of crockery inside overturned. They'd pawed through her drawers, rifled her closets, touched her things.

Their lovely little cottage, the tiny dwelling they'd worked so hard to turn into a home, had been tainted, as sure as Lillias herself had. But then she was a criminal now, wasn't she? A murderer. Why should the magistrate and his men treat her or her home with any respect?

Mairi pulled a chair away from the kitchen table, flinching at the scrape of the legs across the floor, fell into it, and then…just sat there, unsure what to do.

The table where they'd sat for dinner every night, the bed with the green and black tartan quilt they'd made together, the pitcher that held wildflowers every day through the spring and summer were all covered with a thick layer of dust.

Once she'd learned of her grandmother's arrest, she'd gone straight to the toll booth, and from there to the cottage to gather Ian Adair's letters, along with a few bits of clothing. She'd boarded the mail coach for London within the hour, white-knuckled fingers gripping the handles of her valise, every inch of her numb, frozen with shock.

She hadn't been back here since. It wasn't the same as she remembered it. Of course it wasn't. She'd known it wouldn't be, but…she hadn't known it would feel so empty. There'd always been people about before; some had come to have an ailment tended, others just for a chat and a cup of tea.

But now it echoed with emptiness, ached with it.

"You grew up here?" Daniel had followed her inside, but he'd paused at the doorway, his hat between his hands.

"I did." *You did, too.*

She, Daniel, and sometimes Hamish, when Lillias could persuade him to stay.

God, Hamish. The moment she'd told Daniel she didn't know who the brown-eyed boy from his dream was, she'd wished those words back. If she could have plucked the white plumes of her breath from the freezing air, she would have done it. She would have crushed them in her fist.

That didn't make her denial any less deceitful. Maybe it made it more so.

But it wasn't the lie that had made her eyes burn with unshed tears, her lips trembled as she struggled to smother the flood of memories Hamish's name always called up inside her.

She'd told too many lies these last weeks to cry over them anymore.

No, it was that she'd told the lie to *Daniel*, a man who should have remembered Hamish, but didn't. A man who spoke Hamish's name as if he'd never heard it before, as if the syllables felt strange in his mouth. A man who could dream about him, without recalling a thing about Hamish's smile, his voice, his laugh.

Daniel ventured closer, hesitated, then laid a hand on her shoulder. "It's late, lass, and you're tired. You should go to bed."

"You should, as well. The bed's through there." She nodded at the archway to one side of the tiny kitchen. "There's just one, but it's…big."

It was an invitation, of sorts. An awkward one, yes, but she'd never invited a man to her bed before. Was there any way to do it that *wasn't* awkward? Some graceful way to make him understand she wanted to sleep—just sleep—and didn't think she could without another warm body beside hers? Was there a dignified way to explain she didn't know how to be in that bed alone?

His big hand tightened on her shoulder. "Come on, lass."

It was just right, somehow, the way his hand felt on her as he drew her up from the chair. He led her by the hand as if she were a sleepy child, stumbling over her own feet. With a gentle press of her shoulders and a quiet "Sit here," he eased her down onto the edge of the bed.

"There are more blankets in that cupboard, another pillow, and the washbasin…" Where was the washbasin? She looked around the room, but her thoughts had scattered almost as soon as she'd opened her mouth.

"There's time enough to find the washbasin tomorrow."

Yes, that was true, and she was so grateful to him for saying so, for relieving her of the responsibility of the washbasin, it brought tears to her eyes.

Dear God, *more* tears.

She let him take over then, sitting as docilely as a lamb as he untied the ribbon at her neck and drew her cloak from her shoulders, then knelt on the floor and loosened the laces on her boots, and with a gentle tug pulled them from her feet. "Here." He stood and turned down one corner of the quilt, then took her hand and helped her to her feet. "Get in, now."

She did as he told her, nuzzling her cheek against the worn linen of the pillow beneath it, soft now from years of use, her eyelids drifting closed, except...there was something else, wasn't there? Something else she'd wanted, something important—

He lay down beside her, on top of the coverlet, his long legs stretched out, the hard, muscular curve of his shoulder just touching hers, warm and solid.

Oh, yes. She remembered, now.

She'd wanted *him*.

* * * *

It was still dark when she woke. She was unsure how long she'd slept, or what time it was, but it was late, or very early, the night still pressing against her eyelids.

A sound—she'd heard a sound, muted footsteps, the crunch of boot heels over frosted leaves. She rose up onto her elbows, blinking in the gloom, her throat tightening on a muffled gasp as a shadow, darker than the surrounding night, passed by the window opposite the bed.

She crawled free of the coverlet, quickly but quietly, darted across the room on bare feet, her toes going instantly numb from the icy floorboards under her, and pressed close to the glass, breath held.

There was nothing on the other side of the window but darkness.

Gone then, whatever or whoever it had been, if they'd ever been there at all. She might have imagined it, or dreamed it.

It wasn't until she turned to go back to her bed that she remembered Daniel.

She tiptoed across the room and paused beside the bed.

He looked different asleep, more like the boy she remembered, his harsh features relaxed, the hard line of his mouth soft now, his lips slack, a lock of thick, dark hair lying across his forehead.

She swept it aside, her fingers lingering in the silky strands.

It was softer than it looked, softer than she'd thought it would be.

He lay on top of the coverlet, his arms wrapped tightly around himself to ward off the chill. She'd told him where to find the extra blankets, hadn't she? He hadn't bothered with them, if she had, or perhaps he'd fallen asleep too quickly.

Well, that wouldn't do. She darted back across the room to the cupboard, hopping on one foot and then the other to save her poor frozen toes, pulled out a thick bundle of blankets, then darted back to the bed and, one by one, shook each one out and draped them over him.

Yes, that was much better.

She paused for an instant, smiling a little as she looked down at him. She was forever giving this man blankets.

Her fingers were screaming as loudly as her toes now, so she dove back under the covers, careful not to wake him. He was warm, so warm she was tempted to remain close to him, press her body against his to absorb his heat.

She didn't give in to the urge, but she stayed as close beside him as she dared, and let her eyelids drop closed.

Chapter Twenty-two

Sometime in the middle of the night, a weight settled on Daniel's chest. It wasn't heavy, not like it was when he fell uneasily into dreams in London, but soft and light, the warmth of it chasing away the bone-deep chill that had iced the blood in his veins.

He's small in the dream, just a boy, and he's running through a field of wildflowers as high as his waist—fast, faster than lightning, so many colors he can't name them all flying past him in a blur. He turns and looks over his shoulder and sees the back of Mrs. Cameron's cottage, with the little strawberry patch outside the window.

Maybe there are other boys in the field with him, at first—he hears voices coming from far away, bursts of laughter—but they're gone now, all but him and one other boy with curly black hair. He can't see the boy's face because he's too far behind him, but he'll catch up quick, because he's the fastest runner in Coldstream.

But the harder he runs, the farther away the boy gets, which doesn't make sense because the boy is lame, dragging his leg behind him, so Daniel keeps running, but each of the boy's steps are like a dozen of his. His legs are burning, and he's choking on each breath, panting, heaving, gasping breaths that tear at his lungs, but no matter how hard he runs, he can't catch the boy, and he shrinks and shrinks until he's just a hazy shimmer in the distance.

He opens his mouth to shout to the boy, to beg him to wait, but the boy is too far away to hear him, and then the wildflowers melt into a pathway of hard, packed earth under his bare feet, the sunlight peeking through the tree branches above him. He hears a shout behind him, a shriek, a scream, and he opens his mouth to shout back, but it floods with water, his nose and his mouth swamped with water and the thick ooze of mud and dead leaves, choking him—

"Daniel? Daniel!"

Her voice tore him loose from the nightmare and he jolted upright in the bed, sweat trickling from his temples and dripping from the back of his neck down his spine. His linen shirt was damp with it, pasting it to his skin.

"Daniel?" Mairi was hovering beside the bed, her blue eyes wide. "I heard you cry out."

God, he can't breathe, he can't *breathe*, his lungs aching, and his heart is pumping his blood too quickly through his veins.

Mairi reached out her hand to him, but she let it drop without touching him. "Did you have another bad dream?"

Bad? Nay, not at first, but they always ended up that way, sooner or later. This one, though…he shoved his hands under the coverlet to hide their shaking. It was a new one, worse than the usual ones, because for a brief moment, there at the beginning, he'd been happy. It was worse that way, when they started good, then turned dark.

"I dreamed about the boy with the brown eyes again." The boy had been too far away in this dream for Daniel to see his eyes, but somehow he knew it was the same boy he'd dreamt of the night before. "He had dark hair, and a hurt leg."

Mairi looked away from him, but he caught her chin in his hand and turned her face back to his. "Mairi. You know who he is, don't you?"

She swallowed. "Yes. I know him. Knew him. You knew him, too. You really don't remember?"

He did, and he didn't. The boy's brown eyes were familiar to him in the same disturbing way Mairi's blue ones were. "Nay. I don't remember."

"He's…he's Hamish Deacon."

Hamish Deacon. "Last night, I dreamed we were fishing together."

She gave him a sad smile. "You and Hamish called it fishing. Lord Rutherford called it poaching. You'd been warned to keep away from his pond, but neither of you were very good at heeding warnings."

Ah. Some things hadn't changed much in twenty-four years, then.

But they should have heeded the warnings. They should have listened. If they had, Hamish wouldn't be…wouldn't be…

"The boy they pulled out of the pond. The one that's meant to be me. It's Hamish, isn't it?"

"Yes."

That was all. Not, *I'm not sure*, or *I think so*, or *there's no way to know*. One word. Final.

A real man doesn't leave his brother behind.

"Were we brothers?"

She shook her head. "No. Not by blood, but in every way that mattered, you were as close as brothers. You'd even sworn to it, that summer."

Spit-slick palms, clasped hands.

"I should have told you the truth about Hamish yesterday," she went on, "But you said his name as if you were speaking of someone you'd never met before, and I knew you didn't remember him, and I didn't want...he was our friend, and it hurts that you don't remember him."

Our friend. Not just hers, but both of theirs. A friend who'd mattered, or else he wouldn't be dreaming about him. "What happened to him? The whole truth this time, Mairi."

"I don't *know* the whole truth!" She jerked her chin out of his grasp. "Only you and my grandmother know what really happened. She refuses to say, and you don't remember!"

"Shh. It's all right, lass. Just tell me what you do know then."

She drew in a deep breath. "You and Hamish went to Lord Rutherford's pond that day, and neither of you ever came back. My grandmother sent you off with your father, and Hamish, he was just...gone."

Not gone, but tossed into a pond, and not before some blackguard took the time to snap his neck. "Two boys vanish in one day, and not a single person in this entire village thinks the body that floated up from that pond might be Hamish's?"

"They don't remember Hamish, Daniel. Coldstream had its share of beggar children, and they came and went as they pleased. Any one of those boys might have fallen into the fishing pond without anyone in the village ever noticing he'd gone missing."

Ballocks. This damned puzzle was short a few pieces. "Who is the man with the white eye?"

She gasped. "You dreamed of Murdoch?"

"Aye. Who is he?"

"He was the previous Viscount Rutherford's gamekeeper. All of us were afraid of him because of his white eye. He used to whip you and Hamish and the other boys when you poached the viscount's fish. When he could catch you, that is."

"Has he got something to do with the drowned—with Hamish?" He *must* have, because the thought of that milky white eye made Daniel shudder.

"Not that I know of, no. I didn't see him near the pond that day, or anything else other than my grandmother dragging you through the woods. No one saw anything, Daniel, aside from you and Lillias."

"What about that witness? She saw something."

Mairi's lips pursed. "I'd find her account more credible if she'd made the accusation twenty-four years ago. She only mentioned this assault after the body was pulled from the fishing pond."

"Aye, that is strange." Witnesses didn't just appear out of nowhere, and to condemn a respectable woman like Lillias Cameron to the noose on the word of one witness, one who waited twenty-four years to make her accusation?

That was more than strange. It was suspicious.

When they'd left London, he wouldn't have wagered a shilling on Lillias Cameron's innocence. Mairi had insisted she was, but no granddaughter liked to think her grandmother was a cold-blooded murderer, so her word alone wasn't worth a damn.

But there was something wrong here. Someone was keeping secrets, or lying.

"Tell me about this witness."

"Her name is Mrs. Fraser—Elsbeth Fraser. There are dozens of Frasers in the Borders, and have been for centuries, so when Mrs. Fraser makes an accusation, people listen, no matter how unbelievable it is."

"But her accusation about your grandmother in the woods *isn't* unbelievable, lass. You saw the same thing yourself." Still, that was the way of villages. He'd lived in enough of them to know certain people's words carried more weight than others. "No one but this Mrs. Fraser has come forward?"

"Not a soul. I'd like to pay Mrs. Fraser a visit today and see what she has to say."

So, she *did* have a plan. "Then what?"

"I've no idea. We'll figure it out once we hear her story."

Ah. Not much of a plan then.

"The sooner we can speak with her, the better." She rose from the bed and made her way toward the kitchen. "There's tea, and bread with some of my grandmother's strawberry jam. No butter, though, I'm afraid."

She'd been busy this morning, and she looked…rested, in a fresh day dress he hadn't seen before, her hair brushed and woven into a loose braid that hung nearly to her waist. The morning sunshine filled the window behind her, setting the red gold strands that curled around her face alight.

Mairi Cameron was much too pretty for her own good. Too pretty for *his* own good. If this had been another place in another time, or she'd been another lady, he would have taken her back to bed and lost himself inside her sweet, warm body until the dream faded, and his armor grew back over the soft, vulnerable places it had left exposed.

But she wasn't another woman. She was who she was, and even worse, *he* was who *he* was, so he sat up and swung his legs over the side of the bed.

She took a step back as he approached the doorway. "There's warm water in the basin."

"Look that bad, do I?" Likely smelled bad, too.

"I didn't mean…you aren't…I never said you—"

He tried for his usual scowl, but her flustered clucking and the flush in her cheeks forced his mouth into a crooked smile. "Where's the basin, lass?"

She pointed toward a corner of the kitchen. "Just there."

He was grimy from layers of road dirt and sweat, and the hot water felt so good on his hands and face that what began as a quick wash turned into as much of a bath as a man his size could manage in a basin. He peeled off his sweat-soaked shirt and ducked his whole head under the water, then ran the damp cloth over his arms and shoulders and down his bare chest.

By the time he finished, his stomach was growling. "Now then, lass, about this strawberry—"

Jam.

He never got the word out. It got lost in a soft gasp from the other side of the kitchen.

Mairi was standing in front of the stove, a plate of thickly sliced bread in one hand and a toasting fork in the other, but she wasn't looking at her work. She was looking at *him*, mouth open, cheeks on fire, but with so much heat in her eyes her dark blue irises were scorching his skin.

And every bloody inch of him was *burning*. The hair on his arms stood on end, the muscles in his stomach tightened, his nipples rose, stiffening into hard, tight points, and his cock—

It surged against his falls with such ruthless determination the sudden loss of blood made his head wobble on his neck, and he had to jerk the towel dangling from his hands in front of his body to hide his burgeoning erection. "I, er…"

Christ, what did he think he was doing, stripping half-naked in her grandmother's kitchen? Mayhap she understood the male body well enough, being a healer, but that didn't mean she'd seen a man's bits and pieces up close.

He'd just exposed more bare male flesh than she'd likely seen in her lifetime, and his flesh wasn't the prettiest, with its spiderweb of jagged scars from old knife wounds, and one very bad one from a pistol ball that came far closer than he'd liked to his heart, and left a hole the size of the tip of his thumb on the left side of his rib cage.

But Mairi wasn't looking at the scar. She was staring at the place where the waist of his breeches gave way to the skin of his belly. "You, ah…you have a tattoo."

He glanced down at himself, foolishly enough, given he'd seen his own body enough times. "Aye."

She looked up into his face, then back down at his stomach. "May I see it?"

See it? "What, you mean closer than you are now?"

She folded her hands in front of her, the picture of innocence. "Yes. If you don't mind, of course."

He *didn't* mind. Not at all. That was the problem. He kept the towel where it was, but turned slightly so she might see it, silent permission. It was a small tattoo, just two words and a tiny rendering of a boar with a sprig of myrtle in its mouth, half-hidden under the line of his breeches.

He held his breath as she drew closer, and knelt at his feet.

Knelt at his feet. Christ.

He was being punished for some sin or other. One of the mortal ones.

She tilted her head, leaning closer to his torso. He gazed down at the red and gold locks of hair woven into her braid, the thick coil of it so close all it would take was a flick of his wrist to close his fingers around it…

God, give me strength.

His prayers were ignored, because then, dear God, she reached out and brushed her fingertip over his tattoo. His stomach muscles jerked at her touch, but she didn't seem to notice. "*Ne Obliviscaris.* 'Do not forget.' I've heard that motto before, and I've seen this symbol, the boar's head, though I can't recall where exactly. Why do you have it?"

"I got it in memory of my father."

"Is it your family's motto? Is the boar part of your crest?"

Crest? "Do I look like an aristocrat to you, lass? There's nothing noble about my family, Mairi. The Adairs don't have a crest, or a family motto. My father admired the sentiment, and did his best to live by it. Nothing beyond that."

It'd never made much sense, his father's preoccupation with it. He'd never had much use for the nobility, any more than Daniel did, but Daniel had even found drawings of the crest with the motto after his father's death, stuffed inside a rough wooden box hidden among the few things he'd left behind when he died.

"It's a Scottish crest, certainly, or part of one." She traced her finger over the tiny sprig of myrtle caught in the boar's mouth.

"The bread is going cold," he choked out after interminable minutes passed, when it looked as if she might stay there on her knees before him, stroking his stomach forever.

"Oh, yes. Of course." She rose to her feet and hurried back to the stove with her toasting fork, her braid swinging jauntily between her shoulder blades, utterly unaware she'd reduced him to a quivering mass of straining flesh with a single stroke of her fingertip.

Chapter Twenty-three

Mrs. Fraser's interrogation had been a disaster from the start, and it was deteriorating right in front of Mairi's eyes as Daniel's temper slipped further with every word out of the woman's mouth.

He didn't believe a thing she was saying, and he wasn't taking pains to hide it.

"What made you go into the woods that day?" It wasn't the first question he'd put to her—not even the first time he'd put *this* question to her—but Mrs. Fraser was a crafty old thing, and not accustomed to being asked to explain herself.

"What day is that now, lad? My memory isn't what it used to be."

As for Daniel…well, he wasn't accustomed to having to ask for anything twice. Or once, even, as a few snarls and a bit of looming were usually enough to get him what he wanted. The two of them put Mairi in mind of a huge, fierce hunting dog and a sly fox circling each other, hair raised and teeth bared.

"The day Daniel Adair disappeared, Mrs. Fraser. You said you saw Lillias Cameron dragging him through the woods that day. I'm asking what you were doing there at the time. It's an easy enough question to answer."

Unless you have something to hide.

He didn't say it, but Mairi heard it just the same, and apparently so did Elsbeth Fraser, who thrust her grizzled chin up to glare at him. "Well, I can't quite recall, can I? It was years ago now, but I don't see why a body needs a reason to go for a bit of a wander in the woods."

Daniel's jaw pulled as tight as a bowstring with a cocked arrow at the ready. "Seems to me you'd remember everything about that day, since you witnessed an assault. Or do you see an assault every time you take a wander in the woods, Mrs. Fraser?"

Mrs. Fraser jabbed her hands onto her hips. "What did ye say your name was, lad?"

"Macrae." Daniel bit the word out between clenched teeth. "Alister Macrae."

Mairi blinked at him. *Alister Macrae?* Where had that come from?

Mrs. Fraser looked him up and down, taking his measure. "That's a Scottish name, but ye don't sound like any Scot I ever heard. You say you grew up in Coldstream? That's odd, that is, because I don't remember you, and I know the name of everyone who's ever lived in this village."

That cold, beady-eyed stare of hers was enough to silence most people, but Daniel Brixton wasn't most people. Mrs. Fraser had no notion what a hopeless task she'd taken on, attempting to challenge *him*, and Mairi would just as soon the woman never found out, or they'd end up with a door slammed in both their faces.

Daniel didn't seem to have the same concern. "You did just say your memory isn't what it used to be, didn't you, Mrs. Fraser? Mayhap that's why you don't remember me. Mayhap you don't remember what you saw in the woods that day either, eh?"

Mairi frowned. Baiting Mrs. Fraser wasn't going to get them anywhere, and they *needed* to know whatever it was she'd seen that day.

"I never said—"

"If you can't recall well enough to tell me, then how do you know you didn't make a mistake when you told your story to the magistrate? Maybe it wasn't Lillias Cameron you saw at all, but someone else."

The beady black eyes narrowed to slits. "Are you calling me a liar, lad?"

"No!" Mairi stepped between the two of them before Daniel sent this thing careening off a cliff. Finesse was what was needed here, not brute force. "No, of course not, Mrs. Fraser. What Mr. Macrieve meant to say—"

"Macrae, lass. Alister Macrae," Daniel said, the corner of his lip twitching.

Now? He'd decided to be amused *now?* "Er, yes, Macrae. Of course, Macrae. What Mr. Macrae means to say, Mrs. Fraser, is that a lady with as fine a memory as yours must be able to recall in perfect detail what happened that day."

Daniel scowled. "That isn't what I meant to say, lass. No, it was something more like—"

"Ye have a nerve, Mairi Cameron, bringing a scoundrel like this Mr. Macrae—or *whoever* he is—to my doorstep to call me a liar." Mrs. Fraser shook her fist at Daniel. "Now get on your way, the both of you, and don't come back."

"Wait!" Mairi slapped her hand flat against the wood to prevent Mrs. Fraser's door from slamming in their faces. "Please, Mrs. Fraser. You've known my grandmother for decades. You can't really believe she's a murderer. I'm only trying to get to the truth."

"Well..." The door opened a crack wider, and the beady eye appeared in the gap. "I didn't like to have to speak ill of your gran, knowing her these forty years or more as I have, but I saw what I saw."

"All we're asking, Mrs. Fraser, is for you to tell us what you saw."

Mairi held her breath as the beady eye moved between her and Daniel. "Mayhap I do remember more than I thought, but you keep that giant of yours to heel, you understand?"

"Yes, I promise, ma'am." Mairi shot Daniel a warning look before turning her most angelic smile on Mrs. Fraser.

"Well, all right, then." Mrs. Fraser frowned at Daniel, but opened the door and stepped outside. "So, it was like this. I went off to the woods to see if I could find some of those wild blackberries to make a pie for Mr. Fraser. Nothing but my blackberry pie will do for him, especially when his appetite gets tetchy, as it does in the summer. You remember that, Mairi, about Mr. Fraser's appetite?"

"Yes, ma'am."

"Well, so I was just wandering at the tree edge, where the blackberry bushes are, picking berries, when I heard a noise."

"What kind of noise?"

"A boy's shout. It came from over by the pond, and I remember thinking that ragged rabble of boys that were such a nuisance were at the pond again, after the fish. So off I went toward the pond, ready to drag those rapscallions away by their ears, but then I heard another noise, like branches snapping, and that's when I saw your gran with young Daniel Adair."

"And she was dragging him? You saw her doing that?"

"Well, she wasn't so much dragging him as hurrying him along, as you do with naughty boys. He was carrying on a bit, trying to get away, so I figured she was taking him home to his father, who'd whip him for poaching. Not many boys fancy a whipping, no matter how much they deserve it." Mrs. Fraser gave Daniel a sour glance.

"Indeed. Then what happened?"

"I went on my way." Mrs. Fraser shrugged. "Your gran knew how to handle those boys. She had Daniel Adair well in hand, so there wasn't anything for me to do about it."

"Did you see anyone when you passed the pond on your way home?" Mairi held her breath, praying with everything inside her that Mrs. Fraser would say she'd seen Hamish, that she'd have some idea what had happened to him, but in the next breath, her hopes were dashed.

"Nay, no one was there."

Mairi's heart plummeted right down into her slippers. There was nothing new here then. Mrs. Fraser's story was, for the most part, the same as Mairi's own, and that meant it was the truth. Lies changed for the liar's convenience, but the truth was the truth, no matter when it was told, or who it was told to—

"There's one thing here that doesn't make sense, Mrs. Fraser." Daniel had kept quiet while Mrs. Fraser told her story, but now he was back to scrutinizing her with a suspicion so palpable Mairi could feel it against her own skin.

"What's that, then?" Mrs. Fraser asked, her brow furrowing.

"Why did you wait twenty-four years to tell the magistrate you saw Lillias Cameron in the woods with Daniel the day he disappeared?"

Mrs. Fraser blinked. "Why, I didn't think a thing of it at the time. Lillias was always trying to manage those boys, ever since they were old enough to get into trouble—which wasn't very old, I'll tell you that. You're too young to remember, Mairi, but they were a wicked lot, they were."

"Yes, ma'am."

"So, you see, I thought Lillias was taking him off to his father for a whipping, like I said, but somehow the lad ended up in the pond. He was a naughty lad, make no mistake, and likely would have turned into a criminal, but no one wants to see a lad come to such a sad pass, no matter how bad he is."

"No, ma'am."

"It didn't even cross my mind that something could have happened to him, what with Ian Adair going missing from Coldstream at the same time as the boy did. I figured he'd taken the lad off with him somewhere."

"Yes, of course you did," Mairi replied faintly, but all at once her head was spinning.

Ian Adair had been waiting for Lillias to bring Daniel to him that day. She'd already known this, of course—she'd seen Ian waiting on the other side of the woods herself—but until Mrs. Fraser mentioned Daniel's father, she hadn't truly considered the meaning behind it.

Lillias must have gone to fetch Ian *first*, before she went after Daniel. Otherwise, how would Ian have known to be there?

Something else had happened, something that sent Lillias off to fetch Ian Adair before she went out to the pond searching for Daniel. What, though? Mairi's head was too muddled to come up with anything that made sense, except...

Lillias had come to the woods that day to fetch *Daniel*, not Hamish. Otherwise, she wouldn't have taken the time to find Ian Adair, and bid him wait on the road near the woods. Hamish had never been the murderer's target—he'd simply been in the wrong place at the wrong time.

But if that was the case, why had he ended up dead? Who would want to hurt poor Hamish, who never spoke an angry word to anyone, and had nothing to steal? Had he seen something he shouldn't?

For that matter, who would want to murder eight-year-old Daniel Adair?

But someone had, or tried to. Something terrible had happened between the time Mrs. Fraser heard a boy shout and the time Mairi had seen Lillias rushing Daniel through the woods—something that landed Hamish at the bottom of Rutherford Pond with a broken neck.

Perhaps one of the other boys had been at the pond with Daniel and Hamish that day? Had there been some sort of accident, some boyish antics gone dreadfully wrong? But if that was the case, why had neither Mairi nor Mrs. Fraser seen anyone else?

"I never thought Lillias might have done something to the lad until the pond overflowed the banks, and they pulled his poor body out of it," Mrs. Fraser was saying. "She was fond of him, she was. I would have sworn Lillias would never hurt a hair on his head."

She wouldn't have. *She didn't.* Mairi wanted to say it aloud so badly, but what good would it do? Mrs. Fraser had already made up her mind, it seemed.

"But like I told you, Mairi, I saw what I saw. I don't like to believe it of your gran, but I can't help but think of poor Aileen Adair, with all those bairns she lost, one after the other. I thought for sure she'd lose Daniel too, but he came up all hale and hearty, pink and plump as a strawberry."

Mairi, who was frantically sorting through the fragments of memories from that day and piecing them together with what she'd just learned, hardly heard Mrs. Fraser. All she knew for certain was that Hamish had disappeared without anyone seeing anything, without any explanation until, after years of waiting, decades, the crimes of the past had at last caught up to the present, emerging from the deep, as the past always did.

And Lillias had wept that night, and every night afterwards—

"Such love poor Aileen Adair had for that boy!" Mrs. Fraser sighed. "She was so proud of him. I couldn't help but think of her when the lad's remains were found, the happiness on her face when she held that baby boy in her arms. When he turned up all drowned, I knew I had to tell what I saw, and I think I did the right thing, given that other business, with those things Lillias stole from Viscount Rutherford—"

"You can't mean to say you believe that nonsense about my grandmother being a thief, Mrs. Fraser? She never stole anything from anyone in her life!" Murder, and now theft? Had none of these people ever *met* Lillias Cameron? They were making her out to be the worst sort of villain, a monster—

"Well, I don't say I wasn't surprised at it, lass, but it's true enough, or so I hear. It seems Lillias went to the mansion a few months ago to tend to one of the viscount's servants who'd had a fall, and the viscount says she stole something when she was inside the manor house."

Mairi crossed her arms over her chest to stop herself from tearing her hair out. "What did he say she'd stolen?"

Mrs. Fraser frowned. "Now you ask, I can't say for sure. A brooch, maybe? Some jewelry, I think. I never heard much about that after the accusation was made, but Fergus McClellan could tell you. He was there when they searched your gran's cottage."

Fergus McClellan. She'd known Fergus since he was a lad of six years, and used to pull her braids. Fergus was a good deal easier to manage than Mrs. Fraser, and she knew just where to find him.

Chapter Twenty-four

The Sheep's Hide Inn was just as Mairi remembered it—dark and grubby, with a crush of bodies crowded around the bar. Angus Murray, the proprietor, did a brisk business in big, thirsty Scottish lads, but as it was the only pub in Coldstream, a few women could always be found here and there as well, tankards in hand and elbows out, ready to jab any lad who tried to get too friendly.

The whole company was laughing and cursing and shouting at Angus for more ale, with Angus shouting back that they could wait their bloody turns, just like everyone else, the whole picture so familiar it brought an ache to Mairi's throat.

Some of the fine citizens of Coldstream had already tried and convicted her grandmother, but there were small pockets of people tucked in amongst those who doubted who were still Lillias's friends, who refused to believe the worst of her, who hadn't forgotten her kindness and compassion and the loving care she'd always taken of the people here.

Among them were Angus, and Morag Ross, who lifted a hand in greeting when she caught sight of Mairi, and Fergus McClellan, who, for all his youthful teasing and tiresome braid-pulling, had proved himself a steadfast friend.

"I don't like this place." Daniel trudged into the dim, low-ceilinged room after Mairi and glanced around with a scowl. "Why is it so dark in here?"

She was only half-listening to him, already absorbed in searching for Fergus's familiar face among the men lined up at the bar. "Because it's winter in Scotland, and it's been dark outside since noon?"

He grunted. "Not this dark, and where did all these bloody people come from? I thought you said Coldstream was a *small* village."

"It *is* small. It's just that everyone who lives in the village happens to be here right now. Come, I see a place." She grasped his sleeve and tugged him to a small table on the other side of the room. "Sit down, and have a drink. Angus's porter is meant to be very good."

He did as she bid him and sat with his back to the wall, but the promise of a good porter didn't seem to mollify him. "I don't like this seat."

Well, of course he didn't. He didn't like Mrs. Fraser, or the Sheep's Hide, or the darkness, or his seat. "You don't like much of anything right now, do you?"

He glared at her. "There are too many bodies between us and the door."

"Yes, but most of them are only half your size, so it's not really so many as it looks, is it? I won't be long," she added, spying Fergus's tall, lean form at the other end of the room. "Meanwhile I'll have Angus send over a tankard of his porter."

Daniel caught her arm. "Nay, not by yourself, lass. I'm coming with you."

"I don't think that's a good idea." He'd already offended Mrs. Fraser, which was, admittedly, not difficult to do. Fergus was a cheerful soul and slow to take offense, but Daniel in one of his moods was enough to put even Fergus into a strop.

And Daniel looked to be in a mood right now, with his lowered brow and set jaw, and his dark hair standing on end from the way he'd tugged at it during their conversation with Mrs. Fraser.

On another man that disheveled hair might look boyishly charming, but there wasn't a bit of the boy in Daniel Brixton. On him it looked rugged and masculine and menacing—well, as menacing as hair *could* look—yet somehow, still...

Charming. Damn the man. He looked like a disgruntled giant with that spiky hair and a scowl that would terrify the devil himself, and that glower of his sucked up what little light there was in their corner of the room. How in the world could she ever find that appealing? Especially when that demonic glare was pointed directly at her, as it was now?

"Why wouldn't it be a good idea, lass?"

"You'll put him on his guard. I'll be able to charm the information out of him more easily without you there, grumbling and growling at every word."

"Charm him?" His jaw tightened another notch. "What do you plan to do, sit on his lap?"

"No. I don't think it'll come to that, this time."

"This time? *This* time? What the devil do you mean by—"

Oh, for pity's sake. She didn't have the patience for this nonsense. "Just sit down and wait for me here, will you? I'll be right back."

She signaled to Angus to bring Daniel a tankard on her way past, then made her way over to Fergus, who was leaning back against the bar, his elbows propped on top of it, watching her approach with a slow, appreciative smile on his lips. "Well, if it isn't little Mairi Cameron. I thought you'd run off to England, lass."

"I did." She smiled up at him. "And now I've come back."

"Back, and as bonny as ever. Can't bear to be away from me, eh?" Fergus took a long swallow of his ale, looking her up and down over the rim of his mug. "When are ye going to marry me, Mairi?"

Marry him, indeed. Fergus had always had an eye for the ladies, but he wouldn't have the first idea what to do with a wife. "One of these days I'll accept your offer, Fergus, and then what will you do?"

"Why, I'll make you my bride, of course, and count myself among the luckiest men in Scotland." He reached out to tweak one of her braids. "I'm surprised one of those grand English lords didn't snatch you up and run away with you. I hear tell they love pretty red-headed Scottish lasses like you. Or mayhap one did. Who's your friend? Looks a little familiar, he does. Is he the jealous sort?"

Fergus nodded over her shoulder, and she turned to find Daniel glowering at them—yes, *still* glowering—from the other corner of the room. "He's not English, but Scottish, and he is the jealous sort, so you best keep your hands to yourself."

Fergus grinned. "Ach, you break my heart, lassie."

"Stuff and nonsense. You should save your flirtations for one of the ladies in the village who have their eye on you. From what I hear you may have your choice." Fergus was a dark-haired, broad-shouldered lad with merry brown eyes and an infectious grin that had caught the attention of more than one of Coldstream's eligible young ladies.

He clutched at his chest. "You know I don't want any of them, Mairi. My undying devotion is only for you."

"You're a shameless flirt, Fergus." She was one of his favorite targets because she never took a word he said seriously, but she didn't have time for his pretty words right now. "But it's not your devotion I'm interested in tonight."

His brown eyes twinkled. "Well, that sounds promising—"

"It isn't. At least, not in the way you mean. I heard something today that shocked me, and I think you're the man to tell me more about it."

Fergus's smile faded. "This about your gran?"

"My grandmother, and Viscount Rutherford, and some claims he's made against her." Cold was creeping into her chest. "Is it true? Has he really accused her of stealing from him?"

He sighed, and turned to set his tankard of ale on the length of scarred wood that served as a bar at the Sheep's Hide. "Aye, I'm afraid he did."

"Mrs. Fraser says you helped search her cottage."

He looked away from her. "Aye. I didn't have any—"

"You *know* she didn't do it, Fergus!" Despite her efforts, her voice was rising, turning shrill. "You know she'd never steal anything!"

He caught her wrists in his hands. "Hush now, Mairi. 'Course I know it, but what would you have had me do? Viscount Rutherford himself made the complaint against her—took it straight to the magistrate. We had no choice but to have a look. You know that."

She *did* know it, but that didn't make their rifling through her grandmother's things as if Lillias were a common criminal any easier to bear. None of this made sense, and with every day that passed, things were growing more dire for her grandmother. Soon enough the Court of Assizes would convene, and they'd fit a noose around her grandmother's neck—

"We didn't find anything at the cottage," Fergus offered. "If that makes you feel any better."

"What, no stolen goods? Nothing belonging to the viscount?" That *did* make her feel better, because at least it made sense, given there was no way Lillias had stolen anything, but so far it was the only thing that *did* make sense.

"Nay, not a thing. It was strange." Fergus shook his head, his expression troubled. "Viscount Rutherford insisted she'd stolen a ring that belonged to him, but if she did, she hid it well."

"What sort of ring?" She hadn't seen any ring, but Fergus was right. If her grandmother *did* have the ring, she had the perfect place to hide it. Mairi had pawed through that wooden box under the loose floorboard herself to get the letters Ian Adair had sent to her grandmother, but she'd been in a hurry at the time, and she hadn't been looking for a ring.

"A gold mourning ring, a valuable one, with a jewel set into it."

She swallowed. "How valuable?"

Fergus's lips tightened, and his gaze shifted to the floor. "Valuable enough to get her hanged, if she's found innocent of the murder."

Dear God. It was as if Viscount Rutherford was determined to see her grandmother hang, one way or another. "This alleged theft was meant to have happened months ago, according to Mrs. Fraser. Why is the viscount only coming forward now?" It was a suspicious pattern, these witnesses coming out of nowhere, months—even decades—after the crime was meant to have been committed.

"The viscount told the magistrate he'd just found out about it, and he was in a right fit over it, too, from what I heard. It seemed the ring belonged to Malcolm Gordon, his older brother, the viscount as was."

"As grand an estate as that, and Callum Gordon was in that much of a fit over a mourning ring that belonged to his brother? How did he even discover it was missing?"

She didn't begrudge the viscount his property, but his single-minded pursuit of the ring came at the expense of her lovely, compassionate grandmother, who'd been taken up on what appeared to be no more than the whim of a malevolent viscount.

"Mayhap it was a family heirloom? But it's an odd bit of business, I'll grant you that, lass. My mam was housekeeper in the big house for years while Malcolm Gordon was lord, and she always said as the brothers despised each other. She never laid eyes on the younger until the elder was on his deathbed. Arrived in Coldstream just in time to make sure his brother was good and dead, she said."

"Was he?"

"Aye, or close enough to it, I think. Callum Gordon sent all his brother's servants away the night he arrived, then the moment his brother passed he dismissed them all, without references. I'd never seen my mam as angry as she was that day. I was just a wee lad, only six, and it scared the wits out of me."

Callum Gordon had so loathed his brother he couldn't bear to have Malcolm Gordon's servants in the same house with him, yet he was frantic to retrieve this ring that had belonged to that same brother? Willing to see her grandmother sent to prison over it? Sent to the scaffold over it?

And she *would* be. That much was becoming devastatingly clear. Mairi could struggle and claw and fight for Lillias until she dropped, but Viscount Rutherford would have his way in the end, just as noblemen always did.

Who was she, to try and thwart the will of a powerful aristocrat?

No one who mattered.

"My grandmother, Fergus. I think my grandmother is going to hang."

Chapter Twenty-five

There were eight people between Daniel and the door, all of them burly Scottish men with meaty fists. Three of the eight were too sotted to fight, but the other five were steady enough, and of those five, two of them had knives hidden in their boots.

Not the best odds. He'd managed worse, but instead of eyeing a pathway to the door that didn't end with one of those blades buried in his shoulder, he couldn't look away from Mairi and the big, dark-haired Scot who was grinning down at her like he knew something about her no one else did.

The scoundrel couldn't keep his hands to himself, either. He was tugging on Mairi's plait, the long weave of red and gold threads caught between his fingers while Mairi smiled up at him like she *wanted* his hands on her, her soft pink lips curved in invitation.

She'd never smiled at *him* like that, but the Scot was smooth and pretty in much the same way Georgiana's Lord Haslemere was, with that witless sort of grin women lost their heads over. Not like his own dark, sinister face that scattered the lasses like birds at a pistol shot, even when he smiled.

Especially then.

He snatched up the tankard of porter someone had dropped on the table before him, swallowed it in one go, then slammed it back down. Bloody nuisance of a place, Coldstream, with bloody irritating citizens. He'd rather tear every hair from his head than spend another second with Mrs. Fraser, and he'd be happy enough to smash a fist into Fergus McClellan's grinning mouth.

The sooner he settled this business with Lillias Cameron and got back to London, the better. For him, for Mairi, and for Fergus McClellan, the grabby bast—

A blast of frigid air blew through the pub and hit the back of his neck. A man dressed head to toe in black stood in the open doorway for an instant, scanning the crowd, then pushed it closed behind him. He didn't take any notice of Daniel—didn't even glance in his direction—but the hair on Daniel's neck rose, flesh prickling with as dire a warning as if the man had leapt across the pub and pressed the pointed tip of a dagger to his neck.

If the man had spared him even a passing glance, Daniel wouldn't have paid him any mind at all. There was nothing about the man to catch his attention. Just a typical Scot, off to the pub of an evening, like every other man here with a tankard in hand, jostling for space near the crowded bar.

But you could tell as much from what a man *didn't* do as what he did, and this man's disinterest in him was suspicious. Even the most witless of men instinctually took note of a man of Daniel's size and air of menace, if only to know best how to keep away from him.

Then there was the man's dark clothing, perfect for slipping through the shadows undetected, and that hat pulled low to hide his face. Daniel had seen the same thing too many times before to mistake it for anything but the threat it was.

That man had come here looking for *him*.

Here, at a dingy pub in a tiny, remote village in the Scottish borders, where no one knew who he was. It didn't make any bloody sense at all, unless Mrs. Fraser had been offended enough to send some big, sprawling Scottish son or nephew or uncle of hers to teach him some manners by spilling a bit of his blood.

He raised his empty tankard to his lips, tracking the man as he made his way across the pub to the opposite end of the bar. His knees were one weak spot—they were slightly bowed, and would crumple under a kick from a boot heel, and the soft part of his belly would cave with one strike from a fist.

Not much of a fight to be had *there*, though the man was big, tall, and broad through the shoulders, though not as tall as Fergus Mc—

Not as tall as Fergus? Nay, that couldn't be right.

Daniel had a good four or five inches on Fergus himself, and he was broader too, his shoulders roughly twice the width of Fergus's shoulders, and the man in black was a good bit smaller than Fergus was.

Daniel set his tankard down, suddenly uneasy.

The man in black wasn't a big man at all, so why had he seemed so when he'd first walked into the pub? Daniel didn't make mistakes like that, didn't miscalculate a man's size when he knew the evening could end in a brawl, but this time he had.

The man had looked bigger at first. Mayhap the black clothing—
No, it wasn't that. It was something else, something worse.
Daniel felt *smaller.*

The chill from the blast of cold air slid from his neck down his back, icy fingers crawling over each knob of his spine on the way down.

The man accepted a tankard of ale from the barkeep and brought it to his lips. His hand on the tankard, the way his arm moved to raise it—they were familiar, somehow, tugging hard on some secret hidden inside Daniel's head, some edgy feeling in his chest. He stared, throat closing tighter with every twitch of the man's fingers on the tankard's handle, his stomach roiling with each sickening jerk of the man's throat as he swallowed.

Daniel's tankard tipped, fell over onto its side, the clink of metal against wood just loud enough that a few heads turned toward him, but not the man's. He didn't turn either right or left, but stared straight ahead, like he could feel Daniel staring at him, and wanted to avoid meeting his eyes.

That might have been the end of it, if the barkeep hadn't chosen that moment to toss more wood onto the fire. A shower of sparks flew up, the log caught, and the light flared as the flames rose, flickering over the side of the man's face.

That was when Daniel saw it.

The man had a patch covering his left eye.

White flashed in front of Daniel's eyes, so bright he raised his hand to shield them from the glare of the flames, but the flash hadn't come from the fire. He squeezed his eyes closed to shut it out, but it was *inside* him, the image coming to life behind his eyelids, a blind, white eyeball, untethered to its socket, loose and overflowing with evil, wicked spells and curses that could drop a boy to the ground—

He shot to his feet, his chair toppling to the floor with a crash behind him. A man at the table beside his started, then jerked to his feet. Someone cried out his name, but the voice was lost in the roar inside his ears, a boy's scream inside his head.

Tree branches swaying, dappled sunlight, a packed mud pathway beneath his bare feet...

Come on, Hamish. Run!

A boy's feet dangling in the air, inches from the ground, a hand over Daniel's mouth, wagon wheels creaking over a rutted dirt road and fear, a deep, endless chasm of it...

Dread rolled over him, again and again like a punishing wave, tumbling him head over heels, snatching each of his breaths, his lungs heaving, useless, grasping at nothing until at last, at last one breath caught, another, his eyes snapped open, and now the man *was* looking at him, his one working eye wide, terrified.

Terrified.

He took that terror into him, fed on it until the flashes of white darkened to blood red. Rage scalded him, scorching him from the inside out, the blood in his veins fire now, because it wasn't fair, what had happened to Hamish.

It wasn't fair, wasn't *fair*—

Another scream, then a blur of gaping mouths, some grinning, bloodthirsty, others split open in horror. The flickering faces in his periphery was how he knew he was moving, lunging, the roar in his ears back again, or else that was him roaring, his throat raw with it, his world narrowed down to a pinpoint.

That patch over the man's eye—he was going to rip it off so he could see that cursed white eyeball for himself, see if it dropped him dead where he stood now that he was no longer a boy, but a man that other men feared.

Someone grabbed his arm, the heavy drag of it there and then gone as he shook them off, sent them sprawling. Something hit him in the middle of his back, broke into pieces—a tankard of ale, thrown across the pub. Men's bodies appeared in his pathway, there one moment then shoved aside in the next with long sweeps of his arms, right and left, chairs splintering against the wall behind him, a snarl on his lips, frozen there, rusty blood on his tongue, teeth bared, arms flailing.

Ages seemed to pass as he pounded across the floor, but it couldn't have been long, seconds only, until at last his hands found their way around the man in black's throat, his pulse leaping against Daniel's palm, fingers clawing at Daniel's wrists, Daniel's other hand reaching for the patch, his fingers closing around the edges of it—

Then a half-dozen men were on him, tearing his hands away, dragging on his legs, jumping on his back, and he was fighting them, and their bodies were dropping to the floor until a huge fist landed in his eye, opening the gash from Mairi's pistol. Blood poured from the wound, blinding him just as a chair smashed over his back and he crashed to the floor.

There was a flurry of feet rushing toward him, boot heels flashing in front of his eyes, then other feet rushing to pull the first lot of them off him—the man behind the bar, Angus something, and Fergus McClellan, no longer grinning. A boot heel hit his jaw, a weak kick, thank God, then another boot landed in his ribs, that one harder, and a woman's toes came down on his fingers, and there was nothing to do then but curl into a ball to protect his head, his torso, and wait for it either to be over, or wait to be dead, but he wanted to live through it, if only so he'd have a chance to kiss Mairi again, properly this time—

A shout pierced the blur of noise and movement around him, high-pitched, and then the crowd of men on top of him were backing away, some walking, others being tossed, still others lingering, watching him bleed all over the floor, and then, down the center of the parted crowd strode Mairi Cameron, red hair wild around her face, sailing forward like some kind of avenging angel, then dropping to her knees beside him.

Her mouth was moving, but he couldn't hear her, or make any sense of the shapes her lips were making through the blood in his eyes, but before he succumbed to the darkness pressing down on him, he grasped blindly for the one thing inside his head that still made sense, the one thing he knew to be true, the one thing that mattered more than all the other things…

He caught it in his fingers just as the room faded around him, and darkness descended.

She had the loveliest face he'd ever seen.

Chapter Twenty-six

"You owe Fergus McClellan your thanks. If he hadn't dragged those men off you, you'd still be sprawled out on the floor at the Sheep's Hide, your blood seeping into the cracks in the floorboards and a boot print on your forehead."

Instead, he was on her grandmother's bed, his blood seeping into one of Lillias's old blankets. Mairi was holding a towel to his forehead, hoping the gash he'd opened up hurt enough to burn some sense into him.

When those lads had descended on him tonight, fists and feet flying, the contents of her stomach had surged into her throat with one violent heave, threatening to spew from her lips in a flood of sickness. Even now the sour, acid taste of vomit lingered on the back of her tongue, waiting for any excuse to make an appearance.

"Fergus? What, you mean that pretty bloke with the wandering hands?" Daniel cracked one eye open. "Didn't care for him."

She shoved the tip of her tongue between her teeth, but nothing could silence it this time. She'd held it for the entire ride from the pub to the cottage, bumping along the rutted road in the back of Fergus's wagon with Daniel's head in her lap, praying he'd recover with one breath, and cursing his name with the next.

If there was a man more stubborn, reckless, foolish, and wrong-headed than Daniel Brixton, she'd yet to come across him, and she lived in *Scotland*, for pity's sake, land of stubborn, addle-pated men.

He could have been beaten to death, kicked and pummeled until he looked more like raw beef than a man, nothing left of him but a few bits of dark hair, an eyeball or two, and a pulpy, bloody stain on Angus Murray's floor.

But Daniel had the devil's own luck, and his injuries weren't as bad as she'd feared, though that gash she'd given him in London was nasty enough even before he tore it open again. It would leave him with a nice new scar to add to his collection. Aside from that, he had a bruised rib, and one of his fingers was broken, but it was a neat break.

A boot heel would do that.

All told, he'd fared better than he might have on any night prowling about St. Giles, chasing villains. He'd be well enough in a few days.

So, seeing as her prayers had been answered, it was the curses that got loose from her tongue. "You didn't care for him. *You*, who nearly managed to get himself killed tonight, who threw the entire Sheep's Hide into a panic and left a trail of destruction and chaos in your wake. *You* didn't care for *him*."

He scowled. "Nay. I don't like the way he looks at you."

"The way he looks at me?" Dear God, she'd never been more furious with anyone in her life than she was with Daniel right now. "That's ridiculous. He doesn't look at me in any particular way."

"Aye, he does. He looks at you like he thinks you're *his*. He touches you like he thinks he has a right to do as he pleases, like he thinks he owns you."

Owned her? If Daniel thought any man would ever own her, he hadn't been paying attention. "Why, because he tweaked my braid? He's been doing that since we were six years old, Daniel. It doesn't bother me, and it's *my* braid, so there's no reason it should bother *you*."

He grunted, closing his eyes. "Bothered me all the same, whether it should or no."

She tossed the towel aside before she could give in to the urge to shove it into his mouth to silence him. "It's nothing to do with you! We've been friends for years. Fergus would never hurt me."

His cracked lips split open in a grin that looked positively ghastly in his bloodied face. "It's not his *hurting* you that worries me, lass."

"Is that why you tried to tear the Sheep's Hide to pieces tonight then? Because you decided you didn't like the way Fergus McClellan looked at me?"

He pried both eyes open this time, which was quite a feat, given the right one was mostly swollen shut. "Nay."

"Why, then? If you say boredom, or something equally as foolish, I'll black your other eye."

He didn't answer at once, but stared up at her, his eyes dark with shadows, then, "There was a man there tonight, all in black, with a hat pulled low over his eyes."

"Every man there tonight was wearing a hat, and more than a half-dozen were dressed in black."

He shook his head. "Nay, not like this one. He had a patch covering one eye."

"A patch?" She'd only ever known one man who had a need for a patch, but Murdoch had left Coldstream years ago. Decades ago, in fact, and she hadn't laid eyes on him since then. For all she knew, he could be dead, unless—

That dark shape, creeping about the darkness near the cottage last night. Perhaps it hadn't been a figment of her imagination, after all, but Murdoch, returned to Coldstream, as alive as he'd ever been, and sneaking about in the shadows, peering through the windows.

But why would he be watching the cottage?

If he had returned to Coldstream, it couldn't be a coincidence, could it, that he'd reappeared at the same time Daniel had also returned? Or had it not been Murdoch at the Sheep's Hide tonight, but another man with an eye patch?

That seemed unlikely, but she couldn't be certain. She couldn't be certain of anything anymore. Frustration pulled her shoulders tight, an ache blooming between them. Every time she tried to fit a piece into the puzzle, another would fall out.

"It's that gamekeeper. Murdoch." Daniel was no longer looking at her, but staring up at the ceiling without blinking.

She pulled back from him to get a better look at his face. His skin was pale, clammy, tight lines of pain around his mouth. She picked up the cloth, dipped it in the basin, and stroked it over the gash on his forehead. She was furious with him, yes, but she couldn't quite stomach seeing him in pain.

He flinched at the touch of the coarse toweling over his wound. "What happened to Murdoch? Why did he leave Coldstream?"

"He left when Malcolm Gordon died, and Malcolm's younger brother Callum became the viscount. I was too young at the time to remember much about it, but the gossip in the village was that he was sent off by the new viscount, along with most of his brother's other servants."

Fergus had just been talking about this very thing tonight, in fact. As soon as Malcolm was dead, Callum had summoned his own people from his house in London. Apparently, his loathing for his brother had extended to his brother's servants as well.

Quite a stir it had caused among the citizens of Coldstream, too. They hadn't taken kindly to their neighbors and friends being sent off without so much as a thank you, and replaced with uppity English servants. More than one family had been forced to leave the village to seek jobs elsewhere, and those who'd stayed had found little enough reason to approve of Callum Gordon, the Fourth Viscount of Rutherford.

He was an indifferent landlord, that was certain. He'd hardly remained in Coldstream long enough to see his brother buried before he was back off to his luxurious London townhouse, without a care for the land he owned or the livelihood of his tenants.

"What's wrong with Murdoch's eye?" Daniel kept his gaze on the ceiling. "Why does he need the patch?"

"Some sort of accident, I think. We never knew exactly what happened to him, except that he'd lost the sight in his left eye, and it went that strange, opaque white. The nerve must have been damaged, because he couldn't control it. We were afraid of him when we were children. We thought his eye was mystical, that he could—"

"Curse us with it." Daniel was twisting the worn cloth of the blanket between his fingers. "Cast spells with it."

Her hand stilled. She stared down at him, at that pale face, his eyes so haunted she might have believed Murdoch *had* cursed him, and suddenly she was afraid to move, afraid even to breathe. "Do...do you remember Murdoch, Daniel?"

He'd told her he'd seen a man with a white eye in his dream, but an image of a face glimpsed in a dream was not the same as remembering the man himself.

Daniel swallowed. "No. Yes. I remember his eye, but not him. Not... exactly."

She set the cloth aside carefully, as if a sudden move might frighten the memory away, back to the darkness where it had hidden these past twenty-four years. Her only hope of discovering the truth of that day was all there, locked inside his head. She'd witnessed a piece of what had happened, and Mrs. Fraser another piece, but there wasn't enough there to make sense of it, even if she stitched the pieces together.

The only other people who knew anything about what had happened were Lillias, who, for as long as Mairi could remember, had turned her head away whenever Mairi tried to get her to speak of it, and who'd now rather face a noose than breathe a word of the truth; Hamish, long since dead, his voice forever silenced; and Daniel, the only person left who could speak for Hamish, and for himself.

She took Daniel's uninjured hand and pressed it gently between hers. "Do you remember anything else?"

"Trees. Branches above my head. Feet running down a pathway. Mine, I think. That's all." He did meet her eyes then, his expression blank, but it was too late. Some ray of light had lit the darkest places of his mind where his secrets hid. Not all of them, but enough he couldn't hide it. Not from her.

She clasped his fingers in hers, squeezed. "No, it isn't. There's more. Tell me."

"There's nothing more. Just Murdoch and Hamish. That's all."

Hamish. So small and thin, with wide brown eyes and that sweet smile, so innocent still, despite all the ugliness he'd seen, and lame, his smaller, weaker leg always a half-step behind the other.

"But you remember Hamish now?" She leaned over him, too close, perhaps, because he flinched back, away from her. "Can you...did you see what happened to him, in your dream?"

"No. I don't know. I...can't be sure."

"What *did* you see? Tell me, Daniel."

He opened his mouth, then shook his head and closed it.

The part of her that had been living with this mystery for the past twenty-four years wanted to press him, to shake the words out of him, but he looked strange, so lost, so unlike she'd ever seen him that she should have known better.

But she didn't. Not until it was too late.

"Why did you attack Murdoch, Daniel? Is it because of something you remembered? Was he the one who hurt Hamish, or—"

"I told you, I don't know."

"But if you'd just think for a moment, you might remember—"

"I don't *want* to bloody remember!" He jerked away from her and covered his eyes with his hand. "Some villain snaps an eight-year-old boy's neck and tosses him into a pond? You think I want *that* in my head?"

She stared at him, stunned. "But you've done..."

You'd done worse, yourself.

She didn't say it—thank *God*, she didn't say it—but when he lifted his hand away and she got a look at his face, into his eyes—she saw she might as well have screamed it aloud.

"You think I'd hurt a child, Mairi?"

"No!" Oh, what had she said? "No, Daniel—"

"I've hurt people, aye. People like Angel Nash. That's not the same as a boy whose only crime was poaching a few fish out of some nobleman's pond, is it? You think I want to see a boy's murder in my head, Mairi? I don't, and I wouldn't have to, but for you. I wouldn't know my father lied to me for years, that he hid my past from me, but for *you*."

He wasn't shouting now—his voice had gone deathly quiet. "I wish you'd never come to London, never found me. I should have left you in Howe Court that night, and never looked back. If I had it to do over again, I would."

His words were like a blow to the face, the pain sudden and excruciating, leaving her reeling. But it was true, wasn't it? How had she never considered how hard it would be for Daniel to face a past so painful he'd buried it away, hidden it even from himself? She'd thought only of her grandmother, Hamish, and herself, but Daniel had been as dear to her as Hamish.

He still was. How had she never spared a thought for *him*?

"I—I shouldn't have…I beg your pardon." She called on every bit of courage she possessed and dared to slip her hand into his. "I'm sorry, Daniel."

He shook her off, then rolled over onto his side, his back to her. "I don't want to talk anymore tonight."

She knelt beside him for a long time after he turned away, staring at the wild mess of dark curls she'd so loved when he'd been a boy, fumbling to find any words she could say to put things right again.

But there was nothing to say, nothing to do but set aside the washbasin of bloodstained water, turn down the lamp, crawl into her side of the bed, and tuck herself up tight, careful not to touch him.

Chapter Twenty-seven

The field around him is a riot of colors, shapes, and scents—wild garlic, with its stench that wrinkles his nose, the spiky white flowers that look like feathers from far away, columbine, and bright yellow king's cup. White daisies, ribbons of deep purple heather, and Scottish bluebells the same color as Mairi's eyes.

He knows the names of all the wildflowers. That's how he knows it's a dream.

He's lying on his back, the sky above him a blue he's only ever seen in the summertime in Scotland, and Mairi is beside him, the tips of her fingers just touching the tips of his.

They kept the glass jars of lemonade Mrs. Cameron made for them in the creek to keep them cold, but he's just swallowed his in three greedy gulps, and now his lips are puckered and his tongue alive with the sour, sweet taste of lemon. Mairi's jaw is still half full, because she takes dainty, ladylike sips, making the treat last.

He's not a good boy, not sweet like Hamish is. His smile is crooked and wicked, not sunny, and he's wild and rough. He teases Mairi, running away from her, laughing at her when she runs to catch up with them, her red hair in a tangle down her back, tripping over her stubby little legs.

But the wildflowers—*he* did this, planted them for *her*, and now, lying in the field with the prickly thistles digging into his back, and Mairi with that dreamy smile on her lips, it feels like the best thing he's ever done...

Daniel woke slowly this time, his eyelids drifting open one flicker at a time—no jerking awake, or struggling through thick, dark water to reach the surface, but a peaceful float upward, the dream still clinging to him, dissolving gradually like mist in the first rays of morning sunshine, leaving light and heat in its wake.

No terror, no fury, no regrets—not this time, and he keeps still, listening to the quiet beat of his heart, and lets the dream wind through him, sink into him.

He's calm when he turns to Mairi, his breaths deep and steady.

She's asleep, her back to him, huddled into a tight ball on her side of the bed, her fingers curled into the coverlet as if she fell asleep clutching it to keep from tumbling to the floor.

He'd shoved her away, and she'd stayed away, leaving a wide slice of cold, empty bed between them.

Hamish and Murdoch, the horror of what happened at the pond that day, his past now haunting his present, those memories dredged up from the deep, clawing and tearing at him, ripping him open as they slithered upward from the darkness...

There was no escaping them anymore.

That ugliness was inside him now, in his head, a part of him he'd never be free of, but there are fields of wildflowers there too, and cold lemonade, the sharp scent of garlic, Hamish's smile, and Mairi's hand touching his.

Moments of perfect rightness, perfect peace.

His childhood.

She gave him that.

Being free of one part of his past meant losing the other. Would he have made that trade, if he'd been given the choice? It was a cowardly question, and a selfish one. *No one* had that choice. Not Lady Clifford. Not Sophia, Cecilia, Georgiana, or Emma. Not Lillias Cameron, or Elsbeth Fraser. Not Fergus bloody McClellan.

Not Mairi.

She was still struggling with the wreckage from that day, just as much as he was. More so, because the grandmother she loved—the one she'd risked everything for—was waiting to be fitted with a noose for a crime she hadn't committed.

But she hadn't lashed out at him tonight, as he'd done to her, hadn't said a word in reply to his accusations. Instead, she'd hunched into herself, legs drawn up and arms tucked tight against her body, a small, curled bundle balanced on the edge of the bed, only the curve of one shoulder visible in the darkness.

He touched her arm to ease her closer to the middle of the bed so he might warm her body with his heat, but she wasn't the sort of lass a man could move about as he pleased. She jerked awake, fists clenched and hissed, "No, don't touch—"

"Shhh, lass. It's alright. It's me."

"Daniel?" She peered up at him, blinking. "Is it your eye? Has the swelling gotten worse?"

He flexed his fingers, wincing as the split skin tightened over his knuckles. He'd nearly forgotten that a horde of drunken Scots had beaten him to a bloody pulp tonight. Those lads were handy with their fists and boot heels. They had good aim, and their kicks were vicious. They'd torn the gash on his head open, and his ribs were an aching mess of bruises, but he'd take a dozen beatings over the dreams he'd been having.

A beating was less painful. Bruises, broken bones, and slashed skin burned and throbbed and ached, but the pain that came from inside him, the kind he couldn't see or touch, felt like a betrayal, as if he'd turned the knife on himself.

Even the good dreams were a kind of agony, because they were gone too soon.

"Daniel?"

Mairi rose up onto her elbows, and he could just make out the shape of her face in the darkness—the high arch of her cheekbones, and the sweet, stubborn curve of her chin.

"Let me fetch the cloth for you—"

"Nay, I…"

But what could he say to excuse his unfairness to her tonight? He'd never been good with words—he couldn't get them to come out in a way that made sense. He'd cock it up, and she'd shove him away, banish him to the other side of the bed, and he'd go, because that was where a brutal, cold-hearted villain like him belonged.

But he'd try. For her, he'd try. "I beg your pardon, for…"

For what? He hadn't spilled tea on her, or trod on her foot. He'd *hurt* her, cruelly and intentionally. Begging wasn't enough to fix that. Only the *truth* was, but he'd never been good with that, either.

"I didn't mean it, Mairi. What I said tonight, it…I shouldn't have said it." He buried his face in the crook of her neck to inhale her heather scent, burn it into his lungs, because maybe then he'd dream about her again.

She didn't shove him away. Instead, her gentle sigh tickled his ear, and then she was touching him, her fingers in the hair at the back of his neck, toying with the waves, her crooning murmurs soothing him.

He breathed her in, then drew back to look at her. Her red curls were loose, spread out in a wild tangle across the pillow. Her lips still had the same slight pout they'd had when she'd been a child, but there was nothing childlike about her now.

Those pink, plump lips were pure sin, tempting his tongue to steal a taste. "I dreamed of you tonight." He ran his thumb over her lower lip, his belly tightening at the warm glide of her soft skin against it. "You have the same mouth you did as a child, with this sulky lip, only now..."

Now it was seductive, arousing, maddening.

She reached up and touched her finger to the scar on his cheek. "How did you get this?"

"A pistol ball grazed my cheekbone."

Her finger froze. "Dear God, that must have hurt."

"Aye, like the devil, but better my cheek than between my eyes, which is where he was aiming." She'd resumed her stroking, and he closed his eyes to savor the soft brush of her fingertip over his skin.

"Hmmm. And this one?"

She traced the long, thin scar that ran the length of his collarbone, and a pulse of desire made his belly clench. "Knife wound."

"Let me guess. He was aiming for your heart?"

"She. Cecilia—that is, Lady Darlington gave me that when I was teaching her how to throw a knife. I've never seen any lass cry so much over a wee accident."

She was staring up at him, her mouth open. "The Countess of Darlington maimed you in a knife-throwing accident?"

"Marchioness, but she wasn't one then. Just a tenderhearted lass with bad aim."

"Dear God. I knew there was something strange about that school. Someday you'll have to tell me more about it."

"Aye, mayhap I will." But not now. *Please*, not now, not when every inch of his skin was aching for her touch—

"But not now," she murmured, as if she'd read his mind, her fingers dancing across his collarbone. She paused to touch the pad of her thumb to the hollow of his throat, then her hand slid lower, into the open neck of his shirt to—*God help him*—stroke his chest.

"Take this off," she whispered, tugging on the hem of his shirt.

"Off?" he repeated, dazed.

"Yes, Daniel. Off."

"Do you want to touch me, lass?"

"Yes, if you...don't mind."

Mind? He nearly broke his other fingers wrestling his shirt off and tossing it over the side of the bed. It wasn't a good idea, Mairi touching him. She was as much a virgin as she'd ever been, but he wanted her to, was desperate for her touch, had dreamed of her hands on his bare skin, all over him.

But even though they'd slept in the same bed every night since they'd arrived in Coldstream, she'd hardly touched him since he'd made such an arse of himself at the inn in Newcastle.

Tonight, though, she seemed to want it, too, because she was already reaching for him, her warm palms against his back, her curious fingers exploring him.

She paused over every scar, every rough patch, every disfigurement, deep or shallow, small or large, as if she were learning about him by reading his skin. No woman had ever touched him that way before. Her eager caress was nothing like his usual rough, furtive couplings, detached fumbling in the darkness, like scratching an itch.

Mairi touched him as if she wanted to *know* him.

"This can't be another knife wound." She paused over a thick, raised scar that scored the lower part of his rib cage. "A knife wound this size would have killed you."

"Nay, a bullwhip left that one. The tip of it was weighted with iron that caught me right across my ribs."

"My God, Daniel." She was caressing the scar as if trying to soothe the pain it must have inflicted, running her fingers back and forth over it. "What sort of man owns a weighted bullwhip?"

"You don't want to know, lass."

"No, perhaps not." She dragged her fingers between his shoulder blades and right down the center of his spine, her fingernails just grazing him, and his every hair rose to attention, every nerve ending screaming to life under her touch, the caress of her palms so soft against his heated skin.

"Another pistol ball," he murmured when she found the wound in his shoulder. "Boot heel...another boot heel, from the same boot," when she paused over two crescent-shaped scars on his chest. "Just a fist, but he was wearing a heavy, jeweled ring," when she found the small, oval scar on the underside of his chin.

She paused, stroking her fingertip over the indentation, her lips curving in a pleased half-smile, as if she'd uncovered a secret. "I like this one."

He arched his neck, offering her wandering fingers better access to it. "Why's that, lass?"

"Because it's hidden, like a tiny treasure only for those who are permitted to touch you."

That she'd think any part of him was a treasure amazed him, but there wasn't time to dwell on it, because her hand was moving again, a slow sweep down his neck, the tip of her finger dipping into the hollow at the base of his throat and coaxing a groan from his chest, his thoughts fracturing in the wake of her seductive caress.

He closed his eyes then, drowning in her touch, the drift of her palm over his stomach, his muscles twitching and another groan tearing loose when those seeking fingers paused to sift through the tracing of hair low on his belly.

"Do you know what you're about there, lass?" He made himself say the words, bit them out between clenched teeth, but his hips were already shifting toward her, begging for more attention, another stroke of that warm hand.

"Um...no?" She gave him a shy smile. "I thought perhaps you'd show me."

Good Lord, that smile. It stole his breath, and he could do nothing else but lean down to take her mouth, his tongue slipping between her lips, and once he tasted her again, he couldn't stop kissing her, couldn't think of a single reason why he should—couldn't think of anything at all but the flutter of her tongue against his, the plush give of that pouting lower lip when he sucked on it.

The kiss was more than enough to coax his cock to rigid attention. It jutted against his falls, the flushed, swollen head peeking up over the waistband of his breeches.

"Oh." Mairi gazed at him, her blue eyes dark, and God, what a picture she made, her hair in a wild, red tangle around her, her tongue creeping into the corner of her mouth. "May I touch you?"

Please, God please, yes, please touch me...

Had he said the words aloud? Or had she read his need for her in his hoarse, desperate groan, the hot bead of moisture that rose to the crown of his cock?

But it didn't matter how, and it didn't matter why, did it? All that mattered was that she was reaching for him, her fingers on the buttons of his falls, twisting them loose, and then—*Christ*—her soft palm brushed over the damp head of his cock.

"Ah!" His hips jerked, and another bead welled at his tip.

She held him in her hand, her fingers curled around him, her lower lip caught between her teeth. "Show me."

"You want this, lass? Are you...are you sure?" Why should such a fierce, clever, lovely lass like Mairi, with her fine, pale skin and perfect, dainty curves want a big, scarred brute of a man like him?

She let out a quiet laugh, her soft breath drifting over his parted lips. "I'm sure, Daniel. I wouldn't have touched you at all if I weren't."

That sweet laugh sent the last of his doubts scattering, and he closed his large hand around her much smaller one, and showed her how to stroke him, slowly at first, but he was too hungry, too eager, and within minutes he was panting and writhing for her.

"Hold me tighter, lass, like…ah, God, yes." He threw his head back with a hiss as pleasure shot through him, and he was lost to her then, his hips working, thrusting his cock against the smooth warm skin of her palm, low, broken words pouring from his lips. "Yes, just like…ah, Mairi, so good, lass, so good."

She was staring down at her fingers wrapped firmly around his cock, the dripping head shuttling through her fist, her breath coming in quick gasps, and her lips parted in wonder. "It's so *hot*, Daniel, and I can feel you pulsing against my palm."

"You're making me come, lass." He was shaking now, straining against her, his hips working frantically, his cock throbbing in heavy, pulsing beats. "Yes, more—please make me come, Mairi, make me…"

He broke off on a deep, guttural groan, exploding in long, hot bursts into her hand, vaguely registering her soft sound of surprise—he should have warned her, should have explained what would happen…

But she didn't let go, didn't stop stroking him, just gazed down at his spurting cock as if it were the most fascinating thing she'd ever seen until his pleasure receded in dizzying waves, his spine loosening as the last few spurts of his seed spilled into her hand.

He kissed her then, slow and soft and gentle, before leaning over her to fetch the damp cloth from the basin beside the bed. He cleaned her hand and his belly, then took her into his arms, settled her head on his chest and drew the coverlet over both of them.

"That was…I'd like to do that again." She was running her fingers through the hair on his chest. "Soon."

Incredibly, a laugh bubbled up in his throat—not something that had ever happened before when he'd bedded a woman. "Aye, soon." He rolled onto his side, dropped a hand onto her hip and began to inch her skirts up her thigh. "Right now."

His spent cock twitched at the thought of giving her pleasure, hearing her gasp and moan for him, but she stayed his hand. "Not tonight. You had the wits beat out of you just a few hours ago, remember?"

His wits? No man worth anything gave a damn about his wits when the beautiful woman beside him in the bed remained unsatisfied. But his climax had drained all the tension from his body, leaving his limbs heavy and liquid, and his head felt as if it had been stuffed with cotton wool. "Nay, I want to…want—"

"Shhh. You're exhausted." She brushed her fingertips against his eyelids. "Sleep now, Daniel."

She drew back with one final kiss on the underside of his chin, right over the scar she liked best, the one she'd called a treasure.

When she did lie down beside him to sleep, there was nothing accidental about her hand on his chest, his head on her shoulder, her arm around his back, her forearm cradling his neck.

He'd slept with dozens of women, women who'd fallen asleep in his arms, but he'd never before fallen asleep in any of theirs.

Only hers.

Chapter Twenty-eight

Mairi woke the next morning to early morning light pressing gently against her eyelids, and the warm, heavy weight of Daniel's hand resting on the curve of her hip. His broad chest was rising and falling against her back, his deep, even breaths stirring the wisps of hair at her temple.

Disgraceful, really, that she should wake with such a giddy smile when a proper lady would have woken with a blush on her cheeks and a confession on her lips. But propriety was a cold, frigid bedmate, and thus a poor substitute for curled toes, a drowsy, contented smile, and a growling belly, and an even poorer substitute for *Daniel*, who was warm and solid, and wrapped so snugly around her his warmth heated every inch of her skin.

It was like being snuggled up against a great, woolly dog—or no, not *that*. A thick, woolly greatcoat, perhaps, or an enormous fur blanket, but an uncommonly handsome blanket, with hot, dark eyes and soft lips, and a dark trail of hair on his lower belly that tickled her palms.

She might have explored that intriguing line of dark hair again had Daniel not been so soundly asleep, and her stomach rumbling loudly enough to wake the dead.

Cautiously, she wriggled out from under his arm and slid from the bed, then nearly jumped back in again when her toes met the icy floorboards. But her belly wasn't having any of that, so she hurried into her stockings and made her way to the kitchen. She poked the fire back to a roaring blaze, then set the kettle on, sliced up the last of the bread and arranged it on a cloth in front of the hearth.

It was the same breakfast they'd had yesterday, but there was plenty of her grandmother's strawberry jam left, and really, what was more satisfying than toasted bread and hot tea on a chilly morning? Nothing, that she could think of.

Well, almost nothing.

She dropped into one of the kitchen chairs, her long toasting fork in one hand and her chin resting on the other, but the moment she wasn't distracted, doubts about last night began to creep in.

Daniel might not be quite as satisfied with last night's, er, endeavors as she was. He'd been so angry with her before he fell asleep. Waking to find him leaning over her, his big hand on her arm and his gruff whisper in her ear...

I didn't mean it, Mairi. I shouldn't have said it.

It had been...unexpected, so much so she'd thought she was having a dream.

Had he been begging her pardon for losing his temper with her? It had seemed so, but he hadn't been entirely in the wrong, and Daniel wasn't the sort of man who bothered much with regrets.

He didn't beg for anything.

But he'd wanted her hands on him last night, on his shoulders and the long, muscular length of his back, his neck and chest, the flat plane of his stomach. His muscles had twitched and quivered against her fingertips when she'd traced the grooves between his ribs. He'd groaned when she slid her hand lower, below his belly button, her fingers just grazing the top edge of the waistband of his breeches, and then, at the end, when she'd...

He'd said *please*, deep and hoarse and breathless, and then he'd...

She closed her eyes, a hot flush sweeping down her neck.

He'd given her control over his body, and had let her dictate his pleasure. All the power in that strong, muscular body had been at her fingertips, hers to command. To have a man like that, a man who bowed to no one straining for *her*, pulsing in her palm...dear God, just thinking about it made her breaths come more quickly, and she was obliged to press her thighs together to quiet the ache—

"The toast is burning, lass."

"Oh!" She leapt up from the chair and rushed to the hearth, brandishing her fork, and scooped up the bread just in time to save the toast from a fiery, smoking death. "Oh, bother! I set it too close to the flames and singed it nearly black, and we haven't any more bread, so..."

She turned to him, and trailed off with a gulp.

He was leaning one hip against the door frame, his dark hair tousled, his arms crossed over his bare chest, the crisp trail of hair on his lower belly she'd found so fascinating last night even more tempting in the daylight than it had been the night before, now she knew where it led.

His sleepy dark eyes roamed over her, a faint smile on his lips.

He didn't *look* dissatisfied. "How, ah…how long have you been standing there, watching me?"

"Not long enough." He straightened from the doorway, prowled toward her, and caught her by the waist. "I could watch you all day, lass."

She swallowed. "All…all day?"

"Aye. Especially when you're all pink and breathless like you are now." He dipped his head to bite her earlobe. "What were you thinking about that put such a blush on your cheeks?"

"Um, I was thinking about…toast. Yes, toast. Of course, toast." She held up her toasting fork as if it were incontrovertible proof of her words. "See?"

"Toast, eh?" He chuckled, taking up a wayward curl and twisting it around his finger. "Come back to bed, Mairi. I've some unfinished business with you to take care of."

"Un…unfinished business?" What sort of unfinished business? And why did she keep repeating his words back to him? For pity's sake, the man had stolen her wits. "But…the toast."

"Later." He nuzzled her neck, the rough prickle of his beard making her gasp. He took the toasting fork from her, dropped it on the kitchen table and caught her hand, urging her toward the alcove, where the big bed awaited them, the coverlet rumpled and the blanket trailing on the floor.

"Under the coverlet, lass. Your hands are cold."

She *didn't* scramble to do as he bid her, no matter how it looked.

He climbed in after her and took her into his arms, his big body so warm around her chilled one that sleep threatened to steal up on her. Her eyelids dropped, but then snapped open again in a rush of nervous anticipation when Daniel's fingers began working on the buttons at the back of her dress.

She'd still been wearing her day dress when she'd gone to sleep last night, too numb and cold to bother with her night rail. He was making quick work of the long row of buttons down her back, until she lay before him in only her chemise, the chilly air coaxing goosebumps to the bare skin of her arms and chest.

Daniel traced them with a fingertip, the slight roughness of the pad of his finger making her shiver. He was all texture—rough hair, nicks and scars amidst rare, smooth patches of skin. Even his voice was textured, hoarse as a low, pained sound broke from his lips.

"You're perfect, lass." His eyes, dark and heavy-lidded, met hers. "No scars."

"I like your scars." They told the story of his past in the same way a book told a story. Touching him was like reading it.

One corner of his mouth twitched. "Daft lass."

She shook her head, her gaze holding his heated one as his wide, calloused palms swept over the curves of her shoulders. "So pale and pretty." He let his hand rest against her throat, smiling when he felt her pulse rush into a frenzy under his touch. "Is your heart pounding, Mairi?"

"Yes." It was thrashing like a wild thing in her chest, and she couldn't take her eyes off him.

He slid one thick finger down the center of her chest between her breasts, dark eyes gleaming when her nipples peaked for him. He brushed his thumb over one of the taut points, his lips parting when a soft gasp escaped her. "Aye, that's good, lass. I want to hear you," he murmured, leaning over, his hot breath a wicked tease before he took the straining peak into his mouth.

And oh, dear *God*, she'd never felt anything like it before, the slow, delicious drag of his wet tongue over the rosy tip, the rasp of his beard turning the pale skin of her chest a dusky pink, his fingers petting and stroking and pinching gently before he soothed the delicious sting with his lips again.

The odd, drawing sensation in her belly grew tighter with every maddening stroke of his teasing tongue, her nipples high and taut against the thin muslin of her shift, until her back was arching off the bed and damp heat flooded between her legs.

"Daniel." She twisted her fingers in his hair, tugging at him to bring his lips up to hers.

"Nay, Mairi." He caught her wrists and lowered them to the bed, flat against either side of the pillow. "Keep still, and let me take care of you."

Take care of her *how*, or…did it really matter, when she was gripping the edges of the pillow under her as he kissed his way over her throat, then between her breasts, then lower, his mouth a trail of fire across her torso and ribs to her lower belly, one hand fisting the skirt of her shift and dragging it up, higher, and higher still…

Oh. Oh, God in heaven, he was kissing the insides of her thighs, the scratch of his bristled cheeks over that untouched skin the most delicious thing she'd ever felt. Heat gathered in the secret hollow between her legs, making her writhe and twist as sparks shot through her—

"Such a good lass, Mairi, dripping honey for me…"

He surged against her, his hand on her ankle moving one of her legs over his shoulder to make room for his broad back, and then his mouth was *there*, his soft hair brushing the inside of her thighs and his wicked tongue teasing over the tiny knot at her center where she was empty and aching, slow, light strokes with the tip of his tongue.

"Daniel, I…oh, God." She grasped handfuls of his hair to…what? Push him away, because what was she meant to do with such a dark, consuming pleasure as this? But no, she was dragging him closer, holding him to her with her fingers twisted in his hair, her hips rising to meet his wicked tongue. "Don't…don't stop—"

He pinned her hips to the bed with a low growl. "Nay, not until you come hard for me."

His tongue became more demanding then, lashing at her with rough, greedy strokes until she was panting and squirming, her heel digging into his muscular back, and the noises she was making! Gasps and moans and sharp, desperate little whimpers, noises she'd never made in her life before, interspersed with husky pleas for…for…oh, she didn't know what, but Daniel did—he did, because he was giving it to her with every flick of his tongue over her swollen flesh, every nip and playful bite, until she was babbling nonsense, *please,* and his name, *Daniel,* over and over again, and perhaps she was a little embarrassed at first at her utter loss of control, until she realized her every gasp and whimper was spurring him on, his lips and tongue devouring her until…

Pleasure, hot and sharp and sweet rolled over her, her legs shaking with it, her lips opening in a silent cry. Daniel licked madly at her, his hips rocking against the bed. The tight knot of need between her legs unfurled, drawing her body into a rigid arch, her back bowing, the pleasure holding her in a tight grip until it receded in gentle waves, slower than it had come, and she sagged against the bed, stunned, her skin sheened with sweat.

Daniel lay there panting, his head resting on her thigh until he regained his breath, and lifted his head. "All right there, lass?"

She was staring at the ceiling in a daze, still twitching with tiny aftershocks, her ragged breaths sawing in and out of her chest, her mind an utter blank until Daniel kissed her thigh, calling her back to herself, and she reached down and sank her fingers into his hair. "I didn't know you could…I never imagined a man might…I've never heard of such a thing."

He chuckled and nuzzled his face against her thigh. "Is that a complaint, Mairi?"

With a great effort she lifted her head from the pillow, and found him looking up at her, and her breath caught at the wicked twinkle in his dark eyes. "I nearly pulled every hair from your head, so…no, that's not a complaint."

"Ah, that's good, lass." He dropped a kiss on one of her knees, then the other. "Because I like making you squeal and squirm."

"That was…"

What? What did a lady say to a gentleman after *that*?

"Aye?" Daniel gave her knee a playful pinch. "You were saying, lass?"

"That was…much better than toasted bread."

There was a beat of silence, then Daniel threw back his head and roared with laughter—loud, open-mouthed, lose-your-breath laughter so infectious she couldn't hear it without bursting into laughter herself.

She let her head fall back against the pillow, and there it was, the blush she'd scoffed at when she woke this morning, the warm flush of it stealing over her chest and burning her cheeks. "What? I don't see what's so amusing about it. Hush, you wicked man."

"Are you hungry, lass? I thought I heard your belly growling when I was—"

"You most certainly did not," she sniffed, giving his hair a tug. He hadn't heard a blessed thing, if only because her body had been so utterly absorbed by his attention it couldn't have produced the faintest gurgle, much less a growl. "I wouldn't permit such a—"

She broke off with a yelp when he grabbed her hips and with a quick jerk tugged her down the bed and underneath him and braced himself over her. "I'm a wee bit feeble from hunger, myself, but someone burnt the bread this morning, and I don't fancy charred toast for breakfast."

"It's not charred, only a little singed, and you seem sturdy enough to me." Quite sturdy, judging by the arm muscles flexing under her hands. "But we can run over to the Sheep's Hide, if you'd rather. Angus does a nice meal for…"

The Sheep's Hide. How could she have forgotten what Fergus had told her about Lord Rutherford's mourning ring at the Sheep's Hide last night? If that ring was in this cottage, there was only one place it could be where it wouldn't have been found by the magistrate and his men—

"Mairi? What are you thinking about? You've got a strange look on your—"

"Fergus McClellan. Last night he—"

"Fergus McClellan!" Daniel's brows lowered, and lowered, and lowered some more until he wore a scowl darker than midnight itself. "You're lying there thinking of Fergus bloody McClellan right after we—"

"No! No, that's not what I meant. We have to move the bed." She pushed at his shoulder, squirming to get free. "I need to get under the bed and see if—"

"See if Fergus McClellan is under there? He'd better bloody not be, or he'll be damn sorry."

"Never mind Fergus." Goodness, men were foolish creatures. "Come, help me move the bed."

Chapter Twenty-nine

"I don't believe it." Mairi was sitting on the edge of the bed, staring at the tiny ring in her palm, stunned. "Until I found it at the bottom of the box, I didn't believe Lillias actually had it."

Except it hadn't been *just* hidden at the bottom of the box, but in the *false* bottom of the box, *under* a loose floorboard, *under* the bed. They'd only discovered the false bottom was there because they noticed a rattling sound when they'd lifted the heavy box out from under the bed.

Stolen or not, Lillias Cameron had gone to great lengths to hide the ring.

"Do you think…" Mairi swallowed. "Could she have taken it from Lord Rutherford, just as he claimed? Not *stolen* it," she added hastily. "Lillias would never steal anything, but she might have been keeping it for someone."

"It won't matter to the court how she came by it." The law didn't give a damn how someone came to have stolen property hidden under their beds. That Lillias had it at all would be enough to see her hung for theft. "Let me see it, lass."

It was gold, with tiny black stones surrounding a delicate sheet of crystal, a miniature painting of a man's brown eye underneath it, his eyebrow a dark slash above it. "Do you recognize the man?"

"It's difficult to tell much from a single eye, but it doesn't look like any of the Rutherford men. They're all fair-haired, with pale blue eyes."

He held the ring up, studying the black jewels as they caught the light. "What are these stones? Onyx?"

"Jet, I think. It's a dainty thing, likely made for a lady—a petite one, judging by the ring's size. It must have belonged to one of the viscountesses."

"There's no proof it belongs to the Gordon family at all, aside from Viscount Rutherford's say so. There's no crest." He turned it sideways to get a better look at it. A pattern of myrtle was carved onto the outer side of the hand, the gold on the inside worn smooth by a few generations of fingers.

But not entirely smooth. Something was inscribed on it.

He strode to the window and held the ring up to the light. On the inside of the band were a few words in tiny, ornate script, so worn down it was nearly invisible, but it looked like...

Ne Obliviscaris. Do not forget.

The pattern of myrtle carved on the band, and the motto...

No. It couldn't be—

"Daniel?" Mairi leapt up from the bed and hurried across the room to him. "My God, what is it? You look as if you've just seen a ghost."

It was the *same*, his tattoo and his father's drawings carved into the band of a ring that was meant to have come from Viscount Rutherford's house.

No amount of staring at it would make it not so.

"Daniel." Mairi's voice was sharper now, and she gripped his arm with tight fingers. "What's the matter? You're scaring me."

"There's an inscription on the band." He took her hand and dropped the ring into her palm, desperate to get rid of the cursed thing. "Read it."

She stared at him for a moment longer, brow furrowed, but she took the ring and tilted it so the faint inscription would catch the light.

He saw the precise moment when she realized what it said, because that beautiful flush he'd put in her cheeks earlier—a lifetime ago—fled.

"*Ne Obliviscaris.*" Her entire body went still. Her mouth opened, then closed.

It *was* the same, then. He hadn't been imagining it.

"I don't...none of this makes any sense, Daniel!" Mairi closed the ring in her fist, as if she'd crush it in her hand if she could. "Lillias didn't steal this ring—she's no thief—but she *does* have it, and however she came upon it, she made certain no one would ever find it. Lord Rutherford claims the ring belongs to his family, but the motto carved into the band is *your* family's motto, not the Rutherfords."

"Nay, lass. I don't come from a noble family. I told you that. The Brixtons don't have a family motto." But what of the Adair family? If he truly was an Adair, which was beginning to look more likely with every day that passed, then that meant his father was Ian *Adair*, not Ian Brixton. Was that why he'd always been so obsessed with the motto? Because it did belong to his family, after all? Was it part of a lost past?

But there were dozens of different questions that needed answering before that one, starting with, *who the devil was he*? Because he didn't have any bloody idea anymore, and the more this story twisted and wound around itself like a serpent, the less certain he was that he wanted to know.

It would be so much easier to just return to London—to forget Mairi and Lillias Cameron, to forget Daniel Adair and go back to being Daniel Brixton, son of Aileen and Ian Brixton.

Daniel Brixton might be a blackguard, a villain with deadly fists and a pearl-handled dagger hidden in his boot, but he *knew* how to be Daniel Brixton.

But he wasn't blackguard enough, because he couldn't stomach leaving Lillias Cameron to swing for a crime she hadn't committed. Leaving now meant abandoning Lillias, and letting Murdoch escape justice for whatever it was he'd done—something, though Daniel couldn't be sure what—and it meant leaving Hamish's murder unsolved, and unavenged.

It meant leaving Mairi.

The Mairi Cameron he was only just starting to remember had been a wild little lass with fiery, tangled curls, torn pinafores, and knees skinned bloody from chasing after the village lads, determined never to be left behind. Nothing like the lady he'd found that first night in Howe Court, with her smooth, milky skin and refined voice, her long, graceful fingers and delicate curves.

But she'd always been fierce, had always held her own, whether she was facing off with Elsbeth Fraser, or Lady Amanda Clifford, or Fergus McClellan, or Daniel himself. The lass had smashed a chamber pot over the head of a villain three times her size, for God's sake, and not a single strand of that red hair had been out of place.

She wasn't the sort of lady a man left behind.

But this bloody business was as tangled a mess as he'd ever come across, and he'd come across a few in his years in London. It all came down to whatever evil had unfolded at the viscount's fishing pond, but the truth of what had happened that day was trapped inside his head.

He took the ring from Mairi, returned it to the false bottom of the box, and replaced the box under the loose floorboard.

"Daniel?"

"Take me to Viscount Rutherford's fishing pond, Mairi. I want to see it for myself."

* * * *

"What if one of Lord Rutherford's servants sees us poking about his property?"

"Then they can ask us to leave." They could bloody well try to, but they'd have a bigger job frightening him off now than they had when he was an eight-year-old boy. "What are you doing back there, lass? Hiding in the bushes?"

Mairi had paused behind a thick patch of brambles and was crouched down, peeking through the tangled branches. "I used to hide back here and spy on you and Hamish when you sneaked off to the pond without me. I'd climb out the bedroom window there." She waved toward the cottage at the other end of the path. "I'd creep through the strawberry patch, and hide right here."

Daniel couldn't help but smile at the thought of wee, red-haired Mairi wriggling through the window and creeping through the brambles. "Out the window, eh? What did your grandmother think of that?"

"She never knew, or at least, she never told me she did, though I learned when I was older that I didn't have as many secrets from her as I imagined I did." She smiled, thinking of it. "My grandmother understands children. She always knew how best to manage us."

They were both quiet after that, battling through the brambles until they came out on a dirt pathway on the other side. He stared down at his heavy boots slapping against the frozen ground as they made their way toward the pond, fragments of a now familiar memory drifting through his head.

Bare feet pounding over a packed mud pathway...

The dirt was frozen now, but during the summer the mud would be soft until it was flattened by dozens of footsteps. "There's a forest nearby?" He recalled trees swaying in a breeze, a canopy of them, the branches thick overhead.

"Yes, just there, on the other side." Mairi pointed toward a stand of trees, thin and spaced widely apart close to the pond, but becoming thicker as it stretched on.

Cool air, filtered sunlight, the mud between his toes softer under the trees...

A murky, dark-green smell drifted toward them as they got closer to the edge of the pond, the stench of it twisting through his head until a pang of nausea gripped his throat. That smell...he remembered it, the stench of fish and rot, the greenish brown water of the pond, the bank choked with dead leaves and weeds, bits of debris that fell from the trees above resting on the sluggish surface of the water.

"The pathway leads around the pond and through the woods to a dirt road on the other side, but the boys from the village kept near the pond..."

Mairi was still talking, describing how they'd shamelessly poached the viscount's fish, despite repeated warnings and whippings at the hands of Murdoch, who used to chase them, but her voice receded into the depths of his consciousness as other sounds pushed forward, splashes of water, boys laughing and shouting…

Boys shouting.

One boy shouting, screaming—

Come on, Hamish. Run.

Slap-thump, slap-thump, but it's not fast enough, the man is drawing closer with every step, his hand stretching out, reaching, snatching Hamish by the collar and lifting him, shaking him until Hamish goes limp, his feet dangling—

It's too late for Daniel's scream now. Hamish is already gone, dead for years…

He's come here for the face. It's the face he wants, the face of the man who snapped Hamish's neck and tossed his poor, broken body into the water with one mighty heave, then stood and watched as Hamish went down, down, down to the bottom, the mud and rotted leaves filling his nose, his mouth—

Ye go poaching on Lord Rutherford's land again and I'll redden your arse tonight. Ye ken, lad?

Was that why it had happened? Had Hamish drowned because they'd taken a few fish from a viscount's pond?

His palms were like ice, his shins resting on something hard. Mairi had slid an arm around him and…was she helping him to his feet? Had he fallen to his knees? Her hand was on his back and her arm was supporting him, holding him upright and taking him back down the pathway, the brambles pricking his arms and back, one step at a time until the door of Lillias's neat little cottage was in front of him.

Mairi was saying something to him as she led him through the kitchen to the bed beyond. Her words didn't matter, only her soft, soothing voice and her gentle touch on his shoulders as she eased him down onto the edge of the bed.

He pressed his fingertips to his eyes, but the tears were already coursing down his cheeks. Daniel Brixton, the scourge of London's criminal underworld, the man who feared nothing and loved no one, was crying for a boy who'd been gone twenty-four years, a boy he still only remembered in fragments, hazy and broken. A boy who'd been his best friend.

The boy he'd left behind.

His grief was for Hamish, but it was also for himself, for the child he'd been, the years he'd lost, the life he might have had, if things had been different.

He leaned into Mairi, pressed his face into her belly, his arms going around her waist. His deep, shuddering breaths were hurting his lungs, making them ache, but she was holding him tightly, holding him together, her warm hands cupping his cheeks and raising his face to hers.

Mairi understood silence. She didn't try talk to him then, didn't speak at all, but she caught his tears until they dried and he stopped shaking, then her soft fingers drifted over his face, his cheekbones and jaw, brushing his eyebrows, stroking his temples, her gentle touch smoothing away the pain until the pounding in his head eased, and he fell limp against the coverlet, more exhausted from the struggle with himself than he'd ever been in a fight with any other villain.

She kissed him then, his eyelids, his cheeks, his tight jaw softening under her caress, her lips cool against his burning skin, and he...

He let her. He lay motionless beneath her, and accepted everything she offered him. When she kissed his lips and his cock stirred, he didn't grasp her hips, or tumble her to her back. He didn't do anything but open his lips under hers and let her toy with him, tease him breathless, have her way with his mouth.

He'd never much liked being touched, but he wanted *her* to touch him, had wanted it from the first. He didn't understand tenderness, had never known how to give or receive it, but he let *her* stroke him softly, gently, her curls tickling his fingers when he brushed her hair back from her face so he could see her eyes, see into the endless blue of them.

And wait for her to cast her spells on him, lure him to the brink of desire, and take him over the edge.

Chapter Thirty

Daniel's back was soaked with sweat, his shirt clinging to him, the damp linen resisting when Mairi drew it over his head, as if she were peeling away a layer of him, a second skin. His ragged, heaving breaths were hot against her neck, and his hands in her hair were shaking.

She stroked the dark waves back from his face, brushed her fingertips across his eyelids, his lips, the clenched edge of his jaw. To everyone else his face was a forbidding one, his hard, muscular body intimidating, but she'd seen him bleed, *made* him bleed. He was strongest in the places no one else could see.

His heart. It was strong enough to break.

She cupped his chin in her hand and raised his face to hers, but she didn't say anything. What could she say, in the face of such grief? She'd had years to wrestle with that grief, to live with it, and she'd never had to watch as Hamish was broken in two, to see every moment of his murder unfold before her eyes, as Daniel had.

There was no talking away such a thing, no words that were a match for it. There was nothing to do but be there as he passed through it, and promise to be there still when he came out the other side.

But she could touch him, feel the pulse in his neck beat strong and steady against her palm, her other hand against his cheek, her thumb tracing the line of his lips. "Will you come to the bed with me?"

He nodded once.

It was dim in the bedroom, dark clouds having closed in on the sky as the afternoon waned, chasing the sun away, but she drew the draperies over the window still, shutting out what little light there was.

Daniel had dropped onto the edge of the bed when they'd entered, and when she turned from the window, she found him still sitting there, his hands balanced on his thighs, palms up, a lost expression on his face, as if he wasn't sure what he was meant to do with his limbs.

She crossed to him, knelt at his feet, and took one of his heavy, booted feet onto her lap.

"No, Mairi." He tried to draw away, shaking his head. "You don't need to—"

"Hush." She removed his boots one by one, lined them up neatly by the side of the bed, then rose to her feet. "Come here."

He did as she commanded, rising to his feet, and she slid her fingers under the waistband of his breeches, unbuttoning his falls so the fabric hung low around his hips, her knuckles skimming his muscled torso. His skin was still damp when she took him into her arms, but not so chilled as it had been, and he was still shaking, but not with cold or shock any longer.

She swept her hands over his skin—gently, because no one seemed to ever be gentle with this man—learning every mark, every scar, just as she'd done the night before, but with a deeper understanding of what lay beneath the layered muscle and hard bone.

The wounds that never healed, the hurts she couldn't see.

His collarbones were long and heavy, but sleek still, elegant even, for all that he'd scoff at that if she said it aloud. She traced them with her fingers, stroked the thick, strong column of his throat, and sifted her fingertips through the spattering of dark hair over his chest before moving to his waist, murmuring to him until his body eased, and he gave himself over to her, his shoulders dropping, his breaths slowing and deepening, his hands spanning her waist, and his forehead resting against her shoulder.

The hair at the back of his neck was so soft, one of the only soft things about him, like a secret, a treasure hidden there just for her, like the scar under his chin. She let her fingers drift through it, the thick strands curling against her knuckles.

When he'd all but melted in her hands, she reached behind him and pulled back the coverlet. "Lie down."

He lay still, watching her face as she drew the coverlet up to his neck, but when she began to draw away, he caught her wrist. "Don't go, Mairi."

"Shh. I won't go far, just to the kitchen to build up the fire. You need to rest, Daniel."

"Nay, not yet. I don't…" he lowered his eyes, his long, dark lashes brushing his cheeks. "I don't want to have another dream right now. Come lay down beside me."

She couldn't refuse him. Not this. Perhaps not anything, anymore.

He opened his arms to her when she slid under the coverlet, and she went to him without question, letting his warmth wrap around her, feeling his heartbeat thud against her palm. The bed would be so cold, once he'd returned to London. How would she ever fall asleep again?

She didn't sleep now, but lay quietly against him. She'd had no carnal intent in persuading him into the bed, but it was inevitable that they'd gradually awaken to the desire that seemed always to burn between them, their skin heating where their bodies touched, their shared breaths coming more quickly.

When he touched his fingers to her chin and brought his mouth down on hers, it felt like the most natural thing in the world. He kissed her, long, slow, drugging kisses that made her belly clench and her head swim, his chest vibrating in a quiet moan underneath her hand when she opened eagerly for him.

"You taste so sweet, lass." He slid on top of her, his breeches dragging over her thighs, the long expanse of his chest rubbing against hers, making her nipples tighten, his hair-roughened torso and the triangle of his hips sliding between her legs. He buried his face in her hair and inhaled deeply. "Scottish heather."

She pressed her fingertips between his shoulder blades, then dragged them down his spine to his backside, her hands sliding under his breeches to caress the warm skin, smiling when her suggestive touch earned her a husky groan from him. "You may as well take them all the way off."

He pressed another lingering kiss to her lips, then pulled back to search her face. "No telling what could happen if they come off, lass."

"I think we both know what will happen." She rose onto her elbows and pressed a deep kiss to his lips that made his breath catch. "I can't be certain, never having had a lover, but I do believe it's easier with your breeches *off*."

His eyes darkened, black as midnight. "Mairi—"

"Shhh." She pressed her fingers to his lips to hush him. "If you don't want me, say so, but if you're hesitating because you think you're saving me from myself, or from the ire of some mythical future husband, then don't. I've never needed saving, Daniel, and I don't need it now."

"Not want you? Daft lass." He shifted his hips, nudging between her legs. "Does it feel like I don't want you?"

She curled her legs around his hips and pressed harder against him, the heels of her bare feet resting on the back of his thighs. "Then why are you wasting time?"

He held her gaze, his dark eyes burning as he reached under the coverlet and fumbled with his breeches, sliding them down his legs and shoving them off the end of the bed with a determined kick.

Then he settled himself back between her thighs, bare from head to toe.

Just the way she wanted him. The way she'd wanted him ever since their kiss in Mrs. Luddington's innyard in Newcastle. Had that only been a week ago? Everything had changed so much since then she hardly knew herself anymore.

A long, thick finger slid down her cheek, pausing to stroke the corner of her lip before dropping to the neckline of her day dress, the tip tracing the line of the bodice. "Will you have this off, then?"

That teasing finger kept brushing the edges of her bodice, but his tone was oddly formal, and a little hesitant. "Do I detect a note of shyness in your voice, Daniel? Do you think I'd refuse you?"

"Nay, not shy. But I've never asked for..." He waved his hand toward her bodice. "I've never asked for that before."

"What, you mean you usually just fall upon your lovers like a wild animal, and tear their clothing off?" Goodness, what would *that* be like?

"Nay, usually I just hike up...ah, that is, I leave their clothes where they are."

Hike up their skirts. That's what he'd been going to say. He hiked up their skirts, opened his breeches, and did the thing quickly, without any fuss, and likely without a single word exchanged. There was no reason that should make her feel sad, but it did. "Then why start with me?"

He plucked up one of her curls from the pillow and wound it around his finger. "Because you're not them, Mairi."

The heat in his eyes, the slight quiver in his voice—dear God, he was making her wish for things that could never be. She twined her arms around his neck and gathered him close, murmuring, "Take off my clothing, Daniel."

He did, slowly, revealing her skin one inch at a time as if she were a gift he was unwrapping, his throat moving in a rough swallow when she was bare beneath him. "Do all Scottish lasses have such pretty, pale skin?" He cupped her breast in his hand, teasing her nipple with the tip of his thumb.

She caught her breath at the caress. "The redheads, maybe."

"Hmmm." He toyed with her nipple, stroking, then pinching gently, watching as it reddened under his touch, rose high and stiff, begging for more. It was such a light caress, all the more maddening for his restraint.

But his restraint wouldn't last long—she knew that, yet she was still surprised when his hot, demanding mouth closed around the eager nub, his hand slipping between her legs at the same time, his big fingers gently caressing her damp flesh.

She parted her thighs on a gasp. "Daniel…"

"That's it, lass, open for me." He dropped a kiss on the quivering skin of her belly, his fingers still probing, gentle but insistent, petting the hungry little nub between her thighs until it emerged from the protective folds of her body in response to his teasing caress.

All the most sensitive parts of her were rising for him, seeking his touch.

It was so lovely, so easy and natural the way he stroked her, pausing to press a kiss behind her knee, another to the curve of her shoulder, a third between her breasts, not rushed or hurried, as she'd always thought a man would be in the throes of his passion, but slow, lingering kisses, as if he had all the time in the world.

But it couldn't go on this way, could it? Not when he was so thick and hard against her thigh, nudging into her slick folds. She'd seen him, touched him, and, well…it was only natural to be nervous, wasn't it, when such a large appendage was meant to fit into such a very small space? The laws of physics would seem to indicate—

He paused, his fingers stilling. "You've gone tense, Mairi. What are you thinking about?"

"Um…physics?"

"Physics?" Daniel pulled back to search her face, a grin pulling at the corners of his lips. "I must be doing something wrong, then."

"No! No, it's just that I don't see how…" Fear, or arousal, or perhaps a little of both, made her sink her fingernails into his back, hold onto him. "I mean, you're…and I'm…" She gestured vaguely at the lower halves of their bodies, heat climbing into her cheeks.

She wouldn't have blamed him if he'd laughed at her then, but his dark eyes were serious as he gazed down at her. "We'll fit together just fine, but you will feel some pain. It will be quick, but you'll notice it." He touched her chin, raising her face to his. "Do you trust me to take care of you, Mairi?"

She did. He'd been taking care of her since that first night in Howe Court, when he'd thought her a liar. Even then he'd still come back for her, and had still taken care of her, because that was who he was. A protector, a guardian, a man with the tenderest of hearts under that gruff voice, that severe face. "Yes."

She *did* trust him, yet she couldn't help tensing just a little when his fingers took up their wicked teasing again, one sinking into her, then another when she lifted her hips toward him, his thumb circling her core in quick, light strokes, then slow, deep, lazy caresses without rhyme or pattern, but seemingly as the whim struck him, so she never knew when or how he'd touch her next.

It drove her mad, especially when he paused his torment for long moments to kiss her and suckle her nipples, but left her core empty and aching, making her writhe and whimper for him.

But he didn't push inside her. He played and teased and rubbed until her thighs were shaking, and in between harsh, panting breaths he was urging her on, dark, filthy whispers in her ear until she could feel the throbbing ache between her legs everywhere—her temples, her fingertips, her tingling nipples, and with every beat of her heart in her chest.

"So beautiful, lass...*yes*, take your pleasure, come for me, Mairi."

What could she do then but obey? A soft, breathless cry tore from her throat, her legs tensing as he drove her over the edge with one final flick of his fingertip.

"Good girl," he crooned as she gasped and moaned for him, her back arching with the astonishing pleasure he'd coaxed from her body, dizzying waves of it that seemed to go on forever until at last it released her and she lay panting against the bed, the insides of her thighs slick with her own arousal.

Then, while she was still catching her breath, he entered her, a slow, gentle glide at first, then a hard, quick thrust, the stinging pain snatching her breath away a second time, but her body knew what to do, and little by little it shifted to accommodate him, softening and melting around his hard length until she thrust upward, her hips nudging his to urge him into motion.

Only then did he move, careful, shallow thrusts, the impossible size and heat of him unbearable and necessary at once, both pleasure and the sweetest kind of torment until she could no longer distinguish between the two, and her body grew greedier with his every thrust. She wrapped her legs around his waist, entreaties falling from her lips, his name—always his name—and *please, please, please...*

"Ah, God, so good, Mairi." His lips found hers, his kiss rougher now, desperate, his hips pumping harder, low, broken groans rumbling in his chest. "Want you to come for me again."

Could she? It didn't seem possible, as spent as her body was, but he was bringing her closer to the peak with every furious snap of his hips, the hot, hard length of him demanding her release, her surrender, until in the next breath she was screaming with it, her core tightening around him, taking him deep and driving him to his own release, his breath heavy against her neck, a hoarse groan on his lips.

She was still trembling when he kissed her, long and slow and sweet, so sweet. Her body was still twitching with aftershocks when he gathered her into his arms, his chest heaving, damp against her back, her limbs still heavy when he drew the coverlet over them, and whispered, drowsy and deep in her ear, "Sleep."

Chapter Thirty-one

Daniel is quicker than lightning, the fastest runner in Coldstream. Maybe the fastest in the county, but in the end, it won't matter, because nothing—not speed or fury, friendship or love—will be enough to stop what's going to happen.

He'll fly over the mud-packed pathway at his feet, and Hamish will try desperately to keep up, but his wheezing breaths will become heavy, and his footsteps will slow. No matter what Daniel does, it won't be good enough to keep Hamish alive.

Hamish's neck will break, then the dark green water will close over his head, and Daniel's best friend, his brother, will never emerge from that pond again.

But this time, the tree he darts behind is smaller, the trunk narrower, his hands against the rough bark bigger than they've ever been before, his fingers longer and thicker.

This time, he's not a boy anymore.

He's a man with a pearl-handled knife in one hand, the blade gleaming, deadly, his other hand sliding down, fingers closing around the smooth, cold grip of the second knife he's stashed inside his boot.

Slap-thump, slap-thump.

Soon. Any moment now. His stomach tightens, his legs tense to spring.

When the man reaches for Hamish's neck and Hamish screams, Daniel is ready for it.

But when he leaps out from behind the tree, he can't see the man's face. He sees Hamish's mouth twisted in terror, he sees the bulging veins in the man's grasping hand and the edge of a blue coat sleeve at his wrist, but when he looks up where the man's face should be, searching for the milky white eye, there's nothing but a pale blur...

Even before he was fully awake, he was already reaching for Mairi, searching for her sleepy body in the darkness, her warmth the only thing that could chase away the deep chill of his skin, but there was only a cold, empty expanse of bed beside him.

She wasn't there.

"Mairi?" He rose up onto his elbow and peered into the darkness. "Mairi?"

There was no answer. She wasn't in the bed, or the bedchamber.

It was the middle of the night, darker than a rookeries alleyway, the cold so bitter the edge of it could slice flesh into ribbons, the skeletal tree branches thrashing in the biting wind, and she was *not there*.

He slid from the bed and padded into the kitchen, choking back the first thread of fear climbing up from his belly, creeping into his throat. The kettle sat where Mairi had left it earlier, in its usual place on the stove. The braided rugs were spread neatly over the worn patches in the floorboards, and the blue and white pitcher was in the center of the kitchen table.

All was as it should be, but for one thing.

Mairi was gone.

The panic he'd been holding back surged into his chest then, twisted around his lungs, a wave of dread so dark and consuming he staggered back to the empty bedchamber.

Boots, he needed his boots...

But his hands were shaking, his fingers clumsy as he fumbled with them, tugging and cursing, unable to get them on his feet fast enough, the bloody things. He got one foot into one of them, the other halfway there, one arm in the sleeve of his coat, the other sleeve flapping uselessly at his side when he flew through the kitchen door and into the yard beyond, his breath stuttering in his lungs.

The moonlight was weak tonight, half-hidden behind a thick bank of clouds. If it weren't for her night rail, he might not have seen her at all, but a flash of white in the darkness and the flutter of the hem of the skirt flapping around her ankles in the wind caught his eye.

She was wearing her boots. It was no accident she was out here, then.

His relief was short-lived, because right on its heels was fury, the hot, sharp sort of fury born of panic, flaying his insides raw. "Mairi! What are you doing out here?"

She turned at the crunch of his boots across the frosty grass, but instead of answering, she held a finger to her lips. "Quiet!"

Did she just *hush* him?

He stalked toward her, tearing off his coat as he went. "I asked you a question, lass. What the devil do you think you're *doing*, wandering about out here alone? Why aren't you in our…your bed?"

"Shhh!" Mairi grabbed his arm, squeezing in warning. "There's someone out there."

"What did you think you were going to do about it?" He threw his coat over her shoulders, pulled it tight around her, and in a moment of truly miraculous self-restraint, managed *not* to scoop her up, toss her over his shoulder, and take her straight back to bed. "Chase after them in your nightdress? Daft lass."

"I do wish you'd stop saying that. I'm not daft. I'm telling you, I saw a shadow pass close by the window, and I heard the scuff of boots as well."

"Did you see anyone?" He wrapped his arms around her from behind to warm her and shield her from the worst of the wind, and peered over her shoulder, but aside from the faint glow of white frost on the ground, he saw only an uninterrupted band of darkness.

There wasn't a damned thing there.

"Well, no. Not this time, but I'm sure I—"

"*This* time? Christ, lass, you mean this isn't the first time you've seen someone sneaking about the cottage?"

"Er, well, I wouldn't say—"

"The *truth*, Mairi."

She turned to glance at him, her teeth worrying her lower lip. "Oh, all right, then. I thought I saw someone the first night we arrived in Coldstream, but I only caught the briefest glimpse of a shadow, and then it was gone. I didn't mention it because I thought I'd imagined it."

"Some blackguard was creeping about outside the cottage, peering in through the windows, and you never thought to tell me about it?" Christ, even the idea of someone that close to her without him being aware of it made his teeth grind together. "Damn it, Mairi, it isn't safe for you to keep such things to yourself. It could have been anyone."

"It could have been, yes, but whoever it was must have a reason for keeping track of our whereabouts. I can't think of anyone who would, aside from the man who—"

"The man who hurt Hamish! Even more reason to tell me!" A villain who could break an eight-year-old boy's neck would do the same to Mairi without a moment's hesitation. Whoever had been peeking through the windows wasn't just any blackguard, but a brutal murderer.

"I had another dream tonight. Hamish, again." Hamish, so small, running as fast as he could, but not fast enough to save his neck.

"Did you..." Mairi swallowed. "What did you see?"

"Hamish's murder." So calm, his voice, and so cold, as if he didn't give a damn about any of it, but his stomach was twisting into knots, and Hamish's pale face was so real still, as if the nightmare of his murder had been carved into Daniel's skull.

Mairi wasn't fooled by his apparent indifference. She slipped her fingers into his hand and squeezed. "Tell me."

"I saw the murderer grab Hamish, and I saw his coat sleeve, but nothing that tells us anything we didn't already know." Useless bloody dream. Now, when he wanted to make use of the dreams, they refused to tell him anything.

"Dear God." Mairi sucked in a quick breath, her fingers tightening around his arm. "It's Murdoch."

"Nay, I told you, lass, I couldn't see the man's face—"

"No, Daniel. Look." She pointed toward a dark figure hovering beside one of the bare-branched trees, nearly indistinguishable from the surrounding shadows. "There's a man, just there, and I thought I saw..."

"Saw what?" He didn't see anything, but he shifted so his body was between Mairi and the tree.

"I can't be certain, but it looked as if he had a patch covering one of his eyes."

His first instinct was to go after the man, grab him by the throat and squeeze until something useful spilled out of him, but if it was Murdoch, he wasn't moving—just standing beside that skeletal tree, his face turned toward them.

Strange, that, but if Murdoch could wait, then so could Daniel. "Go on inside, lass." He gave Mairi a little push toward the cottage. "I'll deal with him."

"You're mad. I'm not going anywhere."

He opened his mouth to argue with her, then snapped it closed again without saying a word. Arguing with Mairi hadn't ever gotten him what he wanted before, and there was no reason to think it would now. He'd do better to keep his wits about him, and wait for...what?

Was the dark shadow beside the tree Murdoch? If it was, the man was taking a damned foolish risk coming here and letting himself be seen after Daniel had nearly taken his head off at the Sheep's Hide. He must have known Daniel wouldn't hesitate to do the same again. So, why had he come, and what was he waiting for?

The three of them stood frozen, gazes pinned on each other until the thick cloud that had been blocking the moon started to shift, the wind blowing it slowly east, the white glow intensifying bit by bit until the pale light fell across the tree, then the man's face, and his features settled into the familiar pattern Daniel had seen before.

Once. Not in his dream, but the other night, at the Sheep's Hide.

It was Murdoch—no mistaking that black-clad figure with the patch over his eye.

Mairi caught her breath. "What is he doing? What does he want?"

"I don't know." Daniel didn't take his eyes off Murdoch, who also remained where he was, watching them. "But if he had any sense, he'd go while he still has the chance."

But Murdoch didn't go. He stood there for long, silent moments until another bank of clouds shifted closer to the moon, and the light began to fade.

Then he turned, very deliberately, and made his way toward the back of the cottage and through the garden. He paused at the head of the pathway that led through the brambles and onto Lord Rutherford's land—the same pathway that Daniel and Mairi had followed earlier today—then stopped and turned back to face them.

And once again, he waited.

"I think he wants us to follow him, Daniel." Mairi's voice was hushed, her cheeks pale in the ghostly light.

Aye, that was it. He'd come here on purpose to catch their attention and get them to follow him. A challenge, or a trap? It could be either, or both, but it made no difference.

Daniel was going to follow him, no matter which it was.

"Go back inside, lass, and get warm." He turned her back towards the cottage with firm hands on her shoulders. "I won't be long."

Mairi turned back around and planted her hands on her hips, her cheeks reddening with temper. "What have I ever done, Daniel Brixton, to make you think you can order me about?"

"If you think I'm going to let you follow that blackguard into a trap—"

"But you'll follow him into it yourself, alone?"

"I can look after my—"

"Look after yourself? Is that what you were about to say? For your sake, Daniel, I hope you don't mean to imply I can't do the same."

Christ, he was making a bloody mess of this, wasn't he? "I know you can, lass. I figured that out the night we met, when you knocked me flat on my arse."

She raised an eyebrow. "Well, then?"

He didn't know how to tell her this had nothing to do with thinking she couldn't take care of herself, and everything to do with fear.

His fear, a deep, dark, endless chasm of it.

That something would happen to her. That she'd be hurt in some way, just as Hamish had been. That he'd lose her, and would never be able to get over it, or forgive himself for it. That in the few short weeks he'd come to know her again, she'd somehow wriggled her way under his tough hide, and become more important to him than he'd thought any woman ever could be.

But he was hopeless with sweet gestures and tender words, so he said the only thing he could think of in the moment. "You can't go running about in your nightdress. You'll freeze."

She slipped her arms into his coat, pulled it closer about her, and gave him a defiant toss of her head. "I'm perfectly fine. Come, we're wasting time."

"I don't like this, lass. I don't like it at all." But it seemed he wasn't to be given a choice in the matter, because Mairi was hurrying toward the pathway, getting closer to Murdoch with every step, and there was no way he was going to leave her to the mercy of that villain.

"Wait, Mairi." He went after her, caught a fold of his coat in his fist and tugged her backward. "Get behind me."

Mairi rolled her eyes, but she knew which battles to fight and which to let pass, and she fell behind him with a huff.

He reached for her hand, and the two of them followed Murdoch through the thick darkness onto Lord Rutherford's property—followed the man who'd likely murdered Hamish onto the very land where that murder had taken place—without any idea where he was leading them, or what he intended to do when he got them where he wanted them.

What could possibly go wrong?

Chapter Thirty-two

Logically speaking, Daniel was right. Chasing Murdoch across Lord Rutherford's property in the dead of night wearing only her night rail *wasn't* a good idea.

Not that a wild, half-arsed chase after a suspected murderer was *ever* a good idea, but it was especially ill-advised on a night when it was as dark as spilled ink, with hardly a glimmer of moonlight to be seen.

She'd promised herself she'd never again set foot on Lord Rutherford's property after the day Daniel and Hamish vanished. She'd already broken the promise once today, and now here she was again, hurrying past that cursed pond and into his lordship's park under cover of darkness, chasing a man from whom she'd also vowed to keep her distance.

It was far more frightening at night, even with Daniel's large hand wrapped around hers, and the muscular bulk of him reassuringly solid beside her, but it was so curious, so utterly incomprehensible that Murdoch had dared to come to the cottage after what had happened with Daniel at the Sheep's Hide, nothing could have stopped her from going after him.

The man had something to say to them, and after twenty-four years of nothing but deafening silence, she intended to find out what it was.

"Where the devil is he taking us? We've been over half of Rutherford's estate by now."

They'd left the pond, the forest, the eastern end of the parkland, and even the formal gardens behind. The outlines of the manor house—a grim, dark stone affair with dozens of blank windows in rigid rows across the front—was visible in the distance.

Dear God, if there were such a thing as a haunted manor, one didn't need to look any farther than Rutherford House for discontented spirits—

"We're not going into that house, lass." Daniel's voice was tight with warning. "The villain may have half-a-dozen blackguards waiting for us on the other side of the door. There are too many ways to fall prey to mischief there."

Thankfully, it didn't look as if Murdoch were leading them toward the faint glow of lamps lighting the ground floor. He hurried past what was once an elegant rose garden, now a sad collection of bare canes, to a sprawling but empty park beyond.

Every now and again he turned back to check they were still following him, then scurried off again when he found them trailing along in his wake, Daniel muttering dire warnings about blackguards and ambushes as they stumbled through the darkness.

The safety of the cottage was far behind them now, and there was nothing but ominous shadows ahead. Shadows, and Murdoch. It was looking more like a trap with every step they took.

Finally, the tall, narrow spire of the Rutherford family chapel appeared in the distance, and Murdoch paused at the entrance to the churchyard adjacent. "Well, I can't say I expected this." She glanced at Daniel, who was frowning into the gloom, his lips tight. "He, ah…he appears to want us to follow him into the churchyard."

"Nay, lass. Not the churchyard. The mausoleum."

The *mausoleum*? She couldn't think of a single reason why they'd be interested in generations of dead Rutherfords, nor did she fancy a stroll among their remains, but Daniel was right. Murdoch had paused on the shallow steps leading into a dark gray stone building with tall columns flanking a double doorway. A building that looked very much like…

She swallowed.

A mausoleum.

"Well, we've come this far." She gripped Daniel's hand. "It's too late to turn back now."

"No, it bloody isn't. I don't like this, lass."

"Well, I can't say I'm looking forward to it either, but just consider it, Daniel. Murdoch must have a reason for leading us here."

"Aye, he has a reason. He means to bury a pistol ball in each of our foreheads, and end this business with Hamish once and for all."

"No, I don't think that's what this is." Still, it *was* the only explanation that made sense. Murdoch had left Coldstream years ago, only to appear in the village again mere weeks after Lillias's arrest, and within days of their arrival from London.

If he'd had some reason to want to see Daniel Adair dead all those years ago, and had discovered the man staying in the cottage with her wasn't Alister Macrae, as they'd claimed, but was in fact the adult version of the boy he'd tried to kill, mightn't he be tempted to try again?

"Devil of a thing to be wrong about. One thing about a mausoleum like that one, lass? It's a good place to murder someone. No one is about to hear a cry for help." Daniel nodded at the deserted churchyard. "Can't hear a pistol shot through those thick stone walls, either."

Must he keep going on about pistols and shooting?

"We can't be certain Murdoch had anything to do with Hamish's death." The face of the guilty man hadn't yet materialized in the dream. Until it did, the tragedy that had unfolded at the pond that day was still shrouded in mystery.

"Can't be certain he didn't, either."

Murdoch *was* the most likely culprit, at least on the face of it, but then how was it that her grandmother had been taken up for the crime instead? Murdoch's name hadn't once been mentioned in connection to the murder—only Lillias's, the one person in all of Coldstream the *least* likely to have murdered Daniel Adair. "I think someone has a reason to want to be rid of my grandmother, and they discovered a way to see the thing done cleanly, without dirtying their hands."

"Aye." Daniel gave her a reluctant nod. "Hanging is one way to get rid of a dangerous loose end."

"Whatever the truth is, Murdoch knows something about it. I can't bear to let him vanish into the darkness with his secrets, Daniel, not when we're this close to learning what happened to Hamish."

And they were close. She could feel it.

"I want to see an end to this mystery once and for all. I can't..." Bitter, angry tears gathered behind her eyes, the same tears she'd been crying for twenty-four years, for the boy no one remembered. "This can't go on any longer. My grandmother's life is at stake, and Hamish deserves justice."

Hamish, and Daniel, too. All of them.

Daniel touched her chin. "I know, Mairi, but do you really think Murdoch's going to lead you to justice? He's more likely to lead you to a world of trouble."

"I'm willing to accept that risk to see this thing finished. Aren't you? Hamish was your friend, too."

He looked down at her, his dark eyes soft. "I'm willing to risk myself, aye, but I'm not willing to risk *you*, lass."

Oh, dear God, more tears, not for Hamish or Lillias this time, but for Daniel, who was making her heart ache with the gruff sweetness that was his alone.

Daniel Brixton, sweet. A few weeks ago, such a thing seemed impossible, but now...everything had changed. He'd changed, and somehow, he'd changed her along with him. "I promise you I won't let anything happen to me."

He shook his head. "You can't promise that, Mairi."

"Well, no, but I can promise to stay by your side the entire time. Will that do?" That way she could keep an eye on him as well. He might think he didn't need it, but there was no telling what would happen once they went through those towering black iron doors.

"It'll have to, won't it?" He led the way through the churchyard, but when they reached the stone steps of the mausoleum, Murdoch was no longer there. There weren't any places to hide out here, yet a quick search didn't turn him up, either. It was as if he'd dissolved into the mist, and become part of the night itself. "Damn it, where's that blackguard sneaked off to *now*?"

"Well, you *did* try and tear him to bits the last time you met, if you recall." She didn't like this any more than Daniel did, but perhaps it wasn't all that surprising. "I don't know if you realize this, but you can be a trifle intimidating."

He snorted. "Come on then, lass. Let's get this cursed business over with."

The former viscounts and viscountesses of Rutherford and their various offspring died much as they'd lived—luxuriously. The family mausoleum was a handsome old place with a high, arched ceiling made of stone supported with a series of heavy wooden arches, each with a tall, narrow window fitted above it. But like all places that housed the dead, it was cold, dark, and smelled of stale, musty air and rot.

"I don't know where to start. Perhaps with the previous viscount?" He'd be closer to the front, being the most recently interred Rutherford. With any luck, they wouldn't have to venture too far from the door. The back of the tunnel was pitch black, and she didn't like the idea of an accidental stumble into the crypt.

Daniel shrugged. "One aristocrat's much like another."

Malcolm Andrew Gordon, the Third Viscount Rutherford, had been memorialized in death as befitted a wealthy nobleman, in a private burial chamber with its own altar, inside a massive tomb. A white stone likeness of the viscount reclined on the top, with stone draping covering his body, his head resting on a grand white stone cushion.

"Looks comfortable, doesn't he?"

"He does, yes." She studied the impassive white stone face, the white stone hands folded neatly atop his chest. "More so than he deserves." Malcolm Gordon wasn't reputed to be *quite* the reprobate his younger brother Callum was, but her grandmother still got a pinched look about her mouth whenever Malcolm Gordon's name was mentioned.

Daniel was peering down at the white stone viscount, his face as impassive as the statue's. "What finally took him off?"

"A putrid fever. His second wife, Lady Alethea, had succumbed a few weeks earlier to the same fever. Neither of them was a great loss to the village of Coldstream, or so my grandmother always said. Mrs. Alethea Shelby was Malcolm Gordon's long-standing mistress before she became his second wife, and a more vulgar, disagreeable lady never existed. Nothing in Scotland could ever please Lady Alethea—not the village, nor the people, nor the manor house."

"This is all, again, according to your grandmother?"

"Of course. No lady is more fair-minded than my grandmother, but she has no shortage of strong opinions."

He chuckled. "Somehow, lass, that doesn't surprise me."

There was nothing pleasant about a freezing-cold mausoleum stuffed to the rafters with dead aristocrats, but his laugh tugged a grin from her lips. Honestly, one would never guess what a tease he was from that forbidding expression he always wore. "I've no idea what that's meant to mean, Mr. Brixton."

"Do you not, then?"

She tossed her head. "Certainly not."

His answering grin relaxed his face, the hard, straight lines curving, transforming him from harsh and threatening into...well, back into himself, the mischievous but kindhearted lad she remembered from her childhood, and oh, it was good to see that boy again!

"This is Lady Alethea here, beside her husband?" He motioned to a second tomb made of the same extravagant white marble, this one with a statue of a lady kneeling, her hands clasped in front of her breast as if in prayer. "Are those meant to be *wings* on her back?"

"They certainly look like it, don't they?" Mairi slapped a hand over her mouth to smother a very un-Christian smirk at Lady Alethea's expense. It wouldn't do to poke fun at a dead viscountess, particularly while Mairi was standing right beside her tomb, but the idea of Lady Alethea as a celestial being was laughable.

"Angelic, was she?"

"Hardly. I suspect she's raining curses down on our heads even now. It would have infuriated her to have died here in Coldstream. I'm sure she intended a much more fashionable death in London, but alas, one can't choose the time of their...Daniel? What are you doing?"

He'd wandered back towards Lord Rutherford's tomb and leaned closer to the inscription on the stone. "What was the date Hamish and I disappeared from Coldstream, lass?"

"It was July twenty-eighth, seventeen seventy-two." She joined him beside the viscount's tomb, abandoning Lady Alethea to her prayers. "I've always remembered it because it was the day before my sixth birthday."

"That's odd. Lord Rutherford died on that same day." Daniel pointed to the date of death inscribed on the stone. "See here?"

"July twenty-eighth, seventeen seventy-two." She stared, blinked, then blinked again, but it was right there in front of her, carved in stone, no less. "I knew he'd died around the same time, but I didn't realize it was on the exact same *day*. It, ah...it can't possibly be a coincidence, can it?"

"No such thing. There's something to it, sure enough."

"But what? What can Malcolm Gordon's death have to do with you or Hamish?" A dozen different explanations crowded upon her at once, all of them outlandish, but...well, it must mean something.

Was this why Murdoch had led them here tonight? Did he intend for them to find *this*?

Without any inkling what his reasons might be—charitable, nefarious, or otherwise—possibilities flew at her from the darkest corners of her mind, each one more nightmarish than the one before it.

Was her grandmother somehow involved in Malcolm Gordon's death?

No. No, it wasn't that. It couldn't be that, but the idea alone made her jaw clench with foreboding. Lillias would never hurt a soul, but if there was some connection between her and the viscount's death, innocent or not, the law would discover it and twist it until it looked as if it were evidence against her.

She clutched Daniel's arm, her heart racing. "My grandmother...we have to find out what it means, Daniel, before..."

Dear God, she couldn't even say it aloud.

"Aye, I know it, lass. Whatever the Rutherfords have been hiding down in this tomb will come to light, one way or another." He drew her close, tucking her against the warm, solid length of his body. "Let's take a stroll, and see what we can find."

Chapter Thirty-three

Two boys disappear from a small village on the same day a viscount breathes his last breath—the same day his younger brother inherits an ancient title and a massive fortune—and not one person in the small village of Coldstream suspects the two things might be connected?

Twenty-four years later, a boy drifts to the surface of that same viscount's pond, his neck broken, and instead of digging into the circumstances surrounding the viscount's death, the village midwife, a lady who's never committed a crime in her life, is taken up for his murder?

This business was rotten from the head up, and Daniel didn't like it.

He didn't like it at all.

There was no such thing as a coincidence when it came to long-buried secrets, no such thing as chance when it came to murder.

"Where should we look next?" Mairi's voice was trembling, and her fingers were digging into the sleeve of his shirt as if she were a drowning victim herself, fighting to keep her head above water.

"What about Callum Gordon, the current viscount? Are any of his family buried here? A wife, or children?" Because sure as the sun would rise in the east tomorrow, the heir to the Rutherford title and fortune would have a hand in this business, one way or another.

Whatever scoundrel had the most to gain from a murder always did.

This thing had started with Callum Gordon, and it would end with him, too. One way or another.

"No. The last I heard, Lord Callum Rutherford's wife is very much alive, as is his heir and his two younger children, both of them daughters."

Callum had a son then, did he? A son he'd want to see become Viscount Rutherford one day, which wasn't likely to happen if his elder brother lived long enough to have a son of his own. Malcolm Gordon wouldn't be the first man to be murdered for standing between a greedy sibling and a fortune. "What of Malcolm Rutherford's first wife? When did she die?"

"Eight years before her husband? Nine? I'm not entirely certain, but several years before I was born, at any rate."

Damn. At least thirty-two years ago, then. There wasn't much hope her tomb would tell them anything, unless… "What did she die of?" A fall down the stairs, a drowning, another broken neck? It could be that Hamish hadn't been the first victim of Coldstream's murderer—

"I believe my grandmother said it was a fever."

Another fever? The Rutherfords didn't sound like a very hearty lot. Then again… "Was she as disagreeable as the second wife?" If she had been, he wouldn't rule out poisoning.

"Lady Honora? Oh, no. She was lovely, by all accounts, and a great favorite in the village. My grandmother always speaks highly of Lady Honora. She lived in the manor house here by herself, you know, as the viscount was always off in London with his mistress." Mairi glanced around with a frown. "She should be interred beside her husband. I daresay her tomb is nearby."

"Let's have a look, then."

Lady Honora *was* nearby, interred in a lonely alcove off her husband's burial chamber, her tomb a great deal less extravagant than either Malcolm Gordon's or Lady Alethea's. No white marble for the cast-off first wife, no winged angels, but merely a flat stone marker set into the wall with the dates of her birth and death.

Honora Elizabeth Muir Gordon, Third Viscountess of Rutherford, born February twelfth, seventeen thirty-nine, died April eighteenth, seventeen sixty-four, aged twenty-five years.

But that wasn't all. There was more writing below that.

Bram Andrew Muir Gordon, born April eighteenth, seventeen sixty-four, died April eighteenth, seventeen sixty-four.

A child, born and died on the same day, and his mother dead along with him? Daniel's chest squeezed tight, his heart thrashing against his encroaching ribs.

No coincidences…

It hadn't been a fever that had taken Lady Honora off—

"Daniel? What's the matter? You look like you've seen a ghost."

He *had* seen a ghost—the ghost of a child no one seemed to know had ever existed. "Lady Honora didn't die of a fever, lass."

Mairi stepped closer to read the stone for herself, her gaze moving over the inscription until she reached the last line, and let out a gasp. "Dear God, you're right. She died in childbirth. She and her infant son."

"You didn't know of it until now." It wasn't a question. The shock on her face was plain to see.

"I...didn't. Not only did I not know, but I've lived my whole life in Coldstream, and in those twenty-nine years, I've never heard a single word about Lady Honora having ever been with child."

Not a single breath of it, and in a place such as Coldstream, where everyone knew everyone else's business, from Fergus McClellan's braid-pulling to Mr. Fraser's tetchy appetite?

Mairi was shaking her head, dumbfounded. "How could Lady Honora have been carrying a child without anyone knowing of it? How is that possible?"

It *wasn't* possible. Not unless someone had gone to great lengths to make certain it was kept a secret. "Malcolm Gordon must have known. The child's death is clearly marked on Lady Honora's tombstone."

The Rutherfords had plenty of secrets, but the birth and death of Bram Andrew Muir Gordon hadn't been one of them. Malcolm Gordon was still alive when his wife died, and would have been the one to oversee the inscription on the tombstone. Anyone who'd ever been inside the mausoleum would know of the child's existence, as brief as it was.

"Poor thing." Mairi reached out to trace the infant's name with her finger. "Do you suppose he was born on the wrong side of the blanket?"

"Nay. If he were, he wouldn't be buried in the Rutherford vault, on the grounds of their country seat." Malcolm Gordon didn't seem like the type of man to treat his wife's indiscretion with any mercy or generosity.

"But if the child was legitimate, why would Malcolm Gordon wish to keep his wife's pregnancy a secret? The impending birth of a potential heir is no small matter, particularly to a man like Lord Rutherford, with such an ancient title and extensive estates."

"Aye, and it's near impossible to keep such a secret in a place like this, yet no one in Coldstream seems to have known anything about it."

"Someone *did* know of it." Mairi was staring blankly at the child's inscription, the carved letters and numbers blunted at the edges now, moss creeping into the indentations. "One person in Coldstream *must* have known of the child, Daniel."

Someone did. Someone *always* did.

And in this case, the one person in Coldstream who *must* have known Viscountess Rutherford was carrying a child was Lillias Cameron.

Lillias Cameron, who was on the verge of being executed for a crime she was only tied to by the thinnest of threads, because somehow, she'd inexplicably earned the hatred of Callum Rutherford, the current viscount, a man with a powerful title and an enormous fortune at his fingertips.

"My grandmother was the only midwife in this part of the Borders at that time. If Lady Honora gave birth to a child, whether he lived or died, my grandmother *must* have attended her."

Attended her, and then kept the child's birth and death a secret.

"My grandmother isn't one to keep secrets, Daniel."

"It could be that it wasn't her secret to keep, lass." Midwives often knew secrets they'd rather not know. Potentially dangerous secrets, where titles and fortunes were involved.

"You mean someone wishes to see my grandmother sent to the scaffold to keep their secrets?" Mairi shook her head as if she couldn't believe such a thing could be true, but the color the cold had put in her cheeks had fled, replaced with a gray pallor.

"Nay. Not *someone*, lass. Callum Gordon." There was only one reason a man like Viscount Rutherford would target a lady like Lillias Cameron.

She knew his secrets.

"But what secret could she have been keeping, Daniel? If the child had lived, it might have been that Lady Honora asked my grandmother to help her pass the child off as legitimate, but he *didn't* live, and thus was in no danger of taking the title or fortune from Callum Gordon—"

"The child wasn't illegitimate, lass." Daniel felt as if he were on the verge of sinking into that dark green water again, that it was inches away from flooding into his mouth, his nose, but all the pieces of this ugly business were falling together at last, and he couldn't make them stop. "Callum Gordon's at the heart of this thing, and only a legitimate child could be a threat to him. The only reason he has to target your grandmother is if the child is the legitimate heir to the Rutherford title and fortune. The boy was Malcolm Gordon's."

"But the boy *died*, Daniel! How can a dead child inherit—" She broke off, her gaze meeting his. "Oh, my God."

"The child didn't die at birth." Malcolm Gordon had hidden his son's existence for reasons Daniel couldn't even begin to understand, but the boy was still alive when Callum Gordon found out about him.

So Callum had resorted to murder to get rid of him.

And now he was doing everything he could to see Lillias Cameron, the one person who knew the truth, twisting at the end of a noose, and the last of his secrets buried with her.

"Daniel."

It was just one word, his name, but it was enough to make all the hair on his neck stand up. "What is it?"

"The date of the child's birth. April eighteenth, seventeen sixty-four."

"Nay, it can't be." He would have noticed it at once, the first time he read it, only...

He hadn't. He'd missed it because he hadn't *wanted* to see it.

April eighteenth, seventy-sixty-four...

It was his birthday. He'd been born the same day Lady Honora had died, and her infant son had been born. Mairi's grandmother had known of it, and she'd kept it a secret?

Why? What did it mean?

No coincidences—

"There's another thing, Daniel." Mairi touched her finger to a line carved below the date of Bram Gordon's death. The script was much smaller—so small he hadn't noticed it—but there was no mistaking it.

Two words.

Ne Obliviscaris. Do not forget.

"Dear God, I've had it all wrong from the start. When my grandmother told me she'd made a promise to your mother to look out for you, I thought she meant she'd made that promise to Aileen Adair. She didn't. She made it to Lady Honora Gordon."

"No, it's not...it's impossible." He opened his mouth to deny it, to lay out the dozens of reasons why it couldn't be true, but no words came out.

She gripped his sleeve. "You remember what Mrs. Fraser said, about Aileen Adair losing all those babies? She said they all thought she'd lose you too, that it was a miracle you survived. Don't you see? It was no miracle. Aileen Adair *did* lose her child, and so my grandmother gave you to Ian and Aileen Adair to raise as their own, to keep you hidden and safe."

"Not me, lass. Hamish—"

"No, Daniel. It's *you*, not Hamish. Callum must have learned of you somehow—perhaps Malcolm made a deathbed confession? Somehow Lillias found it out, fetched your father, then rushed out into the woods that day to find *you*. Hamish was never the target. It was always you."

"Nay. *Hamish* was the one who—"

"No. Don't you see?" Mairi's words were tumbling over each other now. "Lady Honora must have feared she'd die in childbirth, and so she made my grandmother promise to keep you safe. That's why Lillias won't defend herself from the murder accusation—if she does, your true identity will be revealed, and she swore to your mother she'd protect you at all costs. She never breaks a promise, Daniel."

He shook his head, but the truth of it was sinking into him like a poison, and with it all the other, ugly truths that went with it.

Ian Brixton wasn't his father. The mother he'd struggled so hard to remember hadn't been his mother, either. His entire life had been a lie—

"Callum Gordon sent someone out to the pond to find a dark-haired boy of about eight years old. It couldn't have been Murdoch, because he knew both you and Hamish, and could tell you apart. It was someone else, and he—"

"He found Hamish." Because Hamish was slower than Daniel. Because Daniel had been hiding behind a tree by the time the murderer appeared, and so the villain had seen only one boy, and had assumed it was the boy he sought.

Hamish's neck had been snapped and his poor, broken body tossed into the pond as if he were no better than filth from a slop bucket because he'd happened to be there, and he bore a passing resemblance to Daniel. Nothing more.

Hamish had died because of *him.*

"Lady Honora did everything she could to keep you a secret, even going so far as to have the infant's death recorded on her tombstone." Mairi's brows furrowed. "Malcom Gordon *must* have known the truth, and allowed the tombstone to be done as it was. God knows why."

Daniel hardly heard her.

He wasn't Ian Brixton's son. He was the son of an aristocrat, a man so selfish he'd cast his wife aside to be with his mistress, a man so lacking in honor and feeling he'd renounced his only son, his heir because…Christ, he hadn't any idea why. What had Malcolm Gordon stood to gain by turning his back on his own child?

And this…*this* was his legacy? This was who he was, the son of a father who hadn't wanted him, who'd abandoned him? It was Malcolm Gordon's blood that was running through his veins?

Rutherford blood.

"Daniel." Mairi lay a hand on his arm, her throat working, but whatever it was she was struggling to say was cut off by a crash so deafening the stone walls around them shuddered

It was the sound of a heavy door being slammed closed. Then, a moment later there was a loud clang, a bolt being shot home.

"Dear God." Mairi turned to him, her eyes wide. "Someone's closed us in."

They were trapped inside the mausoleum.

Chapter Thirty-four

"It's not a good idea, lass. You'll break your neck."

Mairi peered up at the narrow slit of the window set into the thick stone wall above the altar. "It can't be *that* far of a drop to the ground. No more than six or seven feet." Of course, a roof did tend to appear to be much closer when one was standing on the ground than the ground appeared to be from atop a roof.

"Aye, if the ground is level, which it won't be, and once you're up there, there's only one way down."

That way being a leap from the roof of the mausoleum to the ground. Of all the challenges this night could have presented, *why* did it have to be heights? She'd rather dig an underground tunnel than toss herself off the edge of a roof.

"There has to be another way out of here."

"We've looked everywhere, Daniel. There isn't." Once they'd discovered they had indeed been locked inside with a passel of dead Rutherfords, they'd searched every inch of this wretched place to find a way out, but every corner and alcove led to another impenetrable stone wall.

It was either out the window, or they'd have to wait until someone found them.

The very narrow, very high window.

Not so high she couldn't manage the drop down, though, and the climb upward from this side looked as if it would be…well, not *easy*, but she could do it. Probably. Once she was standing on the altar, she'd be able to reach the thick, heavy beam set into the wall below the window, and from there it was just a matter of—

"What will you do once you've got a hold of the beam? You'll be caught dangling off it like a fish on a hook."

"Nonsense. I'll simply swing my foot up into the window recess and pull myself up." *If* she could swing her foot that high, that is, and *if* it didn't slip, and *if* she had the arm strength to heave her body from a dead drop into a narrow window recess.

That was rather a lot of *ifs*, wasn't it?

But the real trouble would be kicking the glass free of the window frame so she might crawl through it and onto the roof—

"And that thick sheet of glass set into the window frame, lass?" Daniel demanded, as if he'd read her mind. "You have a plan for that, too, aye?"

"Well, of course, I do. I'll, er…well, I'll figure it out once I get up there." It *was* a plan, just not a very good one.

"You'll topple backward, and end up with a cracked skull."

"I'd prefer we not discuss cracked bones or maimed body parts just now, if it's all the same to you, Daniel. Now, do you have any better idea how to get us out of here?"

Aside from a few servants, the manor house was deserted. Murdoch must still be creeping about the grounds, but given he was likely the one who'd trapped them in here, there would be no help from that quarter, and no one else from the village had any idea where they'd gone.

It was either the window, or they'd be spending all of eternity moldering alongside Viscount Rutherford and his dreadful wife.

If it wasn't *quite* hell, it was close enough to it.

When a flood of alternate routes to freedom didn't pour from Daniel's lips, she held out a hand to him. "Come, help me up onto the altar, won't you?"

"I don't like it, lass."

No, he didn't. That much was clear from his grumbling as he grasped her waist and lifted her onto the altar as if she weighed no more than a communion wafer. She scrambled onto her feet, reached for the beam below the window and, before she could lose her nerve, swung her foot up onto the ledge.

That was when things got difficult.

"Damn it. This is what I was afraid of." Boots thumped across the stone floor below, then Daniel called from directly beneath her, "Drop down, lass, and I'll catch you."

"No!" She'd made it this far, hadn't she? "Just give me a minute, will you?"

The ledge was narrow, and her blasted boot kept slipping off the edge of it before she could get a secure enough foothold to lift herself up. So she ended up just as Daniel had predicted she would—dangling like a fish from a hook while he alternated between muttering darkly, calling out suggestions, and demanding she come down at once.

None of which was at all helpful.

Finally, just when she'd reconciled herself to a drop into his arms and a lecture that would singe her eardrums, she managed to wedge the toe of her boot under the narrow lip of the beam, and with a strength born of a desperate desire *not* to crack a bone, maim a limb, or admit defeat, she heaved herself up one torturous inch at a time until she somehow managed to scramble into the window recess.

It was a nice, lovely deep one, and so she sat there, her back to the glass and her head resting on the wall, snatching breath after breath into her lungs until the blind panic swelling under her breastbone receded.

"Easy with that glass now, lass, or you'll slice your foot to ribbons, and protect your face, as it's more likely to shatter than to come out in one piece, and make sure you…"

He was still nattering on, calling warnings and instructions up to her when she turned toward the window, drew her foot as far back as she could without tumbling backwards, and with all the strength she possessed, slammed her heel into the dead center of the window.

The glass shuddered in the frame, but it held, so she kicked it again. There was an ominous crack this time, but the window remained intact, so she kicked a third time. A crack appeared under her boot heel, so she tried again, kicking as hard as she could. There was a shriek of glass grinding against metal, then the narrow pane popped out of the frame and fell out the window, shattering on the ground below.

A triumphant shout came from below. "Well done, lass!"

It was, by God, very well done, indeed! "I'm going through," she called down to him. "Once I'm down, go round to the front door, and I'll let you out."

But, as with all best laid plans, getting through the final bit proved more difficult than she'd anticipated.

The window frame was narrower than it looked from below. Much narrower. If it had been any narrower, or her hips even a touch wider, it would have ended with her stuck in the aperture for eternity, her upper half dangling in midair, but her backside still trapped inside with the Rutherfords.

She'd never before considered her diminutive size to be an advantage, but then she'd never before attempted to shimmy out the window of a mausoleum, either. It was all a matter of perspectives, just as everything in life—

Oh, no, her hand was cramping! Of all the times for her wretched limbs to betray her! Perhaps it would be best to ponder the fickleness of the human condition when she *wasn't* stuck inside a window frame, her fingernails bloody and her knuckles scraped raw.

She squeezed her eyes closed, counting off the seconds until the painful spasm eased, and she was able to resume her squirming. She'd wriggled another inch forward when her boot fell from her foot and dropped onto the altar below with a thud.

"Mairi!"

A dozen or so other words followed Daniel's shout, but she couldn't make out what he was saying with her head out the window. No doubt he expected she'd follow her boot, though he needn't have worried, as she was in much greater danger of being wedged inside the window frame forever than she was of falling.

She didn't pause to look down, nor did she try to reassure him. He'd figure out she was well enough when she didn't come crashing down onto the altar. As for her boot, let Murdoch—or better yet Callum Gordon—find it there the next time he came to pay his respects to the dead, and wonder.

A bit further…so close…nearly there…

With her hands braced on the slate roof below her and her toes pressing against the wooden beam below the window, she shimmied, wriggled, and squirmed her way to freedom, once tiny inch at a time. Once her hips were free, she dragged her legs through, arms quivering, until at last—*at last*—she landed flat on her face on the roof.

She lay there with her cheek pressed against the damp slate, panting, but there was no time to waste, so she drew a deep breath of the fresh, cold air, sat up and slid on her bottom to the edge of the roof.

Best not to look down. She'd read that somewhere, hadn't she?

Perhaps just a peek. She peered over the edge, and her breath left her lungs in a painful whoosh. That had been a mistake.

But really, it wasn't *that* far. As grand as the Rutherford family mausoleum was, it was a low enough building, and she'd wriggled her way through the window, hadn't she? This was the easy part.

She inched further toward the roof line on her stomach, and, with a muttered prayer, slid her legs over the edge of it. She dangled there for an instant before muttering another prayer for a safe landing, then released her grip.

She hung there for a breathless instant, suspended in midair before the ground rushed up to meet her. She landed on her feet and managed to keep her balance before her legs gave way, and she dropped onto her bottom on the ground with an ignominious plop.

It wasn't the most graceful finish, but as she regained her feet, her heart gave an excited thump. She'd done it! It hadn't been pretty, but she'd made it down.

She wasn't finished yet, however.

The night was as still as the tomb had been, the only sound the tree branches swaying in the wind. The nearby grounds were deserted as well, but Murdoch couldn't be far. She didn't like the idea that he was lurking in the shadows, ready to leap out at her the moment he realized she was alone.

The threat of that evil eye upon her was enough to send her to her feet and darting across the frozen ground—as much as one *could* dart, with only one shoe—to the front of the mausoleum.

Someone had closed the door and locked it with the heavy, iron bolt, no doubt with the intent of trapping them inside, and they must still be nearby, hanging about to see to it she and Daniel didn't escape. An apprehensive glance over her shoulder revealed nothing but darkness, but that didn't mean they weren't there, hiding and watching.

The more quickly this thing was done, the better, but the bolt was nearly as long as her forearm and thicker than three of her fingers put together. She'd never been able to work it loose with just her hands.

A rock. She needed a rock, or something similar, something hard she could strike against the end of the bolt until, little by little it shifted loose. A quick search of the surrounding churchyard turned up a few rocks half-buried in the dirt. She pried them loose, gathered them up into a fold of her skirt, then darted back to the door of the mausoleum.

She smacked one of the rocks against the end of the bolt, using it like a makeshift hammer, but it cracked in her hand after only a few strikes, so she tossed it aside and took up the next one. By now she could hear Daniel on the other side of the door, some indistinct shouting and what sounded like a fist pounding against the heavy iron.

Not a patient man, Daniel Brixton.

She ignored the pounding, and focused on the lock. Her first strikes were awkward and clumsy, but after a few ineffectual blows she discovered firm taps with the end of the rock worked just as well. Each tap moved the iron bar such an infinitesimal amount, she thought at first it wasn't moving at all, but bit by bit the bar edged further and further to the right, until at last a tiny gap appeared, and she wrenched it the rest of the way with her hands.

The moment it slid home with a clank of iron the door heaved open, and she was caught up in Daniel's arms. "Clever, clever lass," he murmured in her ear as he stroked her hair, and she melted against him, relief pouring through her.

But it was short-lived. The soft metallic snick of a safety being released on a pistol made them spring apart, and then without warning, Daniel grabbed her and shoved her behind him.

She turned, expecting to see Murdoch standing there, his pistol pointed straight at Daniel, and her fingers tightened around the rock she still clutched in her hand.

But the man who stood before them wasn't Murdoch. It was a man she'd never seen before, much taller and broader than Murdoch, with a shock of pure white hair, pale, arctic-blue eyes, a long, thin scar from his right temple to the corner of his mouth, and a face...

It was straight out of one of her darkest nightmares. One glance at that face, and she could tell he was the sort of man who'd snap every bone in her body, and leave her where she fell for the wild animals to pick clean.

His pale slash of a mouth pulled into a ghastly smile. "Well, if it isn't little Daniel Adair, come back to Coldstream after all these years. You'd have done well to keep your distance from this place, lad. You escaped me once, but you won't a second time."

Chapter Thirty-five

Daniel had never seen this man's face before, but he knew it still, because he'd seen it on dozens of other men over his years on the London streets. It was the face of a cold, calculating villain, the face of a man who'd slash your throat and watch your life's blood pour out onto the street without a twinge of regret.

The face of a man who'd snap an innocent boy's neck, then let him sink to the bottom of a fishpond, alone and forgotten, without ever giving him a second thought.

"I'm not little Daniel Adair anymore." He wasn't Daniel Adair at all, if the story the gravestones had told them tonight was the truth. "Who are you?"

"Stewart. The viscount's man. I told you, lad, you should have stayed far away from Coldstream. Now you're back here, he's got no choice but to see the job finished."

"And he sent you to do it? He's a bloody fool, then. You cocked it up once, killed the wrong boy. Why should he think you'll get it right the second time?"

Stewart shrugged. "It's too bad about that other lad, but one dark-haired boy looks very much like another. He shouldn't 'a been poaching fish, should he? Guess he learned his lesson."

Mairi was right, then. Callum Gordon had sent this white-haired villain out to kill Daniel, but Stewart had come across Hamish first, and he'd been murdered in Daniel's place. "You murdered an innocent boy, Stewart."

Another careless shrug. "Eh, anyone could have made the same mistake."

"But not anyone *did*. Only you, and now you're going to pay for it."

Stewart threw back his head in a laugh. "You're an arrogant one, especially for a man with a pistol pointed at his head. Lord Rutherford said you would be. He said any man who dared come back here after twenty-four years must be arrogant, as well as stupid."

"Lord Rutherford? What, you mean Callum Gordon? He's not Lord Rutherford. He's not Lord anything." He was as much a murderer as Stewart was, and a coward, who sent another man to do his dirty deeds for him.

"Oh, he'll remain lord, once I'm done with you. Don't think I don't see that pretty little thing hiding behind you, either." Stewart pointed the gun over Daniel's shoulder, even as he never took his eyes off Daniel. "Come on out now, girl, before you get hurt."

"She's not going anywhere near you." Daniel reached behind him to lay a warning hand on Mairi's arm, just in case she took it into her head to try and improve their odds of living through this encounter. Hamish had already died for him. He wasn't going to lose Mairi, too.

If one of them ended this night with a pistol ball in their head, it would be *him*.

But before he could draw away, Mairi grabbed his wrist and pushed something cold and heavy into his hand. It felt like…a rock? He turned it in his palm, weighing it. It was a clumsy weapon, inaccurate and unwieldy, and not heavy enough to kill a man, but if thrown at the right moment and with deadly accuracy, it might inflict enough damage to turn the fight in his favor.

And there *would* be a fight. He'd been in enough of them to recognize the look on Stewart's face and the tension vibrating in the air—that strange stillness moments before it exploded into violence.

"Damn shame you decided to show your face here again, Adair. It was all well enough as long as you stayed away, but you look a bit too much like your grandpa on the Muir side for Lord Rutherford to be easy."

Daniel said nothing, but let Stewart ramble on, his pale lips stretched into a confident smirk. Too confident. The kind of confidence that got a man killed.

Stewart was so certain he was about to end Daniel's life that he was giving away all of Callum Rutherford's secrets, as well. "We can't have a big, coarse brute like you becoming viscount, now can we, Adair?"

Daniel laughed. He'd had worse insults tossed his way, and from far more dangerous men than this one. If Stewart thought a few childish slurs would rattle *him*, he didn't understand who he was dealing with. "I don't see why not. Better a coarse brute than a liar and murderer like Callum Gordon."

The smirk dropped away from Stewart's bloodless lips, and his face turned a dull, angry red. "Lord Rutherford's a gentleman, not a low, crude savage like you, Adair."

"Aye, he's such a gentleman he stole a title and fortune from one boy, and had another one murdered trying to keep it quiet. How did he even find out about me, Stewart? All of Coldstream believed me to be Daniel Adair. How did Callum discover the truth?"

Stewart, great fool that he was, was more than happy to tell that secret, as well. "That high and mighty brother of his got an attack of guilt on his deathbed about his poor, wronged son. Seemed that whore of his didn't like the idea of another boy stealing the fortune and title from whatever mealy pup she might manage to squeeze out between her thighs."

So Malcolm Gordon *had* regretted casting aside his only son, but not until it was too late for any good to come from it. He'd wanted the stain of that sin cleansed from his soul before his death, so he'd confessed to it just in time to expose Bram to Callum Rutherford's wrath.

Malcolm Gordon—his *father*—bore as much of the guilt for Hamish's death as Callum Gordon did.

"He begged his brother to find you and look out for you, but he asked the wrong man, didn't he? The only thing Callum Gordon was ever going to do for you was see to it you met your end right quickly, at the bottom of that pond."

"Except Callum sent the wrong man to do the job, didn't he, Stewart? Such a simple task, too. Kill the boy, and the matter's settled, but you found a way to bungle it. What did he say when he found out? He was none too pleased, I'd wager. Did he give you that scar on your face? Aye, he's a right gentleman, that one."

Ah. That had landed. The deepening flush on Stewart's face was proof he was losing control of his temper.

Good.

"I won't bungle it this time."

Stewart raised the pistol, and Daniel stared down the barrel without flinching, but he gripped the rock, fisting it in his palm, his fingers curling tightly around it. "Get down, lass," he hissed to Mairi.

As soon as she ducked down behind him, out of the pathway of Stewart's pistol, he raised his arm, and with an aim born of years of tossing knives at every blackguard in London, hurled the rock at Stewart.

It hit him in the dead center of his forehead, just where Daniel had hoped it would, but Stewart was a big man, and the rock wasn't heavy enough to do more than stun him. He staggered backward, his hand loosening around the pistol, and for an instant, just a single instant, the muzzle shifted slightly to the left.

It was Daniel's best chance—his only chance—and so, in that instant he let out a bloodcurdling battle cry, and charged.

A deafening crack exploded into the darkness surrounding them—a pistol shot, no mistaking that sound—but he just kept going, expecting every moment to feel the familiar burn in his arm, his shoulder, his chest, or, worst of all, to feel nothing except a tunnel of darkness sucking him down.

But none of those things happened, because Stewart had...missed? Missed him entirely, at that close a range? No, it was impossible, except... oh, God, had the ball hit Mairi? He whirled around, his heart vaulting into his throat, the first prayer he'd uttered in years on his lips.

Please, please, don't let it be her. Please, not her...

Stewart was lying on his back on the ground, his hand slack, the pistol by his foot, and two rocks, one bigger than the other, lay on the ground by his side.

Two rocks?

Where the *devil* had the second rock—

"He's not as sturdy as he looks, is he?" Mairi strode across the ground, paused to kick the empty pistol away from Stewart's hand, then leaned down to peer into his face. "Oh, look! It hit him right in the temple, just where I meant it to. My aim is improving."

She straightened and turned to Daniel, those sweet, pale pink lips of hers curved into a wide smile.

Smiling. The daft lass was *smiling* at him. "You had *two* rocks?"

"No, I had four, but I only *needed* two."

Daniel pointed down at the rocks lying beside Stewart's prone body. "Tell me you gave me the bigger one of the two, lass."

She huffed out a breath. "Now is hardly the time to start arguing over the size of the rocks, Daniel, but if you must know, I kept the biggest one for myself."

Christ, this woman was going to be the death of him. "Why the *devil* would you do that when my arms are twice the size and strength of yours, with twice the reach?"

"Because he was far more likely to suspect *you* of such a trick than he was *me*." She took up a handful of her hair, which was, inexplicably, as smooth and pretty as if she'd been lounging on a tufted cushion sipping tea instead of wriggling through windows and fighting off blackguards. "Fluffy red hair, and a small body, remember? A sweet little thing like me? Why, I would *never* dream of hurling a rock at anyone, would I?"

He stared at her, a long moment stretching between them when he wasn't sure whether to take her over his knee, fall at her feet, or kiss the breath out of her, but in the end, he threw back his head and laughed until his stomach ached and tears were running down his cheeks.

Really, what else was a man to do with such a lass?

His Mairi, so fierce, clever, beautiful, and bloody dangerous.

His life was in utter shambles. The father he'd loved hadn't been his father at all, he'd lost the first eight years of his life, and he didn't have the vaguest idea who he was anymore.

He wasn't even English, for God's sake.

But he had *her*, and she...she was everything.

Thank God she was on his side, or he never would have made it this—

"Well, young Daniel, it looks like you've solved one of your problems."

Daniel froze, but then he dived for the bigger of the two rocks and whirled toward the voice, his arm cocked to throw it.

"First ye try and strangle me, and now you're going to throw rocks at me? Last time I go out of my way to help you, lad."

A man was standing a few feet away, dressed head to toe in black, arms crossed over his chest, and a dark hat pulled low over his face.

But not so low Daniel couldn't see the black patch covering one of his eyes. "Murdoch?"

"Aye, it's me. I can't say you've improved much since I last saw ye. You were a scoundrel then, and you're a scoundrel now, only a much bigger one." Murdoch shrugged. "Mayhap ye would have turned out better if I'd whipped you all those years ago, but I never could catch you. He was a slippery little devil back then, Miss Cameron."

"Yes, I, ah, I remember. How...how do you do, Mr. Murdoch?"

"Ach, well enough, lass. I've been waiting twenty-four years to see this one taken care of." He nudged Stewart's shoulder with the toe of his boot. "He's as bad as he looks, and ye may have noticed he doesn't look too friendly."

Daniel lowered his arm, and the rock dropped from his fingers. "He killed Hamish."

It wasn't what he'd meant to say, but of all the questions he had for Murdoch, all the secrets that still needed explaining, that was what came out of his mouth.

"I know he did, lad. Never thought I'd see him held to account for it, either, until you came back to Coldstream. He's a right villain, he is, but he's like that pistol there." He nodded at Stewart's pistol lying near Daniel's feet. "Harmless enough, until it's put in the wrong hands. Stewart's the weapon, but it's the man who set this thing in motion who wants seeing to."

"Callum Rutherford will be seen to." Daniel would make sure of it.

"Callum Rutherford," Murdoch agreed. "Ye name me a crime, lad, and I can guarantee you Callum Rutherford's committed it. Theft, libel, forgery, conspiracy, murder. There's more, too many to name."

"You knew? All this time, you knew he was behind this?" Daniel was still trying to get his head around the fact that Murdoch had never been his enemy, but an ally—of sorts—all along.

"Aye, I knew. Took me a while to piece it together, though, and even then, I couldn't prove it. No one would have taken my word on it, being as Callum had dismissed me as gamekeeper. Any accusation I made would have looked suspicious, like, as there was bad blood between us."

"Did you witness it? Hamish's...the murder?" Daniel couldn't bring himself to say the word in the same breath as he said Hamish's name. For Mairi and Murdoch, the tragedy of Hamish's death was more than two decades old, but for him, it had only just happened.

"Nay, not the act itself, but I heard Malcolm Gordon tell his brother about you, then before his body was even cold, I see this Stewart fellow here prowling about Coldstream, asking for Daniel Adair. I knew he was up to no good then, and I knew it when I saw him sneaking about the village after you and the lass here arrived from London."

"That's why you led us out here tonight?" Mairi asked. "Because you were hoping we'd read the gravestones, and work out the mystery for ourselves?"

"Aye. It would have been easier just to tell you, you ken, but Daniel here didn't seem pleased to see me when I showed up at the Sheep's Hide, and I'd just as soon keep my neck in one piece, so ye see, I had to find another way to go about it."

He had in fact tried to tear Murdoch's head from his neck that night, so he could hardly complain about the man's strategy, but he wasn't willing to accept everything Murdoch told them without question. "If your only intent was to help us, why did you lock us inside the mausoleum?"

"Nay, it wasn't me. Once I got you out here, I took myself off right quick so as to keep clear of you, lad, but then I saw Stewart creeping about Rutherford's land on my way back to the village. I figured he was up to something, so I came back out to see for myself. He locked you in, and would have left you there until you were as dead as every Rutherford in the place." Murdoch turned to Mairi, his lips twitching. "I'm still not sure how you got through that window and down from that roof in one piece, lass, but the Cameron women are daring ones."

"Indeed. Daring, and wily. There are even some who say we're as wily as a nest of snakes."

Daniel snorted. "Aye, whoever he was, he had the right of it."

Mairi shot him a sly grin, then turned back to Stewart, prodding him with her toe. "What shall we do with him?"

"Leave him in the vault here, I say, until the magistrate can take him," Murdoch said. "Give Lady Honora a chance to haunt him for what he tried to do to her boy."

Daniel didn't have a better idea, and God knew the mausoleum was sealed up tighter than Newgate. So that was what they did, Murdoch and Daniel dragging Stewart's limp body into the mausoleum, then shooting the bolt home, locking him inside.

Mairi was quiet on the walk back to the cottage, huddling into Daniel's coat as if the events of the night had caught up to her at last. He kept one arm wrapped around her, but his gaze kept drifting back to Murdoch, who was walking silently by his side.

"If you'd ever caught me poaching, would you really have whipped me?" he asked as they made their way around the pond to the pathway leading back to Lillias's cottage.

Murdoch grinned, and gave him a hearty slap on the back. "Oh, aye. I'd have stripped the hide right off ye, lad. Ye wouldn't have been able to sit down for a week."

Chapter Thirty-six

Four days later

Freshly baked bread was like golden treacle, or a soft, warm blanket, or fat-bellied puppies and fluffy kittens frolicking in a meadow of fragrant wildflowers.

That is, it was the kind of thing one never grew weary of.

There simply was no such thing as too much freshly baked bread. This wasn't so much Mairi's opinion as it was a fact, one she'd been acting on for the better part of the last six hours.

The two loaves she'd just taken out of the oven were cooling on a rack. She'd wrapped the three loaves she'd finished earlier this afternoon in a cloth and set them on a kitchen shelf to be toasted for this week's breakfast. Two more loaves were in the oven, one batch of dough was rising in a bowl, and she'd just turned what would soon become the eighth loaf onto the wooden countertop, and was pounding the life out of it.

That is, she was kneading it. Vigorously.

Some ladies threw things when they were distressed. Others shrieked or pouted, and still others drank whisky until their heads swam, and they forgot what had distressed them in the first place.

She baked bread.

Not that she was distressed. She wasn't, not at all. It would be ridiculous for her to be distressed, because for the first time since Lillias had been taken up for Daniel's murder, she had nothing to be distressed about.

The labyrinth of secrets and lies Callum Gordon had created hadn't been entirely puzzled out yet. Her grandmother was still locked up in the Coldstream Toll Booth, and Mairi was admittedly a trifle distressed about that, but the magistrate had decided to leave the entire mess in the hands of the Court of Assizes, so Lillias would have to remain where she was until the court granted her freedom.

Which they would do, and soon, because Callum Gordon's intricate plot was unraveling as quickly as a spool of thread in the hands of a sticky-fingered child, in great part thanks to Stewart, who'd made a near-complete confession the night he'd tried to murder them at the Rutherford mausoleum, and in front of three witnesses, no less.

Then there was Murdoch, who knew enough about Stewart's activities on the morning of Malcolm Gordon's death to fill in the gaps in the rare instances where Stewart managed to hold his tongue. They were so rare, in fact, she doubted Stewart would ever see the light of day again.

So that was one villain dealt with.

As for Callum Gordon…well, it wasn't as simple a matter to see an aristocrat brought to justice, but Callum had made a great many enemies in his day, and he had very few defenders.

Time would tell.

The Court of Assizes would convene early next week, and Lillias would be cleared of the charge of murdering Daniel Adair. As for the mourning ring Callum Gordon had claimed she'd stolen from him, well…the magistrate and his men had done a thorough search of the cottage and hadn't turned it up, nor had it ever been found in her possession—at least, not by anyone who might be tempted to reveal it—so she couldn't be proven to have stolen a thing, could she?

So the theft charge against Lillias had been dropped, and there it would stay. Mairi didn't see any sense in risking it being reinstated because of a tiresomely strict adherence to the truth.

So, she *wasn't* distressed. Just…hungry, for freshly baked bread. That was all.

She punched her fist into the soft dough, turned it over on itself, slammed it back down onto the counter, and pounded it with the heels of her hands, then gave it a good pummeling with her knuckles.

Because that was how you made bread, and for no other reason.

Though if she *were* distressed, it would be because of Daniel, if only because she seemed to be incapable these days of experiencing a single emotion that didn't have something to do with Daniel. Joy, desire, irritation, impatience—for better or worse, he was at the center of it all, and since he'd learned the truth about his birth, he hadn't been himself.

He was as tender of her as he'd ever been, and as protective—much too protective, if she were honest. He still held her in his arms every night, still kissed and caressed her with the same ardent passion he had since they'd come together that first time, but inside his head, he was...

Somewhere else, and it was a place she couldn't follow him.

For the past thirty-two years of his life, he'd believed himself to be Daniel Brixton, the only son of Ian and Aileen Brixton. Then, in only a few short weeks, he'd gone from being Daniel Brixton to Daniel Adair, only to discover he wasn't Daniel Adair either, but Bram Andrew Muir Gordon, son of Malcolm Gordon and Lady Honora Muir Gordon, and the current Viscount Rutherford.

It was enough to set anyone off kilter, even someone as unflappable as Daniel, and it was made worse by the fact that he had so far resisted her every attempt to talk to him about it. If she so much as breathed the name Rutherford, he shut down as tightly as a clam guarding a precious pearl.

He knew well how to hold his tongue, too. All those years spent skulking around London had made him a master of silence and subterfuge. Trying to pry her way past his defenses was very much like throwing herself against a stone wall.

She ended up bruised and battered, while the wall carried on much as it had always done—

"What did that dough do to offend you, lass?"

She froze, her fingers clutching at a limp bit of dough. "Oh, I didn't see you there."

Daniel paused in the open doorway of the cottage, sniffing the air. "Are you opening a bakery?"

"No. It's Wednesday. I always bake bread on Wednesdays."

He came inside, closing the door behind him. "It's Thursday, Mairi."

Was it, indeed? "Oh. Well, I guess I'm a bit behind."

"It looks as if you're way ahead to me." He eyed the loaves of bread scattered over every surface, then sauntered across the room to her. "You have flour on your face, just...here." He touched the tip of her nose.

"It does tend to get everywhere." She reached up to rub her nose, but she couldn't tear her gaze away from those dark eyes, the spark of heat in them whenever he looked at her.

It made her breath hitch every time.

"You're all flushed, too, and your hair..." He unwound one of her curls with his finger, a smile drifting over his lips when it twisted again as soon as he released it. "All wild, red curls."

"It's the heat from the stove." She tucked a straggling lock of hair behind her ear. "Where did you go off to today?"

The same place he'd gone yesterday, no doubt, and the day before that, and every day for the past four days.

Off somewhere with Murdoch.

He didn't ask her to accompany him, nor had he told her what they talked about. Daniel's father, perhaps. It would make sense he'd want to know something about Malcolm Gordon, and Murdoch had known the man longer than anyone else in Coldstream.

Daniel didn't owe *her* any explanations as to his whereabouts, of course, or about anything else, really. He might choose to confide in whoever he liked—or *not* confide in them, as the case might be—but they'd been in this thing together from the start, and he'd never before kept secrets from her. It was as if a chasm had suddenly sprung up between them, and she hadn't any idea how to bridge it.

It was…odd. Some might even call it distressing.

Then when he returned to the cottage in the evenings, he was quiet, at best. At worst, he was withdrawn, silent, guarded.

"I went to see Murdoch. He offered to take me about Lord Rutherford's land. He knows it well from all his years there as gamekeeper."

He said *Lord Rutherford,* as if he'd never heard of the man, as if the Rutherford family had nothing to do with him, as if the land he'd surveyed today belonged to a stranger.

But it had taken twenty-four years for the truth about Callum Gordon's perfidy to come to light, so it was only to be expected it would take more than four days for the repercussions to stop echoing, and for everything to be put back to rights.

Or so she kept telling herself. "What did you make of it, then? The land, I mean."

He shrugged. "It's well enough, what I saw of it, which wasn't much. It's too vast to see it all in a single day, or even a year's worth of days. Near seven hundred acres. More than any one man needs."

Such a generously sized country estate would have been a point of pride for any other nobleman, but Daniel didn't think like an aristocrat, and his disgust at such excess was a living, breathing thing, so tangible it was as if another person—an unwelcome one—had entered the kitchen.

"Such a large estate, properly managed will be a boon for the village—"

"Aye, but I haven't any idea how to manage it, Mairi, any more than I have the first idea how to be a viscount. I was never meant to be one."

She swallowed, but there was no dislodging the queasiness that had settled in her belly. "You'll learn how to—"

"I don't want to bloody learn!"

She stumbled backwards, shocked. He'd never spoken to her in such a way before, not even when she'd first arrived in London and he'd thought her a despicable liar.

"I'm sorry, lass. I didn't mean to…" He sucked in a deep breath, and when he spoke again the harshness had bled from his voice. "I've asked Murdoch to act as the estate steward, and he's agreed to do it. He knows the house and lands, and it's…it's better this way."

"But it's *your* land!" His land, his tenant farmers, *his* responsibility. "It's your legacy, Daniel."

"I told you, Mairi." His voice was calm still, but so cold, it was hardly recognizable as his. "I don't want it."

She stared at him, the queasiness in her stomach spreading, the burning taste of bile creeping up her throat. "What are you saying?"

Because it almost sounded like he meant—

"I don't belong here, lass. I was never meant to be Viscount Rutherford." For the first time since they'd arrived in Coldstream, he didn't meet her eyes.

"You're…do you mean to say you're leaving?"

But she knew the answer, even before he opened his mouth, had known it for four days, but every time it crept to the forefront of her mind, she'd shoved it right back into the darkest corner again, where it couldn't hurt her.

She'd known, but instead of facing it, she'd baked bread, and lied to herself.

"Aye. I'm going back to London, Mairi. It's my home now."

"Back to London?" He was running away, then.

"Aye. The manor house, the lands, the money and title…I don't want anything to do with it. I'm Daniel Brixton, Mairi. I was never really Daniel Adair." He dragged a hand through his hair. "And it's too late now for me to become Bram Andrew Muir Gordon."

Did he think he *wasn't* Bram Andrew Muir Gordon if he didn't remain in Coldstream? How could he think turning his back on his birthright somehow changed who he was?

After twenty-four years of lies, twenty-four years of Hamish lying cold and alone at the bottom of that pond, twenty-four years of hoping and praying for the truth to come out, he was simply walking away from it all? Abandoning his tenants, the people who had suffered through years of Callum Gordon's neglect, years of Malcolm Gordon's indifference?

"Say something, lass."

"I don't know what to say." But no, that wasn't the truth, either. Words were crowding into her mouth even now, angry, bitter words she didn't want to say to him swelling into a cry of anger and grief behind the tight seam of her lips.

What of Lillias's sacrifice on his behalf? All those tears she'd wept for Daniel and Hamish, twenty-four-years' worth of tears, and he was going to fly back off to London as if none of it had ever happened?

What made him any better than any of the previous viscounts, then? Any different from Callum or Malcolm, any less selfish than either of them? But no, he was worse, wasn't he, because he wasn't just turning his back on his estate, or the Rutherfords, or Coldstream, or even her.

He was turning his back on *himself.*

"I want you to come to London, Mairi. I want you with me forever. Will you come?" He took her hands in his, his dark eyes pleading.

She stared up at him, too numb to speak. That numbness, the shock… was her expression blank? Was that why he couldn't read her thoughts on her face? Was that how he could ask her such a thing now, talk to her about forever *now*, when he'd just broken her heart in two?

"Mairi? Did you hear me? I can't…I need you, lass. Please, will you come to London with me?"

The part of her that wanted to rage at him, to shriek and wail and claw at him until she'd hurt him as much as he'd just hurt her was surging to furious life inside her.

But the other part of her, the part that heard the roughness in his voice, saw his throat move in a nervous swallow as he awaited her answer—the part that wondered how it would be to never feel that warm, strong hand clasped around her fingers again, never see the spark of desire in his eyes when he looked at her, never again fall asleep in his arms, the part of her that loved him—yes, loved him, fiercely and irrevocably…

That part stopped her, because as angry as she was, as bitterly disappointed in him as she was, there wasn't any part of her that could bear to hurt him.

"Mairi? Will you answer me? I need to hear you say—"

"Shh." She pressed her palm to his cheek. "It's all right. Come to bed, Daniel."

If he knew then what her answer would be, it didn't show on his face. He took the hand she held out to him, and let her lead him into the bedroom, to the bed with the black and green tartan coverlet, where they'd spent every night together since they'd come to Coldstream.

It would end between them, because it had to, but perhaps it had been destined to end from the start. Perhaps he was fated always to leave, and she was fated always to be left behind.

But it wouldn't end yet. Not tonight.

There would be enough time for heartbreak tomorrow.

Chapter Thirty-seven

Had he known, the first time he looked into her deep blue eyes, that he'd lose himself in them, fall into them, and never find his way back out again? That he'd never want to, but would gladly sink into those eyes, and be grateful for the drowning?

"Get into the bed, lass, before you freeze." He raised her hand to his lips, kissed her palm, then turned to the fire. It was warm in the cottage, the scent of yeast and freshly baked bread heavy in the air, but the wind was howling outside, rattling the windows, and it would grow cold again quickly.

Behind him, he heard the rustle of fabric, but when he turned back to her after adding another log to the fire, his throat jerked in a rough swallow.

She'd removed her clothing, but she hadn't yet slid under the coverlet. Instead, she stood just inside the reach of the fire's glow, watching him with those blue, blue eyes, the flicker of the flames limning her fair skin a molten gold.

He crossed the bedchamber to her, slowly, shedding his coat and tugging his shirt over his head as he went. "Not so shy anymore," he murmured, his eyes on hers as he reached out to trace his finger around one of her nipples, his belly tightening with hunger when it rose, stiff and proud, demanding more of his touch.

"It's a bit late for maidenly blushes now." She rested her palm flat against his bare chest and paused there, testing the thudding beat of his heart under his skin before dragging her hand down his torso to his belly, then sliding her fingers under the waistband of his breeches to brush the head of his cock.

He gasped, his belly jerking and his hips thrusting forward. No, there was nothing maidenly about *that* touch. "Not wasting any time tonight, are you?"

"There's no time to waste."

It was an odd thing to say, but he didn't wonder at it, because in the next breath she was stroking him, her gaze on the slow, sinuous glide of her hand over his burgeoning length, her tongue creeping out to touch the corner of her lips when his flushed, swollen head jutted over the edge of his waistband.

He arched his neck, the maddening slide of her soft palm over his aching shaft snatching every thought from his head.

She kept stroking until she'd lured him to the edge of an explosive climax, but she stopped before he could disgrace himself by releasing in his breeches, took him by the hand and led him to the bed. "Lie down."

There was a hint of command in her voice that dragged a ragged groan from his lips, but when he took her waist in his hands and leaned down to take her mouth she eluded him, easing him down onto the bed with a nudge of his shoulders. "No. Take off your breeches, then lie down, flat on your back."

His fierce, demanding Mairi. "Am I allowed to touch you?"

A faint smile drifted over her lips, but her blue eyes were dark, and glittering with a feverish light he'd never seen there before. "Perhaps, if you do as I say."

Such a demanding tone from such a wee, sweet-looking lass, but he knew her now, understood the fierce will that hid beneath that soft skin, those innocent blue eyes. Only *he* had ever had the privilege of seeing her like this, so flushed and eager. A knot of desire gathered at the base of his spine as he toyed with the buttons on his falls. He teased her for a while, his gaze never leaving hers before he unfastened them, let his breeches slide down his hips and lay down on the bed, flat on his back, as she'd bid him.

"Good," she crooned, steadying herself with her hands on his shoulders as she climbed over him, one leg on either side of his hips, the sweet curves of her bottom resting atop his thighs. "This is how I want you tonight."

"You can have me any way you want me, lass. I'm yours." Not just his body, but his heart, his soul, everything he was belonged to her. He reached up to cup her breasts in his palms, circling her pale pink nipples with his thumbs. "And you're mine, Mairi. Every inch of you."

He pinched one of the stiff peaks, heat searing through him when her head fell back on a whimper, her long red curls brushing his legs. "You like that, lass?" He caught her other nipple between his fingers and squeezed a little harder, tormenting the pink tip until it turned a deep, dusky red, and she was squirming against his legs, searching for friction against her damp core. "Aye, you like it when I'm a little rough, don't you? Do you need more? Come here, lass."

He released her swollen nipple and pressed his hands to the smooth, warm skin of her back to bring her closer. Her hands landed on the pillow on either side of his head, her nipples inches from his mouth. He tickled one hard nub with the tip of his tongue, then licked and teased the other, waiting until it peaked for him before he turned his attention back to the first one, sucking it between his lips and drawing hard on it, his hips arching up at her breathless moans and gasps.

"Ah, it drives me mad when you're like this, so wild and desperate for me." He slid his hand between her legs, burrowing into the soft thatch of auburn curls there, delving between her folds to stroke his finger over the center of her desire, his cock giving a needy pulse when she cried out for him. "Yes, so beautiful, Mairi."

He sank one finger inside her, but he didn't thrust. He kept it still while he teased her swollen bud with light, tormenting strokes of his thumb—not enough to bring her to a climax, but enough to keep her dangling on the verge of it, desperate.

God, she was so wet for him, her hot folds so slick against his probing fingers. He wanted to make her come with his mouth, feel her body arch and twitch above him as he brought her to pleasure again and again, but when he grasped her hips to drag her against his lips, she stopped him with tight fingers around his wrists. "No. I want you like this tonight."

She rose up onto her knees over him, slicked her hand down his length once, then again, firm strokes while she held the engorged tip of his cock against her slick, silky entrance.

His groin was heavy with need, his cock on fire, every inch of him straining for her. It was all he could do not to surge upward and thrust into her like a savage. "*Now*, Mairi. Please, lass."

She didn't make him beg again, instead sinking down on him slowly, inch by torturous inch until at last—*at last*—he was buried inside her tantalizing heat. She stilled for a moment, poised above him like some red-headed goddess, her eyes so dark, midnight blue, and then...

Then she started to move, restrained nudges of her hips that drove him mad, the teasing slide of her wet core against his rigid cock both too much and not enough at once. His back arched, his hips working, his chest sheened with sweat as she rode him. She took everything he gave her, every stroke, her mouth open and throat bared, broken cries tearing from her lips until her release hit her and her core pulsed around him, edging him closer to his own release, closer, his cock throbbing, his legs shaking and spine drawing tight...

"Ah, ah, Mairi, *yes*..." He trailed off into a low groan as he came in a hot rush, his hands on her hips, holding her steady for his wild thrusts, then caught her in his arms when she collapsed on top of him. He rolled them to the side, his lips pressed to her temple, her mouth open against his neck, her tongue darting out to taste the salt of his skin.

She drifted at once into sleep after her breathing calmed, one arm thrown over his chest, and he held her against him, stroking her hair and waiting for sleep to take him.

Only...it didn't. He was wide awake, his thoughts careening inside his head, replaying the scene between them when he'd returned to the cottage tonight. Nothing about it had struck him as odd while it was happening, but she'd been troubled before he ever came through the door.

Eight loaves of bread, or was it nine? Every surface of the kitchen was dusted with a fine layer of flour, flour on her nose, and her apron heavy with it. What had possessed her to bake so many loaves?

I guess I'm a little behind.

That wasn't the reason. No, something else had driven her into that frenzy of activity, the same thing that had put a shadow in her eyes, and that was before he told her he intended to return to London, and asked her to go with him.

And she hadn't answered him.

She hadn't answered him.

She'd spoken about the Rutherford land, how he'd learn to manage it, but her expression when he'd told her he didn't want to learn, and didn't want to be the Viscount of Rutherford...

Had she looked angry? Aye, but it was more than that. Shock, when he'd snapped at her, but that wasn't what was making him uneasy. It was something else, some look in her blue eyes he'd never seen before.

He stiffened as it dawned on him, all at once. Disappointment.

She'd looked at him as if she was *disappointed* in him, and then she hadn't answered him when he'd asked her to come with him to London.

Any hope of sleep fled as he jerked upright in bed.

"Daniel?" She peered up at him, blinking groggily. "What's the matter?"

"London, Mairi. You never said whether or not you'd come to London with me."

In an instant she was wide awake and gazing up at him, her head still resting on the pillow, and part of her face hidden in the shadows.

"Mairi?"

"I didn't say I would come with you, because...I can't, Daniel."

He stared at her dumbly, his throat closing. "Why not? Because of your grandmother?"

She sighed as she gathered the coverlet around her, pulling it tight against her neck. "She's part of it, yes. I can't leave her, after everything she's been through."

"I never thought you'd leave her, Mairi. She'll come with us, of course."

Mairi shook her head. "No, she won't. She won't leave Coldstream. Her life here hasn't always been happy—I don't pretend otherwise—but this is her home, Daniel. She'll never agree to leave it."

He said nothing, just waited. He could see in her face there was more, and he needed to hear all of it.

"It isn't just that, though." She let out another sigh, this one tinged with sadness, but she remained quiet for long, agonizing minutes before she drew a deep breath and tipped her chin up to face him, holding his gaze. "You can't hide from who you are, Daniel. You're Bram Andrew Muir Gordon, and that will be true whether you're here in Coldstream, or back in London."

"I told you I'd see to it the village was taken care of, lass. The manor house, the tenants—all of them will be looked after. I won't neglect them like Malcolm Rutherford did, or Callum bloody Rutherford—"

"Shhh. I know it, Daniel, but this isn't about them. It's about you." She took his hand, and laced his fingers with hers. "Do you truly believe you can turn you back on your past? Pretend it never happened? Your history in Coldstream isn't a happy one—"

"Happy?" He choked out a grim laugh. "Hamish was murdered in *my* place, Mairi, on the orders of *my* uncle, a man who'd kill a boy for a fortune and title. Callum Gordon stole my *name*. My childhood, my friends, my past. He took everything from me."

She tightened her fingers around his, tears welling in her eyes. "None of that happened because of anything you did. You're innocent, a victim in all of it, but you can't simply erase it by leaving, and pretend it never happened. Don't you see? The past doesn't disappear because we want it to. It's a part of you, part of who you—"

"Anyone with any sense would run from my past! Christ, Mairi. My father was a selfish coward, my uncle a murderous villain, and from what Murdoch's told me about my ancestors, there wasn't a decent man among them. You think I want to be a Rutherford? You think I want their blood running through my veins?"

"But that's just it, Daniel." Her voice was quiet. "It *is* their blood running through your veins whether you acknowledge it or not, and no matter how far you run from it. It will only bring you heartache to pretend otherwise."

"That's it, then?" He snatched his hand from hers and gripped his hair, tearing at it. "I-I care deeply for you, Mairi. For God's sake, doesn't that count for anything?"

A tear fell down her cheek, just one, but she shook her head. "You care for me now, perhaps, but I'm part of the past you're running from, Daniel. How long will it be before you come to resent me for bringing you back to Coldstream? How long before you look at me like you wish I was someone you could forget?"

God, he didn't know. He wanted to tell her that would never happen, that he'd never feel anything but love for her, but how could he promise that, when he'd seen how quickly a life could be turned upside down?

He couldn't make any promises to anyone. Not anymore.

"If you knew you were going to refuse me, then what was this?" He gestured to the bed, where less than an hour ago they'd been tangled up in each other, with Mairi whispering his name as if he were everything to her.

She gazed at him, eyes dark with anguish, then gently took his hand, and brought it to her lips. Her kiss was brief, fleeting. "It was goodbye, Daniel."

Chapter Thirty-eight

The following week

"Ye haven't learned much since ye were eight years old, have ye, Dan—eh, I mean, Lord Rutherford. That's what I'm meant to call ye now, aye?"

Daniel threw himself into one of the stiff, formal chairs scattered around the drawing room at Rutherford House—bloody uncomfortable, every single one of them—and turned to Murdoch, who was grinning at him like a half-wit. "I don't give a damn what you call me, as long as it isn't Lord Rutherford. Or Viscount Rutherford," he snapped, when Murdoch opened his mouth.

Bram, Adair, Brixton, Gordon—all of them were his names, and at the same time, none of them were his name at all, so what difference did it make what anyone called him?

Except not Rutherford. Never Rutherford, no matter what the courts ultimately decided about the Rutherford viscountcy. It would take months to sort out that wretched business, but until then the courts had given him leave to remain at Rutherford House, as it was his only residence in Coldstream.

So, he was a wealthy viscount now, whether he wanted to be or not.

As for the rest of it, it hadn't taken long for the court to find Callum Gordon and his servant Stewart guilty of murdering Hamish Deacon. The court had also determined Lillias Cameron couldn't be guilty of murdering Daniel Adair, mainly because Daniel Adair was sitting in the toll booth at the time the charge against her was read, still very much alive and breathing.

Breathing wasn't a luxury either Callum or Stewart would be enjoying much longer. They'd both been sentenced to swing.

It was done at last, then, or as done as such a snarled nest of lies ever could be. He doubted he'd ever be truly free of it.

Hamish was still dead. No court could ever change that.

"All right, then, I'll call ye a damned fool. How's that?"

"What are you on about now, old man?" Daniel waved a weary hand at Murdoch. Christ, he was tired. Had he ever been this tired before? "Just say it, will you? God knows you can't hold your tongue worth a damn."

Murdoch eyed him for a moment, then leaned back in his chair, resting his hands on his belly. "All right, then. I'm talking about your sweet little red-haired lass. Mairi Cameron."

"She's not mine." Not anymore. Had she ever been?

"Oh, she's yours, and you're hers, God help the poor lass. So, stop being such a stubborn arse and set things right with her."

Set things right. Become Viscount Rutherford, in other words. The very thought of it turned his stomach. He could think of only one thing that would be even worse than accepting his birthright.

Losing Mairi.

He leapt up from the chair, arse protesting his ever having sat in it in the first place, and paced from one end of the room to the other. He snatched up a pillow as he passed the settee—an orange silk thing with dozens of stiff gold tassels hanging off it. "This is the ugliest pillow I've ever seen. This is the ugliest *room* I've ever seen."

Murdoch glanced around, then shrugged. "Aye, ugly enough. Lady Alethea's doing, I'd wager. The woman didn't have a lick of taste in clothes or furnishings, with everything too grand to be of any use to anyone. She had the same problem with husbands, come to that."

Daniel crushed the silk pillow between his hands, then tossed it aside before he was tempted to pluck all the ridiculous gold tassels off and throw them into the fire. "She didn't look at me once today."

"Who, Lady Alethea? I should hope not, since she's dead."

"Not Lady Alethea, old man. Mairi." All of Coldstream had been waiting outside the toll booth this morning, jostling each other and buzzing with anticipation to hear what the court would decide, but Mairi hadn't said a single word to any of them.

Not to Fergus McClellan, who'd reached out to squeeze her shoulder. Not Angus Murray, who'd murmured something to her as she passed. Not even Elsbeth Fraser, who'd been loudly demanding of anyone who'd listen how it was that scoundrel Mairi Cameron had been dragging about Coldstream could be both Alistair Macrae *and* Bram Gordon, Viscount Rutherford.

Mairi hadn't spared any of them so much as a glance, but had kept her gaze straight in front of her, her face as pale as death as she listened to the charges read out against her grandmother. But she'd kept her head high and her back straight, perched on the edge of her chair as if she were ready to leap into the fray should anyone dare to breathe a word against Lillias.

Such a fierce lass, and so beautiful, even with that pallor and the dark shadows under her eyes. He couldn't bear to look at her again, after the first time. It hurt too much.

"So she didn't look at you. What of it? Ye didn't look at her either. Didn't mean you weren't thinking about her, did it?"

Daniel merely grunted, but Murdoch was smarter than he looked, because he *had* been thinking about her. He was always thinking about her, but thinking wasn't enough to change things between them.

If it were only about him leaving Coldstream and turning his back on the village, or him running from his past he'd have set it to rights with her already.

But it was more than that. It was about him being a Rutherford.

He was a violent man, a coarse brute, just as Stewart had said. He'd always known it, had always been aware of the savagery lurking just under the surface, but he hadn't understood why he was that way. At some point he'd stopped wondering, and just accepted it as his nature.

But now he knew.

It was because he was a Rutherford, one in a long line of violent, savage men.

Lady Clifford had given him the chance to put his feral urges to work for a good purpose, but that didn't change the fact that he'd killed men, sometimes with his bare hands. He'd only ever hurt a person to protect someone who couldn't protect themselves, and he'd even done some good over the years, helping those who otherwise would have remained at the mercy of one blackguard or another.

But those feral instincts were still there, waiting to slither out as soon as the tight control he had over them loosened. And loosen it would, as soon as he accepted his title.

No one had any control over a viscount—particularly one with as much money and property as Viscount Rutherford. He didn't need to look any further than Malcolm and Callum Gordon for proof of that. Their worst instincts had been left to run loose, and they'd done nothing but hurt the people they should have loved and protected.

He had his father's Rutherford blood in his veins, his uncle's blood, and both of them had been utter villains. He had yet to hear of one Rutherford who hadn't been, and he was already part of the way there himself.

What if it hadn't been anything more than circumstance that had kept him from becoming Malcolm Gordon? Or worse, Callum Gordon? If he had inherited the title and fortune all those years ago, what sort of man would he be now?

"Ye look like a thundercloud, ye do. What's got you all grim-faced this time?"

"Callum Gordon."

"Ach, well, a villain like him? That I can understand." Murdoch was quiet for a bit, then he asked, "Did ye take note of his wife and son at the toll booth today? I was watching, and neither of them leaked out a single tear when Callum Gordon was sentenced to hang."

"No?" He'd been too preoccupied with Mairi to take much notice of Lady Rutherford and her son, a boy of about eighteen years or so, by the looks of him, and likely raised to believe he'd become the viscount one day. Daniel expected trouble from that quarter, a squabble over money and titles and property, but if what Murdoch said was true, the relationship between Callum and his family might be more complicated than he'd realized. "Not even his wife?"

"Nay. Sat there stone-faced, the both of them. Mayhap they despise him as much as everyone else does. That boy looks a decent sort. Your cousin, isn't he? And his mother is your aunt, eh?"

His aunt, and his cousin? For an instant his mind went blank.

But Murdoch was right. He had an aunt, and a cousin. Nay, three cousins, because Callum Gordon had two younger children, didn't he? Two daughters.

He had three cousins. A family, of sorts, or the start of one.

"Lord and Lady Muir are on their way to Coldstream. Ye know that, aye, lad? They want to see this long-lost grandson of theirs for themselves, I expect."

Daniel stared at him. "Lord and Lady Muir?"

"Aye, the Earl and Countess of Muir, Lady Honora's parents. They should be here the day after tomorrow. They said in their letter it would take four days to get to Coldstream, and they left Stonehaven three days ago. I hope ye plan to clean yourself up a bit before they arrive."

"Letter? What bloody letter?" His grandfather was an *earl*?

"The letter they wrote in reply to the one I sent them. Now what's that face for this time, eh? Don't you want to meet your grandparents, lad?"

"I...don't know." Two minutes ago, he hadn't even realized he *had* grandparents, and now they were on their way here to meet him? He dropped back into the chair he'd just vacated, then leapt to his feet again to save his arse from further punishment.

Murdoch let out an irritable grunt. "Well, like it or not, you're going to, and the way I hear tell, yer the spitting image of your grandfather. Hard to imagine it, being as he's an earl and yer a bit rough around the edges yet, but I expect ye'll clean up well enough."

Daniel paused by the window, staring out at the park without seeing it, but then an awful thought occurred to him, and he swung back around. "Good Lord. I'm not heir to an earldom, am I?"

Murdoch cackled. "Nay, you've got a half-dozen uncles and aunts and a whole passel of older cousins, some of 'em with children of their own now, from what Lady Muir said in her letter."

"They're not all villains, are they?" If Lady Honora's family was anything like the Gordons, he'd be better off leaving Coldstream before they arrived.

"Who, the Muirs? Nay, lad, they're a good lot, from what I hear. Now, there was a bit of a disagreement between Lord Muir and his daughter over her marrying Malcolm Gordon. They didn't see eye to eye on that, and his lordship held a grudge, and forbade her his home for a time. Otherwise, I expect Lady Honora would have gone back to Stonehaven when she found herself with child."

Uncles, aunts, cousins, second cousins...how was he meant to feel about this? What was he meant to do with them all? Or perhaps the better question was, what would they do with a big, rough man like him? "They're sure to despise me on sight."

"Now you listen to me, lad." Murdoch rose to his feet and pointed a gnarled finger at Daniel. "Lady Muir wrote to me herself, and she sounds like a right sweet lady. All this time she's grieved her daughter and her daughter's dead child, but yer *not* dead, and that poor lady deserves to know her grandson, ye ken?"

Daniel blinked, a wave of memories washing over him. Murdoch sounded just like his father—that is, like Ian Brixton did when he used to scold—and suddenly Daniel was hit with such an intense longing for him it nearly brought him to his knees.

Ian Brixton might not have been his father by blood, but he'd been more of a father to him than any other man could ever hope to be, and he'd been a good man, an honorable man. There was a chance, wasn't there, that he carried some of Ian Brixton's goodness inside him, if not his blood?

"Aye, I ken."

"Good. Now, Lady Muir also said she's bringing some letters with her that she and Lady Honora exchanged, because she thought ye might like to read them, and get to know a little about your mother that way, and I advise ye to read 'em, because your mother was as sweet as an angel. You remember that, eh, before ye go and do something wrong-headed like leave Mairi Cameron behind."

"What's my mother got to do with Mairi?"

Murdoch rolled his eye—actually rolled it. "God above, lad, you think you're so mysterious I can't see what's right in front of my face? There's only one reason I can think of that you'd let that lass get away from you, and that's because ye think ye aren't good enough for her."

Good Lord. Maybe that blind eye of Murdoch's was magical instead of cursed. "I'm *not* good enough for her."

"Ach, well, maybe so, but no man's good enough for a lass like that." Murdoch shrugged. "You'll do well enough, I reckon. You're better than most."

Better? The old man had lost his wits. "No, I'm not. I'm far worse than most. If you knew what I've done—"

"Ye came back here, didn't ye? Ye came back, and saw justice done, not just for Lillias Cameron, but for Hamish Deacon, too, and that's more than most anyone else ever did for that poor lad. Ye did a good thing, Daniel, and proved yourself a loyal friend. That's something, that is, so no matter what else you are, I reckon there's hope for you, yet."

Daniel stared at Murdoch, his throat going tight. Murdoch was the very last person he'd ever imagined could bring him to his senses, but then nothing in his life had turned out to be as black and white as he'd always thought it was.

"Whatever you've done doesn't matter as much as what yer going to do next." Murdoch took his seat again, and fixed his one working eye on Daniel. "Now then, lad. What *are* you going to do next?"

Chapter Thirty-nine

"Well, Mairi. It looks as if you kept up with your baking while I was gone."

Lillias was standing in front of the kitchen shelf, gazing at seven of the eight loaves of bread Mairi had baked last week, all of them lined up like a row of soldiers, each neatly wrapped in a clean cloth.

She'd never before thought of her grandmother as old, but with her forehead puckered and her thin, papery skin pulled tight across her brow, Lillias looked as if she'd spent years under the dark cloud of the murder charge against her, instead of just weeks.

Unjust accusations, ugly rumors, endless gossip, and the days upon days she'd spent locked up in the Coldstream Toll Booth had worn her down, painting her once-vibrant red hair with strands of gray, and slumping her shoulders.

She looked smaller, thinner, as fragile as a bird, and weary down to her bones.

But this was no time to be bitter, or at least no time to show it. The Court of Assizes had released Lillias. She was free. Wasn't that cause for celebration?

"Here, sit down, and I'll fetch us some tea." Mairi pulled out a chair for her grandmother, set the kettle on, then snatched up one of the loaves, along with her knife and toasting fork. "There's butter and jam as well as bread, and your favorite Bohea black tea, of course."

She'd spent hours yesterday seeing the larder was well provided with good, wholesome food, and the cottage in perfect order, just as Lillias had left it. It had kept her busy enough so there'd been no time to mope about, feeling sorry for herself.

Or not much time, anyway. A few tears *might* have slipped out, here and there.

Lillias lowered herself into the chair, but her expression was troubled. "Now, there's no need to fuss over me, Mairi."

Mairi was cutting the bread, but she paused with her knife only partway through a slice. "Yes, there is. You need to rest and eat to regain your strength."

"I'm perfectly well rested, and well enough to fetch my own—"

"No, you're *not*. You're not well at all! You're far too thin and pale, and you look as if you haven't slept in…in…"

Weeks. Because that was how long Lillias had been wasting away in that cold, dreadful cell, and now she looked as if a stiff wind would topple her head over heels, break her into pieces, and…

Damn it. Now she was crying *again*, and after she'd promised herself she wouldn't.

"Oh, Mairi. My poor girl." Lillias rose to her feet and held her arms out. "Come here."

That was all she needed to say. Mairi flew across the kitchen and into her grandmother's arms, just as she'd done hundreds of times when she was young, and cried childish tears over some little slight or disappointment.

She wasn't a child now, but neither was this some small matter easily soothed with a thick slice of bread slathered with strawberry jam. It would take months for her grandmother to recover from the horrors of these past weeks, if she ever did, and…and…

Daniel would be leaving soon. There was no longer any reason for him to stay.

Lillias's good name had been restored, Hamish's death had been avenged, and Stewart and Callum Gordon were going to be held accountable for their heinous crimes.

The tangled mess surrounding the Rutherford estates remained as tangled as ever, but it would take months to unravel that knot, and she didn't suppose Daniel would hang about Coldstream waiting for it. Why should he? He'd made it clear he didn't want the title or the fortune.

He didn't want to be a viscount, or a Rutherford, or Malcolm Gordon's son.

And, well…of course, she was crying. Everything was wretched.

"Ah, Mairi, my sweet, brave girl." Lillias held Mairi tightly to her, crooning as she stroked Mairi's hair. "This has been a dreadful ordeal for you, hasn't it? More so than it has been for me, even."

"No. No one has suffered more than you have." Mairi raised her head from her grandmother's shoulder with a sniffle. "You were falsely accused of a dreadful crime. I only had to—"

"Make your way to London by yourself, track down Daniel Brixton, persuade him to return to Scotland with you, then make the long journey back to Coldstream in time to pick the threads of truth from the mountain of lies Callum Gordon told, before the court sentenced me to—"

Hang.

"Don't say it. Please." She couldn't bear to hear that word on her grandmother's lips.

Not now. Not ever again.

"Why didn't you just tell the truth from the start?" As soon as the words were out of Mairi's mouth more words followed, floods of them, and the next thing she knew she'd wrenched herself free of her grandmother's arms. "I don't understand it! If you'd just told the truth at once, none of this would have—"

She broke off before the bitter anger she'd spent weeks pretending she didn't feel could seep out of her mouth in that same ugly, accusatory tone. Dear God, was she really shouting at her beloved grandmother mere hours after she'd been released from *prison*? What was the *matter* with her?

She bit her lip, hard, until her hateful words slithered back into whatever dark corner they'd escaped from. "I didn't mean...that wasn't what I meant to say. I meant—"

"It *is* what you meant to say, Mairi, and goodness knows you needed to say it. You have every right to be angry with me—"

"But I'm not! I'm *not* angry!"

What sort of monster would be angry at her beloved, emaciated, exhausted grandmother on the very day she was released from prison, for pity's sake? Why, it was impossible, unthinkable, only there did seem to be a hard, hot little kernel of resentment lodged like a stone in the center of her chest, so maybe...

Maybe she *was* a little angry with Lillias.

Or maybe...maybe she was more than a *little* angry.

Lillias had seen it, of course, had known the anger was there even before Mairi did, because Lillias always knew everything. She'd never been able to hide a thing from her grandmother.

"Let's have our tea and toasted bread, shall we?" Lillias smoothed the hair back from Mairi's face. "We can sit here and have a nice, long talk about—"

"Did you steal that mourning ring from Lord Rutherford?" Mairi slapped a hand over her mouth as soon as the question flew out, but it was like when the pond overflowed its banks, and all the things that had been hidden from sight for decades surged to the surface.

Once they'd found their way out, there was no putting them back in again.

But Lillias merely replied, as calmly as ever, "No, I didn't. I don't steal, Mairi. You know that."

She *did* know that. Her grandmother was no thief. Mairi had been shocked to find the ring hidden in the box under the bed, yes, but even then, she'd known there had to be an innocent explanation for its being there. "Of course, I know you didn't *steal* it. What I meant to ask was, how do you happen to have it?"

"I suppose the ring is as good a place to start as any." Lillias dropped into her chair with a sigh. "But perhaps we should have our tea while we talk? There isn't a thing in the world that isn't made better by a generous helping of strawberry jam."

Tea? Oh, yes! She'd forgotten the tea. She scrambled to fetch the tea things, then went back to slicing the bread while Lillias sat quietly at the kitchen table, pulling her thoughts together.

"Lady Honora gave me the ring. Not to keep for myself, of course, but for Daniel—that is, Bram. I confess it's difficult for me to think of him as anything other than Daniel." Lillias let out a small laugh, but it was a sad, forlorn sound.

"Yes, for me, as well. It's understandable, I suppose." He'd always been Daniel to them both, and he'd remain so to her long after he left Coldstream, and she had no reason to ever speak his name again.

Her heart gave a miserable little throb at that thought. She tossed another log on the fire and busied herself arranging the sliced bread on a cloth on the hearth, her face turned away to keep her grandmother from seeing her expression. She'd never been good at hiding what she felt, and Lillias had always been able to read her face.

"The ring wasn't Callum Gordon's, so I couldn't have stolen it from *him*, despite his claims to the contrary. That ring belonged to Lady Honora and had nothing whatsoever to do with the Rutherford title. The motto and the myrtle and boar come from the Muir crest, and the portrait inside is Lady Honora's grandfather. He was known for his handsome dark eyes."

Daniel must have inherited his own handsome dark eyes from his great-grandfather, then.

"That ring is well known to the Muir family. Lady Honora gave it to me to keep for Daniel in case a chance ever arose for him to regain his birthright. She thought it would help to prove to her family Daniel was indeed her son, and they'd help restore him to his title."

"She cared for him very much." Mairi turned the bread over, her back to Lillias still, her gaze fixed on her toasting fork, because it was easier if her grandmother didn't see her heartbreak. The two of them had enough to worry about without *that*.

"She did, Mairi, more than I can tell you. You never knew Lady Honora, but she was truly lovely, and she wanted Daniel—Bram—more than anything. I don't have any love for Malcolm Gordon, but he did do one good thing in an otherwise selfish, wasteful life. That good thing was Daniel."

"Lady Honora…" Mairi cleared her throat. "Did she expect to die in childbirth?"

"We both knew it was a possibility. She'd never been strong, and her lying in was a difficult one. She never ventured outside Rutherford House for her entire pregnancy, you know, not even into the formal gardens. That's how determined she was to keep it a secret."

"From Callum Gordon? But how could she have known—"

"Not from Callum, no. In her worst nightmare she never could have anticipated Callum's monstrous crimes. No, she wanted her child hidden from Alethea Shelby, her husband's mistress. Mrs. Shelby had every intention of becoming Lady Rutherford one day, and she was so determined any son she might bear would inherit the title and fortune that Lady Honora actually feared for Daniel's life."

"And Malcolm Gordon went along with the tale of the child's death because—"

"For the same reason. Malcolm Gordon was a great fool, I'm afraid. He'd lost his head over Alethea Shelby, and he was afraid she'd refuse to marry him if she knew there wasn't a chance her own son would inherit the viscountcy. Either that, or Malcolm Gordon knew what she was, and wanted to protect Daniel from her wrath. I daresay it was a bit of both."

Dear God, poor Daniel, to be born into such ugliness as that, to be treated by his father as nothing more than a pawn on a chessboard, instead of the precious gift he was. Was it really surprising he didn't want to think of Malcolm Gordon as his father?

She poked half-heartedly at the bread with the end of her toasting fork, but her appetite had fled, and her vision was blurred with the tears that were now leaking all over their toast.

Had she made a mistake, insisting Daniel accept his past, and acknowledge his birthright? Who was she, to demand he do anything, when she couldn't possibly understand how he felt?

She'd always known who she was. Since the age of eight, when Lillias had taught her never to let anyone make her ashamed of herself, she'd never questioned her place in the world, but it hadn't been that way for Daniel.

If she found out tomorrow Malcolm Gordon was *her* father, would she be any more eager to acknowledge him than Daniel was?

"I think you know the rest." Lillias's voice was quiet. "Aileen and Ian Adair lost their own boy the day before Daniel was born, and so I gave Lady Honora's son to them to raise. Perhaps it wasn't the right thing to do, but I'd sworn to Lady Honora I'd protect him, and oh, how Aileen and Ian loved that boy! He was everything to them."

Mairi nodded, but she kept her attention on the soggy bread.

"I knew there'd be trouble when Malcolm Gordon caught the fever that took off Lady Alethea, especially when Callum Gordon came charging in to snatch up the title. Malcolm Gordon wasn't as much of a villain as his younger brother, but he was a weak, selfish man."

"So weak and selfish he put his own son in danger to clear his conscience before he died." Lillias might try to excuse him, but Malcolm Gordon was as much a villain as Callum was, just a villain of a different sort.

"Yes, I'm afraid so." Lillias let out a long sigh. "Not even half an hour after Callum Gordon arrived in Coldstream, I saw that awful Stewart in the village, asking after Daniel Adair, and I knew the worst had happened. So I fetched Ian and bid him to wait on the road, then I ran off to the pond to find Daniel."

"Did you..." Mairi dashed a hand across her eyes. "Did you see what happened to Hamish?"

"I—I did," Lillias whispered. "I wish to God I could have stopped it. A day hasn't gone by since that I don't berate myself for being too slow, but it all happened so quickly. By the time I reached them it was too late, and I had Daniel to think of, and I..." Lillias's voice had gone thick with tears. "I did the best I could, but it wasn't enough."

Mairi abandoned the bread then, and darted across the kitchen to wrap her grandmother in her arms. "You couldn't have done anything more than what you did. Didn't you teach me that all you can do is your best, and pray it's enough. If it isn't—"

"If it isn't, then it was never yours to change." Lillias drew in a shaky breath, clinging to Mairi's arm. "But you, Mairi, you and Daniel brought the truth to light."

They had, yes. They'd dragged it out, kicking and screaming. "I couldn't have done any of it if you hadn't had the foresight to ask Ian Brixton to write to you. If it hadn't been for those letters, I never would have found Daniel."

"But you *did* find him. You didn't give up until you'd done everything you could, and this time...this time, it *was* enough. I always prayed Daniel would find his way back to Coldstream someday, that he'd come back to us. I desperately want to see him. I do hope he'll come to me, but I'll let him make that choice."

Mairi pressed a kiss on the top of her grandmother's head. "He will. Of course he will."

He would, too. She believed with all her heart Daniel wouldn't leave Coldstream without seeing Lillias, because for all his gruffness and bluster, he was a man who knew well how to love.

But leave he would, and she...she'd bid him as tender a goodbye as she could, and took comfort in knowing she'd done her best.

Because Lillias was right. Her best was all she could do. All any of them could do.

If it wasn't enough, then Daniel had never been hers to keep.

Chapter Forty

Daniel stood in front of Lillias Cameron's cottage, his hand poised to knock, but he couldn't persuade his fist to meet the wood.

He'd never been the sort to hesitate—fists first, and explanations afterwards had always worked well enough for the likes of him—but since his conversation with Murdoch yesterday, he'd been…thinking.

He'd thought about Lillias Cameron and Ian Brixton, about the Rutherfords, and useless bloody aristocrats—viscounts, mainly—about grand estates and hundreds of acres of land, deer parks and formal gardens, cursed ponds and forests that stretched to infinity.

He'd thought about Coldstream, about Angus Murray and the Sheep's Hide Inn, Fergus McClellan and his wandering hands, Elsbeth Fraser and her scolding tongue. He'd even spared a thought for Mr. Fraser and his tetchy appetite, for God's sake.

But mostly, he thought about Mairi, and himself.

Thinking didn't suit him, really. Action—leaping into the midst of a brawl, squeezing a confession from some villain's throat, kicking his way through a crowd of blackguards—aye, that was all easy enough.

Declaring his love to the lass who'd stolen his heart? Bloody terrifying.

But here he was, standing in front of Lillias's door, heart pounding and sweat gathering on the back of his neck, frozen in place like a damned fool, afraid to knock because once he did Mairi might answer, and he hadn't any idea what to say to her.

He *wasn't* good enough for her, but then maybe Murdoch was right, and no other man was either, and in the end he was as selfish a brute as he'd always been. He wanted Mairi, and he would have her, no matter what it cost him, and no matter if he didn't deserve to kiss those soft pink lips, or run his hands through those wild red curls—

The door flew open, and a lady with faded red hair and laugh lines etched into the corners of her dark blue eyes stood in the open doorway. "Daniel Adair. You've, ah...you've grown up, haven't you, lad?"

His dreams hadn't brought Lillias Cameron's face back to him. He'd known her at once yesterday, the moment she entered the toll booth, but now, standing this close to her, his heart remembered her in a way his mind never could have.

Lillias had held him in her arms when he'd wept over his mother's death. She'd scolded him and laughed with him, taught him the names of all the wildflowers in the meadow behind the cottage, and made him repeat his prayers until he knew them by heart.

She's as much your grandmother as she is mine, Daniel...

He hadn't believed Mairi when she'd told him that on their first night together in Howe Court, but it had been the truth. Back then, Lillias Cameron had been the grandmother of every lost child in Coldstream, in one way or another. But especially his and Hamish's, because they'd needed her more than most.

It was still the truth, now, and so he did something he'd never done before, for anyone.

He opened his arms to her.

She didn't hesitate, but stepped into his embrace, tears in her eyes but a smile on her face like she'd just come home. "My goodness, Daniel, but you've become a big, strapping man, haven't you?"

"Aye, big enough." Good Lord, he sounded like a fool, but even as he shifted from one foot to the other, much as he'd done when he was a boy, he couldn't keep from grinning.

Lillias didn't ask him to come inside, but simply took his hand and led him through the door. "Have you had breakfast? I have tea, and more bread than I know what to do with."

"Aye, mayhap some tea." He made a quick sweep of the cottage when he entered, his grin fading when he realized it was empty.

Mairi wasn't here.

"Mairi went off for a walk." Lillias's sharp blue eyes were on his face, likely reading the disappointment there. She'd never been one to miss things. "I daresay she'll be back by the time we finish our tea."

Or else she'd peek through the window, see him sitting at her kitchen table, and run as far away as she could get from him.

"I was a bit worried you wouldn't want to see me, Daniel." Lillias piled the tea things onto a tray and set it down in the middle of the table.

"Wouldn't want to see you?" Did she think he'd forgotten all she'd done for him? "Why would you think that?"

Lillias was quiet as she poured the tea, so quiet the soft click of her teaspoon against her teacup seemed too loud in the silent cottage. "Because I changed the course of your life, lad, and you never had a say in any of it. I thought you might be angry with me—"

"Angry with you for saving my life? For giving me a mother and a father? For trying to protect me from Callum Gordon after I'd grown into a man, even though it meant you'd face the noose?"

Lillias's refusal to speak up on her own behalf had confused and hurt Mairi, and anything that hurt Mairi, hurt him, but he could never be angry at Lillias. Everything she'd done, she'd done to protect him.

She gave him a faint smile. "Well, if I'd known you'd grow into such a big man, mayhap I would have let you handle Callum yourself."

"I would have done, and gladly." He had, in fact, spent a good deal of time thinking about all the ways in which he might have handled Callum Gordon.

"I did what I believed your mother would have wanted. I swore to her I'd keep you safe from the Rutherfords. Your well-being was the most important thing to her, and so it was the most important thing to me, as well. More important than Callum Gordon's crimes."

When my grandmother makes a promise, she keeps it.

That Mairi's wee little grandmother would sacrifice everything to keep a brute like him safe was humbling and...aye, a bit absurd, but the Cameron women were daring ones, just as Murdoch had said.

Daring, and *fierce.*

"Callum Gordon is...well, you know yourself what he is. I had no idea what he'd resort to if he discovered you were still alive." Lillias kept her eyes on her teacup, turning it in her hands. "The sort of man who'd have a boy murdered so he could steal his title would stop at nothing to keep that title."

"Aye. He wouldn't, at that."

"But once Stewart was taken up, and I found out you'd returned to Coldstream, there was no reason for me to keep the secret any longer." Lillias sighed. "It's going to take time before Mairi finds it in herself to forgive me for my silence."

"Nay, that lass's heart is as tender as a newborn babe. You'll have her pardon before the sun goes down tonight."

"Hmm. You may be right." Lillias set aside her teacup and pinned him with those knowing blue eyes. "Mairi tells me you're leaving Coldstream. Is that true, Daniel?"

He didn't answer right away. He was clumsy with words, and he wanted to get this right, so he took a moment to choose them carefully. "I don't pretend to be happy about being Malcolm Gordon's son. I've never had much use for noblemen, especially villains like the Gordons, but Mairi wants to stay in Coldstream, and I could never leave her. I'm in love with her."

It was short, and a bit awkward, and not at all the sort of flowery declaration a man in love was supposed to make, but Lillias didn't seem to mind.

She clasped his hand in hers, and looked him straight in the eye. "Here's one thing to keep in mind, Daniel, when you get to fretting over Malcolm Gordon. You're not just *his* son. You're Lady Honora Elizabeth Muir Gordon's son as well, and a sweeter, lovelier lady never lived. Her blood is flowing through your veins too, just as surely as his is."

His heart leapt at the fierce light in her eyes, the gentle pressure of her hand on his. "Aye. I'll remember."

"Good lad." She gave his hand another pat. "I can't think what could be keeping Mairi. Maybe you'd best go after her, Daniel. She hasn't had her breakfast, and I don't like her to miss a meal, as wee as she is."

Daniel was on his feet before she finished speaking. "Aye, I'll go."

Lillias hid a smile under the rim of her teacup. "She's in the wildflower meadow, behind the cottage. There aren't many wildflowers to see now, of course, but they'll be out come spring. You'll see them then, I expect. Such a beautiful array of colors, you can't imagine them all! I daresay you'll grow to love them as much as Mairi does." Another smile, then she waved a hand toward the door. "Go on, then. Get on with you."

It had snowed the night before. Shallow drifts of it still covered the frozen ground behind the cottage, and it crunched under his boots as he made his way past the strawberry patch, the window Mairi used to crawl out of right above it.

His heart was pounding with nerves and anticipation, but a grin stole over his lips, all the same. Daft lass, tumbling out windows like that. She hadn't changed much since she was a wee girl, had she?

Just as well, because she'd been made for him from the start. That was why he'd dreamed about her, even before he remembered her, dreamed of her face, before he recognized it as hers. In some ways, he'd been in love with her his whole life.

He stopped when he saw her, the crunch of his boots over the snow giving way to a silence that was louder, somehow, than it had been before. She was wearing her worn brown cloak, her hood covering her hair, but the few wild curls that could never be tamed were blowing against her cheeks, the red strands brighter than the sun against the bland, cold whiteness that surrounded her.

And it was perfect, that she should be the brightest thing he'd seen this morning, the brightest thing he'd seen *every* morning since he'd found her again.

"Your grandmother is worried about you, lass." His voice was deeper than usual, as if it had worked its way loose from the furthest reaches of his chest.

Mairi whirled around. "Daniel! I didn't hear you coming."

"She's got your breakfast ready." He ventured a few steps closer. "It's your favorite, lass. Toasted bread."

A ghost of a smile drifted over her lips, but it was a weak, pathetic little thing, and as he drew closer, he saw her eyes and nose were red, and a trace of tears stained her pale cheeks.

Ah, she was tearing his heart in two.

If it hadn't been for the crunch of snow under his boots, he wouldn't have known he was moving, drawing closer to her with every step until he caught a fold of her cloak in his hand, the wool rough against his palm, and then the warm, smooth skin of her cheek was under his fingers, and his fingertips were damp with her tears. "Don't cry, lass."

"I always cry at goodbyes." She used the excuse of wiping her eyes to pull gently away from him. "Did you see Lillias?"

"Aye. She's much like I remember her."

"You do remember her, then?"

"I didn't, really, until I saw her this morning, but as soon as I did…" He caught her hand in his, unable to keep himself from touching her. "I remembered. She's as much my grandmother as she is yours, just like you said."

Ah, now that brought a smile to her lips—a real one this time. "At one time or another, she's been a daughter, a sister, a mother, and a grandmother to everyone in this village."

"Aye, that's so."

But he hadn't come here to talk about Lillias. He'd come here for one woman only—the woman who was edging away from him right now, her small, booted feet turning back toward the cottage. "I, ah…I hope your journey back to London is a pleasant one. You'll give Mrs. Luddington from the King's Head my compliments, won't you?" She tried to laugh, but it came out sounding more like a sob.

"See, that's the thing, lass." He caught her hand before she could put any more distance between them, and held it tightly between his to warm the small, cold fingers pressed against his palm. "I don't fancy another skirmish with Mrs. Luddington, so maybe it would be best if I stayed in Coldstream for a bit."

"You...you want to stay in Coldstream?" The pale pink lips he loved so well curved upward in a smile so tiny, so cautious, it broke his heart all over again.

"Aye. I thought I wanted to go, but that was before your grandmother told me this meadow is filled with wildflowers in the spring."

She shook her head, but the tiny smile was widening, growing more hopeful. "You already knew about the wildflowers. You planted them. Remember, I told you?"

"I remember you told me, but I don't remember what they look like." He'd dreamed of lying in a field of wildflowers with her, the tips of their fingers touching and the taste of lemonade on his tongue, but dreams were no longer enough for him.

He wanted a *life*, one sweeter even than his wildest dreams.

He wanted her.

"I need to see these wildflowers for myself." He tightened his fingers around hers and drew her closer, so she was tucked against his chest. "Did you really think I could leave you, lass? I love you, Mairi."

"Daniel..." she whispered, then her voice broke, and tears filled her eyes.

"No more tears, Mairi." He kissed her eyelids, one and then the other, and let his forehead rest against hers. "I think you knocked something loose inside my brain with that pistol of yours, because I've lost my head over you. I love you so much, lass."

"I knew I'd aimed that blow just right." She took his face between her two cold hands and touched her fingertip to the scar under his chin. "It seems growly, dark-haired Scots are my weakness. I love you, too, Daniel. With all my heart."

"You'll have me, then? I don't know much about being a viscount, but I expect I'll need a lady, and the Rutherfords could do with some fierce, blue-eyed, red-headed viscountesses to keep them in line."

"But I'm not a lady. Aren't viscounts supposed to marry—"

He pressed a finger to her lips. "You *are* a lady, lass. *My* lady."

"I will have you, then, because I can't think of anything I'd rather be than yours." She rose up to her tiptoes and pressed her mouth to his.

"My Mairi," he whispered against her lips, then he kissed her until their panting breaths turned the cold air around them white, the frosty clouds drifting upward into the tree branches above before vanishing into the clear blue sky.

Epilogue

One year later

"Lord Rutherford! I've got a salmon on the line! Oh, he's a big one, too. Look at him squirm!" Graham Campbell, one of the younger boys, jerked on the line to show off the size of the fish wriggling on the end of it.

Thursday was fishing day at Rutherford Pond.

Mairi was perched on a blanket spread out on a grassy knoll a safe distance away—young boys and fishing being a soggy endeavor—one of her hands on little Hamish's plump belly, but the rest of her attention fixed on her husband, who looked handsomer than any viscount she'd ever seen, in his buckskin breeches and billowing linen shirt, a wide smile on his full lips.

"Aye, that's a salmon, all right." Daniel strode toward the bank and laid a hand on Graham's shoulder. "Careful with him now, Graham, or he'll pull you right off your feet and into the pond."

"How in the world do they know it's a salmon?" Lillias, who was sitting beside Mairi, watched as Graham wrangled his fish, her hand shading her eyes from the sun. "It's silver with scales and gills, just like all the other fish."

"I don't have the vaguest idea." Mairi couldn't tell one fish from another, but Daniel had taught the gaggle of village boys who came every Thursday how to differentiate between the fish he'd stocked in the estate pond. He'd even bought a trim little rowboat, so the boys might fish the deeper water in the middle of the pond.

Daniel paused beside another boy, this one very small, watched him cast, then held out his hand for the boy's fishing rod. "Try snapping your wrist. It'll send the line out further. Like this." With an expert flick of his wrist, he sent the line streaming out into the water, then handed the rod back to the boy with a grin. "You just need to practice, and you'll have it in no time, eh?"

"Aye, my lord." The little fair-haired lad—Iain, she thought his name was—gave Daniel an adoring look. "Thank you, my lord."

"I never thought I'd see any Viscount Rutherford mucking about with the village lads as Daniel does." Lillias paused in her cooing at Hamish to cast an approving look at Daniel, with his little gang of ruddy-cheeked boys, all of them shouting, splashing, and laughing at once. "Those little boys worship him. See how they listen when he speaks?"

"Oh, it's the other way around, I assure you. Those lads have the grand Viscount of Rutherford wrapped around their grubby little fingers."

Lillias gave her a sly smile. "You say so now, but no man is truly wrapped around a child's finger until he has a daughter."

"Oh, there will be a daughter, by and by. A wee, fierce, red-headed one, if Daniel has his way."

"I daresay he will have his way, come to that. He *is* a viscount now." Lillias threw back her head in a laugh at Mairi's arched eyebrow. "Ach, well, I think a little red-headed lass would be lovely."

Mairi quite wanted a little girl herself one day—after all, the Camerons had a legacy of wily, daring women to uphold—but there was plenty of time yet to give Daniel the little girl he longed for.

Meanwhile, they had their precious son Hamish, named after the friend they'd lost, and still grieved. Their sadness had softened somewhat over the past year, the sharp edges of it blunted with time and the arrival of his namesake, but they'd taken the Muir family motto to heart.

Ne Obliviscaris. Do not forget.

Hamish Daniel Bram Muir Gordon was the first Viscount Rutherford to bear that name, but he wouldn't be the last. There would be no more Callums, Malcolms, or any of the other names that had been traditionally bestowed on the Rutherford sons for generations. It was well past time for a change, and what better place to start than with their firstborn son's name?

Of course, some things never changed.

The village of Coldstream was, for better or worse, still Coldstream. Fergus McClellan was still an incorrigible flirt, Elsbeth Fraser still had a tongue sharper than a dagger, Angus Murray still made the best porter in the Scottish Borders, and Mr. Fraser's appetite still became tetchy in the summer months.

Mairi loved Coldstream as much as she ever had, despite its foibles. Even Daniel had made his peace with it, though he still didn't care for

Elsbeth Fraser, and he'd never entirely forgiven Fergus McClellan for his braid-tweaking and otherwise "wandering hands."

That was nonsense, of course, but Fergus wasn't inclined to challenge Viscount Rutherford, for all that Daniel didn't act a thing like a stuffy viscount. He and Murdoch could often be found at the Sheep's Hide of an evening, tankards of porter in hand, arguing over a chess board.

But some things in Coldstream had changed. There was no more talk of poaching, and no mention of whippings. The tragedy that had unfolded all those years ago was only a bad memory now, one that faded further with every day that passed.

"I think Hamish and I will go for a wee ramble." Lillias rose to her feet, brushing the dried leaves from her skirts. "Would you like to go for a walk with grandmother, sweet boy?"

"He would, indeed." At least, that was how Mairi chose to interpret her son's enthusiastic kicking and wriggling. He was much like his father, never able to be still for more than a handful of moments at a time.

He had his father's eyes, too—lovely and dark, with impossibly long, thick lashes. It was a bit too soon yet to tell what color his hair would be, as he still had just a tracing of it, but Daniel insisted it would be red, just like his mother's.

Who was she to gainsay the Viscount of Rutherford?

"Come along then, lad." Lillias reached down and plucked up her great-grandson with all the ease of a lady who knew how to handle babies, and bore him off like the prize he was, chatting about birds and trees and fish to him as they went, with Hamish tugging on her hair and gurgling his agreement.

"You look very pretty this morning, my lady."

Mairi turned back toward the pond to find Daniel making his way up the bank, his dark eyes warm as they rested on her. "Oh, I look a fright." She'd wanted to watch the boys at their angling, and hadn't bothered to take the time to braid her hair that morning, so it was flying about in the brisk wind coming off the pond.

"Nay, it's lovely like this." Daniel joined her on the blanket, reaching out to wrap one of her curls around his finger. "It makes me think of how it looked spread out all wild on my pillow this morn—"

"Hush, you wicked man." But even as she scolded him, her lips curved in a smile, and warmth rushed into her cheeks at the heat in Daniel's eyes.

He laughed softly at her deepening blush, then brought her curl to his lips to kiss it. "Not as wicked as I'd like to be," he murmured, sliding his hand under the hem of her skirts and wrapping his fingers around her ankle.

There was a scattering of muffled laughter, and Mairi peeked over his shoulder, her grin widening when she found a few of the boys watching them. "Careful, my lord. Your lads are snickering at us."

"Maybe I'd better take you inside, then." He stroked a fingertip over her ankle bone, his eyes darkening when she shivered under his touch.

"But won't the boys be disappointed if you finish early?" There was nothing she wanted more than to steal some private time with her husband, but she didn't like to disappoint the boys.

"Nay. Graham scared off all the fish with his thrashing, so Murdoch's going to take them out in the boat." He rose to his feet and held out a hand to her. "Come here. I've missed you, lass."

She took his hand, and let him help her to her feet. "How can you have missed me? We've been together all morning."

Yet she knew how, because she felt just the same as he did. As if every moment they spent apart was endless, and every moment together more precious than the one before it. Each day she woke thinking it was impossible for her to love him more, until the next morning proved her wrong.

"Unless you're in my arms, I always miss you, Mairi." He drew her closer and touched the back of his fingers to her cheek. "Before I even remembered you, I missed you so much, I dreamed of your face."

Author's Notes

Bennett, Rachel E. *Capital Punishment and the Criminal Corpse in Scotland*, 1740–1834. London: Palgrave Macmillan, 2018. Chapter 4, "Scottish Women and the Hangman's Noose." https://www.ncbi.nlm.nih.gov/books/NBK481730/ doi: 10.1007/978-3-319-62018-3_4.

Harper, Charles G. *The Great Northern Road: London to York, the Old Mail Road to Scotland*. Project Gutenberg eBook. August 2014. https://www.gutenberg.org/files/46716/46716-h/46716-h.htm.

Johnson, Helen. *Assizes: Our Criminal Ancestors.* University of Hull. https://ourcriminalancestors.org/assizes.

Kane, Kathryn. *For Love or Death: Locket Rings.* The Regency Redingnote, February 2017. https://regencyredingote.wordpress.com/2017/02/10/for-love-or-death-locket-rings.

Thomas, Gail B. *Midwifery in Britain: Pre-Twentieth Century.* Memories of Nursing. 2003. https://memoriesofnursing.uk/articles/midwifery-in-britain-pre-twentieth-century.

Printed in the United States
by Baker & Taylor Publisher Services